The Wyandotte

The Wyandotte

Frank J. Irgang

James C. Winston
Publishing Company, Inc.

Trade Division of Winston-Derek Publishers Group, Inc.

TO SOW THE FALLOW SOIL

First printing

PUBLISHED BY JAMES C. WINSTON PUBLISHING COMPANY, INC.
Trade Division of Winston-Derek Publishers Group, Inc.
Nashville, Tennessee 37205

Library of Congress Catalog Card No: 95-61852
ISBN: 1-55523-770-3

Printed in the United States of America

To those who long ago lived in harmony with nature in the gloomy pine forests in the north, the steamy swamplands of the south, and the vast prairielands of the west.

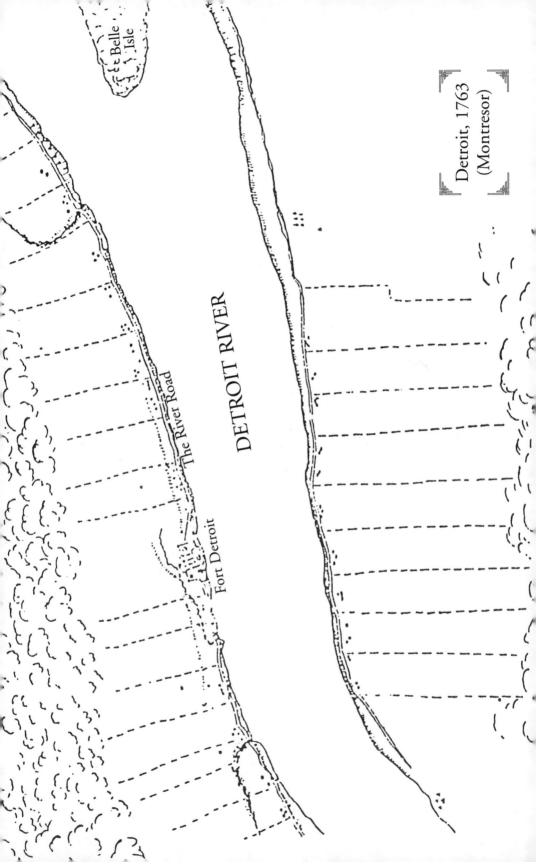

Belle Isle

DETROIT RIVER

The River Road

Fort Detroit

Detroit, 1763
(Montresor)

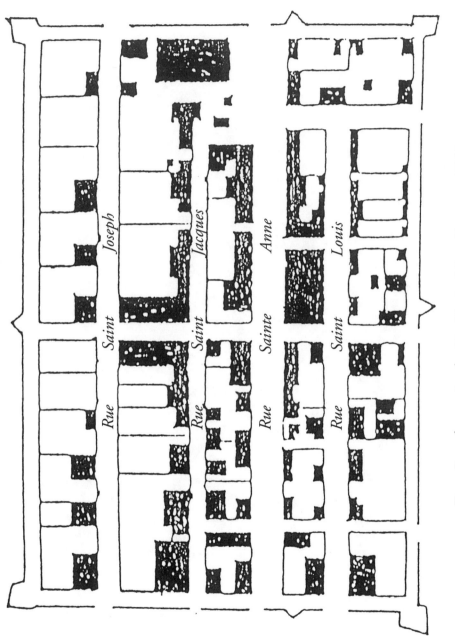

Fort Ponchartrain du De Troit, New France, 1749
(DeLery)

Contents

Prologue:

The Time Before—
1241 A.D.

Tokah stood in front of his *abnaki* and looked at the entrance of the bark-covered pole house in the distance. The air was heavy and damp, but the dense fog was beginning to lift. He self-consciously looked down at the glossy quills of his breastplate, then reached up and stroked the long braids of his moist, graying hair. The braids, indicating his rank, stood out from the usual inverted bowl-style haircuts of the lower tribal members. Guiding his fingers around his leather headband, he anxiously touched its gray timber wolf emblem to be sure the symbol of his authority was centered on the flared bangs of his forehead. Fearful these burly invaders would demand tribute before they departed, he wanted to look his best to emphasize the strength and power of his tribe. He hoped they would not take the maidens nor insist that warrior-hunters accompany them as slaves. Just then the entrance flap of the pole house was pushed aside, and the twelve tall men filed out. He watched with awe and admiration as their leader, Rothaar, led them directly to him. The harsh winter was over, and the blonde visitors were ready to continue their journey.

The villagers gathered around them. They liked to hear the deep, loud, rasping voice of the leader. Despite the clumsy phrasing and obvious accent, his meaning was clear. "Captain Rothaar and his warriors wish to thank the great chief, Tokah, and his Wyandotte people for letting us winter in their village." He had learned to communicate with surprising speed.

Tokah studied the Norseman's face, noting traces of pemmican eaten for breakfast clinging to his thick, curly beard. He looked at the leather armor that protected much of Rothaar's hairy arms and legs. It intrigued him because it made the big-boned visitor look larger than he was. And there was the white wolf's head that adorned Rothaar's horned helmet. Tokah had never seen wolf's fur so snowy white. "The Wyandotte people are pleased the Great Spirit granted them the privilege of helping their white brothers," he replied, his jaw set with a steely hardness.

He recalled the day the tall ones first appeared at the far western edge of the village during a howling blizzard. They were hungry and very cold. After a brief conference in the council lodge, the village elders had informed the people the strangers were spirits of dead ancestors who had returned. They were treated with a very deep reverence until the elders discovered they had to eat to live and defecated a foul substance just like the red men. Reassessing, the elders concluded they were mortals, but indeed, sent by the Great Spirit.

Tokah was determined that he, as chief, would make certain the generations of Wyandottes that followed would know about their white brothers' stay in their village. He and his people had learned many things from these burly men. They had watched the construction of a great pole house of new design and strength, had seen strange new knives and arrowheads, and had touched breastplates so hard the finest flint arrowheads would not pierce them. Yes, much had been gained.

Another thing had impressed Tokah. Although some young braves were not pleased, eleven Wyandotte maidens were now carrying seeds from the bearded visitors in their bellies. These white warriors were unusually virile. The infusion of strong bones, thick blood, and brave spirits would strengthen the Wyandotte tribe so they could more easily defeat the treacherous Potawatomi and numerous Chippewa.

Rothaar thrust two bronze arrowheads into Tokah's hand. "Take these symbols of our brotherhood!" his voice boomed. "As long as the Wyandotte chief possesses them, his people will never go hungry nor be defeated in battle. Some day Rothaar's people will return and bring many more!"

Tokah held them in his open palm. If only his people knew where to find the hard, yellow material. But Rothaar had said that was sacred knowledge not to be shared at this time. He looked up and scanned the other men behind Rothaar. Two wore horned leather helmets. The others had fur caps they had made from animals while hunting with the Wyandotte braves. He was about to speak when the fog suddenly parted and a bright beam of sunlight shone down upon them. It highlighted the white wolf's head and flashed against Rothaar's copper breastplate, the glare hurting Tokah's eyes. He knew it was an omen of great significance. He hesitated, then said, "The Great Spirit unites us in brotherhood. Someday you will return from beyond the great waterfall in your big canoe that travels with the wind. Then we meet again!"

Chapter 1

Old World— 1748 A.D.

Sam Locke pulled the heavy oak door closed behind him and stepped out into the darkened street. Looking up, he scanned the densely overcast sky and saw the leading ribbons of a thick, gray fog creeping in from the channel. He buttoned his coat and turned to admire a copper lantern hanging from its wrought iron bracket. The light of its candle glowed orange on his clean-shaven face. He smiled. He was proud of that lantern.

It was eleven o'clock, an hour later than he usually left the Red Sails Tavern on a Saturday night. But no matter, he had been talking with a sailor.

While standing at the bar waiting to be served, he heard the sailor tell another man about the New World. "You been there?" Sam asked.

"Sure 'ave, mate," the sailor replied, turning to face him. " 'Tis a land o' real opportunity."

"What's it like there?"

"Much different than 'ere, m' friend," the sailor replied, pleased that someone wanted to listen. "Cities springin' up all over." He took a swallow of warm ale from his tankard, then continued. "And the farms. Stake as much as ye want. Trees and open flatlands as fer as the eye can see. Grows punkins big as wagon wheels, rye shoulder high. And the deer and rabbits, can shoot 'em from yer back stoop."

Sam had heard similar stories from others and wondered how true they were. They stirred his imagination and aroused a desire within. He looked the sailor in the eye. "And where did you see this?"

"Just got back from Yorktown, Colony of Virginia."

As long as he could remember, Sam wanted to be a farmer. Just own a few acres of land that he could walk across. He liked to turn the soil, feel it run through his fingers and inhale its earthy odor. He wanted to plant fields of rye and oats and watch them grow in the warm sun. But as long as he remained in Weymouth he would never have the means to buy a farm. Like his father and his father's father, he would work day in and day out as the village blacksmith to earn a meager living for his wife and son.

He jammed his hands into his pockets and started down the street. Walking unsteadily on the rough cobblestones, he approached the Stagecoach Inn. He didn't like the place but had to pass it on the way home. He stopped, and his eyes traced the driveway to the well-lighted front of the half-timbered structure. The clamor of music and boisterous laughter made him set his jaw. During the past two years it had become a hostelry for noble gentry who wanted to spend a weekend of merrymaking away from their wives and the confines of the city. They disturbed the tranquility of his peaceful village. He didn't like it.

A rotund man wearing a beaver hat rode up, dismounted with a grunt, and handed the reins to the stableboy. As he started toward the entrance, he stumbled and brushed against Sam. "Out of the way, peasant!" he said.

Sam detected a strong odor of brandy on the man's breath. "Bastard!" he yelled. "Bloody bastard!"

Surprised, the man stopped and turned to face him. "Watch your tongue, rogue!" he said, weaving unsteadily on his feet. "You're speakin' ta the Earl o' Wixton!"

"You and your friends should stay in London, where you belong!" Sam told him, shaking his fist. He turned to leave, then stopped. "And take your whores with you!"

"You can't talk like that to a gentleman!" the man shouted, waving his riding crop.

Sam felt the blood surging through his body and wanted to beat the man with his fists. He knew he could administer a good thrashing because he was tall and wiry and his muscles were strong. But he also knew that if he did the constable would be knocking on his door before daybreak. He recalled the arrest of George Carter who used a hoe handle on a drunken group from the Inn when they trampled his garden on horseback. London headquarters had issued orders granting the gentry protection from such interference. Sam clenched his fists and walked quickly into the darkness.

The next morning Fanny Locke put a platter of scrambled eggs, ham, and biscuits on the table for breakfast. Since Richard was still asleep in the overhead loft, she ladled small portions onto a plate for him, covered it with another plate, and put in on the back of the stove to keep warm. She poured tea into cups, then sat down with Sam to eat.

Fanny looked at her husband, then put her hand behind her head and lifted the soft brown ringlets of hair from her slender neck. A calm, diminutive person, she rarely asked questions or raised her gentle voice. But she knew her husband was troubled. He had not slept well during the night, and his face looked grim this morning. She took a sip of tea, then asked, "More trouble at the Inn?"

Sam nodded. "A bunch o' blighters," he said, placing a small amount of egg on the back of his fork with his knife. "They just come here for weekend hell-raising." Elevating his voice, he added, "Just a bunch of pompous asses!"

Fanny shook her head and pointed toward the loft. She didn't want their son to hear profanity in his home. Trying to calm Sam, she said, "Maybe they'll tire of it here and go elsewhere."

"They've been doing it for two years," he countered caustically, "and it's gettin' worse." He paused, swallowed a mouthful of food, then looked across the table into her clear, blue eyes. "Like I told you before, we ought to leave here. We could get a start somewhere else.

And maybe Richard could do something besides blacksmithing—something to give him a better hold on life."

Sam, an ambitious, hard-working, God-fearing man, was a respected craftsman. His mother died when he was born, and when he was twenty-two, his father was kicked in the head by a horse and passed away a few days later. Sam took over the business, doing wrought iron work for merchants and horse shoeing and hoof clipping for farmers. He learned to work with copper and became a specialist in the design and fabrication of ornamental shields and small caldrons. He had made several lanterns that hung at the entrances of local shops, but the demand for such services was limited among a people who struggled to eke out a meager living.

That evening Sam sat in his rocker in front of the fireplace watching tiny blue flames consume a small pile of coal. He was thinking about the New World. Looking over at the table, he studied his wife and son. Fanny had been taught to read and write by a nobleman uncle and wanted to teach Richard what she could. Each evening, by the light of a tallow candle, she had him read and write passages from the Bible. Sam was pleased with his son's progress. Looking back at the fire, he was determined that Richard would not have to be a blacksmith.

Several weeks later Sam stamped his feet, tugged at the latchstring, and stepped into his cozy cottage. It was a chilly night and the warmth felt good on his face. "Been a bit crowded down there," he said, hanging his hat on a peg.

Fanny, sitting in the oak rocker in front of the fireplace, looked up momentarily, then continued with her sewing.

While drinking ale at the Red Sails, he had been listening to stories of storms and serpents and distant lands. Although Fanny looked upon such tales as tavern talk by rum-soaked sailors, Richard was enthralled by them.

Sitting down at the table with his son, Sam related what he had heard. As he spoke, the wide-eyed youngster asked for details so he could find the places on a parchment map his mother had given him. Fanny, sewing a patch on the knee of a pair of Richard's trousers, occasionally shook her head as she listened.

Suddenly there was a loud clatter outside the cottage. Sam rose to his feet and walked quickly to the door. As he reached for the latch, Fanny and Richard watched with rapt attention.

With a resounding crack, the door burst open, and Sam was knocked violently backwards. Tumbling toward the fireplace, he upset the rocker, tossing Fanny onto the floor. When he looked up, he saw the rump of a thrashing roan horse backing toward him.

Fanny thought of Richard still sitting at the table. She got up as quickly as she could and rushed toward him. Just as she grabbed the hand of the astounded lad, a gust of wind blew out the candle. Jerking hard enough to lift him off the chair, she retreated toward the bedroom, pulling him after her.

Sam sprang to his feet, pushed the overturned rocker out of the way, and seized a poker that was leaning against the fireplace. In the dim light of the blazing coal, he could see the frightened horse repeatedly try to rear up on its hind legs only to be thwarted by the low ceiling. With each painful thump it uttered a terrified cry and emitted a loud burst of pungent gas from its backside. Near the door, he saw the figure of the drunken rider stumbling about, yanking viciously at the reins.

Wishing the end of the poker was as red hot as the day he shaped it at his forge, Sam swung it forcefully against the rear of the animal. The horse bucked and snorted, tossing the rider onto the table. As the table collapsed, the rider's head hit the wall with a dull thud.

Again, Sam brought the poker down upon the horse. With a loud snort and shriek, the animal bolted out the door, taking part of the casing with it. Not far away, Sam could see the shadowy outline of the rider struggling to his feet. Using both hands, he grabbed the sleeve of the man's velvet coat and heaved him out the door. "Leave us alone, you bloody bastards!" he yelled, tossing the man's torn coat sleeve and beaver hat after him.

He quickly located a candle, lit it in the fireplace, then rushed to the bedroom. "You all right?" he asked, peering inside.

"Yes, we're all right," Fanny answered soberly, her body shaking as she spoke. She still held Richard's hand.

"You can come out now," Sam said, placing his arm around her shoulders. "He's gone."

Sam, sweating profusely, placed the door in its opening as well as he could and lit another candle. While Fanny tried to straighten the room, he continued to vent his anger. "Bastards!" he shouted. "Those bloomin' bloody bastards will never stop their hell-raising here!"

Fanny did not try to stem the profanity. Not only was she frightened, but she was angry that abuse by the ill-mannered noblemen continued to grow. Each time they came to town, they kowtowed the constable and engaged in an orgy of shameful behavior and property wrecking. Only last week she learned that three local maidens had been carried off, seduced, then abandoned in the center of town when the bleary-eyed revelers mounted their horses and carriages for the trip home.

Sam picked up the pieces of the broken table, then turned to Fanny. "Enough of this!" he said, stamping his foot. "We're going! Living among savages in the New World can't be any worse than putting up with these barbarians!"

Fanny looked at him and reluctantly nodded agreement.

Chapter 2

New World

When Arthur Harrington visited Fredericksburg the first time in the summer of 1741, he saw a few graying, unpainted, wooden houses along a slight bend on the south bank of the Rappahannock. He was convinced its unique location gave it the potential of considerable expansion and development. It was surrounded by miles of rich, level farmland, could be used as a division point for emigrants headed north, south, or west, and seagoing ships could reach it if they desired.

Arthur's father had been a lower echelon English nobleman who tried to impress his peers by educating his son at Cambridge University. When Arthur finished his law studies, however, he did not take the job as a London solicitor his father had arranged. Instead, he went directly to the busy docks on the sewage laden Thames and, hiding his pale, uncallused hands in his pockets, signed on as deckhand to a ship sailing for New York. "And just why are ye leavin' England?" the crusty Captain had inquired.

Arthur was through suppressing his frustration. He looked the captain straight in the eye. "I'm sick and tired of wipin' the noses and kissin' the asses of every drunken, stuffed-shirt duke and lord just to please my family."

He spent several days in New York assessing the possibility of opening a law office, but decided the city was too settled and organized for him. In Philadelphia he found conditions much the same. His money gone, he went to work dipping candles in a small shop. Although the hours were long and the pay low, for the first time in his life he discovered the pleasant satisfaction of working with his hands over the hot caldrons of molten wax and tallow.

At the candle shop he met Sarah, an attractive, demure young lady who had been taken in by the shop owner and his wife. Orphaned by the great fever epidemic that swept Philadelphia, she had been raised as their own and was carefully educated and groomed in the ways of colonial womanhood. Arthur was smitten with her but realized he must establish himself before asking for her hand. He worked three months, then bought a horse so he could look for a young settlement where he could start a business of his own. He promised Sarah he would come back for her someday, but wondered if she would wait. She cared for him. He knew that. But there were many eligible men in Philadelphia looking for wives, including some older, wealthy ones who had lost their spouses. He decided to act quickly to find a niche for himself.

A few days later he reined up on a small bluff overlooking the Rappahannock and looked at the scattering of houses on the other side. The quiet air echoed with the banging of carpenters hammers as men worked on two new buildings. In the distance he could see rising plumes of white smoke where farmers were clearing more land. The signs of growth pleased him.

Arthur urged his horse forward and descended a narrow trail to the ferry landing. He had to wait thirty minutes for the raft to be brought from the other side.

When it came, he wondered if he should board it. It was made of rough-cut pine lumber fastened together with square, hand wrought nails. Looking down at the badly worn plank deck, he noted the notches around its edges where a railing once existed. The craft was small, barely large enough to carry a team of horses or a short, lightly laden wagon. It might carry a horse and buggy with passengers. He was sure no maintenance had ever been performed on it. And the shabby, sway-back mule that staggered back and forth in an ever deepening path as it worked the cables, showed similar lack of care.

The operator, a short, gnarled, graying individual with an extensive vocabulary of profanity, lived in a small, cluttered shack at the river's edge. He went by the name of Semi, although no one seemed to know why. Some local residents whispered it referred to his intelligence. He didn't bother to wash, shave, or comb his hair, and whenever he donned a piece of clothing, it was never removed until, by worn-out necessity, it was replaced by another.

Arthur led his horse onto the shaky craft and wondered if the animal would break through the splintered deck or possibly capsize the battered vessel.

As he stepped ashore a few hundred yards below the town, he gave a sigh of relief. There should be a better conveyance here, he thought.

He rode slowly past a cluster of stores and shops. Several blocks of dirt streets had been laid out in a grid pattern, but business buildings fronted on only one block. Beyond that were a few homes and other shops.

He dismounted at the small, wooden shed of a blacksmith and walked inside. The smith, covering the hot coals of his forge with a shovelful of ashes, watched as he approached.

"Good day, sir," Arthur said, extending his hand. "My name is Arthur Harrington. I'm a barrister."

The smith eyed him cautiously, then shook his hand slowly. "Stover. Sidney Stover. I'm the village smithy." He stared at Arthur suspiciously.

"I'm thinking of opening an office." Arthur could see the tension ease on Stover's face. "Any need for a lawyer here?"

"Not much," Stover replied, shaking his head. "Might be afore long, though. The place is growing fast."

Arthur spent two days around Fredericksburg. It would be difficult to earn a living from a law practice. But, if the town was becoming a gateway to the western wilderness as some had told him, a business might provide more money. And he recalled the satisfaction of working with his hands. It was more pleasing than dealing with books and papers.

He rode several miles up and down the river looking for something he could do. Finally, he returned to the ferry and sat on the riverbank a few yards from the landing. As he watched, he wondered how it worked at all.

When a customer approached, Semi, lying on a rag-covered cot beside his shack, asked, "Goin' cross?" If the reply was affirmative, he ordered, "Git on board," or "Unload and we'll take the wagon over first." He didn't rise from the cot until the customer was on the raft. Then he picked up a willow switch lying beside the cot and shuffled over to his skinny mule that was leaning against its traces. Whacking it on the rump, he yelled, "Gitty up, Danny, goddamit!"

As the mule plodded slowly along the dung covered rut it had carved in the sod, Semi walked alongside spewing forth a stream of threats and cuss words which were ignored by the mule. After the round trip had been completed and the mule returned to its starting position, Semi blew his nose on the ground, rubbed his nose with the back of his hand, then wiped the hand on the already slick and shiny leg of his trousers.

Arthur approached the cot. Without opening his eyes, Semi asked, "Goin' cross?"

"No. Just want to talk," Arthur replied, sitting down on a keg a few feet from the cot.

"Who are ye?" asked Semi, displaying a squint-eyed suspicion as he reared up on one elbow.

"My name's Arthur Harrington. Came from London. I'm looking for something I can do around here."

"Wastin' yer goddamn time here," replied Semi, lying back again. "Nothin' here."

"You seem to have quite an outfit here."

"Ain't worth a shit! No goddamn good!"

"What makes you say that?"

"I'm a woodcutter. This ain't fer me," roared Semi, coming to a full sitting position. "Machinery! Hell, I can't work no goddamn machinery!"

"Would you like to sell it?" Arthur asked with masked enthusiasm.

"Ye goddamn right—to any sonofabitch that'll take it!"

They agreed on a price of fifty guineas. Arthur had but twenty. "Hell, that's all right," Semi said with a broad grin. "I'll come back in a few months fer the rest."

Arthur Harrington was elated. He was owner of the Fredericksburg ferry, including a scrawny mule and junk littered shack.

He replaced the mule with his horse. If the tired, sad-eyed animal was to be of service, it had to rest and regain its stamina. Over the next few days he greased the pulleys, repaired the raft, and cleaned up the shack.

Then he wrote a letter to Sarah describing the town and the countryside, and he told her of his newly acquired enterprise. In closing, he asked her to wait for him. If she would, he promised to return in the spring and ask for her hand in marriage.

During the winter he constructed a raft large enough so heavily laden wagons would not have to unload. It was too heavy, however, for his light horse and aging mule to operate. So he tied it to some large pilings until he could afford a team of draft horses. In the spring he purchased a pair of matched Clydesdales.

Arthur went to Philadelphia and married Sarah as he had promised. When he brought her to Fredericksburg, they moved into a little wooden house he rented on George Street. He was exceedingly proud of her and pleased to have her for a wife. Although the household furnishings were sparse, Sarah arranged the place into a cozy dwelling. She made friends with the neighbors and found her new home a delightful place to live.

◆

The warm afternoon sun was still well up in the sky. Ferry traffic had been heavy but there was a lull for the moment, so Arthur removed his hat to wipe his brow. When he looked up, he saw Semi plodding along the dusty road toward him. He watched until the gnarled little man was a few feet away, then said, "Hello, Semi. Been wondering when you'd come around."

Semi didn't answer. He walked up to the big raft, placed his hands on his hips and looked it over. Then he spit a tremendous slug into the river. "Well, I'll be damned!" he exclaimed. "I'll be goddamned ta hell!" He turned to Arthur. "Been doin' right proud fer y'self, ain't ye?"

"Made a few changes."

"Ya sure as hell have!"

"Where have you been?" Arthur asked, noting the appearance of the old man hadn't changed.

"Down 'round Richmond," came the slurred reply. "Been doin' odd jobs. Mostly round livery stables."

"They say Richmond's a nice town," Arthur ventured, handing Semi a small bag containing the guineas he still owed him.

"Tain't worth a shit!" Semi replied, looking out across the river as he fingered the coins. "Too many snobbish bastards. Always lookin' down on people. Always kickin' hell outa poor workin' people."

Arthur looked at him for a moment. "Semi," he said, "there's something I've been wanting to ask you."

Semi eyed him seriously. "What's on yer mind?"

"Wondered where you got the name, Semi?"

"Usually don't tell folks," Semi replied. "But hell, I'll tell you. Name's Somner—Somner Shane. When I was a young'un me friends couldn't say Somner. They called me Semi. Stuck with me ever since." He looked into the distance, then added, "It's not a bad name."

"No, it's not," Arthur agreed. Then he asked, "Where are you going from here?"

Semi wiped his nose with the back of his hand. "Goin' ta New York Territory. Yessiree, New York Territory. That's where they treat ya like a human bein'."

A customer drove up and Semi, indicating he wanted to see some friends in town, shuffled off, mumbling as he went.

◆

Years before, a few days after Richard's tenth birthday, the Locke family disposed of all their possessions in England except the clothing they wore and a few sentimental items packed in a copper banded wooden trunk and caught a ride on a fishing boat to

16

Plymouth. There they boarded a larger ship, the *Scythian*, that was sailing for the colony of Virginia. No longer would they have to suffer the indignities committed against them by pompous gentry.

The family was assigned quarters in a dingy area below deck near the stern and slept on a pad of folded canvas placed on the floor by a sympathetic crewman. At first, the creaking and scratching of the whipstaff and tiller just above their heads made sleep difficult. But after a few days it blended with flapping canvas, chafing ropes, and squeaking pulleys to form a low-level din that lulled their senses.

During the second day at sea, Richard explored the ship, cautiously staying out of the way as he watched crewmen tying down cargo and climbing the rigging. They were very busy, he thought, but took up an awful lot of room as they swaggered through the passageways and across the decks. Several were cantankerous complainers, objecting to the amount work, unhappy with their rations of rum, and resentful of the officers who gave orders. He tried to avoid them.

On a lower deck he heard loud voices. Peering warily from behind a stack of barrels, he saw two sailors arguing. Suddenly, the larger of the two began beating the other with a bung starter. The smaller man whipped out a large knife and slashed a deep gash across the face of his aggressor. With blood soaking into his white shirt, the large man beat his opponent unconscious, then proceeded to stomp his body.

The wide-eyed Richard was more frightened than he had ever been before. He ran back to the protection of his mother and father, but fearing they would not let him roam the ship anymore if they knew, he did not mention what he had witnessed.

But a few days later he became acquainted with three other sailors who spoke with pleasant voices. They kept him enthralled with an endless series of sea tales while letting him help with their tasks. He had concluded the adventurous life of a sailor was for him when, on the twenty-third day, a turbulent storm arose, making him violently ill. And when his bed would not stop pitching so he could get well, he changed his mind, deciding a life ashore would be more to his liking.

◆

The family settled on the south bank of the Rappahannock River six miles below the village of Fredericksburg where the river made a broad turn to the north. Sam Locke staked his claim of eighty acres, including a quarter mile of river frontage, then quickly constructed a small log cabin with thatched roof of reeds. As Fanny put the cabin in livable order, he cut heavy grass with a sickle and turned the rich soil with a shovel, creating a tilled plot for corn, potatoes, and rye. Afterwards, adjacent to the cabin, he prepared a smaller area for his wife's garden and a few tobacco plants.

"I'm glad to be out of that tent," Fanny said as the family sat down to a dinner of rabbit stew at a roughly hewn table.

Sam nodded agreement. "With such fine soil and timber, it should be easy to make a go of it." He was optimistic, but wanted to stress the point since he knew she was growing weary of the hard work.

Richard, enthusiastic about his new life, added, "Next we can get some animals."

"Someday," Sam replied, not wanting to diminish his son's eagerness. "But first we'd better repay the neighbors for what they lent us."

During the remainder of the summer as her husband and son toiled with the field crops and cleared more land, Fanny Locke tended her garden and worked about the cabin. She kept the fire burning, sewed burlap drapes, and made pillows and cushions.

One warm day while sitting on the floor stuffing dried corn-husks into a mattress cover, she heard a buzzing sound overhead. Looking up, she saw a bumblebee probing the thatched ceiling for a nest sight. She feared bees, so she laid back quietly to watch the persistent insect, hoping it would leave. As a girl she had been stung by a wasp while visiting her grandmother. She recalled that the elderly lady put wet tea leaves on the swelling, then wiped away her tears and told her, "You must be kind to all living things. They are part of God's plan." She missed those days. She missed England.

She looked down at her scratched arms, torn fingernails, and callused hands. They had never been in such poor condition. Tears welled up in her eyes. Perhaps she didn't possess the stamina for such a rugged life. Lord, here she was in a strange new world and afraid of some silly bee. Then she heard the voices of Sam and Richard as they approached the cabin. Looking up at the ceiling, she saw the bee was gone. She wiped her eyes with her apron, rose slowly to her feet, and walked to the door to greet them.

◆

The broad, fenceless expanse of the farm was a source of wonder and pleasure for Richard. The forest was filled with animals more curious than afraid, and he enjoyed watching the birds peck and scratch for the crawling things that scooted and wiggled in the newly plowed soil. He liked to work in the earth, to smell its fresh dampness, to feel the sun-warmed clods crumble beneath his bare feet. And he had room to run, walk, and romp, without feeling he was under the watchful eye of those living a few yards away. It gave him a sense of freedom he'd not experienced in England, where little compact plots of land were boxed in by stone fences.

However, he did not like what the farm was doing to his mother. She had always worked hard, but since coming to Virginia, her life had turned to one of endless, exhausting labor. Her eyes, no longer clear and blue, had become yellowed and bloodshot; the ringlets of her soft brown hair had lost their sheen, and the warm glow of her cheeks had been replaced by tightly drawn flesh that appeared pale and lifeless. He knew she was terribly tired, but realized she would insist on working from dawn until after dark.

Then one day he saw her strength fail. It was early fall, and he was helping her gather blue clay from the grassy bank of the Rappahannock to line the fireplace and chink cracks in the cabin. She was on the path just ahead of him carrying two loaded buckets when he saw her stagger, then sit down on a stump. Dropping his buckets to the ground, he ran to her side.

"What's the matter, mother?" he asked, panic showing in his face.

"It's nothing, son," she replied, trying to calm him. "I'll be all right in a minute." Her breath was coming in rapid, shallow puffs.

"Shall I get father?"

"No!" she ordered. Then, trying to assure him, she wiped the cold perspiration from her face. "I'll get moving soon."

After a short time she rose slowly to her feet, picked up the buckets and started up the path. But Richard could not forget the fright he experienced.

When winter came, Sam was proud his family was snug and secure. The cabin windows were shuttered with clapboard and sealed with deerskin, and a Dutch door at the entrance provided adequate light when it was opened. The harvest had been bountiful, and the forest was teeming with game. And he had a cow which he kept in a small barn, and ample hay to feed it.

Richard helped his father with the chores. He chopped wood, carried water from the river, and hunted and fished for food. In the evenings before the fireplace, he also studied his reading and writing lessons.

But each day continued to be long for Fanny. Even on a Sabbath, when the cold dampness of January made her joints ache, she rose early. She knew farm work was making her age too fast, but she put the thought out of her mind. It was Sunday, a day reserved for prayer and worship, and she had to make breakfast and lay out the dress clothes for her husband and son.

Sam had fueled the fireplace with an armful of wood before he and Richard went to the barn, and the crackling heat warmed the cabin. Fanny put water and cornmeal in an iron kettle, then added two pinches of salt. She gave the mixture a stir and hung it on the iron bar next to the blazing fire to cook.

After breakfast, as the sun tried to lift a blanket of haze that covered the area, the family walked a mile along the river trail to a small, weather-beaten chapel. Pockets of dense fog still obscured the sheltered recesses along the river. The occasional cawing of a crow was the only sound that broke the silence.

Just before walking up the steps of the little chapel, Sam paused, removed his tricorn hat, then turned to his son. "Remember," he warned, "in the church, nothin' can distract from the Lord." Fanny and Richard nodded.

He had made the same declaration on prior occasions, but thought it his duty to mention it again. He was head of the household and, as such, was responsible for their behavior in the eyes of other members of the community.

He held the door open for them to enter. "You must think only holy thoughts in here," he said in a low voice. His breath showed in the cold air as he spoke.

A circuit riding minister from Fredericksburg came the first Sunday of each month to deliver an inspirational sermon, but this was the third week and the small congregation had to organize their devotional services themselves. During the chilly winter months, worship in the unheated chapel was shortened considerably, although there were some who remained to *give the Lord His full measure.*

The services opened with a long prayer expressing reverence; then they sang several hymns. Next came five minutes of silent meditation and a closing prayer.

Just before the final prayer, Richard's eyes wandered to the row in front of him. A louse had crawled out of a tightly wound braid on the head of a woman seated before him. He watched it work its way up the braid to her fur covered hat. Then it scurried along the decorative edge to the tip of a long turkey feather that graced its top. There, it held on precariously, as the feather vibrated with a snap at each throb of the woman's pulse.

Richard rose from his seat and poised his hands to kill the parasite. Before he could clap them together, however, his father, who had observed the entire incident, seized him by the coat and slammed him down on the bench with a resounding thud. Richard's face reddened. He set his jaw, closed his eyes, and bowed his head. The well-disciplined congregation remained silent and unmoved.

———————◆———————

During the second summer, the warm sun and fertile soil provided rapid growth for everything the Lockes planted. Sam surveyed the fields carefully. There would be an abundant harvest of hay and grain. He could now buy four pigs and six sheep from Jason Willows who owned the property in the woods behind his farm. As a gesture of friendship, Willows, a widower with a young daughter, gave Mrs. Locke six baby chicks. "They'll be layin' and broodin' by fall," he told her.

Fanny continued to work long hours picking berries, which she dried, gathering nuts, and smoking the fish and venison Sam and Richard brought in. To ease the burden of heavier work, Sam bought a blocky Percheron gelding and light wagon from the livery in Fredericksburg. That meant the barn had to be enlarged.

To Richard, it seemed there would never be a letup in the work. However, even though the days were long and tiring, he found time to relax during warm evenings by fishing the Rappahannock. The river made a slight turn as it passed the Locke property, creating a wide swirl near the shore. It attracted large numbers of chubs and trout. Along the path that led to the river, he gathered an assortment of crickets, grubs, and worms for bait. And by climbing down the bank, he could sit on a large, flat rock his father had placed at the water's edge and fish until the sun dropped below the horizon. When darkness came, it brought swarms of mosquitoes from their daytime forest sanctuary and forced him to retreat to the shelter of the cabin.

On a mild fall day, Richard accompanied his father on one of Sam's infrequent trips to Fredericksburg. Each breath he inhaled was filled with the fragrance of crops to be gathered. Orchards were heavy with apples and pears waiting to be picked, a second cutting of hay was drying in the fields, and plump, ripe blackberries hung in clusters from vines that lined the roads and lanes. Richard liked going to town. It was more than a respite from work. It gave him the opportunity to meet other people, to see how they lived and what they did. And now he was old enough to walk the streets by himself.

He hopped off the wagon and stood at the beginning of a three block section of River Street that had been paved with gray granite cobblestones. Scanning its length, he saw that it was covered with dust and littered with horse droppings. Beyond the cobblestones, its compacted dirt surface had been rutted by carts and wagons when it was muddy.

He made his way slowly past the stone-faced shops, stopping occasionally to look at a cluttered window display. A crow, irritated by the staccato of a carpenter's hammer on a new building, cawed defiance from a nearby tree. Suddenly, he looked up and saw a rosy cheeked girl about his age watching him. She was dressed in a bright blue dress and wore a white ribbon in her hair.

"Hello," he began, thrusting his hands deeply into the pockets of his brown corduroy pants.

She looked him up and down slowly, then lowered her blue eyes. "Hello," she responded shyly.

"My name is Richard Locke. What's yours?"

"Elizabeth." She lowered her eyes again. "Elizabeth Harrington."

He looked at her seriously. "Where do you live?" he asked.

"Over there," she stated, indicating one of several houses down a side street. "Where do you live?"

"Way down the river," he replied, motioning toward the east.

They walked along slowly until they came to the blacksmith shop. Dangling their arms over the hitching rail, they watched the smith as he made a pair of iron hinges. On the dirt floor near his feet were several piles of recently made nails.

"That's Mr. Stover," Elizabeth said. "He's a nice man."

"My father can do that," Richard bragged.

"Not as good as Mr. Stover," challenged Elizabeth, determination showing in her sparkling eyes.

"Yessir!" countered Richard, standing upright to face her. "That's what he did in Weymouth."

"How come he's not doing it now?" she asked. Her voice was more subdued.

"Because he likes farming better."

They returned slowly to the intersection of William Street. Richard liked Elizabeth and wanted to see her again, but felt a sense of awkwardness about suggesting it. And he knew it was time to return to his father's wagon. "Will you be coming down here again?" he asked cautiously.

She nodded.

"Good!" he said, feeling relieved. "I'll look for you the next time my father brings me."

◆

Arthur's daughter, Elizabeth Mary Harrington, had been born on a humid Saturday morning, August 24, 1743, in the small frame house on Charles Street. The stout midwife who delivered her moved in and took charge of the household. She treated Sarah like an invalid. " 'Tis a confinement case," she said as she bustled about the house. "And in a confinement case, mothers hafta stay abed fer seven days."

Elizabeth took her first step on her first birthday and was simultaneously weaned from her mother's breast. This was a good sign, according to the watchful older women of the neighborhood who referred to her as *the Harrington's girl, Elizabeth*. Her mother insisted she be called Elizabeth, and would tolerate no nicknames or abbreviations. She corrected those who tried.

Each Sunday, Elizabeth attended the Congregational church with her parents, where she was coached in proper church behavior. Since the ferry did not operate on the Sabbath, the family usually strolled through the neighborhood on their way home. It gave Arthur and Sarah the opportunity to stop and chat with others who were enjoying the day walking about or sitting on their porches. They were proud of their daughter and beamed when others commented on her neat apparel or good behavior. Sarah made an effort to keep Elizabeth spotlessly attired in colorful little dresses she made.

One afternoon, when Elizabeth was old enough to run errands, Sarah handed her a crock of tea and told her to take it to her father.

Arthur had just brought a wagon across the river and halted the horses beneath a shade tree, when he looked up and saw her approaching. "Hello, Elizabeth," he said, delighted to see her. "What does my girl have there?"

"I brought you some tea, Daddy."

While Arthur drank the tea, Elizabeth wandered onto the deck of the raft, then followed the cables to the horses. Although she was fascinated by the ferry and studied the pulley mechanism to see how it worked, it was the horses she liked best. They were so big and strong, yet so gentle. She liked to pet them and feel the velvet softness of their noses.

Arthur directed a horse and buggy onto the raft, then walked over to the tree to pick up the reins. Elizabeth was still standing beside one of the horses. "Would you like to ride him?"

24

Elizabeth's face lit up. "Oh, yes!" she said eagerly.

"Hang onto the mane," he said, placing her astride the blocky animal.

This was much different from her mornings at Mrs. Wright's house. She, and eight others, attended the Classical School for Girls where they were taught to read, write, and cipher. They were also taught proper grooming and how to walk, talk, and act in the presence of others. Although Sarah thought it unlikely her daughter could move up in the structured British class system, she was aware of the growing wealth of colonial merchants. She wanted Elizabeth adequately prepared in social graces should an opportunity arise to marry someone of wealth and prominence.

After thirty minutes on the horse, Elizabeth's legs became irritated by the sweaty hair. As her father lifted her from the animal, he asked, "Going home?"

"Can I stay?"

"Yes. Just be careful." He was pleased to have her with him.

Elizabeth liked playing at the ferry landing. It was different from the delicate role of a girl that was expected at home or in school. She chased frogs and crayfish at the river's edge and sat beside a large piling while she played in the slippery blue clay. She made islands and peninsulas, canals and bridges, cities and farmyards, and other imaginary things she had studied or read about.

When she was ready to go home, she looked down at her mudcoated clothing, then up at her father. "Oh, that's all right," he told her. "Change them when you get home."

She loved him for that.

Most of Elizabeth's friends were her schoolmates. They liked to play in her backyard where they could ride a swing Arthur made in a towering poplar tree. The rope was long enough for them to swing high and see over the fences into several back yards. A contest frequently developed as to who could boast the spiciest observation. Ofttimes it was imagined or exaggerated.

Late one afternoon one of Elizabeth's friends on the swing saw Mr. Stover make a dash to his outhouse clothed only in his underwear. When she went home she mentioned the incident to her mother, stating that he didn't have his clothes on. Two weeks later as the blacksmith sat in the Gray Fox Tavern drinking a pint of ale, Dr. Hart came through the door and walked up to the table where he was sitting. He placed a hand on Stover's shoulder and bent down to talk. "Sid, hear you been cavorting in your backyard without any clothes on."

Stover looked up at him. "When was this?" he asked.

"Couple weeks ago," the doctor replied. Then he patted Stover on the shoulder and walked over to the bar.

Sidney Stover raised his eyebrows and thought for a moment. Then he nodded and smiled. When the doctor returned with a tankard and sat down across from him, he said, "Oh, hell! It's those damned girls!" He shook his head. "Was home in bed with a big bellyache and a case o' the scours. All of a sudden m' pucker string loosened up, and I had ta make a run fer it. Had m' long handle drawers on, though."

Dr. Hart nodded knowingly and smiled. "Three months ago they had Mrs. Wright wearing bright red underwear. Respectable women just don't wear red underwear. And I oughta know."

"Ought ta 'ave their little 'ides tanned," Stover said, setting his jaw.

"They're just going through a stage," the doctor replied, trying to down play the incident.

◆

One Saturday, Elizabeth asked her mother if she could visit Mary Moore. Mary was the same age and in the same grade as Elizabeth. They often spent time together studying, talking, and sharing secrets.

Sarah, who was preparing a batch of navy beans for soaking, nodded approval. "Be back in time to set the supper table," she said. She wanted to remind Elizabeth that she still had obligations at home.

"I will," Elizabeth replied as she walked toward the door.

It was a few days before Elizabeth's thirteenth birthday. The sun was hot and humidity high, so she walked along the gravel street slowly. As she passed the livery stable, she thought of Richard. She wondered when he would come to town again. Although a number of her classmates knew he was her friend, she didn't want them to know how fond she was of him. They would tease her about her farmer boy if they knew. She had confided to Mary that she liked him a lot. Of course, she knew Mary could be trusted to keep a secret.

The girls were playing hopscotch under a large elm in Mary's yard when Elizabeth experienced a warm flush surge through her body. Feeling unsteady on her feet, she sat down on the porch.

"What's the matter?" Mary asked, looking puzzled.

"I don't know," Elizabeth replied, her eyes showing fear as beads of perspiration appeared on her forehead. "I feel a bit tired."

"I bet I know," hummed Mary. "You're getting the monthly sickness"

"What's that?" Elizabeth's eyes opened wide enough to crease her moist forehead.

"You're going to start having periods."

"Oh, that," came the relieved reply. She had heard other girls talk about it.

When Elizabeth, as casually as she could, mentioned this new development to her mother, Sarah surveyed her daughter's enlarging nipples. "All girls get this," she told Elizabeth. "I'll tell you what to do so you can take care of it when it happens."

She went to the linen closet and brought out two long bands of white muslin she had been saving for this day. Using one of them, she showed her how it should be used.

The new development brought significant changes in Elizabeth's behavior during the next few weeks. Her self image became that of a mother's partner around the house, rather than a child who had to be watched and supervised. And she rarely played with the younger girls except in a superior and aloof manner. Instead of skipping rope and standing in the swing, she and Mary walked sedately down the street or casually sat in the swing as they talked, generating a minimum of motion.

Her grooming also became much more important. She dressed carefully and avoided exposure to the hot sun. She wanted to develop the soft white skin texture her mother said was the essence of beauty. Her hair, now a deep brown with reddish highlights, was painstakingly brushed so it hung to her shoulders in soft waves and ringlets. And she wore long, full-skirted dresses to hide adolescent legs and hips that were developing a distinct feminine shape. As she walked down the street, she enjoyed the second glances from males, young and old, who suddenly realized she was no longer *the Harrington's little girl, Elizabeth.*

Elizabeth slept on a cot in one corner of the living room in their single bedroom home. A small chest of drawers in the bedroom provided storage for her things and gave reason for her to enter the room and change clothes. For years she hadn't bothered to close the door, but with her new status she could close it without question. Sometimes she paused before putting on her clothes to examine her growing breasts, carefully pressing them with her fingers, eliciting a tingling sensation from the pink nipples. There was also the crop of down-like hair that was beginning to hide the coral protuberance at the junction of her long legs. She was pleased that at last the mystifying changes were under way.

Whenever Richard visited Fredericksburg with his father, the ride home over the lonely Rappahannock trail, although pleasant, always seemed long. Occasionally they met a rider on horseback or a farmer returning home from the fields, but mostly the silence was broken only by squeaking harness, the dull rattle of axle hubs, and the mating calls of birds and frogs. Once in a while they saw a trout leap clear of the river to snatch a flying insect, leaving concentric circles of ripples drifting lazily along the slow moving, glass-like surface.

It was nearly nightfall when they pulled up in front of the cabin to unload the provisions Mr. Locke had purchased. Fanny had supper waiting and came outside to meet them. After the household items were unloaded, Sam reached beneath the wagon seat and removed a package wrapped in brown paper. "This is for you," he said with a grin as he handed it to her. Then he stood back and waited for her reaction.

In the past, he sometimes brought her a tin of cookies or a small sack of candy, but this was larger. "For me?" she asked, a broad smile covering her thin face as she weighed it in her hands.

"For you," he said warmly.

Richard stood beside him eagerly waiting for her to open it.

When the paper was unwrapped, she found several pieces of printed broadcloth. She held the stack of folded materials in the palm of her hand and carefully examined them in the fading light. "Oh, these are wonderful!" she declared, her moist eyes glistening as she looked up at her husband. "They'll look so good made up."

She had been taught not to show affection openly, but she threw her arms around his neck and kissed him squarely on the mouth. Then she drew Richard close to her and kissed him on the cheek. Rarely did she have a chance to show off her new creations, but she always relished the admiring comments of her husband and son. She could hardly wait to start sewing.

◆

Sam was pleased with his accomplishments, but was not one to show it. With each successive season he had cleared more land, increased the number of domestic animals, and acquired additional labor saving equipment. He had added a bedroom to the cabin, constructed a root cellar, and installed glass in the windows. His family was becoming known in the area and, with additional settlers claiming land farther down the river, more neighbors dropped in for casual visits. He already had more than he thought he would ever possess, more than any English commoner could dream of owning. He was glad he had left Weymouth. He wished his friends there could see him now.

Still he was not content to relax his efforts. Sometimes in the evening as he sat in his chair after a hard days work, he thought of leaving a great legacy for his son. There would be a large white house and barn, and acres of productive land worked by hired hands. In his old age he could watch his son supervise its operation. Now he wished he had staked more land when he came, maybe a hundred and sixty acres, or even a half section.

In spite of all his progress, however, when he looked at his growing herd of cows he realized he still did not own a bull. One evening, after offering the blessing at the supper table, he said to his wife, "We need a seed bull to service the cows and heifers."

Fanny was shocked. They had discussed it twice before but never in the presence of Richard. She stared at him, then frowned.

"It's all right," Sam assured her. "He's old enough to know about these things."

Richard's face reddened, and he twisted the soles of his bare feet hard against the floor. He knew about the mating of animals, but had never discussed it with anyone. Noisily, he began serving himself from a bowl of beans.

"Sam," Mrs. Locke said sternly, "you know how I feel about this. I don't want a bull on our property."

"But things have changed," Sam pleaded. "And I think I can handle it."

"No!" She was adamant. "You well remember how many farmers were killed and maimed around Weymouth." She paused briefly, then added, "And I don't want anything to happen to you." Tears welled up in her eyes as she slowly turned her head from side to side. "England is so far away," she said softly.

Sam knew, if anything happened to him, she would return to Weymouth. It wasn't that she didn't like it here; she did. But only as long as it was with him.

A week later a heifer came in season. Sam slipped a halter over her head and, accompanied by Richard, led the agitated animal a mile into the hinterland to the farm of Jason Willows. Willows kept a large, virile bull that was used by several nearby farmers who paid two shillings for each live calf born.

Sam ordered Richard to go to the house and visit with Willow's daughter, Linda, while he and Willows placed the two animals in a pen attached to the barn. She was a year older than Richard and had been helping her father with the farm work since her mother died three years before.

By the time Sam had led the heifer into the pen and the bull had been released from the barn, Linda and Richard were positioned in a hazelnut bush so they could watch.

"We're supposed to be in the house," Richard protested. He didn't mind watching but felt embarrassed with Linda at his side.

"We'll go back in a few minutes," she assured him, enjoying his uneasiness. She had watched alone on several occasions. Each time, she became highly stimulated and enjoyed the vicarious pleasure it gave her.

As soon as the panting bull had completed his third run on the wide-eyed heifer, Linda, who had been oblivious to the abashed Richard beside her, whispered, "We'd better go now."

They scampered back to the far side of the house. "Wait here," Linda said hurriedly.

She trotted off down a footpath that led to a small clapboard privy. Richard watched as she entered and released the latchstring.

In a few minutes Richard heard his father calling.

———————◆———————

Fanny Locke looked out of the cabin window and saw that the sun was nearly down in the western sky. Supper had to be started. She went to her garden and gathered some string beans and carrots in her apron. While stamping the dirt from her shoes, she looked toward the cornfield and saw Richard approaching. He had a hoe slung over his shoulder and walked with a bouncing gait.

She observed his gangly arms, nut brown in color, and noted that they had grown rapidly during the past few months. Looking at his trousers, she saw that the cuffs, which used to cover his ankles, hung much too high above his bare feet.

"Hello, Mother," he said, his voice fluctuating between that of a boy and a young man.

"Hello, Son," she replied with a smile. Although reluctant to admit it, she had to concede that he was growing up. And she knew he would make her proud of him.

He leaned the hoe against the cabin and strode off toward the river to rinse off the sweat and grime.

She put a small amount of kindling on the ash-coated embers in the fireplace. Richard was keeping himself cleaner these days, she mused. He was especially careful about his grooming when he went to town. Then she wondered about Elizabeth, the girl Sam had mentioned on several occasions.

Richard had created a swimming hole by cleaning debris from a quiet eddy pool at the edge of the river and often went there to refresh himself after a day of hard work in the fields. After swimming for a short time in the clear, blue water, he stretched out to dry on a large, flat rock that had been warmed by the sun. While his senses were soothed by the pleasantness of the moment, he thought about Elizabeth. He pictured her clear skin and sparkling eyes and remembered the neatness of her freshly laundered dresses. He wondered if she would consent to live on a farm.

Sometimes he thought about Linda, too. But she seemed to be a perplexing puzzle to him.

———————◆———————

In early summer, shortly after Richard's fifteenth birthday, his mother gave birth to a baby daughter she named Martha. He was elated to have a little sister and envisioned her growing into a beautiful girl like Elizabeth. Fate intervened in the fall, however, when lung congestion developed in the infant, then turned to pneumonia.

The little body, dressed in crisp new clothing that had been hand sewn by Fanny, was placed in a small, padded wicker basket. The basket was sealed in a rough box hewn by Richard and his father. In a simple family ceremony, the child was laid to rest beneath a feathery-leafed locust tree that grew on a slight rise five hundred feet behind the cabin. Mr. Locke stood with his arms around his wife and son as he quoted passages from the Scripture. He concluded by reciting a verse from the Book of Psalms.

The three of them stood for some time with heads bowed, while the tears fell on the newly turned soil. Sam, wanting to ease the suffering of his family, tightened his grip on their shoulders. "Let's go down to the house," he said, his voice cracking with emotion.

Richard felt his father muster the strength of Samson as they turned to take the long, sad walk back to the cabin.

With a quill pen, Fanny recorded the event on the last page of the family Bible.

◆

Many days travel from the Locke farm, deep in the gloomy pine forests of the north in a land spotted with swamps and lakes, a young brave stood in a smoke-filled longhouse watching his mother and sister roast husk-covered ears of corn on a bed of ash-coated coals from a dying fire. Although not many moons beyond his puberty rites, he was already a seasoned warrior who had recently distinguished himself in a furious battle with an age-old enemy, the Potawatomi. In the dim light he noted the beauty of the women of the longhouse. They possessed light skin and fine facial features, qualities that set them apart from the neighboring tribes. His thoughts wandered to Lahana, the lithesome maiden the elders had chosen to someday warm his bed. How he adored her soft warm arms, supple breasts, and the scent of juniper oil she exuded after she had bathed in the stream behind the longhouse. But he could not have her until there was a unity ceremony. And it would be some time before the Great Spirit would place all of nature's signs in the proper configuration.

Recalling the story his father had often reiterated, he remembered how, as a small boy, he had stood for long periods of time on the bank of the great river that flowed past the village and watched for the promised return of the burly warriors who had imparted the light skin and brave spirit to his people. Often he had wondered if the Frenchmen who tilled the farms to the north might be the ones. But his father had informed that they were not, because they had dark complexions like the Chippewa and Ottawa. He was told he must wait for a long boat coming up the river being paddled by men with white skin, their heads and faces covered with straw-colored hair.

The mother rose to her feet and faced her young son. To her he was but a boy, not old enough to be a warrior. Noting the pink protrusion of a lengthy scar stretching across the side of his neck, a frightful reminder of the razor-sharp head of a flint-tipped Potawatomi arrow that had just missed his throat, she brushed it lightly with her hand. "Naseeka, my son," she said, "we must have peace with our neighbors. Your father ages. You must save yourself so you can become chief of the Wyandottes."

Naseeka looked at her sternly. He thought of the feisty Potawatomi, the overbearing Chippewa and Ottawa, and the deceitful marauders, the Huron. "There can be no peace," he stated. "The others scorn us because we look different."

He studied her softly rounded cheeks as they glistened in the dim light. "And," he continued, "they live in many villages in great numbers. We are so few. We can hope for peace, but must always be ready to fight." He knew the Potawatomi understood the fury of Wyandotte warriors, but any sign of weakness would invite another attempt to overwhelm his village. Looking down into her dark eyes, he added, "Someday our warrior ancestors will return. Then we will not have to live in fear!"

Chapter 3

The Lure of the Untamed

The winter of Richard's fifteenth year was especially spiritless for him. His mother, always an impelling force around the cabin, had lost her drive. She no longer bustled about or gave orders on tasks that had to be done. Actually, she seldom spoke. When she did, the sparkle was missing from her eyes, and her voice lacked its determination.

In the past, winter had been a time of evening lessons in reading, writing, and ciphering. But now he seldom had to recite to her. Instead, she preferred to sew or read the Bible. Sensing that she was still troubled by the loss of little Martha, he tried to avoid disturbing her.

One evening he helped his father carve a wooden spoon and ladle for her. She was sitting in a rocker by the fireplace, a lap robe covering her legs, when he handed them to her. She looked up with an expressionless face. "Thank you," she said weakly.

Disappointed by her response, he lit the oil lamp that hung above the dinner table and sat down to read.

Unable to concentrate on the reading, he got up and put on his coat and hat. "I'm going for a walk by the river," he said.

His father nodded, but Fanny remained motionless.

The blue-gray light of the moon flooded the barren fields and leafless trees, making the landscape appear lifeless. He sat down on a stump and watched several cottontail rabbits hopping about in the eerie light. A red fox barked in the distance.

As frequently happened, his thoughts turned to Elizabeth. He was terribly fond of her, maybe in love. He really didn't know. And he was certain she cared for him. Why else would she make an effort to see him when he rode into town? If he only lived nearer to Fredericksburg, he could spend more time with her.

He rose to his feet, shivered, then pulled his coat more tightly around his body. He knew his father expected him to remain on the farm, to become a partner, to eventually take over its operation. He wasn't sure he wanted to do that. He liked farming all right, but there were many jobs in town that appealed to him. He could become a blacksmith, work as a carpenter, or learn to operate Mr. Harrington's ferry at the river crossing. Disappointing his parents was a dreadful thought, but in another year or two he would be old enough to try some of these things. Would they understand then? An awful agony was gnawing within. Turning on his heel, he started to walk slowly toward the cabin. An owl in a nearby oak hooted softly.

During the next few days he noticed that his mother was developing a slight, almost imperceptible cough that caused her to clear her throat continually. Late in December she came down with a cold. His father gave her onion cough syrup and applied hot poultices to her chest, but the cold would not clear up. Then Mr. Locke ordered her to remain in bed and fed her hot turtle soup, and to keep her warm, he heated rocks in a fireplace caldron, wrapped them in cloth, and placed them around her feet and legs.

After two weeks, Sam could see no improvement in Fanny's condition. When he looked at her closely, he saw she was struggling to breathe. Frightened, he yelled to Richard, "Go get Dr. Hart! Mother needs him! Quick!"

Richard hurriedly slipped a bridle on a roan gelding and headed up the river trail at a hard gallop. The brisk onrushing air numbed his cheeks. Twice he let the animal walk to catch its wind, but as soon as the violent heaving of the gelding's rib cage subsided, he urged it to speed on.

He dismounted at the hitching post in front of the doctor's office, looped the reins over the rail and charged noisily through the newly stained doorway. The doctor, sitting behind a cluttered desk, looked up from a book he was reading. "You seem to be in a hurry," he stated calmly.

"Yes, sir," Richard replied, removing his hat. "It's my...."

He was cut off by the penetrating voice of the small, gray-haired man.

"Been ridin' hard."

"Yes, sir," Richard repeated, impatiently wondering when this man was going to listen to his emergency.

"Know how I can tell?"

"I suppose... ," Richard began, again being interrupted.

"It's your wet pants. Soaked with horse sweat."

"Yes, sir."

"Now, what brings you here?"

"My mother. She's sick," Richard replied, feeling relieved that the doctor was finally listening to his problem.

"In bed?"

"Yes, sir."

"And who might you be?" Dr. Hart asked, his voice softening.

"Richard Locke. My mother's Fanny Locke."

"Oh, yes. Sam Locke's wife. Out on the river road."

"Yes, sir."

"What seems to be wrong?

"I don't know." Richard paused a moment. "But she's terribly sick."

The doctor looked at the floor, then back at the desk. "Well, I guess I can go out there now."

He put on his hat and coat, picked up his leather bag from behind the desk, and escorted Richard out the back door to a sagging wooden shed. The boy helped him hitch a gray filly to a surrey and lead it into the alley. When they reached the street, Richard tied his roan to the back of the surrey, then climbed up and sat down beside the waiting doctor.

After nearly an hour of trotting along the tree-lined trail, they reached the cabin. Sam was waiting at the door. While the doctor went inside, Richard took charge of the animals.

Dr. Hart dropped his coat and hat on a wooden chair and went directly into the bedroom, closing the door behind him. When he emerged nearly thirty minutes later, Sam offered him a cup of tea.

"How is she, doctor?" Sam asked as he poured the tea into the cups he had placed on the table.

The doctor sat down, took a deep breath and shook his head. Looking the elder Locke squarely in the eye, he stated, "She's pretty sick."

"What's wrong?" Sam asked, his mouth failing to close when he finished.

"Consumption—the white plague," the doctor said in a low voice.

Sam looked down at the table. He listened as the sound of a light, muffled cough escaped the partially opened bedroom door.

The doctor got up, closed the door, then returned to the table.

"What's her chances?" asked Sam, his face showing grave concern.

"Hard to say. But she's pretty far along. Just keep her warm and make her rest. Could be a while, and she's not going to have any strength. Absolutely no work!"

———————◆———————

Fanny Locke passed away during spring planting and was buried beside her baby, Martha.

Fortunately for Richard and his father, the following weeks of long daylight hours were extremely busy for them. They plowed, harrowed, and planted. Sometimes, they paused and looked across the fields through the quivering heat toward the feathery-leafed locust tree on the knoll behind the cabin. It reminded them that now they were alone.

In warm evenings as shadows lengthened, Sam walked the little path his booted feet had made to the carefully tended burial plot. He raked the two dark mounds to keep the weeds from growing, then stood with bowed head in silent prayer. He lingered until reminded by the call of a whippoorwill that the sun had dropped below the horizon.

Neighbors on their way to Fredericksburg stopped in for brief visits. It broke the periods of loneliness for the Lockes. Usually they left an item of baked goods or a cooked dish that brought a welcome change from the soup and stew Richard and his father found so convenient to prepare.

Linda Willows was a frequent visitor. Two or three times each week she emerged from the dense woods at the rear of the Locke farm carrying a small kettle containing a dozen cookies. Richard watched for her so he could meet her at the cabin. After placing the cookies in the pantry, he took her back to the place where he was working. He enjoyed being with Linda, but had to continue with his work to satisfy his father.

◆

The hot sun and warm rain of July made the corn leaf out and grow rapidly. It also brought on the ragweeds and thistles that Richard had to uproot with a hoe. He liked to have Linda visit him in the cornfield because it afforded privacy from his father who now worked nearer the house. Besides, the revealing clothes she wore aroused a curiosity within him. When she stood with her legs apart and her arms folded, stretching her faded broadcloth dress tightly across her buttocks, it made the blood rush through his veins. The distinct outline of her body was revealed, and it pushed her ample breasts upward so the cleavage was clearly visible. He was certain she did it to draw attention to her body.

At the far side of the cornfield stood a tall oak, its large trunk covered with shaggy bark. The lower branches drooped nearly to the ground, providing a pleasant, shaded spot for Richard to rest after weeding each long row of corn. It also made a nice place for Linda to visit him. At first they merely sat and talked beneath it, but as the corn grew to conceal them, they playfully pushed and shoved one another.

During one hot August day, Richard was working in the head-high corn. He removed his floppy hat to wipe his brow with the sleeve of his shirt when he saw Linda, in bare feet, carefully making her way toward him. Tossing the smooth handle of the hoe over his shoulder, he walked directly to her, took her soft, small-boned wrist in his callused hand, and led her to the shade of the oak. He dropped to his knees, pulled her down beside him, and kissed her awkwardly on the cheek.

She surprised him by seizing his face between the warm palms of her hands and kissing him squarely on the lips. He tried to withdraw, but she held firm. Soon he relaxed and felt the pressure of her breast against his chest.

Again and again they kissed until he sensed her hand guiding his in a circular motion to the fullness of her abdomen. As he continued the caressing, he became aware of his state of erection and knew that she could feel the throbbing muscle against her hip. Alarmed, he wondered what to do. He halted the movement of his hand and looked at her face as if to speak when she, with eyes closed, sighed, "Oh, Richard, rub it more."

He felt beads of perspiration developing on his upper lip and forehead as his erection began to subside. Again she sighed, raised her hips to hike her soiled skirt, and placed his cool hand on her pubic hair.

"Press harder," she urged, spreading her legs.

Suddenly he withdrew his hand and flipped the folds of her skirt down.

She opened her eyes. "What's the matter?" she asked, searching his face for an answer.

"I don't know," he replied, wrinkling his brow. "I don't feel right about it."

"Oh, Richard!" she declared disappointedly. "This is fun!"

"Maybe," he stammered, "maybe we'd better think about it."

For several long minutes they held hands and stared quietly at the leafy canopy overhead. Then, after squeezing her hand and kissing her on the cheek, he rose to his feet and pulled her up after him.

"I hope you're not angry with me," she pleaded, brushing the grass and leaves from her dress.

"Oh, no," he assured her, putting his arms about her neck. "It's just that it's so new to me."

40

They stepped apart and walked into the warm sunshine.

"Well, I'll go now," she said, smoothing her dress. "But I'll be back in a couple of days."

"All right," he replied as he retrieved his hoe. Then he watched as she disappeared into the tall corn.

That night he did not sleep well.

Two days later, after breakfast, Mr. Locke hitched the team to the wagon and climbed onto the seat. He was going to Fredericksburg and wanted to get back by early afternoon. It was the time of the year when every hour of daylight was needed to get the work done. "Rinse off the dishes and finish weeding the corn," he said to Richard as he snapped the reins to start the horses.

The ripening period was just ahead, and Richard knew that corn roots must not be disturbed then. It would be the last weeding of the season. He had spent dozens of hours at the tedious task and was pleased that the end was in sight.

After working three hours, enough to complete half of his assignment, he heard the rustle of someone threading a path through the withering corn. It was Linda, wearing a loose-fitting dress of green printed broadcloth. Her eyes sparkled, and her blond hair hung unconfined over her shoulders.

"Ho!" he greeted with a broad grin.

"Hello, Richard," she replied, a partial smile making shallow dimples in her pink cheeks. "Ready for a little rest?"

"Yes, I was just about to take one."

He took her by the hand as they walked across the warm soil toward the oak. Neither spoke until they were seated on the flattened grass beneath its sheltering limbs.

"Richard," Linda began, "I'm glad you still like me."

"Shouldn't I?" he asked, looking at her questioningly.

"After the other day, I mean."

"Oh, that." He paused for a moment, then smiled. "It was all right with me."

"Good!" She brightened. "Let's lay back and rest."

In a few minutes he was caressing her lower abdomen. She placed her hand on his and carefully directed the finger to the small, fibrous button of her clitoris. "There," she whispered. "Right there."

A short time later he opened his eyes and looked up at the motionless leaves above. Bewildered, he listened to the slow, rhythmic breathing next to him and remembered making love to her. When he reached down, he felt the sticky wetness of his trousers.

Slowly, he turned his head and looked at the array of soft blond hair nestled against his shoulder that partially obscured Linda's closed eyes. Her delicately molded lips were turned slightly upward in a smile of contentment. Suddenly he was frightened.

Richard continued to see Linda for the next several weeks, but his interest was waning. She was a good friend. He liked that, but thought she was expecting him to fall in love with her. That was something he could not do. She was so different from Elizabeth. Her soiled clothing, body odor, and coarse mannerisms bothered him. Each time they met, he felt more guilty for not being honest with her about his feelings.

By contrast, he was elated after a visit with Elizabeth. She attended school, so she could read, write, and understand the history of her country. And her mother was carefully training her in the art of homemaking. Whenever he saw her, she was tidy and clean, giving her a delicate neatness that appealed to him. He had held her hand only once, but was sure she would let him do it again.

◆

Richard turned seventeen in the spring. He had developed into a tall, wiry young man. Already five feet eight inches tall, he weighed 145 pounds. Working the fields in the bright summer sun deeply tanned his face, arms, and neck, and the muscles of his forearms rippled when he moved the fingers of his strong hands. He was a kind person, shy in the presence of strangers, but his actions showed the maturity he was acquiring. When he spoke, his piercing blue eyes and firm-set jaw gave conviction to his statements. He was also developing a spirit of independence and, with it, a yearning to extend beyond the confines of a farm on the Rappahannock.

When the fall harvest was complete, Sam gave Richard fifteen gold guineas, a quarter of the money he received from the sale of two cows and a wagonload of corn and rye. "There should be more than that next year," the elder Locke said with a smile, slapping his son on the shoulder.

Richard was pleased with the money and put it in a small wooden box in his dresser drawer. He was troubled, nevertheless, because his father still assumed he would take over the farm. For some time now, he had great misgivings about his future. The feeling haunted him. Someday he would have to explain to his father that he may want to do something else. But not today.

When November came, the leaves colored and fell from the trees. The fields, cleared of their harvest, would remain fallow until spring. Richard no longer had to spend long hours working in them. Although the animals still had to be cared for and wood had to be chopped, it took but a few hours each day. With time to himself, he decided to spend a day in Fredericksburg.

He took his brown corduroy breeches and heavy gray linen coat from the closet. They would make him look more like a city dweller than a farmer. After putting them on, he pulled on a pair of leather boots. He took a guinea from his drawer, flipped it in the air and caught it in his open palm. After studying its shiny face, he dropped it into his pocket.

"I'm going into town for a while," he told his father, who was drinking a cup of tea at the kitchen table.

"Gonna be back in time for chores?" his father asked. He was sure he would be, but was concerned that a young man with time on his hands and money in his pocket could drift into trouble.

"I will," Richard answered, slipping his new hat from its peg.

In town, he tied his horse to the rail in front of the livery stable next to Stover's blacksmith shop. If Elizabeth walked out onto her porch and looked down the street, he knew she would recognize the roan by the ivory rings on its reins. She had noticed the unique decorations on a previous occasion.

At Mrs. Dixon's Lodge on Hanover Street he drank a glass of ginger beer and bought a stick of taffy. Then he walked slowly up River Street. It was obvious that the horse and foot traffic had increased during the past two years. The activity fascinated him, so he lingered at the blacksmith shop to listen to the conversation of waiting customers. Several were making plans to move to western

Pennsylvania. "Can stake out bigger farms," a burly young man told Sidney Stover. "And the game's still thick there, too." Others standing nearby nodded agreement.

Suddenly he caught a glimpse of Elizabeth, wearing a blue shawl and long, dark coat, entering a store down the street. Hurrying, he got there just as she was emerging.

She dropped two spools of thread into a cloth handbag, then looked up, trying to act surprised. "Why hello, Richard," she said, her face coloring slightly. "What are you doing here?"

"Had some time. Just thought I'd ride into town."

"I'm getting some thread for a quilt I'm working on."

Richard jammed his hands into his pockets. "Can I walk you home?"

"Why, yes," she said, handing him the bag.

As they made their way up the street, Richard struggled for something to say. "The quilt," he said, "who is it for?"

Elizabeth carried herself erect, her head held high. She knew there were people watching from houses on both sides of the street. "I'm making it for my hope chest," she replied. "Mother thinks I should have two of them."

"Oh," Richard said. "That's nice."

"And how's your father?" Elizabeth inquired, turning her head to look at him.

"He's fine," Richard replied, feeling more relaxed. He looked at the smooth features of her face. "He'll rest up in the winter. But come spring, the work will pick up again."

When they reached the landing at the Harrington porch, they stopped. Elizabeth held out her hand for the bag. He hoped she would stay and talk with him, but Elizabeth, mindful of her mother's concern about appearances, said, "I must go in now. Mother needs my help."

"Oh?" Richard said.

Elizabeth saw the disappointed look on his face. She brightened and asked, "But why don't you call on me the next time you come to town?"

His face beamed. He shook her hand and felt pressure when she squeezed his before releasing it. As she walked up the steps, he

44

turned and hurried down the street. Although he wanted to jump with joy, he tried to walk as naturally as possible. He could feel a dozen eyes watching from behind shuttered windows.

◆

Richard drove a light wagon to town to buy rivets. He made the purchase at the harness shop, then decided to ride past Elizabeth's house. After all, he had been seen walking with her a number of times and she was nearly fifteen. Instead of continuing on as he had planned, however, he reined up in front of the house in the shade of one of the graceful young elms that lined each side of the street.

Elizabeth heard the clatter of the horse and wagon and looked out of the front window. When she stepped out onto the porch, her heart was pumping hard enough to bring a slight flush to her cheeks.

"Hello," called Richard, nervously fingering the reins.

"Hello, Richard," came the soft, reserved reply.

"What are you doing?" he asked, fumbling for something to say.

"I was just about to take a crock of tea to daddy," she stated, descending the steps as gracefully as possible.

He dropped the reins over the seat and hopped down beside her, pretending to check the gray animal's harness. "Just came in for some harness rivets."

At that moment Sarah opened the front door and called out, "Elizabeth, the tea is ready!" Then she saw Richard. "Oh, hello!" she said, waving to him.

"Hello, Mrs. Harrington," Richard replied, removing his hat. Turning to Elizabeth, he said, "I can take you if you like."

She looked at the dark eyebrows arching over his clear blue eyes. They seemed to emphasize an enthusiasm he was trying to disguise. "I'd like that," she responded with a smile.

She walked rapidly to the porch for the tea. "Mother, Richard offered to drive me to the ferry and back," she said softly.

"Fine, but come right home."

The springs beneath the weathered seat flexed easily as they turned onto the cobblestones of Caroline Street. To impress Elizabeth, he sat very erect and quickly maneuvered the rig through the traffic. When they reached the bumpy turnoff to the ferry, he took the crock of tea from her and placed it on the floor between his feet so she could hold onto the seat with both hands.

"Daddy fills these holes," she apologized, "but they come back still bigger after every rain."

When Arthur Harrington saw the wagon approach, he unhooked the cable across the entrance to the ferry. But when he looked up and saw his daughter, he replaced the hook and waited for them.

Elizabeth handed him the tea. "Richard gave me a ride. Wasn't that nice of him?"

"Yes. Fine." Arthur wondered about Richard's intentions.

Richard was disappointed by Mr. Harrington's cool response. Perhaps the son of a farmer wasn't good enough for his daughter. He waited for Elizabeth to get to the ground, then jumped down and walked over to Arthur's team. The sheen of their coats and silkiness of their buff manes and tails showed they were well cared for. "Sure good horseflesh," he ventured, patting one on the rump.

"It takes a good team to work this ferry," Arthur said as he walked toward Richard. He had a warm smile on his face.

After they talked a few minutes, Richard felt that Mr. Harrington liked him. And when he and Elizabeth were ready to leave, Arthur shook his hand. "Nice meeting you, Richard. Drop by again."

Richard knew he was accepted.

He turned the wagon around in front of Elizabeth's house and brought the horses to a halt. She sprang nimbly to the ground. "Thank you, Richard, very much."

"Yes'm," he replied. "You're welcome." He wanted to show good manners. Then, looking shyly away, he said, "I'll come by again the next time I'm in town."

She looked up at him. "I'd like that," she said with a smile.

She dashed up the steps and into the house. He was going to be her man. She'd see to it.

◆

Elizabeth got her own room when her father bought a larger, two bedroom brick house on Charles Street. It provided the privacy a young lady needed to bathe and dress, and she could spend more time in front of the large mirror to be certain she was presentable.

She had grown to a height of five feet two inches, with fine bones and coordinated muscles that made her lithe and nimble. Now her abdomen was flat, and the firmness of her supple breasts forced the protruding nipples to point slightly up and outward. She had a slender, velvety-white neck she protected from the elements with high collars and broad-brimmed hats that drew attention to her oval face and deep-set eyes. And high cheek bones created small creases at the sides of her mouth when she laughed. She tried different styles with her shoulder length hair, but thought it looked best parted in the middle and held back loosely with a satin ribbon tied so the ends streamed down between her shoulders.

A few days after they moved in she heard the rattle of wagon wheels and the clip-clap of a horse approaching on the dirt street. She looked out the window and saw Richard stopping out front. After checking herself in the mirror, she walked out onto the porch. "Hello, Richard. Come see our new house."

"I'd like to," he said, removing his hat.

Elizabeth felt elated as she showed him the large room that served as a dining and sitting room. The sitting section had a blue camelback settee against one wall and two straight-backed chairs with needlepoint seats between it and the fireplace. In one corner sat a hardwood rocker.

Richard stepped gingerly across the fringed, wine-colored carpet to the polished plank floor of the dining area. He reached across one of the ladderback chairs and rubbed the smooth surface of the heavy oak table. "Nice," he said, looking up at Elizabeth. "Mighty nice."

He noted the dishes in the large sideboard, then looked back into the sitting area. It was so different from the plainness of the little house he shared with his father. Perhaps if his mother had lived, they would have built a large home. His thoughts were interrupted by Elizabeth. "Look at the kitchen," she said, beckoning him through a large archway.

Mrs. Harrington was cooking over a wood-burning stove. "Hello, Richard," she said, looking up with a smile.

"Yes'm," Richard replied with a nod. He liked her. She was always so nice to him.

Then turning, Elizabeth said, "Here, I'll show you the bedrooms."

They glanced into her parent's room, then entered hers. Elizabeth walked over to the bed. "Daddy bought me this for my birthday," she said proudly.

Made of honey-colored maple, it had turned legs and a delicately carved headboard.

"That's a pretty quilt," Richard said, pointing to the multicolored bed covering.

"I like it. My mother and I made it."

Suddenly, Richard realized he had to get back to help his father with the evening chores. "I've got to go now," he said, heading for the door. "Could I take you for a ride Sunday afternoon?"

"Oh, yes," Elizabeth replied, her eyes sparkling with delight.

Elizabeth was waiting in her room when Richard wheeled the light wagon around in front of the house and tied his gray Percheron gelding to the iron hitching post. She watched him mount the steps, then heard a knock on the heavy oak door.

Mr. Harrington, reading a book at the dining room table, slowly got to his feet and let Richard in. "Elizabeth," he called. "Richard's here."

"Thank you, Daddy," she replied, trying hard to contain her excitement.

Richard waited by the door, hat in hand, as Mr. Harrington returned to the dining area. Then Elizabeth came out of her room.

"Oh, hello, Richard," she began as she walked toward him, her long yellow skirt nearly touching the floor. She emitted a faint fragrance of the lavender sachet kept in her closet and dresser drawers. Her pink cheeks, which she had pinched a few seconds before, gave the rest of her creamy velvet face a radiant look.

Her mother appeared at the archway separating the kitchen from the dining area. "Hello, Richard." Her face was graced with a broad smile. "A very nice day for a ride."

"Yes'm," he replied, twisting his hat in his hands.

Turning to Elizabeth, she cautioned, "Be sure to take your bonnet."

"Yes, Mother. I have it," Elizabeth answered, holding up a pale blue head covering with long ties. Turning to Richard, she said, "Ready?"

"Have a nice time!" Mrs. Harrington called out as they went through the front door.

Arthur continued to read.

They turned south on Hanover Street and headed out of town. Except for a few strollers, the streets were empty. Most were still eating dinner or enjoying the warm afternoon in the shade of their backyards. The street funneled down to a narrow lane overhung with trees populated with chirping jays and tanagers. A multitude of fox squirrels were using the scaly limbs as raceways. Neither Elizabeth nor Richard spoke as he soberly managed the reins, but they held hands on the seat between them, the folds of her dress hiding this act of affection from public view.

After fording a shallow stream, Richard tapped the muscular animal with the reins to begin an ascent up a slanted bluff to a forested overlook. At the top, he tied the horse to a sapling and then, grasping Elizabeth by the waist, helped her down, enjoying the warm softness of her body.

Holding hands while they walked, they went a short distance to a clearing where they could look out over the town. A few plumes of white smoke from scattered chimneys rose high into the azure sky before being carried eastward by an upper level current. The shiny blue ribbon of the Rappahannock formed a graceful curve around the town, then traveled on until it blended with the distant horizon. Richard was certain he could see where it passed his father's farm.

"I can see our house!" Elizabeth exclaimed excitedly. "Over there." She pointed.

"Have you ever been here before?" Richard asked.

"No."

They walked beneath the oaks and maples, shuffling through a carpet of last year's dried leaves. At one point, they had to circumvent a massive tangle of wild grape. Richard brushed off the trunk of a fallen tree and they sat down. A cottontail scampered into the brush.

"I like this," Elizabeth said, squeezing Richard's hand.

He placed his arm around her shoulder and she responded by resting her head against his neck. The warmth of his closeness felt good to her. And if her friend, Mary, asked whether he hugged her, she could truthfully say he had.

After a while he took her by the hand and started back toward the wagon. On the way, he slipped his hand around her waist and asked, "May I kiss you?"

She felt a flush in her cheeks. "Yes," she whispered.

As they kissed, ever so briefly, she quivered.

"Again?" he asked.

"Yes."

He held her close enough to feel the pressure of her breasts and thighs.

She placed her arms around his neck and closed her eyes.

Her temples began to throb. Suddenly, she pushed back, took his hand and said, "Let's go now."

On the way back they stopped at Mrs. Dixon's Lodge and had some ginger beer and vanilla cookies.

◆

In October they took another ride to the heights. The oaks and maples were aflame with reds, golds, and yellows, and the ground was covered with a new crop of pliable, leather-textured leaves. It made walking quieter and felt softer beneath their feet. Elizabeth spread a light lunch on a cloth in the speckled sunlight beneath a large maple tree. As they ate, a brightly colored leaf occasionally dropped upon them.

After awhile, they laid back on the lunch cloth and held hands. They looked up through the gray branches at the thinning leaves and bright blue sky. The air was filled with the sharp cries of an agitated blue jay and the ceaseless chatter of scampering squirrels. Richard rolled over and embraced her. Then he caressed her arms and shoulders and kissed her several times.

Elizabeth's breathing quickened. She was not supposed to enjoy the wonderful sensations surging through her body. Her mother had told her such pleasures would occur only after she was married—and maybe not even then. She grasped Richard's hands and held them against her chest. "Richard," she said earnestly, "I love you. But I don't feel right about this."

Memories of Linda flashed through Richard's mind. Elizabeth was different. He didn't want to change that. "I understand," he said. He kissed her, then pulled her to her feet.

◆

Riding out of Fredericksburg in midwinter, Richard noticed a sign tacked to the livery stable door. It read, *Help Wanted*. After riding to the edge of town, he wheeled his horse around and came back.

Sidney Stover was working his forge as Richard approached. "What can I do fer ye?" he asked, continuing to work the bellows.

Richard pointed to the stable. "The sign says you need help."

"That I do," Stover replied. "Too much work fer one man ta handle now." He looked at Richard. "You're the Locke boy, ain't ye?"

"Yes, sir."

"Job's yours, if ye want it. Takin' care o' the stable. Ten shillings a week and ye'll sleep in the back."

Richard was surprised at the quick turn of events. "When do I start?"

"Next week, Monday."

Richard went directly to his father and told him what he had done. His father looked at him stoically, then said, "Been expecting it. Thought maybe the city's gettin' to ya." He paused, then added, "Can probably get by the winter myself. But come spring, will need some help. Maybe I'll get a sharecropper." He looked out the window. "Remember, Son, there's a place for you here anytime you want it. But I understand."

"I'll remember that, Father," Richard said, extending his arm to shake Sam's hand.

◆

Late in the spring, a British army sergeant rode up to the livery stable and tacked a printed notice on the door. Richard, who was oiling and polishing a harness inside, came out when he heard the hammering. The sergeant mounted his horse and watched as Richard read the poster aloud. "By order of His Majesty, King George II, the Braddock Road will be made serviceable from the town of Winchester to Fort Pitt. Hardy workers are needed for the task. Any man willing to render such patriotic duty in the service of His Majesty should report to Fort Frederick during the first week of June, 1759. In addition to his keep, a worker will be paid one shilling for each day worked."

Richard turned to the sergeant. "Is that the wilderness?" he asked, his face beaming with eagerness.

"Aye. 'Tis the beginnin' o' the wilderness," the sergeant replied as he turned his horse.

A summer of work on the frontier appealed to Richard. Winter at the livery stable had enabled him to meet people migrating west. They told him fanciful stories of lofty dreams that could be fulfilled on the ever-widening frontier.

And there was something else. He had an underlying feeling of foreignness about living in Fredericksburg. Although he was well accepted by those who knew him, they were not many. The educated young men of prominent families looked down upon him as a farm boy, one who belonged in a social stratum below them. Others tended toward drinking, carousing, and hell-raising—something he wished to avoid. All he needed was a chance to prove his worthiness. Service in the king's cause would provide the opportunity. And maybe, just maybe, he would find his destiny.

A few days later, he rode out to inform his father of his decision. Apple trees were in full bloom, and farmers were already working their fields. It bothered him to leave his father this time of the year, but he had to take advantage of the situation. It wouldn't present itself again. And his father was well enough established to manage without him if he had to.

Sam sat with Richard at the dining table sipping a mixture of vinegar, sugar, and cold water as the young man haltingly described his plans.

When Richard finished, he looked up into his father's eyes.

Sam had listened attentively and watched the enthusiastic expressions on his son's face, recalling his own yearnings as a youth. Richard could certainly take care of himself; he knew that. Perhaps he would be ready to settle down on the farm when he returned. Sam nodded. "Sounds like some good experience," he said, pursing his lips.

Surprised by Sam's response, Richard asked, "You don't mind?"

"Not if that's what you want." Then Sam added, "Jason Willows has agreed to farm the back field on shares. And then you can come back here when you're done. That is, if you want to."

They stood and shook hands. "Be careful, Son," Sam said soberly. "That's a damn rough world out there."

The next day Richard took Elizabeth for a buggy ride along the river to tell her of his planned departure. He was certain she would understand and would wait for him to return. "Elizabeth," he said looking at her, "I want to tell you what I plan to do."

Her face brightened, and she slid over closer to him on the seat. Although it had never been mentioned, she had a feeling they would get married within the next year. Perhaps he wanted to say something about it now. "I'm listening," she said.

"I'm going to work in the king's service on the Braddock Road," he said, forcing a smile.

She leaned back and looked at him. The expression on her face changed from that of shock to anger, then to hurt. "But, Richard," she gasped, "I thought you loved me!" Tears filled her eyes.

"I do," he explained, halting the horse and taking her hands in his. "Someday I want you to be my wife. But I can't ask for that while working in a stable." He drew her close. The tears ran down her cheeks and spotted her dress.

"That place is filled with savages! They kill people! General Braddock was killed. Colonel Washington was defeated." She knew her history well.

"But it's all been retaken now," he countered. "Besides, the army will guard us." He paused. "I'll only be gone two months, and it'll give me more money. Might even lead to a better job."

She looked into his eyes. "Richard, I don't care what kind of work you do. I just want to be with you."

"You will be," he vowed, wiping the tears from her cheeks with his thumbs. He kissed her on the forehead, nose, and mouth, then pressed his forehead and nose against hers. "I promise you."

◆

He bought a new musket, one with a rifled bore, packed his clothes into a small bundle, and climbed onto his gray gelding. Elizabeth and Sarah followed him in a buggy to the ferry crossing. He shook hands with Arthur and kissed the two women.

"I'll wait for you," Elizabeth promised, tears welling up in her eyes.

"I'll be back soon."

He boarded the ferry to start his journey to Fort Frederick.

Chapter 4

Braddock Road

Richard tapped his gelding in the ribs, urging it across a shallow, rocky ford and up the bank on the far side of the Potomac. Halting the stalwart animal, he scanned the area about him, then heaved a large sigh of relief. He was on the broad, hard surface of the much-traveled Frederick Pike. It was the widest and straightest road he had ever seen. For three days he had been riding through the densely wooded countryside crossing streams, dodging branches, fighting gnats, and watching for Indians. Travel would be easier and safer now.

The road, twenty feet of packed clay and gravel with a narrow apron of clearing on each side, had been cut through the forest three years before. It was littered with the debris of heavy travel. Broken wagon parts, pieces of harness, and the shoes of horses and oxen were scattered along its edge. Animal droppings spotted its surface.

The sun was midway down in the western sky. Richard shaded his eyes and looked down the road into its glare. He wasn't sure how far it was to the fort but wanted to reach it before nightfall. Behind him, barely discernible in the distance, was a caravan of two wagons and a small herd of animals. It would take too long to wait for it. He flipped the reins and started the horse at an easy lope.

A mile down the road he came to a half-timbered structure with several British soldiers clustered in front. A wooden sign hanging in a wrought iron frame identified it as Ye Olde Tank Inn. A short distance ahead, looming in the late afternoon haze, was the log palisade of the fort.

Fort Frederick was located on high ground overlooking the Potomac. To Richard, it was an awesome structure. Its thick inner walls, made of brick and stone masonry, were designed to thwart Indian fire-arrow attacks. He rode through its large open doors and was halted by two red-coated sentries. Dismounting, he announced, "I'm Richard Locke. I've come to work on the Braddock Road."

"Aye," came the stiff reply, "ye and a dozen others." Turning, the sentry pointed to an opening in the inner wall. "Right through there and ask for Sergeant Turner."

Sergeant Turner, a wiry young man with a pointed chin and high cheekbones, was seated on a plank bench in front of a company headquarters. His black hat lay beside him, and his snug fitting trousers, their once shiny white twill now aged a dull cream color, were neatly tucked into a pair of lightly scuffed, black leather boots. "Damn nice horse," he stated after Richard introduced himself. "But you'll 'ave ta get rid of it."

"I've had him a long time, and I'd like to keep him," Richard protested.

"We furnish all pack and transport," the sergeant stated firmly. Then pointing, he added, "Take 'im to the stables for now. After that, go to that building and pick a bed. Then go over to the mess hall and eat.

The barracks, a long, low structure made of close-fitting limestone blocks, was located near the thick inner wall on the far side of the compound. Inside, closely spaced wooden bunk beds with slatted bottoms lined each wall. A narrow center aisle ran the length of a compacted dirt floor. Small open windows, which could be closed with their heavy wooden shutters, furnished illumination and fresh air.

Richard searched for several minutes before finding a bed that was not taken. He placed his roll of clothing on it, then went to the mess hall. A kitchen helper wearing a grimy apron ladled him a bowlful of thick beef stew. He carried it to a plank table and sat down.

"Eat 'er up, lad," welcomed a toothless man across the table as he wiped his whiskers on the sleeve of a tattered tweed coat. "It's damned good fare!"

Richard looked at the man's deeply furrowed face and graying hair. He had seen men like this who drifted through Fredericksburg. Illiterate and outwardly coarse, they wandered from place to place, doing whatever appealed to them and then only the minimum necessary to feed and clothe themselves. He would be courteous but wanted to become acquainted with someone nearer his own age. "Tastes good," he said soberly.

The man, sensing Richard's uneasiness, smiled. "Me name's John Harmon. Come from Yorkshire eight year ago. Done a lot o' things, but like work crews best."

Richard extended his hand. "Richard Locke. It's my first time with a work crew."

John took an immediate liking to Richard. He explained that he preferred being near the frontier to avoid the demands of settled, organized areas. "Not near enough ta be attacked, mind ya. Ain't lived thirty-seven years without bein' careful."

The weathered look of his bewhiskered face made him appear much older to Richard. But there was also a feeling that beneath his roughness the man possessed the gentleness of a grandfather.

He told John about his horse. "It's a nice animal. But they say I have to get rid of it."

"Won't be hard ta sell," John said. "There's a steady stream o' people runnin' this here pike every day. Lots o' them is buyin' everything in sight, 'specially those headed west."

"I hate to let him go," Richard said ruefully.

"Yah, I know," John sympathized. "A horse can be a good friend."

The following day Richard sold his gelding to a farmer who planned to settle near Fort Cumberland. "Ya can tell they're a good family," John said, trying to console his young friend. "They'll take good care of 'im." Then he put his hand on Richard's shoulder. "Let's walk to the barrel house down the road fer a sip o' ale."

As they sat down at a table in the rustic tavern, Richard said, "I rode past here on my way in."

"How'd ye come?" John asked. "By way o' Baltimore, or Philadelphia?"

"Neither," Richard replied, wiping foam from his upper lip. "Used the cross country trail over the Shenandoah."

"Good God!" exclaimed John, slamming his pewter tankard down on the table. Squinting, he stared at Richard. "No Indian trouble?"

"Only gnats and mosquitoes," Richard said with a shrug.

A soldier at the next table leaned over and told John, "It's not so bad now. Most of the 'ostiles 'ave crossed over to the other side of the mountain."

"But I 'eard 'twas crawlin' with 'em," replied John, munching his gums.

"That was two years ago," countered the soldier. "Some regulars and Virginia Militia routed 'em." He paused, then added, "O' course, ya never know!"

◆

On Monday, June 11, 1759, Richard left the safe confines of Fort Frederick. He was part of a convoy of one hundred civilian workers, two hundred British soldiers, and ten horse-drawn wagons under command of Major Henry Bowman. The pleasant scent of spring was everywhere, and the forest was alive with birds and animals tending their young. Alongside the road, clusters of daisies were being caressed by gentle zephyrs. Leading the long column were twenty British officers, brightly dressed in red and white uniforms, their gleaming trappings reflecting the bright sun as they rode astride trim, white stallions. Although the Indians in the area were considered friendly, several families moving west followed the convoy for protection.

Richard looked back and noted a commotion a short distance behind him. A family was having difficulty keeping one of their cows in the herd. He dropped back and, after a brief chase through the woods, caught the errant animal. The owner then slipped a halter over its head and tied it to the rear of his wagon with a short rope.

"Much obliged," wheezed the winded man.

"Pleased to help," Richard replied, tipping his hat to the man's wife while turning to rejoin the column of workers.

Late in the morning the convoy pulled onto a sandbar where Tonoloway Creek rushed to join the Potomac. " 'Tis as far as we go on the Pike," Major Bowman informed the families. Then, noting the look of concern on their faces, he said, " 'Tis perfectly safe. No danger between here and Fort Cumberland."

While the families moved on, tables from the supply wagons were spread so the officers could sit in the shade and eat their ration of cold roast lamb, bread and tea. Others sat on the ground to eat.

"Must be afraid of staining their white britches," Richard mused aloud, nodding toward the officers table.

"Hope ta 'ell they stain 'em on the inside," quipped John with a laugh. "They think they're so damned mighty!"

The Winchester Trail was a narrow, crooked path suited for foot or mounted traffic. The supply wagons straddled stumps, were forced between trees, and became mired in the black ooze of soggy depressions. A dozen men with axes removed low hanging limbs and intruding vines.

When evening approached, the convoy halted beside a cluster of bubbling hot springs.

"Them's mineral springs," John informed Richard as they stood over one of the fissures in the sod from which the steaming water issued.

"Sure stinks," replied Richard, squatting to watch the water boil up then flow down a reddish brown rut into a nearby freshwater stream.

"Yah, but it's good fer ye," voiced John, drinking some from his cupped hand. He stood, then wiped his chin with his sleeve. "Indians roll in that brown mud. Keeps 'em strong and healthy. Makes 'em so's they can outrun a deer."

Tents were erected for the officers and kitchen, horses were tethered, and guards posted. Soldiers placed their bedrolls on the ground in a preselected area while workers took theirs to another.

"I don't give a damn where ya sleep," shouted Sergeant Turner as he stood among the workers, "but ya best not go too far out!"

After supper John sat down near Richard. He propped his back against a small tree and took a roll of soiled cloth from his coat pocket. Richard watched intently as he extracted a short, nicotine-stained clay pipe from it.

"I'd try a bath in the mud pot," John said, examining the pipe, "but I'm afeared the night air'd chill me blood."

"I'm going down to the creek and wash up," Richard said. "My feet feel tired."

"I'll sit 'ere and wait," said John, taking a leather tobacco pouch from another pocket.

Richard walked to where the small, clear stream left the woods to meander across a grassy meadow. He rinsed the sweaty grime from his face and arms, then removed his shoes. While enjoying the refreshing feeling of the water on his feet, he looked up to see a family of deer filing leisurely along a well-worn path toward the meadow. It reminded him of the farm in Fredericksburg. Regardless of how hot and sultry the day, evening brought a pleasant coolness to the forest floor inviting the wild creatures to venture forth for food and to drink from the lacy edge of a stream.

The deer suddenly halted and stared with big brown eyes in his direction. Standing motionless with their ears pointed alertly upward, they sniffed at the mixed odors of burning wood, tobacco smoke, and sweat that drifted toward them. When they smelled the spiciness of venison stew that lingered over the area, they turned and walked rapidly on.

Richard remained for several minutes listening to the babble and shouts of the work crew and thinking about home, and he thought about Elizabeth and smiled.

He slept fitfully that night, irritated by bumps on the hard ground and mosquitoes that probed openings in the folds of his blanket. In addition, horses neighed, soldiers snored, workers farted, and he could hear the constant shuffle of men moving about.

◆

Three sergeants, under command of the engineer officers, roused the workers early, herded them to breakfast, then split them into three crews. A half dozen volunteers were selected to remain at the camp to repair harness and hunt game for the cooks.

"Bring on those red-assed bastards!" shouted one worker, waving a sickle above his head.

John leaned toward Richard. "Yah," he said in a low voice. "Probably shit 'is baggy drawers if he saw one acomin'."

One crew was assigned to work on the road surface while the other two worked the berms. Although the section of the Braddock Road from Winchester to Fort Cumberland had seen occasional use, the surface had to be smoothed, leveled, and cleared of saplings, roots, and other impediments that had developed during the past two years, and the narrow berms had become overhung with low branches and clogged by a profusion of tall weeds.

Officers, mounted on neatly groomed horses, ordered a group of soldiers forward to guard against Indians. Then they rode about giving directions with an occasional comment or wave of a riding crop. The sergeants, who were the most knowledgeable road builders, struggled to keep the sweating, joking, grumbling workers at the task.

Late in the afternoon the work was halted for the day and everyone returned to camp. Richard washed his face and hands in a pond then spread his bedroll on a cushion of dry needles beneath the low-hanging branches of a pine tree.

"Just be sure 'tain't a roostin' place fer the birds," John warned as he approached with his bedroll.

Suddenly the sky darkened and the calm air became alive with the beating whir of thousands of fluttering wings.

"What in God's name is that?" asked one of the workers, jumping to his feet.

"Birds!" replied Richard, shouting to be heard above the din.

"Well, I'll be damned!" exclaimed John, rising to watch the noisy, dark cloud passing overhead in a solid mass.

"They're comin' down right over there!" shouted Sergeant Turner, pointing to a scattering of large oaks and maples in a clearing a short distance from the camp. "Let's 'ave a look."

Richard and John joined the small group led by the sergeant. They walked through the brush and bramble as cautiously as possible, trying to stay beneath trees to avoid the rain of droppings. At the edge of the clearing they stood in awe, while thousands of birds landed in the large trees.

"Passenger pigeons!" announced the sergeant, yelling to be heard.

Richard looked at him with a puzzled expression on his face.

"Aye. Seen 'em many times down on the Monongahela."

The pigeons continued to arrive, changing the trees from a bright green to a dark gray. Limbs drooped steadily lower until birds near the tips slid off and had to reposition themselves. When a large branch, unable to support its heavy burden, snapped with a resounding crack, a dark, fluttering cloud of squawking, cooing, chirping birds arose and circled.

After returning to camp, John walked over to the cook. "Let's get some birds ta eat fer tomorrow," he said.

"We'll take care o' it in the mornin', just afore dawn," the cook replied, hooking his thumbs in the neckstrap of his food-stained apron. "That's when they'll be their juiciest and tenderest."

"Are ya sure?" asked another worker.

"Aye! That's when ta kill birds. We've done it afore."

For the remainder of the evening, until campfire flames had subsided into beds of glowing coals, Richard listened to embellished stories about birds.

◆

Stars still sparkled in the dark purple canopy overhead when Richard was awakened by a rustle of movement in the soldiers' sleeping area. He sat up quietly and looked about. Others were also rising to a sitting position. He reached over and jostled John.

"What's the matter?" John asked sleepily.

"Sh!" Richard cautioned. "The hunters are going after the birds."

Fifteen minutes later they heard three distinct booms. Shots that followed were blended with echoes and reverberations that rolled back and forth among the hills and trees. As the booming subsided, they could hear the frantic fluttering of wings and alarmed cries of thousands of frightened birds taking to the air.

The noise gradually died away, and the camp waited for the hunters to return. Just as the eastern sky was turning a light gray, they came back carrying several sacks filled with pigeons.

When breakfast was finished, Richard and John joined a group of workers who wanted to visit the roosting site. After struggling through a tangle of waist-high blackberry plants that surrounded the hardwood clearing, they approached a large oak tree. Several branches had been broken and were hanging by tough, stringy sapwood fibers.

"What say ye, lad?" asked John, breathing heavily from the walk. " 'Twas a sight ta behold, weren't it?"

"It was," Richard agreed, looking over the area. "I did not know there were that many birds in the world."

"Those shots musta scared 'ell outa 'em," volunteered one of the men, pointing to the heavy layer of droppings that obscured the ground beneath the tree. "Just look at that pile o' shit!"

John guffawed.

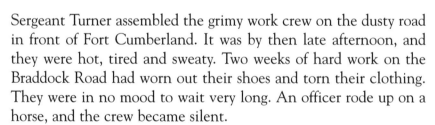

Sergeant Turner assembled the grimy work crew on the dusty road in front of Fort Cumberland. It was by then late afternoon, and they were hot, tired and sweaty. Two weeks of hard work on the Braddock Road had worn out their shoes and torn their clothing. They were in no mood to wait very long. An officer rode up on a horse, and the crew became silent.

"Major Scott would like ta 'ave a few words with ye!" the sergeant shouted.

"Men," the major began, surveying the group from left to right. "ye've done a right fine job and deserve a rest. We'll be 'ere two days." He paused briefly, then continued, "I've 'eard some o' ye want ta quit. We're sorry ta lose ye. But the paymaster will give ya what's due ye. For those 'ardy men among ye who want ta see the job finished, ye'll be paid at Fort Pitt. What e'er ye might need now, ye can charge against it." Again he looked them over. "We'll gather again in two days."

As the major rode off, John turned to Richard. "So says is royal 'ighness," he said with a snap of his head.

Fort Cumberland was a cluster of wooden houses, barracks and sheds surrounded by a stockade of pointed poles set vertically around its perimeter. It was considerably more primitive than Fort Frederick and, from a defense standpoint, not well situated.

It occupied a small clearing on the north bank of the Potomac and was nearly surrounded by forested highlands. Garrisoned by fifty British regulars, it also housed civilians, mostly transients on their way to establish farms in the nearby valleys. They were the settlers who had not yet acquired the woodsman's skill and hatred of Indians—the rawhide toughness necessary to be cunning bush-fighters able to stand alone in the wilderness. And there were the drifters, drunks, and vagrants, both Indian and white, who mingled with the inhabitants or camped along the approaches to beg, sell, or steal.

Inside the fort, Richard looked through a pile of shirts on a table at the trading post. When he raised his head, he saw a tall, handsome young man dressed in buckskins across from him. "Trying to find a shirt," he explained to the man. "Ripped mine working on the road." He pointed to a large triangular tear on the shoulder.

The stranger eyed him with cool blue eyes. "Just joined the crew myself," he responded.

"I heard that a dozen quit," Richard said, walking around the table. He extended his hand. "My name's Richard Locke."

The man grasped the hand firmly. "Wade. Phillip Wade. My friends call me Flip."

There was something about Flip's demeanor that Richard liked. He wasn't exactly sure what it was, but had a feeling it was their destiny to meet. The man spoke with a measured cadence that gave a ring of authority to what he said, and his precise enunciation of words in a learned accent showed evidence of schooling and culture. "Flip it will be," Richard assured him.

Richard selected a shirt, then looked at some shoes. "Where do you come from?" he asked.

"Boston," Flip replied as he watched Richard examine the shoes.

"And you joined *this* work crew?" Richard asked, shaking his head. "Sure a long way from Boston."

"Haven't been there for many a year. Heard about this job when I was selling a batch of pelts at Fort Ligonier. So I hotfooted it to Fort Frederick." He shook his head. "Was too late, but they said I could catch you here."

They talked for several minutes, then walked slowly back to the barracks.

Flip Wade had spent much of his thirty-two years trading among the English, French, and Indians. His body appeared agile and swift and radiated a determination to arrive anywhere he set out to reach. Some squint wrinkles rimmed his eyes, and a few vertical lines were beginning to show on the otherwise smooth, tan skin of his face. A heavy crop of black hair nearly covered his ears and trailed off down the nape of his neck. Although he didn't talk much about it, Richard got the impression he understood life on the frontier very well.

◆

The sun had risen above the trees just enough to warm the backs of the assembled work crew. Richard and Flip stood to one side as those without weapons were issued muskets, powder horns, and short lengths of lead rod from which they could bite shot.

Nearby, drivers hitched their horses to the wagons.

"Tie your musket to your bedroll and put 'em in this wagon!" a sergeant bellowed, pointing to one of the waiting vehicles.

"Must be expecting a fight," Richard said, rolling his bedding around the musket he'd brought from Fredericksburg.

"Best we're ready," Flip stated coolly. He patted his musket. "Carried 'er four years. Ain't misfired yet."

"Ever kill anybody with it?" Richard asked, a frown of concern showing on his face.

"Yes. One Frenchman and four Indians." Flip reflected for a moment. "But I always use ball shot."

John, who had been issued a musket, approached as Flip spoke. He looked down at his weapon, then up at the two men. "B'gawd, I hope we don't run inta somethin'," he groaned. "If I'd wanted ta fight I'd 'ave joined the militia."

They placed their bedrolls in the wagon, then walked toward the head of the column. Suddenly, John thrust his arms out to halt them. "Look at that!" he said, pointing to the lead wagon. They're loadin' in four women!"

They're Indian girls," Flip said calmly. "To keep the officers' quarters in order"

"Ha!" John snorted. "They'll all 'ave a British seed in their bellies by the time they get ta Fort Pitt!"

Flip, enjoying John's state of irritation, prodded him again. "And they're taking two Indian scouts along, too."

"Oh, hell!" John said, spitting on the ground. "We'll 'ave trouble fer sure!"

For the first three miles, the road traversed a fertile valley occupied by several farm families. Then, after skirting Wills Mountain, it went over a series of steep hills where landslides had to be removed and washouts filled. At Wills Creek, a bridge had to be constructed over a gorge.

While axmen fell trees which were hauled to the site by horses and oxen, dozens of workers cleared, leveled and compacted the bridge approaches. They tossed animal bones, broken harness and smashed wheels onto a growing pile of wrecked materiel Braddock had expended in a gigantic effort to haul heavy artillery over the mountains.

"Hope ta hell we don't have too much of this," complained Flip, removing his hat to wipe the sweat from his face. "This damn shovel handle just don't fit my hand very well."

"Shouldn't be this rough very long," Richard replied, trying to assure his friend that most of the work would not be this strenuous.

They knelt at the edge of the rapidly flowing little stream, rinsed their faces, and drank from the cool water.

"Cheer up, me lads," teased John as he watched them return to pick up their shovels. "There's only a hundred and ten miles ta go."

Although evenings were cooler in the highlands, the nuisance of gnats and mosquitoes did not diminish. And security had to be tightened when the two Indian scouts ran off. "They'll tell their friends," Flip warned. "Tell 'em, what we have and how we guard the camp."

As a precaution each night, the men were gathered into a small area with the supply wagons at their center. The number of guards was doubled and in the morning, before work was begun, scouting parties were sent out to be certain the area was clear of Indians.

A few nights after the scouts had fled, Richard was awakened by a damp chill. He shivered, then pulled his blanket up around his neck. It was after midnight and the campfires had been reduced to piles of ash-covered coals. Most of the men, tired after a long day of hard work, were sleeping soundly beneath the dark canopy of tree limbs that blocked the sky from view. Suddenly, a shot rang out. Then another.

Richard tossed his blanket aside, sprang to his knees and grabbed the loaded musket lying beside his bed. In the darkness he could see shadows of shouting men darting about trying to get their muskets from the supply wagon. He was glad Flip had told him to keep his weapon beside his bed.

As his eyes searched the darkness, he could feel his heart thundering inside his chest. Amid the shouting he heard someone say that an Indian had tried to steal a horse. A guard saw him, fired and missed. The red man fled into the forest.

In a few minutes a fire was blazing and the disorder subsided. Off duty soldiers dressed and took their stations, surrounding the camp with a ring of freshly loaded muskets bristling with burnished bayonets.

Richard stood and looked down at Flip, who sat calmly in his bed. "Where's your musket?" he asked excitedly. He could still feel his temples throbbing.

"Right here beside me," Flip replied as he looked around.

"It's Indians!" Richard warned.

"No Indians for a mile now," Flip said assuringly. "Probably some young buck trying to show his bravery to the elders."

Richard slid into his bed but could not go to sleep. He heard only the restless coughing and shuffling of others who could not sleep.

When the light of dawn finally came, it brought relief from the spell of imagined fear that gripped him. He would talk to Flip to learn more about Indian ways. Perhaps then, he could sleep better.

◆

In mid-July the work crew finished the tortuous stretch of road over the Laurel Mountains and broke out onto the grassy flatlands of Great Meadows. "Men," said Sergeant Turner, "the worst is behind us. And we're goin' ta rest 'ere fer two days."

The weary men burst forth with loud shouts of jubilation. John rubbed his face. "Been out o' the sun fer so long I've got moss growin' in m' whiskers." He chuckled and looked at Richard.

Richard grinned, and John's eyes gleamed. John liked to impress the young Virginian with his quips.

Richard and Flip spread their bedrolls near a large beaver pond at the edge of the camp. Then Richard removed his shirt and sat down on a stump to mend it. The bright sunlight made him squint as he threaded a bone needle.

"Wouldn't have ta do that if ya had buckskins," said Flip, walking over to sit on the ground beside him.

Richard looked over at a hungry horse filling its shrunken stomach with the lush bluegrass. "Do you have to wash buckskins?" he asked.

"No," Flip replied. He pushed a stem of grass through his teeth. "Only time they get wet is when it rains or I get chased across a river." He smiled.

Sergeant Turner walked up. "Flip Wade, aren't ye?" he asked, looking down at Flip.

Flip nodded.

"Scouts report a small camp of Indians in the woods on the other side." The sergeant pointed across the pond. "The major wants ta give 'em some presents ta keep 'em friendly. Needs someone ta talk with 'em. Somebody said you know Indians."

Flip chewed on the grass stem and looked across the pond.

"I'll go," he agreed. "But we'd better lay some plans first."

"We'll leave in an hour or so," Sergeant Turner said, turning to go.

"The Indians I've met just don't like having an armed party comin' late afternoon or evenin'," Flip replied.

The sergeant faced Flip again. " 'ow much Indian experience ye 'ad?"

"Lived among 'em on and off two years."

"Which ones?"

"Hurons, Mohawks, and Senecas," answered Flip.

"You lived right with the Indians?" Richard asked, his face showing surprise.

"Yes," Flip replied calmly. "Met a lot of different ones. Up around Lake Erie, mostly."

That night the grassland camp was ringed with soldier guards. Fires were kept small, and the workers talked excitedly about contacting the Indians.

"Didn't know you knew Indians so well," Richard said as he sat with Flip in a small cluster of men.

"Oh, sure," Flip said. "I've hunted, fished, traded, and trapped all around the Alleghenys and up along the lake."

"But the French are up there," one of the workers snapped indignantly.

"French, English, Indians—it don't matter to me," explained Flip, poking the fire with a stick. "I just go about my own business." There was a long moment of silence then, pointing across the pond, he added, "Tomorrow we'll go over and see how friendly they are over there."

"Be up ta me," spouted one of the workers, "I'd go o'er and run em ta 'ell out!"

"I'd say ta just move on and let em be," concluded John, puffing noisily on his gurgling pipe.

◆

The next morning after a late breakfast, twenty of the king's regulars and four civilian workers, including Flip and Richard, assembled to visit the Indian camp. The regulars were commanded by Lieutenant Whiteman, who wore a gleaming gorget on his breast. His soldiers were neatly dressed in their bright uniforms and fully prepared for battle. Walking up and down before them, he eyed them carefully. Then, turning on his heel, he faced them. "Men," he began, "empty your muskets and recharge them with fresh powder. We'll 'ope fer the best and prepare fer the worst. Gotta give em a show of strength."

In a column of twos led by Flip and the lieutenant, they walked through knee-high grass still damp with dew. A spray of brown grasshoppers fled before them, the larger ones clicking loudly as they fluttered down a few yards ahead.

When they skirted the pond, a pair of blue jays and several crows set up a chorus of squawking and cawing. Some leopard frogs jumped from the coarse grass and rushed to the safety of the mud beneath the shallow water, sending a series of ripples across the glassy surface. And the fat, croaking bullfrogs suddenly became silent.

Flip and the lieutenant strained to see some kind of movement among the bark lodges, but there was only smoke issuing from crevices along the rooflines.

"Must still be asleep," said Richard softly, as he followed a few steps behind Flip.

"Ya can bet there's a dozen eyes watchin' ya right now," Flip replied without turning his head.

They came to the brink of a small hill that descended to the narrow stream below the beaver dam. Focusing on a commotion in the tall grass, they watched as two small boys scrambled up the incline on the other side and disappeared into a scattering of trees near the lodges. In their frightened haste, the boys had abandoned a small, bewildered companion who was naked below the waist.

Flip spun around and raised both hands, halting the column. He turned to the lieutenant. "Have them sit down—quick!"

Lieutenant Whiteman motioned with his arms and the troopers squatted on their haunches. He and Flip continued to stand and watch the little boy.

"Should we go down and 'elp the little bloke?" asked the lieutenant.

"No. Just wait here," cautioned Flip, looking toward the lodges.

Three Indians dressed in buckskin clothing arose from the grass directly across the cut from them. Their facial features were not clear since they stood in the shade of scrub oak growing behind them. Flip and the lieutenant remained motionless.

"Popped up outa nowhere," whispered the lieutenant.

"I'm sure there's more," replied Flip, continuing to look straight ahead.

The Indians stepped forward into the sunlight, folded their arms across their chests, and stared at the strangers. The fierce look in their dark eyes frightened Richard, but he forced himself to remain calm.

"Cherokee," whispered Flip as he raised his right hand with an open palm. "Can tell by the bands and red marks on their neck and sleeve."

One of the Indians responded by raising his hand in a similar manner. He then shouted over his shoulder, and a rotund woman came from the trees and ran down the bank to retrieve the little boy. Quickly, she grabbed him up under one arm, turned, then struggled as she waddled back up the incline. The luster of her braided, jet-black hair reflected the morning sun.

Lieutenant Whiteman signaled his men to come forward and spread out on a line along the brink of the cut.

The three Indians remained motionless as Flip again raised his hand. Then, he and the lieutenant crossed the stream to meet them, halting ten feet from where they stood.

Two of the braves appeared very young to Flip, perhaps sixteen. Their shoulder length hair hung loosely about their short necks.

The third, a bit older, had longer hair fastened behind his head with a leather thong. A braided leather band held two crow feathers erect at the back of his head. All three wore ill-fitting buckskins and emitted a strong odor of wood smoke. Flip imagined a thousand eyes were watching. He could feel the hair rise on the nape of his neck.

"Ask 'em who is the chief," suggested the lieutenant.

"None of these, for sure," answered Flip as he asked for their leader in sign language.

Flip saw that the two younger ones did not understand, but the older one responded immediately.

"He says the chief is in the lodge and cannot be disturbed."

After several exchanges, Flip concluded that the chief was not going to appear. "Let's leave the presents with these three," he told the lieutenant.

Whiteman motioned for the gift couriers to come forward. Two blankets, a sack of glass beads, several bright metal buttons, and three small mirrors were stacked at the Cherokees' feet.

Flip again spoke in sign language. "These gifts are for your chief and his people. They are gifts of friendship and peace from your friends across the pond in the meadow. The white warriors will leave in two days. The chief and his people are welcome to visit the white man's camp."

The older brave nodded in straight-faced gratitude and approval.

After the troopers were assembled for the return to camp, Lieutenant Whiteman stood at the front of the column. "Let's get ta 'ell out of 'ere!" he exclaimed, stepping off briskly.

"No fear," Flip assured him. "They're not in a hostile mood."

"Still makes me feel uneasy."

When Whiteman dismissed his men and reported to the tent of Major Bowman, the troopers were besieged with questions from those who had remained at the camp. "First time I was ever near an Indian camp," Richard confessed as he and Flip sat down near their beds. "I was wondering what they were going to do when you walked up to them. Were you scared?"

"A bit," Flip admitted. "But they showed no weapons or paint. Besides, Indians around here have had the hell beat or scared out of 'em a couple years ago."

"Do they always smell like that?"

"Usually. Lodges are almost always full of smoke. That's why an Indian has ta sneak up on ya from downwind." Flip paused a moment to look across the pond. "They probably built a fire ta warm up this morning."

◆

Work on the road moved rapidly in the flatlands. Horses and oxen ate their fill of grass each day, and the heightened spirits of the men made them more energetic. Several talked about reaching Fort Pitt in a few days. "There's still some rough stretches ahead," warned Sergeant Turner. He wanted to maintain their eagerness but feared it would falter in the wooded hills ahead.

One evening they camped beside the slow, meandering waters of Indian Run, directly across from the ruins of Fort Necessity. After supper, Richard and Flip leaped over the little stream and walked through the partially burned tangle of split oak logs and brace poles. The area seemed eerie, almost foreboding to them.

"This place isn't any bigger than our barnyard back home," Richard stated soberly as he looked at its circular outline.

"Musta had a terrible time defendin' it," Flip said, stumbling as he walked through the ruins.

Suddenly, a voice behind them exclaimed, "So this is where old Georgie Wash got his ass licked!"

Turning, they saw John, his toothless mouth puckered around the stem of his pipe. He was standing on one of the long, V-shaped mounds which protected the trenches around the stockade.

While Flip probed the ruins, Richard jumped over a caved-in trench and stood beside John. Quietly, they scanned a forested hill a few hundred yards away, then focused on a grassy area to the north. It was spotted with tree stumps.

"Musta been a little grove o' trees where they got the logs," John said pointing with his pipe.

At that moment four British officers walked around the ruins to a small, grass-covered mound located between the stockade and a perimeter trench. A large granite fieldstone had been placed at one end of the mound. The officers removed their hats and stood quietly, side by side, with bowed heads. As Richard, Flip, and John walked toward them, the officers replaced their hats and turned to leave. One of them looked at Richard and said solemnly, "The grave of General Braddock."

The three men remained for several minutes among the lengthening shadows before Richard broke the silence. "What a lonely, desolate, godforsaken place to fight for your life."

"But," Flip responded, "sometimes man's not given a choice where ta die."

◆

Deep in the dense forest, the work crew arrived at a shallow crossing of the Youghioheny River. Although the men preferred the coolness of the shade, the troopers held an intense fear of the forest and what it could hide. By day, patrols ranged left and right, front and rear. At night they were so edgy they frequently aroused and alerted the camp at the sound of walking deer or hooting owls.

"Why not camp on the other side?" Richard asked as he and Flip looked across the fast moving water. "Would have all night to dry off."

"Always keep water between you and the unknown when ya can," Flip answered, squinting to see past the thick brush on the other side.

"Do you see something?"

"There's something there all right," Flip answered quietly.

"I see it," Richard said. He could sense his pulse quicken.

Out of the brush stepped two men dressed in buckskins. The shorter one cupped his hands to his mouth and shouted, "Can we join you?"

Six armed troopers trotted to the water's edge, looked them over, then signaled for them to cross. Under careful scrutiny of the soldiers the two men waded through the knee-deep water. As they walked, murky ribbons of silt rose around their feet and blended with the clear water rushing downstream.

"Sure glad ta see ya, lads," the short one said in a thick Irish brogue as he walked up to the troopers. He was lean and wiry, and wore a floppy, gray, broad-brimmed hat pushed back on his head. His narrow, gopher-like face was covered with a thin blond stubble of beard he stroked nervously as he talked. "The name's O'Toole. Been three days on the road and seen nary a soul." A high pitched voice and protruding front teeth made certain words end with a whistle.

"Where are you from?" asked Richard, holding the man's musket while he removed his backpack and placed it on the ground.

"Acomin' from Fort Pitt," he replied.

The second man was a swarthy, heavy-set individual with a coonskin hat who stood beside O'Toole but said nothing. The pants of his buckskin outfit were new, but the jacket was so old it was shiny black in several places and most of the fringe was missing. He smelled like rancid fat.

"Get in line with the others," Sergeant Turner said sternly. "The cook will give ye a plate o' rabbit stew and biscuits."

When they sat on a log to eat, Flip sat near them. He wanted to ask them some questions, figuring if he knew them better he might sleep easier. "How's the road between here and Fort Pitt?" he began.

O'Toole swallowed a big mouthful. "Not bad. Not bad 'tall." He took a bite of biscuit. "Tore up in some spots, but not bad 'tall."

"What's happenin' at Fort Pitt?" Flip asked.

"Well, me and Lance here, we spent the winter along the Juanita. Then we sold our pelts at Raystown." He waved his fork as he spoke. "That's east o' Pitt. Then we spent a week at Pitt." He looked at Flip, shook his head and smiled. "Spent most o' our money, too." He paused to dab a piece of biscuit in the gravy on his plate. "Thought we'd go through the Cumberland Gap and spend next winter in the mountains o' West Virginia. Oughta be a lot a good pelts just fer the takin'. Get provisioned at Fort Cumberland afore we go."

Lance nodded and continued to eat.

Richard and Flip walked away to a small campfire John had started near their beds. "Ever see them before?" Richard asked. To him, O'Toole seemed no different than most of those in the work crew. But Lance had shifty eyes that seemed to dart about, focusing on one thing then quickly changing to another

"No," Flip replied, sitting down at the fire. "There's a lot of trappers around. They're probably tellin' the truth. Just watch 'em, though."

They sat for several minutes watching the fire as it hissed and popped. Then John broke the silence. "They seem good enough ta me," he said, looking at Flip for a response.

"It won't hurt ta watch 'em," Flip said as he added two small pieces of wood to the fire. "I always make it a habit ta keep an eye on strangers fer awhile. Never know what they'll do." He paused, then added, "Besides, you'll probably never see 'em again."

That night Richard and Flip slept with muskets against their sides and hunting knives in their bedrolls.

The next morning after breakfast, O'Toole, with Lance at his side, shook hands with Sergeant Turner. "We thank ye fer feedin' us and keepin' us overnight." They turned, took a few steps, then turned back again. "And thanks fer fixin' the road. It'll make travelin' a bit easier."

They started off again, halting once to wave back before disappearing around a turn in the road.

"Damn nice chaps," said the sergeant. Then he removed his hat and waved it above his head. "Let's get across the river!" he bellowed.

While a group of men stepped into the cold water and plodded across, Richard and Flip sat down and removed their shoes and socks.

"That water feels good on the feet," Richard said, treading carefully on the muddy bottom.

"Yah," Flip agreed, wincing as he stepped on a sharp stone. "Feet get tender when the shoes get thin."

John carefully wrapped his pipe in its old rag and stuffed it into his coat pocket. Then, with an air of indifference, he raised the bottom of his coat and walked directly across. After making his way up the gravel slope on the far side and onto a flat carpet of leaves and grass, he stamped his feet several times. Turning to Richard, who had watched him, he nodded his head in a show of satisfaction. "Feet's washed and they'll be dry by noon! Feels good!"

"Your feet needed a washin'," Flip said with a chuckle.

◆

When the work crew came to a bog a half mile wide and a hundred yards across, the officer engineers surveyed the area carefully. "We'll cross this with a corduroy road," one of them told Major Bowman.

For three grueling days the men and animals struggled to span the bog with four hundred large pine logs. Laid side by side crossways to the road direction, they were covered with a foot of clay and gravel.

John, his shirt saturated with perspiration until salt rings had formed around his underarms, tossed one last shovelful of dirt onto the road. Then he walked over to where Richard sat scraping mud from his shoes. Together, they looked back over the newly completed section. "Looks good," Richard said, his face beaming with satisfaction.

"Might look good, but 'twon't last." John scoffed. "No sir, goddamit. 'Twon't last."

"Looks solid to me," Richard replied questioningly. "Those logs will float to support it."

"Yah, they'll float all right—right to the top. Hell, next spring the frost'll heave 'em. That's why they call it corduroy. Just bumpier than hell!"

Richard sat down to stuff more dry grass into his worn shoes. He looked at his clothes and shook his head. They were still two days from the final crossing of the Monongahela, and everything he owned was nearly unusable. He had patched and repatched his clothes until little was left of the original material. Pockets and sleeves were gone, and he used rabbit skin for the last patch on the knee of his trousers.

He looked around at clusters of others. Their clothing was in tatters, too, and they were complaining of food staples running low and the cooks sifting weevils from the flour to make biscuits. They had eaten so much rabbit, squirrel, and deer that several were going to ask Sergeant Turner to slaughter a work ox so they could eat some meat that didn't have a strong, wild taste. And there were the comforts and pleasures enjoyed by the officers. "Bet them Indian women all got their bellies full!" one of the workers exclaimed.

A round of laughter echoed through the trees.

Just then Flip walked up. Richard looked at him and smiled wryly. "Next time, get buckskins," Flip said matter-of-factly.

Richard nodded. He knew that Flip rarely complained. He respected him for that.

"According to Sergeant Turner," Flip said, sitting down beside him, "when we cross the Monongahela, there'll be just eight easy miles ta go. Then ya get paid."

It was late afternoon when the work crew reached the Monongahela. The ford was so shallow that two rows of large rocks marked the way across the rapidly flowing water. Sergeant Turner ordered the men to cross.

Richard turned to Flip. "Why are we crossing so late in the day?

"I suppose we're close enough to Fort Pitt to be safe," Flip answered with a shrug.

After the crossing, Sergeant Turner gathered the men together. "Men, we'll camp here." He paused for a long moment, then said, "A few hundred yards ahead is where General Braddock's troops were overwhelmed four years ago. Then, the French bastards turned the Shawnee and Iroquois loose ta butcher 'em."

After supper, Richard, Flip, and John walked north to the battlefield. Others followed in small groups.

There was a fringe of thick shrubs along the twelve-foot bank of the river, but the rest of the slightly irregular terrain formed a glade that was lightly forested with oak and chestnut trees. The blooms of white daisies and pink June clover stood above the short grass, giving the calm, evening air a pleasant, sweet odor. A few bees still gathered nectar in the lingering sunlight as songs of meadowlarks floated across the fields from different directions.

A quarter mile from the camp they came upon a few partially exposed bones lying in the grass. Richard kicked one loose from the soil, assuming it was that of a deer. A few steps farther he saw more—hundreds more.

The three men stopped and looked around. "People and animals," Flip said quietly as he looked at the clusters of scattered skeletons. Then he pointed to a small skull. "A youngster," he said, shaking his head.

They walked about the area for several minutes, being careful where they stepped. Then they sat down on a dead limb that had fallen from a large tree and watched as others looked at the gruesome scene.

Sergeant Turner walked up. "These were supposed to be buried," he told them. "The bloody French just let 'em lay. But when we took Fort Pitt, a detail was sent out ta bury 'em. Laid out 'ere two years then. Musta missed a few."

Richard shuddered. He was shocked by the grisly find. He looked at Sergeant Turner. "How could they miss all of these?"

"Maybe buried 'em too shallow," the sergeant said flatly.

"How many were killed here?" Flip asked.

"Oh, 'bout six 'undred. Some families with 'em, too." Turner paused a moment. "General Braddock 'isself got it 'ere. Took 'im back to Great Meadows and buried 'im in the middle o' the road so's the savages couldn't find 'im."

Richard and Flip walked away and sat down on the edge of a small gully that ran across the field. They watched quietly as a dozen men from the crew wandered about, occasionally stooping to pick up an item. Some of the things were pocketed; others were tossed back onto the ground.

Richard looked down into the gully at a narrow trail of bent grass used by small animals going to the river. His eyes traced it a short distance until he saw an object that caught his attention. He stepped forward, retrieved it, then back-stepped and sat down again. It was a brass button attached to a small, torn remnant of faded blue cloth. After rubbing the tarnish from the face of the button with his thumb, he held it up for Flip to see.

"French," Flip said. That's their emblem, the *fleur-de-lis*."

Richard examined it closely. He wondered what happened to the man who wore it. Certainly he had a mother. Maybe he came from a large family. Had he been killed? These things bothered Richard. He would keep it so it wouldn't lie on the ground anymore.

They sat silently for a long time as others drifted back toward the camp. A small herd of browsing deer appeared in the distance, frequently jerking their heads up to keep an eye on the strangers who were in their territory. A fox barked, an owl hooted, and stars appeared in the eastern sky. A short distance away, John bent down to pick up an object and let roar a loud fart.

"You're gonna blow sand into your shoes!" Flip yelled.

John looked at him with a sheepish grin. "Damn beans! Just gotta be heard from."

Flip swatted at a mosquito on his cheek. "Let's head back," he said, drawing his feet beneath him so he could stand.

That evening the three of them joined a group of workers sitting around a blazing campfire. As tongues of flame danced and leaped into the air, they listened to stories of the battle told by those who had heard about it months before. Several men passed around corroded buckles, rusty knives, and horseshoes with bent nails they had picked up from the battlefield.

Flip leaned toward Richard. "Don't hear 'em complainin' about working conditions now, do ya?" he whispered.

The next morning Sergeant Turner paced back and forth before the assembled workers. "Men," he began, " 'tis our duty ta see to it that the remains of those killed by those bloomin' French bastards and butchered by the bloody savages get a decent burial. Then they'll be able ta rest in peace." He stopped and turned to face them. The men were nodding approval. "I'm askin' ye ta gather up their bones so we can bury 'em." He looked left and right. "And if ya dig up any while fixin' the road through there, we'll do the same with 'em."

A deep hole was dug beneath the sheltering limbs of a giant chestnut tree. Thousands of bones were placed in the large grave and covered with earth. On top of the neatly packed mound they stacked broken wagon wheels, weathered boards, rotted leather pouches, and the exploded remains of a brass cannon.

Major Bowman walked up to the grave and removed his hat. The workers became silent. They bared their heads and lowered their eyes. In a loud voice the major said, "May God show them the mercy they so richly deserve. May they rest in peace and their souls reside eternally in the Kingdom of Heaven." He replaced his hat and walked away.

John removed a bone fragment from his pocket and tossed it onto the grave. "Was gonna keep it as a remembrance," he told Flip. "But I changed me mind." He turned to leave, then stopped and faced the grave again. "And may those French bastards rot in 'ell!" he exclaimed, shaking his fist.

———————◆———————

Richard returned his pewter plate and cup to the kitchen. He was in a good mood. Although he had eaten another ration of cold venison, hard biscuits, and tea, Fort Pitt was only a few days away. There he would eat a hot lunch, sleep in a bed, and replace his worn out clothes, and he could return to Fredericksburg.

He joined Flip and John as they walked back to their work stations. "Can't wait ta get me paws on that pay," said John, rubbing his hands together.

"Better save it," warned Flip. "Jobs are scarce around here."

Richard bent down to pick up his shovel just as a great shout of jubilation echoed through the forest. He stood up and, with Flip, squinted to search the road ahead where the sound seemed to originate. Suddenly, their faces brightened. Three troopers from the camp's advanced guard were leading a small caravan of cows and pack horses toward them.

As they passed, Flip and Richard looked up at a mounted guardsman. "Where'd ya find them?" Flip asked.

"A present from Fort Pitt," the guard replied. He smiled, then added, "We're gonna eat tonight."

When the crew finished work for the day, they returned to camp in a jovial mood. Richard watched their faces brighten when they saw the beef roasting on a spit and smelled the baking corn bread. Most went to the river and washed. Several shaved for the first time in weeks. And they stood in clusters, talking and laughing. Suddenly, Sergeant Turner's voice could be heard above the noise. They fell silent.

"Men!" the sergeant shouted. "I've got good news fer ye! All the beef and corn bread ye can eat. And Major Bowman says ye'll be fed first!"

A chorus of shouts and applause arose from the men.

As they got in line to be served, John turned to Richard. "Damn decent o' the brass asses," he snorted, grinning so broadly his upper and lower gums showed.

"Gonna share their Indian wenches, too," Flip teased, slapping John on the shoulder.

A thickset sergeant standing beside them leaned over and said, "Indeed, now! A sweaty wrinkle is about all ye lads'll find on those fat ones."

A coarse chuckle arose from the men standing nearby.

That evening when the campfires were started, the men were issued a scoop of tobacco and double ration of rum. One man took a Jew's harp from his pocket and began to play it. Others gathered around to sing and dance.

Richard laid back on his elbows near his bedroll and stared at the fire. The large meal and cup of rum gave him a warm, contented feeling he had not experienced before. He didn't like the taste of rum and usually gave his ration to John. But tonight was special. He wanted to enjoy the way the rum soothed his mind and muscles.

A man sitting beside him was telling others about hunting in the Catskill Mountains. But Richard did not listen. He looked at Flip, noting how his smooth face reflected the light of the dancing flames. He admired this man of the forest and wanted to learn more from him about living in the wilderness. Something inside told him that one day they would be as close as brothers.

Richard looked over at an older man, Adam Towne, who was explaining why he was working on the Braddock Road. "Was farming a small piece o' land I'd cleared in upper New York. 'Twas near Albany." He paused to break a twig from a stick he held. "Small pox took me wife and two little girls. Walked away and never looked back." Tears welled up in his eyes.

The group fell silent and looked at Adam. John, feeling uneasy about Adam's sorrow, spoke. "Ain't never been tied down by relatives or property," he said. "No plans ta settle down in one location." He paused and pulled a long draw on his pipe. "Yessiree, when I stop walkin' these pikes, b'gawd, they can cover me over. Just can't stand seein' the same damn people and places every day."

A man walked up and dropped an armful of dried wood on the fire. Richard leaned back and watched a flurry of sparks rise with the smoke. It made him think about the mysteries of the vast wilderness. And he wondered what it would be like to spend the winter with Flip, trapping around Lake Erie.

When he went to bed, he found it difficult to go to sleep. Work on the road had made him miss Fredericksburg very little, but he would be returning soon. The new road would make traveling easier. He was grateful for that. He thought of his father, the farm, and the livery stable. And there was Elizabeth, lovely Elizabeth. If only she was here with him so he could smell the fragrance of her hair and feel the softness of her body.

When he fell asleep, the camp was quiet and the fires had been reduced to beds of dying coals.

◆

The work crew burst out of a dense strip of forest onto a flat, level area where cows grazed contentedly in lush, green, stump-dotted pastures. Roofs of cabins protruded from fields of heading wheat and ripening corn alongside the Monongahela. The air was fresh and clean and laden with the sweet smell of vetch and wild roses. It was early August, and the surrounding woods no longer held the fear of an unseen enemy.

Richard stood in the warm sunshine and shivered. A feeling of exhilaration swept over his body as he looked across the cultivated fields and watched the grazing animals.

Flip walked up beside him. "What do ya see?" he asked.

Richard inhaled deeply. "Sure is nice," he said.

"Yah," agreed Flip. "Sure is. But now we'll run into people—damn people and all their damn rules."

"Is that bad?" asked Richard, turning to look at his friend.

"Well, maybe not for some. But fer me," Flip shook his head, "I like to do things without havin' ta see if it's all right with some sonofabitch first."

A colonel from Fort Pitt, dressed in a scarlet coat and sitting astride a prancing, snow-white stallion, rode past. As he looked at the work the men were doing, he pulled a white silk handkerchief from his cuff and dabbed his nose.

Major Bowman walked out to meet him. The colonel reined to a halt. Sitting pompously on his horse, he gazed into the distance. "Looks as if ye 'ired the dregs o' creation to work fer ye, Major," he said.

"But, sir, these men 'ave been livin' outdoors fer weeks without proper supplies."

The colonel sniffed the air. "So they 'ave," he said, turning his mount to leave.

Soon others—peddlers, drifters, and the curious—were wandering among the workers. Sergeant Turner attempted to drive them off with threats, but they simply moved a short distance and stopped again. Irritated by their interference, he had the guards run them off.

In the evening, Lieutenant Whiteman saw a dozen half-breed prostitutes a short distance from the camp. He assembled the troops.

"There's a batch o' whores hangin' around," he told them. "Fifty lashes to any o' ye caught rollin' in the weeds with those infected sluts!"

The troopers chorused a low moan.

"Mind ye! Fifty lashes!" he shouted.

Soon afterwards, John saw several workers walk over to the prostitutes. He watched them talk briefly and saw each man hand a woman a pouch of tobacco or a trinket. Then they disappeared into a cornfield.

He walked over to Richard. "They'll be scratchin' their asses tomorrow," he chuckled. "Mosquitoes'll see ta that!"

———————◆———————

Fort Pitt, located a few hundred yards back from the point of a triangular piece of land formed by the confluence of the Allegheny and Monongahela, was in its final stages of construction. Shaped like a pentagon, it was protected from the rear by a deep, heavily fortified ditch. In addition to the military installations, it also had shops, stores, and a few houses.

On the day the Braddock Road crew arrived, a hundred workmen were still smoothing and sodding the exterior slopes of its earthen ramparts, tarring roofs of masonry barracks, and setting the last rows of bricks on the revetments. Others were tearing down the thirty, fire-blackened chimneys that stood like gaunt sentinels on the low, sandy point of land where the rivers converged. They were all that remained of the once proud Fort Duquesne of the Blessed Virgin at the Beautiful River.

The Fort Pitt paymaster sat at a table in the warm sunshine at one end of the parade ground. As Sergeant Turner, with Lieutenant Whiteman at his side, called each man's name, the workman stepped forward to receive his money.

At the same time, across the field, Major Bowman inspected his troops. He smiled and said, "Men, I wish ta compliment ye on a job well done." He paced back and forth, then faced them again. "But we cannot lose sight of the fact that ye represent the king's finest. And ye must look it!" He paused, then set his jaw. "Ye'll wash yer clothes, shine yer boots, and put pipe clay on yer shoulder belts—I want 'em white!" He looked sternly from left to right. "Lieutenant Whiteman will see that unserviceable items are replaced. Dismissed!"

As Richard stepped up to the table, the paymaster squinted at his roster. "Fifty-six shillings, less five for goods at Cumberland." He paused, then said, "And here's a letter."

Richard recognized the writing as Elizabeth's. He tore it open and scanned its brief message. Then he walked over to a barracks building and sat on the ground with his back against the wall so he could read it again.

It stated that things in Fredericksburg were all right and continuing as usual. His eyes focused on the last line. "I'm waiting for your return. Affectionately, Elizabeth."

A shiver raced through his body as he looked off into the distance. He would leave as soon as possible for home.

In a small, hot, clapboard trading post just outside the fort, he found an ill-fitting shirt, pair of pants, and a jacket.

"Usually don't sell ta them's goin' back," apologized the merchant, a bearded, balding man who didn't wear a shirt over his heavy underwear. "Mostly ta them's goin' on."

Flip stood back and observed his friend. "You look like a frontiersman," he said with a smile. "Now, let's find ya a horse."

They walked for nearly a mile, talking to farmers whose little houses dotted the cleared land. But no horses were available. "Can't even loan ye one," said one man who was cutting hay with a scythe. "Too near harvest time."

As they returned to the fort, Flip explained how pleasant it was to walk along the shore of Lake Erie and paddle the canoe up the many rivers that laced the area. He suggested Richard join him on his next trip.

"How far would we go?" asked Richard.

"Oh, I don't know," said Flip with a wave of his hand. "As far as we want. Maybe as far as Detroit."

They encountered a small group of the work crew carrying large packs high on their backs.

"Where ya goin ? " Flip inquired.

"East," they chorused.

"Takin' Forbes Road," one of them added.

That evening at the supper table, they sat across from John. He was neatly dressed in dark blue trousers and a red flannel shirt. "Look nice in those clothes," said Richard with a nod of his head.

"Where ya goin' now, John?" Flip asked, looking him in the eye.

"Oh, I'll stay here a while." His eyes sparkled and a sly grin grew on his clean-shaven face. "Got me a widder down the road a stretch. Gonna move in tonight." Then, feeling embarrassed, he sobered. "But hell, 'tain't fer me. Just a good, fat, little beddin'. I'll head east afore winter."

Richard and Flip climbed to the top of the fort's wide ramparts and strolled among the mounted cannons and patrolling sentries. From a bastion on the western perimeter, they stood and looked out over the glassy surface where the waters of the two rivers joined. The sun hung like a dull, red ball just above the tops of the dark green trees on the other side of the Monongahela.

"What say, Richard? I think it would be a wonderful experience. We can make a lot of money from the pelts."

Richard looked at the forest on the far side of the Allegheny. It appeared black in the fading light. Thoughts chased one another through his mind. Flip was a good friend. He respected him and admired his poise, his calmness, and his knowledge of the wilderness. Such trust and faith tugged at his sense of judgment. But then there was Fredericksburg, his father, and Elizabeth.

"I'll tell ya what," said Flip, interrupting Richard's train of thought. "I'm going ta make a trip to Fort Ligonier for some traps. Then I'll come back. That'll give you time ta make up your mind. If you're comin , we'll leave here one month from today. If not, I'll go alone."

"Well," replied Richard, thinking one month was hardly enough time to make a round trip, "could we make it six weeks?"

"I'm afraid that's too close to winter."

"If I can't make it back in a month, how about next summer?"

Flip scratched his head and stared off into the distance.

"That might work. Sure. I should be here most of June. Let's figure one month from now. If not, next June."

Richard turned and faced him. "It's a deal," he said, extending his hand.

Chapter 5

White Woman of the Senecas

A thin layer of steamy vapor was suspended a few feet above the smooth-flowing water of the Monongahela as Richard, musket in hand, left Fort Pitt and started back to Fredericksburg on the Braddock Road. The grass was heavy with dew, and thin plumes of fresh white smoke rose from the cabins of farmers whose long day of work had begun. Occasionally, he waved to one who was releasing cows from overnight barnyard confinement or slopping a group of squealing hogs.

By the time the sun was halfway up in the morning sky, he had left the inhabited area and was rapidly making his way through the quiet Braddock battlefield. He looked over at the somber chestnut tree sheltering the grave where he and his companions had interred the bones of the battle's dead. Suddenly frightened by the loneliness he felt, he wondered if he should turn back and take the longer but safer Forbes Road. Then he shook his head. He could take care of himself. Besides, he wanted to get home as quickly as possible.

As he crossed the river at the shallow ford, he filled his tin cup with water, then sat down beneath the thick, spreading limbs of a large white oak laden with ripening acorns. From a leather pouch hanging at his side he withdrew a piece of dried beef and a hardened biscuit.

The meal was finished quickly, but he remained for several minutes, enjoying the pleasant feeling the vastness of the wilderness gave him. He sighed, reluctantly drew his feet beneath him, and stood. Noting that the birds and squirrels had suddenly become silent, he listened, thinking he heard a strange noise. Holding his breath, he slowly turned his head to catch the sound, but the throbbing pulse in his temples made hearing difficult. Then he heard it again, carried along with the rustle of leaves on a gentle zephyr. Grabbing his musket and bedroll, he went farther from the road and dropped down behind a large, half-rotted log crawling with carpenter ants.

In a few minutes the scarlet uniforms of mounted British troopers were discernible through the foliage. He stood up, slapped the dust from his clothes, and walked out to meet them.

There were twelve mounted soldiers, six front and six rear, escorting ten freight wagons. The soldiers tugged at the reins of their sweating horses, halting the train.

"Where ye goin'?" the lead trooper asked in a firm voice.

"Fort Cumberland," Richard replied. "Just left Fort Pitt."

"How long ye been?"

"Just left this morning."

"Good!" The trooper turned his head and shouted over his shoulder, "We'll be there by nightfall!"

Those behind smiled and nodded.

"Any trouble along the way?" Richard asked, looking at the impatient freight drivers.

"Nothin'," came the emphatic reply. "Absolutely clear sailin'."

The lead soldier waved his hand, and the train began to roll again.

When the shadows began to lengthen rapidly and deer emerged from their resting place in the thicket, Richard looked for a place to spend the night. He estimated he was twenty-five miles from Fort Pitt. It was a good first day.

A short distance from the road, he found a large pine with low-hanging branches. He made his bed beneath it, then shot and skinned a cottontail rabbit. After placing the rabbit on a makeshift spit over a small fire of dried twigs, he took a potato from his pouch and pushed it into the blazing coals.

When the sun went down, he scattered the fire and crawled into bed. As he watched a twinkling star move slowly across a little purple opening in the branches above, his eyelids became heavy. Suddenly, there was a muscular wiggling beneath the small of his back that shocked him into consciousness. It quickly subsided. He waited, breathless with fear.

Slowly, he started to breathe again. Then it came again, pressing with even greater vigor across the width of his back. Like a tightly compressed spring suddenly released, he bounded from the bed, sending his blanket flying several feet through the air. He took a dozen quick steps and spun about, crouching to challenge whatever was there.

For several minutes he watched intently, but could not see or hear anything unusual. Then, slowly, carefully, he crept back and examined the pad of pine needles where he was sleeping. Pressing with his hand, he felt the soft outline of a mole tunnel. When he collapsed it, it was immediately reestablished by the muscular little animal. He sighed and grinned wryly, then moved his bed farther around the tree.

On the fourth day Richard was less than five miles from Fort Cumberland when nightfall came. It would be better to spend the night there, he thought, than along the road. He would press on.

A few minutes later, he heard a garbled, boisterous conversation filtering through the trees ahead. He was still two miles from the inhabited farm area, but felt no reason for concern or alarm.

Clearing a turn in the road, he saw the silhouettes of shoving, stumbling humans in the milky-gray distance. The deep guttural shouts were those of savages. They must have spent the day loitering around the fort and were returning to their village. He cursed under his breath, something he would not have done before working with the Braddock Road crew.

A large, uprooted tree had fallen so its top nearly reached the road. It happened so many years ago that all the branches had dropped off, leaving an immense log which terminated with a soil-laden root mass. Richard took refuge in the leaf-filled hole located in the shadow of the rootball.

Peering cautiously from his hiding place, he watched as the Indians approached. Their naked bodies shone dully in the blue-white glow of the warm summer evening. Suddenly, one sent forth a loud shout, bolted from the group, then leaped upon the fallen tree trunk. He raced toward the root mass above Richard.

Richard hugged the ground, burying his face in the decomposing leaves. He thought of easing his hand to the scabbard that held his hunting knife but was afraid the movement would betray his position. As his heart thundered in his chest, he opened his mouth to lessen the sound of his heavy breathing, and he tried to think of a way to escape if discovered.

The Indian mounted the rootball and, swaying unsteadily, pulled aside his leather loincloth and discharged a generous stream into the pit below. Richard remained motionless as the warm fluid saturated his back.

Then the Indian, still swaying atop the rootball, thumped his chest and gave forth a tremendous yell that intensified in volume with each syllable. "Ahm-mahn-ghan-deeha!" he shrieked. As the loud cry echoed through the forest, he ran down the log and rejoined the others.

Richard crawled from his hiding place and watched them disappear down the road.

◆

Astride the horse he had purchased at Fort Cumberland, Richard reined up at the Fredericksburg ferry landing. He looked down at the operator, a middle-aged man he had not seen before, then dismounted. "Where's Mr. Harrington?" he inquired.

"Home, I suppose," the man replied, unhooking the chain so Richard could lead his horse aboard. "Hired me last month ta help out."

When Richard mounted his horse again on the south bank of the river, he had a strong desire to go directly to the Harrington house. But he looked down at his clothing, then shook his head and started the animal on the road to his father's farm. If he was to impress Elizabeth, he had to make himself more presentable.

As he approached the tidy entrance to the log house he had helped to build so many years before, he saw his father cutting a stand of ripening corn in a field a short distance away. Upon seeing his son, Mr. Locke paled and dropped his sickle. Richard rushed to his side and assisted him back to the house. "You'll work no more today," he ordered.

Richard hung the teakettle on the fireplace iron. "How long has this been going on?" he asked, looking into his father's sallow face.

"Only happens once in a while," Sam said evasively. "Just don't have the strength I used to."

While the tea steeped, Richard sat down across the table and studied the older man's dull, tired eyes. Grave and absorbed in anxious thoughts, he wondered if his father was eating well enough. Or perhaps it was the loneliness. Nevertheless, now that he was home, he would work the farm, and his father could rest. And his father would eat well. He would see to it.

The next morning, Richard rode to Fredericksburg. There was a sensitivity about the area he had not experienced before. He looked at the tall, green trees, smelled the ripening apples, and squinted into the sun's glare on the glossy surface of the Rappahannock. It seemed good to be home in a place that was safe and placid and comfortable. It was a beautiful spot to live and a wonderful day to enjoy it. Then, puzzled, his brow wrinkled. He wondered why he sometimes got an urge to leave.

At the Harrington house, he bounded up the steps and knocked on the door. Elizabeth opened it and let out a squeal.

"Richard!" she said, grasping his hands and pulling him inside. Her eyes sparkled as she kissed him on the mouth. Then she called out, "Mother! It's Richard!"

Mrs. Harrington appeared at the kitchen doorway, hesitated momentarily, then rushed over to shake his hand. "It's nice to have you back, Richard," she said, struggling to be calm. "I'll get some cookies."

Elizabeth took his hand and led him to the couch. He sat down on the edge, careful not to put pressure on the back. It seem so delicate compared to the heavy wooden furniture at the farm.

"Oh, Richard," she said, dabbing her eyes with a lace-edged handkerchief. "I worried so much about you out there alone with those wild beasts and savages."

"But I wasn't alone," Richard assured her as he patted her hand. "There were hundreds with me. Some were soldiers with muskets."

"Well," stated Mrs. Harrington as she placed a tray of tea and cookies before them, "we heard some terrible tales of what the savages do to white people."

Richard noticed wet streaks on her cheeks. "The only Indians I saw," he said with a shrug, "were peaceful and quiet." He didn't want to mention the ones he encountered on the way back. "Besides, everyone was armed."

"Well, anyway, we're glad you're back," said Elizabeth, forcing a smile as she squeezed his hand.

◆

Richard lit a fire to ward off the evening chill, then sat back to watch the flame grow. He had been home eight weeks and was pleased with the way things had gone. The harvest was nearly complete, and his father's health had improved considerably. He was grateful for that.

The room was quiet except for the crackling blaze. He looked over at Sam darning a hole in a sock at the table. It was apparent his father's attitude toward him had changed. He was being treated like an adult partner instead of an adolescent son. If a task had to be done, he was asked to do it. That was better than being ordered to do it. And when the wagon axle had collapsed two weeks before, he was the one who had to make the decision whether to repair it or buy a new one.

Pleased with his new status, Richard wondered how long it would last. Sam was a proud and determined man; he knew that, and he realized that he, too, had changed. Work at the livery and on the Braddock Road had given him confidence in himself, and Flip had convinced him that he could stand alone if he had to.

He placed a small log on the fire, then laid his head back and looked at the overhead beams. He thought of last Saturday night and the dance at Stover's stable. It was his first. He remembered the embarrassment when Elizabeth pulled him onto the straw-covered floor. In a few minutes, the embarrassment was gone, and he was dancing. And it was fun. In two weeks, there would be a husking bee at Taylor's farm east of town. He would ask her to go with him.

◆

When the harvest was finished and the dull gray of winter set in, Richard felt restless. The barren, harsh appearance of the land-scape and confining cold weather dissipated the appeal of living at home. During the long evenings, he watched his father sit before the fire, frequently napping but seldom speaking. It was so differ-ent from the Braddock Road. He tried reading passages from the Bible aloud, but Sam showed little interest, so he stopped and read silently to himself. Outside, he took care of the animals, repaired harness, and sharpened the axe, saws, and sickles.

◆

Richard tugged at the reins to halt the roan in front of the Harrington house. He sniffed the warm April air. It smelled clean and fresh. Hopping down from the wagon, he was met at the porch by Elizabeth. She had a lunch basket in one hand and her bonnet in the other.

"Good morning, Richard," she said cheerily.

"Hello," Richard replied with a smile.

He took the basket and helped her climb onto the wagon seat.

At a forested overlook on Marye's Heights, he tied the gelding to a cottonwood sapling. They walked along a footpath, still soft with moisture from winter's snow, to the base of a large pine. Richard spread a blanket on the cushion of dead pine needles and steadied Elizabeth's hand as she sat down. Then he lowered himself beside her.

For several minutes they looked out over the town through the bare branches of oaks and maples. Elizabeth noted that the twig tips were swelling with the first signs of life. Winter was over, and Richard still didn't seem ready to get married. He'd told her many times he wanted her for a wife, but never said when. She had discussed it with her mother. Her parents were fond of Richard. And she was seventeen, an age when most of her friends were getting married.

She recalled how happy Richard was to be back from working on the Braddock Road. He had saved the money, a nest egg he called it, to use when they got married. But during the winter he told her about the wilderness and extolled the opportunities of living on the frontier. She knew she didn't understand life on the frontier, but she loved him. She would be happy with him anywhere.

A squirrel chattered, and she glanced at Richard. He was looking at her admiringly. Then she remembered that she'd brought a lunch to eat.

After they had eaten, Richard leaned over and kissed her on the cheek. She placed her arms about his neck, and they fell back onto the blanket. He looked at her for a long moment and noted how the soft, brown ringlets of highlighted hair formed a wreath about the creamy white flesh of her face. Then, gently cupping her chin in his hand, he placed his mouth over hers and tenderly kissed her. He raised his head slightly and looked at the white teeth showing through the narrow opening of her parted lips and observed the long, dark lashes gracing her closed eyes. "I love you," he whispered.

"I know," she replied, still keeping her eyes closed. "I love you, too."

When he slipped his hand inside her underpants, she stiffened. He thought she was going to rebuff him. Then, she relaxed.

"Don't let anyone see us," she whispered.

"They won't," he assured her, gently massaging her.

Suddenly she thrust her hips upward and gasped, then relaxed. He straightened her dress and pulled her body close to his. A small tear glistened in the corner of each of her closed eyes. A trace of guilt surged through his mind, but he felt closer to her than ever.

◆

Early in May they went to Mrs. Dixon's Lodge for cookies and ginger beer. Afterwards he took her for a ride along the river road. It would be a good time to tell her he was going back to Fort Pitt, he thought.

Although she assumed he might want to return, she was still very put out by his decision. "Why do you want to go there?" she asked sharply.

Richard noted a fiery look in her eyes, something he had not seen before. "I can make a lot of money hunting and trapping. Then we will be able to get married," he told her.

"If you really loved me, you wouldn't run off and leave me like this!" she yelled. She reached over and pulled at the reins until the wagon stopped. "And you won't find me waiting when you return!" She jumped down from the wagon and ran toward the woods.

Richard secured the reins and ran after her. When he caught her, he spun her around and looked into her tear-filled eyes. Holding her firmly by the shoulders, he said, "I love you more than anyone in this world, and I always will!" He kissed her harshly on the mouth as she stared in rapt amazement. "And, by the grace of God, I intend to marry you when I get back!"

They embraced, and she whispered in his ear, "I'll wait for you." Then, with tears welling up in her eyes, she added, "Forever, if I have to."

The following week he went to Elizabeth's house to see her before leaving for Fort Pitt. Her parents were away, but he stayed anyway. Elizabeth took him to her room to show him quilts, shawls, and a chair seat and arm covers she had made to use when they set up housekeeping. Then, pointing to a small, framed sampler hanging on the wall beside her bed, she giggled and said, "That proves I'm ready."

He took her into his arms, and their lips met in a passionate embrace. After rolling back the patchwork spread, he placed her on the bed and removed her underpants. She lay quietly, fists clenched and eyes so tightly closed her forehead and temples were wrinkled. Dropping his trousers, he carefully climbed onto her. She held her thighs tightly together.

"Do you really want to?" she asked, seeking assurance it was all right.

"Yes," he replied, breathing heavily. "Very much."

She spread her legs and felt him probe her opening. There was immediate pain which continued to grow in intensity until she thought she must cry out. She bit her lip so hard it seemed her teeth would surely go through it. But she was determined not to make a sound. She was a woman, his woman, a full grown woman, and this was nature's way. Even mother had told her so.

With a sudden, searing flash, it was over. The pain subsided and she felt him inside her. Surprisingly, it felt good.

Afterwards, Richard noted small beads of perspiration on her upper lip and forehead. He looked into her clear, blue eyes and told her, "From now on, my darling, it's not you and me. It's us—just us."

When they arose, the center of the muslin sheet was stained with a small red spot.

------------◆------------

Richard arrived at Fort Pitt in the early afternoon of Friday, June 6th. A gentle west wind was heavy with the sweet scent of wild roses and choke cherry blossoms.

Once through the massive gates, he went directly to the Crown Point Trading Post and asked the proprietor if he had seen Flip. The man shook his head. "Trappers are still comin' in, though," he said. "Could arrive any day." As Richard turned to leave, he added, "That is, providin' the bears or Indians didn't get 'im."

Confident Flip would meet him, Richard decided to wait at The Red Fox, a boisterous roadhouse a half mile east of the fort. His small, dingy room had rough-sawed plank walls and a pole bed wedged into one corner. A little window, shuttered by a door hinged on leather straps, looked out over a stump-dotted field behind the building. Beneath it, a blue porcelain basin, along with a wooden bucket half full of water and a short beeswax candle, sat on top of a hand-hewn table.

Richard washed and shaved, then laid down on the musty blankets of the bed to rest. As he looked at the cobwebs in the rafters, he wondered if Flip was all right. The statement of the man at the trading post concerned him. Flip was an able frontiersman; he knew that, and he was a man of his word. Anyway, it was foolish to worry, so he closed his eyes to put it out of his mind.

When he awoke, he went to the tavern area and asked the short, unshaven innkeeper if he could get something to eat.

"Sure can," the man replied, placing both hands on the bar. "Gotta pot o' sow belly and beans."

As he walked to his table, Richard ranged his eyes around the room. Two men with bushy beards and heavy coats sat on the far side. Blood and grease on their clothes identified them as trappers. They halted their conversation and eyed him carefully, then started talking again when he sat down.

After he had eaten, Richard walked over to them. Their fetid odor filled his nostrils. He wondered if they were wilderness cut-throats. "Seen a trapper called Flip Wade?" he asked.

They calmly looked him up and down, shrugged indifferently, then looked at each other before shaking their heads.

Approaching the bartender, he asked, "Ever hear of a fellow by the name of John Harmon?"

"Aye!" The bartender's eyes lit up. "Lives just down the road a piece—'bout ten minutes walk—'e and the missus."

"Married?" Richard asked, showing surprise.

"Aye. And a nice wife she is."

"Well," said Richard, stepping back from the bar. "I'll go see him."

"You a friend?"

"Yes. Worked on the Braddock Road together."

"East a quarter mile." The bartender nodded in that direction. "Nice little house back from the road on the right."

Two hours of daylight still remained as he walked the dirt road that was rapidly being covered by the creeping shade of trees lining its side. A few insects flitted about, and the quiet air held traces of smoke from fires used to clear the land.

A narrow, grassy lane led to a log cabin and barn surrounded by a lush pasture and newly seeded plots of black soil. The sound of a bell drew his attention to the barn from which a half dozen cows emerged. He knew they had been milked and would spend the night in the barnyard.

Approaching the doorway, he suddenly came face to face with John. "Hello, John," he said, stopping to await recognition.

John stood fixed, squinting as he stared at the young man before him. "Well, I'll be damned!" he shouted, taking several quick steps to grasp Richard's outstretched hand with both of his. "I'll be goddamned! If it ain't Richard. I'll be goddamned ta hell!"

"It's me all right, John," Richard assured him. "Found out at The Red Fox you were here."

John was clean shaven; his hair was neatly trimmed, and he wore expertly patched clothes. As they walked toward the house, Richard explained his return to Fort Pitt. John stopped and looked at him. "That can be dangerous," he said soberly.

"I think we'll be all right," Richard said, nodding his head. Then he pointed to the milk buckets John was carrying. "Want me to carry one of them?"

"No. The two of them keeps me balanced."

"Becky!" John called, as they approached the small log cabin. "I've got a friend I want ya ta meet!"

A short, stout, middle-aged woman appeared at the door, wiping her hands on a gray, cotton apron.

"Becky, this is Richard." He paused after taking the last steps to the doorway. "You know, the young Virginian I've told ya about."

She was nearly as tall as John and bore herself straight and proud. Her brown hair, showing streaks of gray, was neatly braided and tightly coiled into a knot on the back of her head. Richard sensed she was a hard working, orderly person.

"Oh, sure," she replied cheerily, extending a tanned, callused hand.

Richard grasped it firmly and felt the coarse contrast to that of Elizabeth's. It reminded him of the hands of his mother.

"I'll set this milk inside," said John, stepping sideways through the doorway.

The cabin, one tidy room with a dirt floor, reminded Richard of the one his father had built when they first came to Virginia. The furnishings, however, were finely crafted pieces like those he had seen in a catalog for homes of the wealthy. It made him think that Becky had been a woman of class.

The two men reminisced about the Braddock Road for a few minutes, then the conversation turned to John's farm. "Been doin' mighty fine," bragged John, a contented smile unpuckering his toothless mouth. "And Becky's a good wife." He looked over at her as she poured the milk into a cooling container, then added, "And a good farm worker, too."

John lit his clay pipe, and they went outside.

"And you said marriage wasn't for you," Richard teased as they walked toward the barn. "Sure as hell made you over."

"Ya know," John said slowly, "when ya reach my age ya oughta settle down. It's quiet and peaceful, and with a little work, you're well taken care of."

They approached the pole fence that enclosed the barnyard.

"Nice herd," Richard complimented.

"Yeah," John agreed. Then his forehead wrinkled. "Something wrong with one o' them, though. See that black and white one?" He pointed. "Hasn't eat nothin' in three days."

They entered the barnyard and walked over to the animal. She stood quietly, occasionally switching her tail to drive off flies. Richard examined her carefully, feeling the fullness of her stomach and the leanness of her legs and hips. He stood up and looked squarely at John over the animal's back. "John," he said, "I think she's lost her cud."

"Never heard o' such a thing," John replied doubtfully.

"Sometimes it just drops out of their mouth if they're bumped or scared. Used to happen once in awhile at home. If she doesn't have one to swallow, she can't bring up the next batch to chew."

"I'll be damned," said John. "What can ya do about that?"

"Got any salt pork?"

"Sure. Left over from last winter."

A few minutes later, Richard slid a salty wad of diced pork into her mouth. She hesitated momentarily, then began to chew. When she swallowed, they watched the return mouthful ripple up through her neck.

"How the hell did you know about that?" queried John, scratching his head.

"My father taught me. Don't know where he got it."

John and Becky stood in the doorway and watched as Richard left. "Don't forget to come back!" John shouted. "And remember, bring that sinner, Flip, around when ya find 'im!"

◆

Richard sat on a bench just inside the east wall of the fort, wondering if something had happened to Flip. Occasionally he stood, stretched, and paced about to overcome the drowsiness caused by the warm rays of the afternoon sun. Four times during the three days he had been here, the northeast blockhouse sentry had called out that a canoe was approaching. Each time, he hurried to the landing dock, only to find it was someone else.

And now the sentry called again, "Two canoes upriver!"

Drawing his feet under him, he stood and stretched, then sauntered through the east gate. As he walked unhurriedly the hundred yards to the dock, he could see two heavily-laden bark canoes coming across the Allegheny. A man in buckskins knelt in the forward vessel and paddled with long, forceful strokes to tow the second through the swift current. It was Flip. Richard recognized him immediately.

"Sure glad you got here," Richard beamed as he held the prow of the lead canoe against the dock.

"No need. Heavy take. Loaded to the gunnels."

Richard looked at the canoes, then back at his friend. It was apparent that Flip was very tired. His face was covered with a stubble of beard, and the creases in his skin were filled with a sweaty grime. Flip looked up at him and said, "I'll need some help to get 'em to the trading post. They have a rig there we can borrow."

A short time later Richard returned with a weathered light wagon drawn by a skinny horse that was shedding its winter coat. Flip had unloaded one canoe and was working on the second. Richard jumped down from the wagon and looked at the piles of furs stacked on the dock. "You catch all of these?" he asked.

"Some," Flip replied, halting to wipe his perspiring forehead with the back of his wrist. "Traded with other trappers and Indians, mostly." He shook his head. "Then had ta watch they didn't steal 'em back."

They pulled the canoes from the water and took the pelts to the trading post. Flip removed a soiled piece of paper from his pocket. "Here's the inventory," he said, handing it to the lanky proprietor. "Most are prime."

Richard watched as the man leafed through the odoriferous skins. "I'll give ye a hundred pounds," the man told Flip. "Give ye the rest after I've graded 'em."

The value of the pelts surprised Richard. If they are this abundant on the frontier, he reasoned, he could return to Fredericksburg next spring with plenty of money to marry Elizabeth. Suddenly, he was anxious to get started.

Flip picked out new socks, moccasins, and buckskins. He put them under his arm, then told the proprietor, "We're goin to The Red Fox. Be back in a couple days." He brushed a persistent fly from his face, then turned to Richard. "Sure gonna feel good ta sleep under a roof tonight. Won't have to look and listen for everything that moves and breathes, either."

<hr>

Richard and Flip sat at a small table with John in one corner of the smoky tavern. It was the evening before their departure, and they wanted to drink some ale with their friend before they left.

"Don't do this much anymore," John said, wiping the foam from his lip.

Flip watched him savor another swallow. "John," he said, "I just can't picture you as a farmer."

John knew he had boasted he was a free spirit, that he would never stay in one place for long. But that was before he discovered how pleasant it was to be served good meals and sleep in a warm bed every night. "By God, it'll happen ta both of you!" he snorted, puckering his mouth and snapping his head to emphasize the point.

"Becky is really a fine woman," Richard said, trying to soothe his uneasiness.

John looked at him thoughtfully, then smiled. "Trouble is, she won't have anything stronger than tea in the house." He chuckled. "Says, if the Lord'd wanted ya ta drink spoiled juice, he'd a growed it that way." He paused a moment, thinking he should add something positive. "She's a damn good housekeeper, though."

When they finished their fourth round of drinks, Flip suggested they call it a day. John's talk was louder and his gestures more pronounced. He didn't want to send his friend home drunk. Besides, he and Richard planned to get an early start in the morning, and they needed clear heads for wilderness travel.

"Hell, no!" John said, slamming his empty tankard down on the table. He looked around at the noisy crowd and smiled with satisfaction. "Becky'll love me, drunk or sober," he said with a wink. Then he waved for the bartender.

A short time later, they turned to look at a portly, middle-aged gentleman who had just walked through the open door. He wore a white ruffled shirt, blue satin trousers, and a black, three-quarter length velvet coat. Halting momentarily, the newcomer surveyed the dimly lit room, then removed his tall, felt hat. The tavern patrons paid little attention, but the proprietor recognized him as a gentleman of the city. In Richard's view, he brought back painful memories of the estated gentry of England.

Coming quickly from behind the bar, the tavern owner escorted the man to a small, round, wire-legged table at one side of the room. He took the man's hat and pigskin gloves, then darted back to the bar to get a candle for the table.

The man tucked a red checked bib under his bulging chin to eat the evening's fare of venison stew and biscuits. When served a tankard of ale, he motioned with his stubby finger for the proprietor to come closer. "Did ye know the king is dead?"

"No," the proprietor replied calmly. "We get very little news here."

"Just found out in Philadelphia last week m'self," the gentleman said, looking somber as he dabbed his mouth with his napkin.

The proprietor stood up. "Gentlemen!" he called out. The room fell silent. "This distinguished visitor reports that his majesty, King George, is dead!"

There followed a brief moment of silence. It was not in reverence for the king, but because announcements were not made at The Red Fox. A few men shrugged their shoulders and began talking or playing cards again. Others, not knowing what was expected of them, continued to stare at the rotund visitor sitting pompously at his table.

John slammed his tankard down on the table and shouted, "It's about time that simple old fart kicked in! No damned good, anyway."

The visitor threw his napkin forcefully onto his table and rose to his feet. An indignant scowl covered his face. "Sir!" he yelled. "How dare you be so disrespectful of the crown!"

The room again became silent as the patrons watched.

John rose unsteadily to his feet. "The crown, hell! I'm talking about that capon, George the second! No guts ta do anything!"

"I'll 'ave ye know 'e sired his successor, George the third!" replied the gentleman, snapping his head to emphasize the point.

"A bastard! Nothin' but a bloody bastard!" said John, shaking his finger as he started toward the man. Flip grabbed his hand, but he pulled free. "Somebody else got 'is 'airy 'and in the queen's britches!"

The proprietor stepped in front of John, placed his hands on the swaying farmer's chest, and told him to sit down. John glared at the indignant visitor, who stood boldly at his table. He could see the man's pig-like eyes, pushed nearly shut by his fat cheeks, glistening in the dim light.

John pushed past the proprietor, lost his balance and stumbled forward into the man's table. The table flew across the room, and John landed on his knees at the man's feet. Seeing his adversary on the floor, the man kicked wildly at him. John grabbed the foot, bringing the man's heavy bulk down onto the dirty floor with a resounding grunt.

Several others rushed over to assist the proprietor in separating the two struggling men. Richard and Flip attempted to halt them. "Let them settle it themselves!" Flip shouted.

In a few minutes, the shouting and shoving became a wild disorder. Tables, chairs, dishes, and tankards flew across the darkened room. Flip and Richard grabbed John by the arms and pulled him through the tumultuous disturbance and out the door.

"Let me at 'im!" John protested, struggling weakly against the strong grip that held him. "I'll clean 'is bloody works!"

They dragged and carried him well into the lane leading to his cabin. "You sure as hell fixed things there," Flip said, shaking his head disgustedly.

"And we've got to go back and get our stuff from our rooms," added Richard.

"Oh, hell, they'll get over it," John said, weaving unsteadily as the three of them stood in the dark catching their breath.

Two hours later Flip and Richard were able to slip unnoticed into their rooms at The Red Fox.

◆

The first orange streak of dawn brought with it the command to open the heavy gates of Fort Pitt. Flip and Richard were waiting. They went directly to the storage shed adjacent to the trading post where they had stacked their supplies. Using the horse and wagon, they quickly and quietly transferred the load to the center of one of Flip's canoes. While Richard returned the rig, Flip balanced and tied the load, then covered it with a canvas.

The rays of an early morning sun felt warm on their backs as they silently dipped their paddles to guide the heavily-laden vessel through the deep, swirling eddies created by the turbulent marriage of the Allegheny and Monongahela. "Let's get closer to the north bank," Flip called to Richard, who was kneeling in the prow watching for floating obstacles in the dark green water as he paddled. "Then we can slack off and let the current carry us."

Flip knelt in the stern, taking long, powerful strokes, halting each momentarily at the end with a twist of the wrist to maintain proper course. In this manner, he left only a quiet trail of small eddies that were quickly swallowed up by the strong current of the widening Ohio. He liked traveling on a broad river. It gave him a sense of freedom and security. The canoe was silent and swift, and it left no tracks. He had learned to use it well.

As a boy, he'd liked to row a skiff in Boston Harbor, but gave it up when a sudden squall upset the little vessel. An overly protective mother forbade him from entering the water again. His father, Jeremiah Wade, had been a captain of a whaling ship that foundered with the loss of all hands when Flip was eight years old. Two years later, his still grieving mother was stricken with a fever that left her partially deaf and completely bald. It placed her in a state of depression. She drew the blinds, closed the shutters, and vowed never to go outside again. Two maiden aunts had taken young Phillip to live with them. He never saw his mother again, but attended her funeral six months later.

The aunts hovered over him, making certain he was well clothed, had a bath each week, and wore clean underwear, "Just in case you get hurt and someone has to look at you." They'd insisted he attend school regularly, spend an hour each Sunday in church, learn to cipher, and be able to read and write English and Latin. And he had to take lessons on the piano.

It was the piano lessons he hated more than anything else. He was especially resentful of the performances he had to give before the aunt's women friends each time he learned a new piece. Frequently, after he left the room, he'd overheard them offering advise and counsel on how to rear *the young Wade boy.*

He looked at Richard working the paddle in the prow and imagined the excitement he must feel. He remembered the first time he'd entered the wilderness and how awed he was by it. Only seventeen at the time, he was fed up with school, tired of not having an adult male to imitate, and frustrated by the oppressive constraints of a bevy of prissy, possessive women. He had run off to serve as a flunky for a pair of Catskill Mountain trappers. They'd trapped, traded, and lived among the Senecas and Mohawks. He'd studied the habits of animals, became a sharpshooter with a musket, and learned to deal with the Indians. After two years, confident he could stand on his own, he'd decided to move westward with the advancing frontier where trapping was better and Indians less debased by the white man.

As the fort faded from view in the misty morning, Flip called out, "Let the current carry it!"

The smoothly flowing water took over the task of propelling the burdened vessel, allowing the men to change to a sitting position. Only occasionally did they dip their paddles into the dark water to maintain a downstream heading of the prow.

Richard sighed as he tried to relax. Then he quivered as a feeling of newly found freedom raced through his tissues.

———————◆———————

The second day out of Fort Pitt, the bright sun was approaching its zenith as they put ashore near a sandy knoll just above Beaver Creek. It was the land of Chief Sheninjee and his band of Senecas. Flip had traded with him and considered him a friend. With the chief's approval, he knew the Senecas would protect them as they traveled up Beaver Creek.

Richard stepped out as the prow of the canoe nudged the ragged shore. He looked anxiously at the path leading into the dense forest and wondered about their safety. There was no army to protect them now, and if they were captured or killed, how would anyone ever know? He would have to put his trust in Flip. He looked down at the deep tracks his moccasined feet made in the blue clay. It reminded him of the Rappahannock.

"This Sheninjee is really a Delaware," Flip explained as he slipped the leather straps of his pouch and powder horn over his head. "But he runs this bunch of Senecas out here." He picked up his musket and straightened up. "Just want to stay on the good side of him."

A group of naked children who had been watching from a clump of witch hazel, suddenly darted out and disappeared up the path. Flip turned to Richard. "Remember," he said, "walk like you know where you're going. Don't look around and don't smile."

A few yards up the path they came to a clearing of dead, bark-ringed trees. Several women with sticks were scratching the soil amid plantings of sunflowers, beans, and squash. Unmindful of the strangers, the women continued with their work.

Looking neither left nor right and walking erect with a strong, determined stride, they continued on to a cluster of basswood and elms that provided shade to a dozen bark-covered lodges. Suddenly, the deerskin draped entrance to one of them parted. A statuesque Indian, neatly clothed in fringed buckskins, stepped out. He looked at them coolly with a pair of deep-seated, penetrating black eyes highlighted by prominent bronze cheekbones. His mop of coarse black hair, brushed fiercely back and topped with four eagle feathers, made him appear tall and awesome. He took three steps forward, folded his arms, and waited.

Without breaking stride, Flip walked up to him, stopped abruptly, then offered his hand.

Richard stood behind Flip, cradling his musket in his arms. He could feel the blood racing through his body.

Sheninjee grasped the hand firmly and gave it two hard jerks, jarring Flip's head and shoulders.

"My good friend, Sheninjee," Flip greeted as the hands were released.

"Again, you are welcome to my village," the Indian replied in English. His voice was deep and resonant.

Richard was introduced and, as a few adolescent boys and naked children looked on from a distance, the three of them entered the chief's lodge. They sat cross-legged on soft animal skins around a stone fire ring containing cold ashes of a blaze long since dead. Flip explained they wished to travel through the chief's territory on their way to the Big Water. The chief consented, but insisted he furnish four guides.

Flip was surprised and puzzled. In the past when he wanted assistance, he had to request it and bargain for it. "We know the way," Flip said. "We do not need help."

Sheninjee ignored his statement. "They will be ready to go with you in two days." His dark eyes searched Flip's face for a reaction.

"We planned to leave tomorrow morning," Flip protested.

"Tomorrow I take a wife!" the Indian stated sternly. "Nobody leaves village!" His hand reached for the handle of his knife.

"We will be pleased to stay for your marriage," Flip agreed.

Richard nodded approval. He could see the chief was dead serious and realized there was no other choice. He wondered if they were now in deep trouble.

That evening, braves lit a circle of small fires around a clearing that faced the diminutive, deerskin bridal tepee. Bare-chested men and women danced and sang to the rhythmic cadence of taut skin drums. It would cleanse the area of evil spirits and prepare the prospective bride to receive a man.

As the dancing continued, others from the village brought pieces of dried wood to form a large stack in the center of the circle. Women then placed several freshly killed deer and numerous rabbits around the stack.

By midnight a full moon had risen to a point directly overhead, its pale blue rays shining through a hole in the apex of the tepee. A circle of eerie light bathed the bride-to-be as she sat nude on the cushioned white pelt of a timber wolf. Four matrons had washed her in warm water scented with steeped juniper berries and covered her with bear grease.

As the matrons combed and separated her long, flaxen hair, she wondered if there was some way to get away, some way to avoid the marriage. One of the matrons had mentioned that two white men were in the camp. For two years she had hoped and prayed for rescue when white men came, but nothing happened.

She recalled the raid by French troops on Marsh Creek Valley. She was fourteen then, and her name was Mary Jemison. She, along with her mother, father, and two younger brothers, had been taken captive, and as they'd watched their cabin burn, the French had turned them over to the accompanying Senecas. She remembered the long walk south to the Ohio and recalled the red-haired scalp of her mother and that of her father stretched on wooden hoops, drying. She had been named *Dehgewanus* and was forbidden to speak English again.

Tears came to her eyes.

"Do not cry," a matron warned. "The chief needs a strong wife." Then, she stepped outside and raised both hands above her head. The beating of drums halted and the crowd fell silent.

The medicine man emerged from the shadows and walked up to the matron. He wore a skunk skin hat and had four squirrel pelts hanging from a waistband. His aged, deeply wrinkled face was decorated with blue and white stripes. From his belt he pulled the carved and polished thighbone of a deer and held it high for all to see. Its marble-like head shone dully in the dancing firelight. The matron stepped aside to let him enter, then closed the entrance flap.

The villagers stood motionless, their eyes fixed on the tepee, their ears straining for the slightest sound that might emanate from the ceremonial structure. For several minutes they remained frozen like statues, the silence broken only by the crackling fires and the mating call of a distant owl.

Suddenly, the flap opened, and the stern faced medicine man emerged, throwing an aura of expectant awe over the waiting crowd. Dramatically thrusting his arm above his head, he displayed the bone phallus, its moist, blood-stained shaft glistening in the dim light. The prospective bride had been deflowered without uttering a sound. She would make a good wife for their chief.

On her wedding day, the Great Spirit would look down kindly upon Dehgewanus. In the deep blue heavens this night, it had placed the stars and moon in a configuration that foretold her destiny. She would become the most powerful and influential member of the tribe. The world would come to know her as the White Woman of the Senecas.

A tumultuous cry arose from the crowd. Using brands selected from the ring of small fires, they ignited the large stack of wood in the center. Then they began a wild celebration of chanting and dancing.

"Let's get some sleep," suggested Flip.

They made their beds near the canoe, but sleep was difficult. The clamor of the celebration echoed through the trees and troubled thoughts raced through their minds. They wondered about tomorrow.

◆

At midmorning Sheninjee stepped from his lodge, halting the frenzied singing and dancing. He was still dressed in buckskins but now wore a long necklace of bear claws and wolf teeth. The ring of small fires was gone, their ashes having been thrown onto the remains of the center blaze. The animal carcasses piled on top, bubbled, oozed, and dripped into the glowing coals, sending thin plumes of blue smoke lazily upward.

Sheninjee circled the clearing with a deliberate and measured stride. Then he took a position in front of his lodge.

"Looks like he's ready," Richard said, nudging Flip who was sitting beside him on a log at the edge of the clearing.

"I hope so," Flip replied with a sigh. "I'd like to get going again."

At that moment, the flap of the bridal tepee opened, and a matron emerged leading Dehgewanus by the hand. A series of grunts arose from the approving spectators. While she was being escorted to the side of Sheninjee, who was waiting with the medicine man, Flip and Richard stood to see over the heads of those standing before them.

"My God, she's white!" gasped Richard, turning his head toward Flip.

"Don't act surprised—don't say anything," Flip whispered out of the side of his mouth.

The petite bride, barely four and a half feet tall, was dressed in soft, white doeskin generously adorned with brightly colored shells and beads. Her hair was neatly parted along the center of her head and formed into carefully woven braids that hung to the mounds of her breasts. Light blonde eyebrows formed gentle arches over a pair of delicate blue eyes that were highlighted by a small nose and dainty chin shiny with bear grease.

She scanned the crowd, her face showing no sign of emotion or recognition. When she caught sight of Flip and Richard, her eyes focused, and she gazed stoically at them for a long moment. The two men sensed her pleading but felt helpless.

The matrons handed the medicine man a cape made from softened hides that had been taken from a buck and doe deer and sewn together with a narrow thong. He placed it carefully over the couple's shoulders so the white tail of the buck hung at the small of Sheninjee's back and that of the doe reached the same position on his bride. Then, standing before them, he seized her right hand, pushed it into Sheninjee's left palm, and slipped a small, braided reed hoop over their wrists.

As members of the village watched in silence, he spoke the marriage declaration in the language of the Seneca.

"You will now share a shelter and a bed as you do this garment. This union will bring strength and vigor to the Seneca tribe of the Iroquois nation."

As the great shout of jubilation arose from the hoarse throats of the villagers, Flip and Richard pushed forward and laid a neatly folded red wool blanket at the feet of the newlyweds. Then they placed a new hunting knife and string of blue glass beads on top of it.

"Thank you, my brothers," said Sheninjee. "We are grateful."

Dehgewanus looked down at the presents, then at the two men. Again, they felt the pleading of her eyes.

Turning, Flip and Richard threaded their way through the celebrating crowd. The villagers seemed to be in a state of trance, their voices hoarse, their bodies dripping with offensive sweat. The two men stopped to watch the Indians rip pieces from the cooking carcasses and stuff the charred flesh forcefully into their mouths. Richard looked back at Sheninjee and Dehgewanus. Sheninjee was talking to a brave, but Dehgewanus was watching him and Flip. "What are we going to do to help that poor girl?" he asked.

"Not a damned thing!" Flip replied emphatically. "Sheninjee is a sly bastard; If we tried anything, as sure as there is a God in heaven, we'd be slit and gutted like a dressed deer. We're being escorted by four braves to make damned sure we don't turn back for help. By the time they leave us, she'll be long gone."

Chapter 6

Naseeka

The heavy runoff from a storm that had passed to the north two days before filled Beaver Creek to the top of its banks, and its yellow, silt-laden waters were surging to the center of the smooth flowing Ohio before being carried off downstream. With a half dozen quick, angular strokes of their paddles, Richard and Flip turned the heavy prow of the canoe abruptly to the north and headed into the roily water. Kneeling, they dipped deep and pulled determinedly to gather momentum for the upstream run. In a few minutes they had settled into a steady, uniform cadence of powerful strokes that propelled the craft rapidly forward, eliciting grunts of surprised approval from the four Indians watching on a path along the east bank.

"We'll be hungry tonight!" shouted Flip from his position in the stern. Beads of sweat were showing on his tanned forehead.

"Sure makes a difference going upstream," Richard complained as he pushed an onrushing limb aside with his paddle. "Why can't those Indians help with a line?"

"They've been given strict orders what to do," stated Flip, squinting at the sun's reflection from the water. "They'll let us know, if the time should come."

The Indians sauntered along the path, keeping abreast of the canoe, occasionally stopping to pick wintergreen berries or watch the antics of a scolding blue jay. Three of them were dressed in a motley, ill-fitting combination of leather, fur, and a coarsely woven cloth that was draped across one shoulder and hung loosely to their knees. They wore no foot coverings but hid their genitals with a red loincloth of soft doeskin. A quiver of arrows hung on their backs below a pair of crow feathers that dangled from their plaited hair.

The fourth, dressed in buckskins tailored for someone much larger, wore knee length moccasins and carried a rusty musket. His head was shaved except for a circular shock of blue-black hair jutting from its center. The hair was bound at its base with a beaded leather thong, making it stand erect, its ends arching in all directions.

"You can bet some poor trapper's bones are bleachin' somewhere because of that savage sonofabitch," Flip observed as they rested while holding the canoe in a quiet eddy pool near the bank.

Richard looked up and saw the piercing black eyes of the one in buckskins darting about, scanning them suspiciously. He turned to Flip and said quietly, "That one's a wild looking bastard. Wonder if he knows how to use that musket?"

"I doubt it," Flip answered easily. "He hasn't any powder and probably no shot. Hell, the only real weapon he's got is that skinnin' knife."

As they talked, the black, beady eyes zeroed in on Richard, making him feel uneasy. He turned to Flip. "Let's get going," he said, checking the position of his musket as he picked up his paddle.

By late afternoon, they had reached a point above the effects of the now distant storm. The water ran clear and was not as deep nor as swift. And the channel had narrowed so branches of trees along its banks overlapped, forming an arched canopy of green foliage that eliminated the sun's rays.

While Richard moored the canoe for the night and gathered wood for a fire, the Indians sat cross-legged on the forest floor a short distance away watching him intently. They made him uneasy, and he wished Flip would return. Flip had gone hunting for rabbits, stating he wouldn't be far away. "Three or four is all we need," he'd told Richard when he left. "And they're plentiful."

Richard knew Flip was an excellent marksman, so after counting three shots he studied the thick growth for some kind of movement, some sign he was returning. Glancing warily at the Indians, he saw that they were still watching him carefully. He knew he was supposed to trust them, that they served not only as guides but as protectors from other Indians, as well. Yet, he wondered if they could suddenly change, unexpectedly revert to their savage ways.

The loud report of a fourth shot rang out. Flip emerged, carrying three rabbits and a squirrel. "How many of these do we need?" he asked, tossing the game onto the ground near Richard.

"Just two rabbits," Richard replied, poking the fire to make a flat spot for a small skillet.

When Flip placed the remaining rabbit and squirrel before the Indians, they grunted a raspy, deep-throated approval but didn't move from their seated position. He returned again with an armful of wood and a firebrand starter. They jumped quickly to their feet.

While Richard sat hunched on a moss-covered log by the fire intent on cooking the pieces of meat in a sizzling skillet, Flip dipped a small pot of tea water from the creek and nestled it against the developing coals. Then he sat down and watched the thin column of blue-white smoke as it rose rapidly for a few feet before drifting lazily through the upper branches of dense growth. He was glad he had asked the young Virginian to come with him. Richard was good company and rapidly becoming adept at living in the wilderness. He knew his friend was still fearful of Indians, but he recalled his first encounter with the Mohawks and remembered how nervous he was. Richard seemed much calmer.

He glanced over at the Indians. They were sitting around their small fire eating chunks of raw flesh cut from the carcasses of the animals he had given them. When he turned back, he saw that Richard was also watching.

"What would they do if you didn't give them anything?" Richard asked.

"Oh, hell," Flip replied. "Indians don't keep track of eating time. They just eat when they get hungry. Eat anything they find handy. Look at the blood runnin' off their chins." He laid two more pieces of wood on the fire. "They're a rough damned bunch. Probably got a batch of jerked venison hanging on 'em somewhere."

Richard watched the one in buckskins stuff a portion of dripping entrails into his mouth. "Good God!" he exclaimed, shaking his head. "He *is* a savage." Once again, he turned his attention to the skillet.

After they had eaten, he rubbed the skillet and tin plates with dry pine needles, then rinsed them in the water. Flip tossed the food scraps and bones into the stream to avoid attracting skunks and mice. Then they placed their open bedrolls on a pile of leaves and pine needles they had scraped together and sat down by the fire to drink another cup of tea.

Summer dawn came early north of the Ohio. Although the sun had difficulty penetrating the dense forest growth, the stirring of small animals and bickering of jays and mockingbirds made sleeping beyond the first gray light of morning impossible. Flip and Richard sat up and looked over at the Indians. They were squatting about the remains of their small fire, coaxing it back to life with pine needles and dry wood chips.

"How do you feel?" asked Flip, getting to his feet.

"Stiff and sore," replied Richard, reluctant to leave the warmth of his bed.

"Fifteen minutes in the canoe will cure that."

By midafternoon, they had reached a point on Beaver Creek where shallow water made them select their course very carefully. Broken tree limbs and dead vines frequently had to be dragged aside to let them pass. When they reached a large, uprooted tree that blocked their passage, Flip declared, "We'll camp here tonight. Then tomorrow we'll start our portage to the Cuyahoga."

As Richard stepped out of the canoe, he hesitated, looking at its load. Flip noticed his concern. "We can make it in two trips," he said. "Supplies in one, canoe in the other."

"That shouldn't be too bad," Richard said with a shrug.

"Trouble is, it'll probably take a week."

"Why a week?"

"It's some distance to the Cuyahoga."

Richard stared at the ground thoughtfully, then looked up at Flip. "Well," he said, "so be it!"

They shared their supper of biscuits and quail with the Indians, then laid their bedrolls beside the dusty footpath on a pile of bronze-colored pine needles they had scraped together. When they returned to the tethered canoe to unload and bundle the cargo for backpacking, the Indians rushed to their side. By arm and body gestures, the red men indicated they were to help with the portage.

"Well, I'll be damned!" exclaimed Richard, looking at Flip for a reaction.

"They're following orders," Flip said, suddenly bemused. "Now we can make it in one trip." He turned to the Indians and explained that he would make up the packs.

The Indians, not satisfied with the arrangement, indicated with unflinching determination that they must help.

Flip thought for a full minute, looking first at the neatly loaded canoe and then into the resolute face and uncompromising eyes of their buckskin-clad leader. He welcomed their help but knew from previous experience they lacked a sense of order. They would have to be carefully controlled to avoid confusion and a resulting mess.

Richard stood nearby, uncertain what he should do. He would wait for Flip's orders.

Flip looked at him, then said, "You unload and hand it to them so they can carry it over to me." He thought for a moment, then added, "Give me time to square things away over here so I can stack it in four piles."

He removed the tarpaulins from the canoe and spread them on the ground beside the trail.

"Watch those overanxious bastards," he warned, as Richard put one foot in the canoe.

At Flip's signal, Richard handed the Indians small amounts to carry to him. When the task was finished, Flip tied two packs so they were ready to go. The remaining two would have to wait until morning for the camping gear.

The Indian in buckskins walked over to the canoe. He grunted an order, and two of his companions picked up the finished packs.

The third rushed to his side and began helping him pull the canoe from the water.

"Stop those crazy asses!" Flip yelled, nodding his head in the direction of those loading packs on their backs while he rushed to restrain the ones at the canoe.

Richard spun about and yanked the pack from the hands of the Indian nearest to him. The Indian struggled to regain it but was no match for Richard's superior strength. Their attention was abruptly diverted by the noisy confrontation at the canoe.

It took ten minutes of wild gesturing and firm talking for Flip to convince the Indians they must wait until morning to begin the trek. Angrily, they walked away, three of them shouting at their leader.

"Just like a bunch of little children," Flip sighed.

Richard walked over and stood beside Flip. He could still feel his muscles trembling, but was proud that he had stood up to the Indian. "I should think they'd realize there isn't enough daylight left to travel any distance at all."

"Hell, they don't pay any attention to the clock. An Indian eats when he's hungry, sleeps when he's tired, travels when he feels like it. They don't do any plannin' or figurin'. They just go. Gotta treat 'em like little children." He paused for a moment, then, looking Richard in the eye, added, "I like the way you took the pack from that one. Ya see, they're not so strong, leastways not for a fellow as big as you. You've gotta be strict with 'em. They'll respect ya for it."

Richard was pleased with Flip's praise. "I'll keep on them," he said with a smile.

Still, the commotion had alarmed him. He reloaded his musket with a fresh charge of powder, then sat down on a rock facing Flip.

"These Indians won't let anything happen," Flip assured him. "They've been told to take us so far before going back. Anything comes this way, they'll let us know ahead of time."

When Richard crawled into bed, he placed his musket close to his side. He closed his eyes, but sleep would not come. Listening, he heard the movement of the Indians and the munching of foraging deer, sounds he had heard before. Now, they seemed louder and more strange.

He raised his head and looked at the Indians sprawled on the ground a short distance away. He had never dealt with savages before and didn't understand their way of thinking, their code of honor, and the strictness of following the orders of their chief. And, there was the frightening thought of others traveling the trail at night.

He looked over at Flip. The rise and fall of his blankets coupled to his heavy breathing indicated he was asleep. Again, Richard lowered his head and closed his eyes.

◆

Impelled by the impatient tramping of the Indians, they arose when there was barely enough light by which to see. They ate a cold breakfast of leftover quail and hard biscuits, then loaded the packs onto the backs of the Indians. Then they tied their muskets to the ribs of the canoe and flipped the vessel over their heads.

"Not as heavy as I expected," Richard said, adjusting the load to his shoulders. "But I hope you know where you're going, because I sure as hell can't see much."

After a few steps, there was a noisy shuffling beside them. Flip saw the feet of the Indians hurrying past. "Stop, you crazy bastards!" he yelled, lowering his end of the canoe to the ground.

He ran ahead and grabbed the one in buckskins by the sleeve. The Indian stopped and turned to face him. "You must stay behind!" Flip shouted, waving his hand vigorously toward the rear.

At first, the Indian shook his head in a negative manner, but when he saw the show of determination on Flip's face, he agreed to stay behind the canoe.

"They're in one hell of a hurry," Flip complained, breathing heavily as he placed the canoe back on his shoulders.

"Maybe we should let them carry the canoe," Richard suggested, picking up the cadence of Flip's stride.

"Oh, no. They'd let it get all punched full of holes."

◆

By noon of the third day after leaving Beaver Creek, they reached a sandy bar at a bend of the Cuyahoga where the water was deep enough to float their loaded canoe. A small hole, however, had been ripped in its bark skin, so they laid it on its side in the sand. When the Indians took the heavy packs from their backs and placed them beside it, Flip gave each a small skinning knife as a present and informed them to thank their chief for his help.

As they started down the trail at a brisk run, he turned to Richard. "They're in a big hurry to get back," he stated, exhaling audibly. "Damned glad we don't have to supervise them any longer."

"How long will it take them to make it?" asked Richard, watching them disappear around a bend.

"Oh, they'll run all night. Be there tomorrow morning."

Richard shot a look at Flip. "Didn't you say the chief would move the village as soon as we left?"

"Yeah. But they'll find signs," Flip replied, looking down at the canoe. "Let's get this thing fixed."

He cut a patch from a birch tree and handed it to Richard. "Here, sew this over the hole," he said. "I'll find some balsam pitch to seal it."

After placing the canoe in the water, he and Richard loaded it with their supplies. "There," he said, smiling as he looked down the river. He turned to Richard, and his face became serious. He wanted to tell his friend of the dangers they now faced, but didn't want to frighten him. Again, he looked down the river. "We're on our own, now," he began.

Richard looked at him soberly. There was a gravity in Flip's voice that concerned him.

Flip continued. "We'll take no chances. Just try to stay out of the way of everybody."

"Who's likely to give us trouble?" Richard asked solemnly, looking around them.

"We probably won't run on ta anybody." Flip replied, wondering if he'd overemphasized the dangers. "Never had any trouble myself. But, been told there's cutthroat trappers as well as bands of marauding Indians roaming the wilderness." He paused, then added, "And there's the *voyageurs*, those half-breed French who wander everywhere."

Richard nodded his head slowly. "We'll just have to be careful," he said, turning to look through the trees around them.

They selected a campsite on the west bank where the overhead foliage was so thick there was little plant growth at ground level. It provided a clear view through the surrounding tract of large trunk shafts that stood like sentinels, erect and silent, offering protection to those seeking sanctuary beneath their sheltering limbs. They used dry wood for a fire of minimum smoke and hoped the sound of their muskets and odor of food had not reached the senses of anyone who would track them down.

After bathing, shaving and eating, they sat staring into the pile of glowing coals with its fingers of little blue flame that consumed the escaping gases. Silently, they immersed themselves into their own private thoughts.

For the first time since leaving the Rappahannock, Richard felt the total isolation and loneliness of the primeval forest. Suddenly, he realized he was many miles into an endless sea of trees and foliage so extensive and so dense that a man could travel for days without seeing the sun, where a sense of direction becomes confused and lost so that the only reliable method of guidance is that of flowing water. He thought of Fredericksburg, of his father, and of the soft white arms of Elizabeth. He shuddered and wondered what she was doing.

Looking over at Flip thoughtfully drawing smoke from the short stem of a corncob pipe, he noted the reflection of the fire on the smooth skin of his face and neck. Flip was at home in the wilderness, a man who enjoyed the quiet solitude and feeling of independence it gave. A man who had the skill, knowledge, and strength few men possessed for such a life. And he radiated a calmness and confidence that Richard admired. He was grateful he had such a friend in which to place his trust.

They sat quietly for some time, absorbing the warmth from the ash-coated embers. Then, Flip broke the silence. "Let's turn in," he suggested, "so we can get an early start. With a little luck, maybe we can reach Lake Erie tomorrow."

After scattering the fire they crawled into their beds, spaced a short distance apart, with muskets at their sides. "Stay alert for an hour," Flip warned. "Just in case somebody's been watching. It's so dark nobody else could find us."

In the morning, they pushed the canoe into the rapidly flowing Cuyahoga. It was still narrow enough to keep them from seeing the sky, but by paddling at an easy cadence, they moved swiftly along its smooth surface. There was something about the speed of movement that eased Richard's fear of the unknown. It gave him a confidence of being able to outrun an attacker. He would feel better, however, when they got out into the open where he could see beyond the endless green canopy that had covered them like a shroud for nearly two weeks.

He looked up and saw a line of Indians walking toward them along the path on the east bank. Startled, he looked back at Flip. Flip, who had already seen them, nodded calmly, indicating there was nothing to fear.

The Indians were led by two elderly men. They were followed by a dozen women carrying heavy backpacks. Several children and dogs romped and played among them.

"Headed for a new campground," Flip said, waving to them. "We'll just keep movin'. Their warriors will be out of sight on the other side of them."

The Indians plodded on, showing no sign of recognition.

They skirted a misty falls; then the river made a big turn and suddenly widened. Its water flowed flat and serene, and the green canopy overhead parted, then disappeared.

After negotiating a double line of large stepping stones that served the heavy foot traffic of the Lake Erie shoreline trail, they glided through a short, cattail-lined estuary, startling a group of red-winged blackbirds. Suddenly they were rolling on gentle green waves and feeling the mild breeze of Lake Erie against their faces.

The openness gave Richard a sense of freedom and happiness, as if a heavy burden had been removed from atop his body. He looked out across the expanse of fresh, blue-green water, then up at an azure sky, its color accented by fleecy clouds and soaring gulls. Inhaling deeply, a smile broadened to a grin as he observed small waves lapping a beach that appeared to go on forever. How fresh and new. How different from the dankness of the forest.

"We'll stay out a ways," Flip stated matter of factly as they turned west to parallel the white sandy shoreline. "Never sure what's in the woods. Out here they can't surprise us."

The lake was contained by a ridge of sand thirty feet high created over the centuries by the thrust of huge blocks of ice driven inland during raging winter storms. A scattering of scrawny poplars, struggling for a foothold, grew along the top and down its back slope to the forest floor. There, rot and humus nurtured the heavy growth of vines and evergreens. It was at this juncture that the traffic of the shoreline trail chose to travel. It kept them from the dankness of the inland forest and afforded a solid footing the sandy ridge could not give.

After paddling along the shoreline for an hour, Flip and Richard stopped to locate a campsite for the night. They drew the canoe onto the beach just enough to prevent wave action from rocking it free, then walked up the slope of soft sand. It felt good to the soles of their moccasined feet. They staggered slightly from the effects of kneeling in the canoe, but they were in no hurry. They peered at their tracks and watched the fine grains of sand fill them again. They picked up halves of clamshells, studied them momentarily, then dropped them. Looking into the glare of the afternoon sun, they saw a scattering of driftwood in the distance.

At the top of the ridge, Flip relieved himself against the trunk of a twisted sapling, then puckered and spit downwind. Richard shot a look at him, then pointed toward the woods. "Let's get the muskets and go down for a look," he said.

"Right by me," Flip agreed, refastening his pants.

When they reached the flatland, they took a few steps through the thickening undergrowth and emerged on a heavily traveled trail. Standing motionless, they looked to the left and right. Tracks indicated horses, cattle, and humans, barefooted and with shoes, had used it since the last rain.

Out of the corner of his eye, Richard thought he saw something not far away that looked unusual. Squinting to allow his lashes to more clearly direct the shade-filtered light into his eyes, he exclaimed in a barely audible voice as he pointed, "Good God!"

Both men dropped to their haunches, Flip's eyes following the direction of the still pointing finger. There, less than fifty feet from them, a naked Indian was suspended upside down between two hickory saplings.

They waited a full two minutes, looking around and listening intently, before approaching the red man.

He was a young brave, not more than thirty years of age, lean and muscular in build, whose smooth, reddish-bronze skin was marred by a thin X slashed across his chest. A half dozen welts from a beating crisscrossed his back. Attached to the two slender trees that had been forced toward each other to create tension, he was held by strips of leather around his wrists and ankles so that his long, black braids hung a few inches off the ground. His head and the neck of his scrotum had been tautly bound with several turns of doeskin thong that was gradually tightening as it absorbed the cold perspiration oozing from his tortured body. Although unconscious, his half-opened eyes still glistened with moisture. Their lids fluttered slightly as the two men approached.

With their knives, they quickly cleaved through his bindings and eased his limp, unclothed body to the ground. Using care not to cut the skin, they sliced through the thongs which had become imbedded in his forehead and around his cold, purple genitals.

In a few seconds, the brave regained consciousness. His body stiffened, and his eyes stared in stark terror as he focused on the two white men, knives in their hands, kneeling beside him. Flip quickly raised his right hand in an open position and placed the other gently on the Indian's heaving chest. The Indian again lapsed into unconsciousness, relaxing his tense muscles.

"Now what?" Richard asked, looking about suspiciously.

"Get ta hell out of here, Flip stated emphatically. "He hasn't been up there more than fifteen or twenty minutes." He thought momentarily, then added, "If they come back they'll string us all up."

"What about him?" asked Richard, voicing concern for the red man's life.

The brave stirred, then opened his eyes again.

"He'd better get out of here, too," Flip warned. Knowing that the Indian would be killed if the enemy returned, he didn't want to abandon him, but he wondered if they had time to help.

Turning to the red man, he tried to question him by using words of the Seneca, but the Indian did not answer. He used the language of the Iroquois and of the Mohawk, but the young brave, who was trying to sit up, still did not respond. Finally, in exasperation he muttered, "*Mon dieu!*"

The Indian immediately brightened. "Please, help me, my friends," he pleaded in French. His dark eyes searched each of theirs for some sign of compassion.

"Let's go," said Flip as he picked up his musket and got to his feet.

With the aid of his rescuers, the weakened man struggled to his feet. In a low crouch, they slipped hurriedly through the sparse growth and made their way up the sandy incline At the top, the Indian's knees buckled, then his head dropped forward and lolled to the center of gravity. They placed his arms around their necks and carried him to the canoe. Again, his eyes fluttered and opened. He could stand again. Flip ordered him to lie face down on top of the loaded craft.

"Can we give him some clothes first?" Richard asked.

"No time," came Flip's terse reply.

He was quickly covered with an oilskin tarpaulin.

They paddled strenuously for two miles before finding a suitable break in the shoreline. Turning abruptly, they entered a sheltered cove lined with a dense growth of reeds and thicket.

While Richard unloaded their needs for the night, Flip tended the Indian's wounds. He carefully washed the cuts and contusions with water, then swabbed them with turpentine, a practice he had been taught by other trappers. He knew that it would sting open cuts, but it had been known to save lives. He was surprised, however, when it did not elicit the slightest reaction from the Indian.

Using his thumb, he massaged the red furrows still etched across the brave's bronze forehead, then felt his testicles to see if the circulation had returned. "As good as new," he told him. Then, without turning his head, he added in English loud enough for Richard to hear, "A little turpentine on those hot balls would make him take notice!"

Richard, busy covering the canoe with reeds and cattails, looked over at Flip and chuckled.

The Indian thanked them for their help and started to leave.

Flip had been impressed by the red man. To him, he looked lighter in color than other Indians he had known and much less savage, and he spoke French fluently. Intrigued, Flip wanted to have him stay for a while so he could learn more about him.

"Why don't you stay with us for a few days until you are stronger," Flip suggested.

"I would like that," came the grateful reply.

Turning to Richard, Flip said, "This is no ordinary savage. I think he's a different class." He paused a moment, then said, "Let's see what we can find out about him."

"Sure," Richard replied. "Somebody sure wanted him to suffer."

"He would have died in another half hour."

They tramped reeds and grass into bed pads; then Richard distributed a generous amount of jerked beef and hard biscuits for their supper. The Indian bolted his down, then drank some water from the lake. When he returned to sit with them again, Flip looked him in the eye. "You are our friend. Who are you?" he asked sternly.

"I am Naseeka," the red man replied soberly. He hoped his rescuers were true friends who would help him return to his village. He did not know how far it was, but it was a great distance. His past raced through his mind as he looked at them. It bolstered his strength and made him confident he *would* get back. "Naseeka is a Wyandotte," he said, searching their faces for a reaction.

Naseeka explained to the two men that he was fishing a half hour's walk below his village, using a reed net his betrothed had woven for him, when a small band of renegade Hurons had captured him.

"They stripped me of my buckskins and bound my wrists behind me," he told them. "I could smell brandy on their breath.

"They fastened a leash around my neck, then pushed, prodded and kicked me while making their way noisily along the trail. Sometimes they stopped to rest and talk, but they continued to drink liquor from a moose bladder one of them carried. I hoped that when they had sated themselves by using me as a source of amusement, they would turn me loose. Or, if they got drunk enough, perhaps I could escape.

"But every time they stopped, they tied the end of the leash to one of their ankles." He shook his head. "I was very concerned when they reached the south shore of Lake Erie and headed east.

"On two separate occasions they started back, but each time an argument ensued and they would head east again. They fed me nothing and rarely permitted me to quench my thirst from the many streams we crossed. Other groups of Indians they met on the trail were amused at their actions. And they chose to hide from six heavily armed Frenchmen who were driving a small herd of cattle westward."

Naseeka got another drink of water, then sat down again.

"Late one afternoon, they sat in a circle on the trail to decide what to do with me. They ridiculed me about my light skin and said they could see my muscles through it. They said my face was not that of a true red man.

"Finally, they decided to string me up beside the trail. They would weaken my body by choking the flow of strength from my testicles. And they would make me cry out in pain by binding my head. This would bring the animals and birds to peck and chew at my carcass." The young brave looked off into the distance. He set his jaw and took in a deep breath. "Again, I told them, 'I am Naseeka, son of a Wyandotte chief.' They scoffed and sneered. 'You are Wyandotte!' they said. 'You are white Indian!' Then they went away."

After Flip had finished translating the last sentence for Richard, Naseeka again expressed his appreciation for being rescued. He told them he trusted them and felt safe in their company. Then he asked why two British subjects would venture so far into French territory, especially since a war was being carried on between the two countries.

"The French have been defeated," Flip informed him. "They have surrendered all their territory to the British."

Naseeka shook his head in disbelief. "The French were good to us. I hope the British will be, too."

"They will be," Flip assured him.

Just before the sun dropped below the horizon, Naseeka's keen ears sensed a far-off sound, and he raised his hand in a request for silence. Placing his ear against the ground, he listened momentarily, then stated in a whisper, "They come."

When Richard and Flip placed their ears to the ground, they, too, could hear the distinct sound of running footsteps.

Sitting quietly, they waited with their muskets ready. The thicket and tall grass should conceal them and a southerly breeze would place them downwind from anyone on the trail. In a few minutes, a group Flip estimated to be four fleet-footed braves approached. Instead of trotting past, they stopped.

Flip dropped to his elbows and, holding his breath, cocked his weapon. Naseeka, who was slightly ahead of him, rose to a low crouch and tried to peer through the thick growth. Flip patted him on the back and motioned for him to get down.

Naseeka, embarrassed, quickly lowered his haunches onto his heels. He knew better. His elders had told him that curiosity had caused many white men to lose their scalps. "If you can see your enemy, your enemy can see you," they said.

Flip quietly removed his knife from its sheath and slipped it into Naseeka's hand.

The four Indians were conversing and bantering in low, guttural tones. Occasionally, one of them would yelp or howl.

Naseeka listened intently. "Huron," he whispered.

The Indians became quiet. Richard could hear the spatter of them urinating into water at the edge of the lake. He held his breath and nervously fingered the trigger guard of his cocked musket. It had been two days since he had reloaded it with fresh powder. He wondered what to do if it misfired.

A strange fear suddenly gripped him, a fear he did not comprehend. He had faced Indians before, but this seemed different. Perhaps it was because he was so far from home. His breath became labored and heavy. He hoped it would subside, but it grew more intense. Although the Indians were thirty feet away, he was afraid they could hear him. He opened his mouth to reduce the noise from the rapid passage of air.

His pulse throbbed in his temples, making it difficult to hear, and his heart was thundering in his chest. Thoughts raced through his mind. If he was killed here, his father and Elizabeth would never know what happened to him. He looked at Naseeka and saw the knife in the young brave's hand. Could Naseeka have been a lure, and now his four friends were returning to do the white men in?

His fearful chain of thoughts was suddenly interrupted by a whoop from one of the Hurons as they trotted off. When their deep, throaty tones had faded away, he released the hammer of his musket.

Although he was soaked with perspiration, his breathing had returned to normal. Turning, he saw Naseeka giving the knife to Flip. A feeling of guilt surged over him for having doubted the Wyandotte.

———————◆———————

It took seven more days, with Naseeka paddling in the center of the canoe, to reach the western limits of Lake Erie.

Shortly after turning northward they encountered a flotilla of fifteen *bateaux* loaded with armed, blue-coated French soldiers. They were being escorted from Detroit by ten British soldiers trailing in their own bateau. The vessels, each using six men with paddles, were evenly spaced along a single line. The color of the French uniforms made a striking contrast with the bright red of those worn by the British.

Sitting proudly erect and looking straight ahead in the third bateau was the French commandant, Marie Francois Picote de Bellestre, dressed in a brilliant blue, white and gold uniform.

Naseeka recognized one of the soldiers in the lead vessel. "Hello, Henri!" he called out, his paddle trailing in the water. "Where do you go?"

Richard and Flip stopped paddling to accommodate the conversation.

"We go to Philadelphia!" Henri replied with a forced smile, as he passed without a change of cadence.

Other soldiers, curious at the conversation, looked toward them momentarily, then paddled on.

"I will see you when you return!" Naseeka said cheerfully.

"I will see you no more!" came the hurried reply.

"Why?" asked Naseeka, shouting ever louder because of the growing distance between them.

"The British have come!" Henri shouted back. His voice seemed to have a ring of gladness at the prospect of leaving the wilderness.

Paddling slowly, they waited for the British soldiers to approach. "Are the British at Detroit?" Flip asked.

Surprised at the sound of spoken English, one of the soldiers replied cheerily, "Right ye be, me lad!"

"And why do the French have their weapons?"

"They've got no place ta run ta, and we may need their 'elp ta boot. Besides, they surrendered as gentlemen."

As the trio picked up the rhythm of paddling again, Naseeka shook his head and sighed. He twisted his body to look back at Flip. "You are right," he declared. "The British are here."

The tension he had felt for many days had left Naseeka. He was within the range of his hunting and fishing grounds. "You are safe now, my friends," he told Richard and Flip, as their canoe sliced through smooth water. "The Wyandottes will protect you."

They looked at him, then nodded. They were not certain about the Wyandottes, but knowing that a British garrison was not far away made them feel better.

They built a roaring fire on the beach against a foot-high bank of rock-imbedded clay where stunted sumac and saw grass grew. After feasting on rabbit, squirrel, and hot biscuits, they relaxed around the fire to savor the pleasantness spreading through their tired bodies.

Richard sat on the bank and removed his moccasins and socks, then worked his feet into the cool sand. He looked across the fire at Flip, who was calmly puffing a clay pipe and staring absently at the rapidly changing shadows of the dense forest. Flip's guidance and confidence meant a lot to him. Without it, he would have turned back long ago.

He laid back on the ground, still enjoying the feeling of the sand around his toes, and looked up at the darkening canopy above. One fluffy pink cloud seemed to be suspended from a vast false ceiling. Thoughts chased themselves through his mind. He felt a certain excitement about approaching the outpost at Detroit, but he was concerned about Naseeka's promise to bring them to the Wyandotte village.

He was beginning to know and trust the red man and could understand some of his French, and he was able to teach Naseeka the names of several dozen objects in English. But still, the village would be that of savages.

Closing his eyes, his thoughts drifted back to Fredericksburg. It gave him a good visceral feeling. But when he thought of Elizabeth, he experienced a surge of guilt. Instead of being in the wilderness, he should be back there, close to her, making plans to marry and settle down as he had promised. But then, that was why he was here. He wanted to earn a fat purse in the fur trade so he could marry her. Perhaps he could find a good place to live on the frontier like his father had in Virginia.

His mind wandered, and he began reliving his moments with her. If he could only smell the fragrance of her hair, taste the sweetness of her lips, and feel the softness of her thighs. A quiver in his loins made him sit up in time to see Naseeka returning from a walk along the water's edge.

"In two days we see my village," the Indian declared, lowering himself to a cross-legged sitting position near the fire.

Richard smiled. He understood without Flip translating.

They sat quietly for some time, watching the fire burn down to ash-covered coals. Flip shook the remaining blackened tobacco from his pipe, blew into the stem making a gurgling sound, then tucked it into his breast pocket. He felt at peace with the world, for this was his element. The hustle and noise of cities annoyed him. He had lived for several years among trappers and Indians and had learned to be cunning and skillful in the forest. Out here, one must observe carefully and reason adroitly in order to anticipate what is going to happen, or all could be lost. He would teach these skills to Richard, for Richard was a good friend and had an aptitude for living in the wilderness.

◆

As they neared the shore on their approach to the Wyandotte village, they were ignored by two women filling leather-lined wicker baskets with water. There were several lightly clad children playing with sticks and a rawhide ball on the beach. Naseeka waved to them, but received only momentary attention. Then, he shouted a greeting in their native tongue. Halting their play, they shielded their eyes and squinted inquisitively into the bright, water-reflected rays.

"Look! It's me, Naseeka!" he shouted, kneeling upright as he waved again.

The children dropped their sticks and scurried off, yelling as they ran, "Naseeka! Naseeka!"

The women looked up, then turned and walked slowly toward a plume of smoke that was rising among the trees.

Richard and Flip were relieved at the prospect of a respite from their paddles. They had left Lake Erie and, for the last three miles, had been struggling against the choppy waters of a broad river.

Naseeka directed them into the mouth of a shallow creek. They went a few yards, then tied up among a dozen other canoes and rafts in a small cove that was sheltered by reeds and willows. He stood up and stepped onto a well-worn path that led toward the village. Suddenly, he was surrounded by a crowd of jubilant Wyandottes. Several adults bowed and shook his hand, then stepped back to cautiously look at Flip and Richard.

A group of children, chatting noisily, grabbed his arms and patted his head and back. "They are my relatives," he explained, looking back at Richard and Flip.

An older woman, dressed in a beaded tan buckskin dress that hung nearly to the ground, shuffled up. As she approached, the crowd parted and became silent. She walked up to Naseeka and faced him squarely. Placing her gnarled right hand on his left shoulder, she uttered something that made him smile. He responded with a single syllable. Tears appeared in the corner of her dark eyes, then rippled down the leathery surface of her deeply wrinkled, sun-browned cheeks.

Flip watched intently. He wondered who she was and what she said. He had never seen a display of emotion by an Indian before.

Richard, concerned about the number of Indians around him, cradled his musket in his arms and nervously shifted his weight from foot to foot. Searching for direction, he looked at Flip, but saw that his friend was absorbed in watching Naseeka's reception. He raised his voice above the din. "Better get your muskets," he urged.

Flip looked over and noted his friend's uneasiness. Smiling, he said, "No need for it here." He thought for a moment, then walked over to the canoe and picked up his weapon. "We'll keep 'em with us, just the same."

The Wyandottes started down the path toward a cluster of long-houses and wigwams that were discernible through the trees. Naseeka turned toward his white companions and motioned with his hand. "Come," he said in English. Then, he added in French, "I must learn English if your people command at Detroit." Observing their hesitation, he said, "Your canoe will be watched and guarded. It will be safe."

As they walked, Naseeka told them that the two hundred Wyandottes of this village were the last of a once powerful woodland tribe. They came here to establish a permanent settlement and surrounded it with a protective palisade of poles and sticks. "Since we ran off the Potawatomis, we have no need for such a fence." He pointed to a section that had toppled. "It is of no use now."

As Naseeka talked, Richard tried to see through the oaks and pines that sheltered the village. Although the crowd seemed friendly enough, he sensed that dozens of hidden eyes were watching them suspiciously.

Ahead, six longhouses caught his attention. To him, each looked like half a watermelon with walls and roofs of bark. They were held together by a framework of poles that had been bent and tied together with vines and strips of hides. Interspersed among them were a dozen wigwams and tepees covered with the skins of dogs, deer and bear.

They walked across a hard dirt carpet to a centrally located fire pit. Several young women were removing green husks from ears of corn before tossing them into a battered, soot-covered, copper caldron of boiling water. A half dozen skinny, mongrel dogs stood near them, waiting for something they could carry off to eat or bury.

Naseeka conferred briefly with the women, then turned and said, "You will come with me to our guest abnaki where you will rest for a time. *Abnaki*, that is our word for dwelling."

He led them to a large tepee at the edge of the village. "Stay here. I will come for you later."

The floor of the tepee was covered with the skins of bear and deer. A small, stone fire ring was located on bare earth in the center. Along the back wall was a sitting log, covered with the haired pelt of a large black bear. Placed before it in a neat row were several circular reed trays of hazel nuts, shelled corn, venison strips, smoked fish, and roasted acorns.

They walked across the floor and could feel the soft cushion of pine needles that had been spread beneath the skins. "It's certainly clean," Richard ventured. "But," he added, sniffing the air and pointing to the wall, "it's a good thing the flesh side of those skins is on the outside."

"You'll get used to it after a while. They usually put their newer skins on the visitor's lodge to show respect and to impress him."

"I feel like a prisoner," Richard said, sitting down on the log.

"You aren't. But if they felt like it, you would be."

They ate some food from the trays, then stretched out on the floor. In a few minutes, Flip was asleep. Richard looked through the smoke hole at the apex and saw a small patch of blue sky through the limbs of a pine tree. He reflected on the events of the day and wondered if their lives were as safe as Flip insisted. Each day found them deeper into the wilderness and more distant from the people of their kind, people they could trust. British soldiers at Detroit would be a welcome relief. He hoped they were there.

◆

Nasingah, having watched the decimation of his once proud and powerful nation by winter famine, white man's diseases, and brutally savage attacks from the Chippewa, Ottawa, and Huron, was old for his years. The skin on his face looked like bronze leather, pock-marked and deeply furrowed. Sitting hunched and impassive on his brightly painted stump chair, his body appeared drained of the vigor it once possessed. His eyes, however, were as clear and piercing as those of a young man, and his mind was sharp and uncluttered.

He was dressed in a soft, buff-colored mantle, extensively fringed and beaded, that was gathered at the waist with a belt of human hair. Long braids of steel gray hair, neatly braided and tied at the ends with bands of red glass beads, hung down his chest halfway to his waist. Two strands of bear claws encircled his crepy throat.

Naseeka translated as he spoke to the two white men standing before him. "You have done the Wyandottes a great service by saving the life of a brave warrior. He is my son. But beyond that, he is a member of the tribal council. The Wyandotte people listen to his word and follow his advice. For this deed, you will be given one hundred beaver skins and will always be welcome as a friend."

"Thank you," Richard and Flip said in unison. Then Flip added, "We are proud to be friends of the Wyandotte."

Richard nodded agreement.

Other members of the council appeared, and Naseeka took a place between his white friends. They formed a circle, then sat cross-legged on the ground before the chief. Nasingah raised his hand, and several women brought the men reed baskets heaped with roasted passenger pigeon, blackberries, and crab apples.

Again Nasingah raised his hand. "And now, my friends, the village elders will tell you the story of my son, Naseeka."

An old man sitting in the circle wrenched a leg from a pigeon, then told of the birth of the young brave. When he finished, another took up the narration.

Behind them, other members of the village grabbed handfuls of food the women had placed on a large mat near the big fire pit.

------------◆------------

He had been born twenty-eight summers before on the west bank of the sluggish Maumee River to one of the wives of Nasingah, chief of the Wyandottes. They named him Naseeka, the quiet, intelligent one, for someday he would sit on the governing council that guided the tribe through its encounters with the larger, more hostile Indian confederations and dealt with the encroaching white man. At one time they were a very large tribe living in many villages that were spread over a vast territory. But the diseases of the white man, coupled with savage battles fought with the Ottawas and Hurons, had reduced their numbers so only one village remained.

The Wyandottes, handsome, intelligent natives, were tall, fine-boned, and smooth featured. They produced fierce, brave warriors, unaggressive by nature, who preferred to hunt and fish rather than seek a fight. If provoked, however, they displayed a degree of vigor, violence, and fury in battle that could not be matched by their enemies.

135

As a small boy, Naseeka had often heard the legend from the lips of his mother and grandmother of the twelve flaxen-haired *Wampana*. They'd had round blue eyes, bushy blonde beards, and heavy leather breastplates. Long, long ago, they had wintered with the tribe and pleasured with the women. Then, there came many Wyandottes with light hair and blue eyes. But through successive generations the dark eyes and black hair had returned.

The legacy of many things remained, however. Members of the tribe were taller. And they had slender noses and lighter skin, features that set them apart from the neighboring Ottawas, Hurons, and Miamis. This created a jealous discord and brought on an occasional battle.

They got along well with the French, especially the *couriers de bois*, who traversed the area in big canoes, fairly bartering beads, knives, and axes for furs. And when Antoine de la Mothe Cadillac built Fort Pontchartrain at a place he called *de troit*, where the cold, clear waters of the north hastened on their way to Lake Erie, the tribe made arrangements to barter pelts, squash, corn, and wild rice for guns, blankets, and brandy with the traders and settlers.

To maintain independence from the encroaching white man, the village was moved a few miles below the fort. Chief Nasingah was careful to allow enough distance between his tribe and the long, narrow farms fronting on the water that had been cleared of trees and were being cultivated and grazed by the pioneering Frenchmen. A few months after the move, a group of Potawatomis, jealous of the friendly relationship the Wyandottes established with the French, built a village of bark-covered longhouses between the Wyandottes and French farmers, hoping they could gain a favored position with the white man.

The Potawatomis began a campaign of harassment by stealing and sniping to make it difficult for the Wyandottes to communicate with the fort, and when additional settlers came and staked out their farms, the Potawatomis were forced to move farther south, thus increasing the friction between the two tribes.

One day, a group of Potawatomi bucks grabbed three Wyandotte women who were working in their corn and squash patch and dragged them off to their village. The next day, the Wyandottes descended upon the Potawatomis with the fury of a pack of mad wolverines. They killed one hundred of their number, burned the longhouses to the ground, and drove the remaining Potawatomis into the inland wilderness.

Although he was only fifteen at the time he participated in the Potawatomi battle, Naseeka was considered a fearless brave and a grown man by the tribal elders. They had guided him through puberty rites three years before, had sent him on extended hunting and trapping missions, and watched him skillfully bargain with the couriers in their village and the merchants at the fort.

He sat with them around the council fire during the long night before the raid, voting on the decision and then preparing himself for battle. At the beginning of the fighting, he led a small band of braves dressed only in breechclouts, whose bodies had been greased with bear fat and painted with white clay, charcoal and vermilion, into the center of the Potawatomi village to rescue the three women. When this had been accomplished, they assisted others who were burning every structure and, using spears, knives and tomahawks, killed everyone who resisted. Nearly half of the inhabitants, however, escaped to Potawatomi villages in the distant hinterland.

After the flames died down, Naseeka stood in the center of the smoking ruins and watched the Wyandotte women search for food and utensils they could use. The men tossed the scalped and mutilated bodies of their enemy into the chilly waters of the river. That night everyone danced and sang around a huge bonfire while sating themselves with venison, fish, and passenger pigeon.

◆

When the elders had finished, Naseeka appeared pleased. Then he turned to Flip. "We have many beaver pelts," he said, taking a bite of pigeon. "But they are not for you. They are are not prime." He chewed for a moment. "I will see that you get prime ones, but you will have to wait for winter."

Flip nodded. He knew it took two months of cold weather to produce thick, durable pelts. "Winter is not far away," he said. "We must go soon to find a good place to trap."

Richard looked at him. "I'm ready anytime," he said, gesturing impatiently.

Naseeka finished eating an apple. He tossed the core on a growing pile of bones, corncobs, and nutshells in front of them. "Naseeka will show you where to trap," he said.

"We would like that," Flip replied, reaching over to shake his hand. "But first we must get our winter supplies."

Three of the Indians in the circle seemed to be in a heated argument. They were ignored by others who were in a jovial mood celebrating the return of Naseeka. One sat motionless, staring at the ground in front of him. He appeared mesmerized by the clamor.

The sun went down, stars emerged, and more wood was thrown into the big fire pit. Richard knew he was experiencing a favorite pastime of the Indians, that of prolonged eating and endless talking and storytelling. He no longer feared being in the Indian village, and he had learned enough French to converse with Naseeka. Still, he was tired of it and wondered when it would end. He looked at Flip and heaved a heavy sigh.

Flip had done this with the Senecas and understood it. It was recreation for them, a means of relaxing, of impressing their friends with their deeds, and of passing on the history and legends of their people. As he listened, he found that he could understand much of what was being said. It was not greatly different from the language of the Huron of upper New York. "Be patient. No one dares to leave until the chief leaves." He smiled. "And his people are still enjoying it."

Leaping tongues of flame from the fire pit made grotesque shadows that flitted and darted through the trees and across the structures of the village. Richard watched them for several minutes, then turned to Flip. "My ass is cold and sore. Besides, I could use some sleep."

It was still early in the evening when Nasingah stood. Without a word, he turned slowly and made his way around the stump chair, then disappeared into a large tepee a short distance away. Those in the circle stood, nodded acknowledgment to Richard and Flip, then wandered off.

At the guest lodge, the two men found a mound of hot coals in the fire ring and, on each side of it, beds of bearskin and coarsely woven wool blankets.

"Just like the Hotel St. James in Boston, by God!" Flip exclaimed, standing with his hands on his hips.

"Pretty damned nice," Richard agreed, kneeling to examine one of the beds. He looked up at Flip, whose face reflected the glowing light of the fire ring. "They must think a lot of us."

"They do. We brought back an important member of the tribe." He sat down. "Don't forget, though, they're savages. Can turn quick if something happens they don't like. Leaders'll keep their word, but the rest can turn into a pack of wolves."

The next morning, they arose early. While Flip packed his pipe for a smoke, Richard stepped outside. The sun was trying to lift a light autumn fog that had blanketed the area. In a few hours it would warm the leaves and grass and evaporate the dew that covered them like little jewels.

Two naked children shivering with cold, their faces smeared with dirt from running noses, wandered about poking at the ground. A small plume of white smoke rose lazily from the pile of ashes in the large fire pit. Nearby, the large copper kettle rested upside down, the ground around it moist from its water, and several dogs, their tails between their legs, pawed and chewed at the pile of garbage from the feast.

The two men walked to their canoe. Finding it intact, they followed a path to the sandy shoreline of the big river that flowed past the village. Looking across its glassy, blue-green surface through the haze of morning sun, they could make out the shadow-darkened shore of a large island.

"Looks real big for a river island," Flip said, squinting as he searched its tree-lined shore for activity. "Naseeka says the French called it *Grosse Isle*."

He tossed a pebble into the water and watched the concentric circles float rapidly away. "Wish ta hell he would finish what he has in mind so we could get to Detroit."

"Why don't we just go," suggested Richard.

"We are very good friends of these people." Flip squinted as he looked around. "We may need their help someday, and it would be an insult to walk off. It won't be long, because Naseeka knows what we want ta do."

They walked back to the village and saw several matronly women gossiping in the warm sun while waiting for the rekindled blaze to build in the fire pit. A chubby man with a fat, baby face waddled up to them. He was dressed in an oversized loincloth and draped with a soiled blue cape that had been used as a carpet. They greeted him with a single word. He acknowledged them with a nod. Then, they returned to their conversation.

Naseeka emerged from one of the longhouses and walked over to the two men. He no longer wore the buckskins they had given him, but was clothed in some that were not as well fitted nor as neatly sewn. He saw that they were watching the women at the fire pit. These men were his friends, and he wanted them to know his people and understand their ways. "The women keep the fire going so the village will always have starter coals," he explained. "When rains come, they transfer a small fire to a longhouse." He paused as Richard and Flip nodded that they understood. "And they also cook and smoke fish and meat out here."

He led them to the women, where he spoke a word of greeting. The older, more wrinkled of the group responded with a toothless smile, then nodded in the direction of Flip and Richard. "She is in charge," he stated. Then, turning toward the fat man, he continued. "This is Chobo, the arrowsmith. He was one of our village sentries who was captured by the Ottawa several years ago. They castrated him. Seems to get along better with the women than the men."

Two women with vessels of food to heat approached. When they hesitated, Naseeka beckoned them forward. As they placed the containers close to the fire, two braves carrying muskets and blankets after a night of guard duty, walked up and began eating from the food containers. The women voiced objection and waved them away. The braves shrugged their shoulders, smiled, then walked off.

---◆---

At midmorning, Naseeka took the two men to the entrance of a longhouse. He lifted the draped hide that covered the small entrance and threw it up over a wooden peg. Then, he turned to them. "My father lives in the chief's tepee," he said. "I live here with the rest of my family."

Inside, the smoky, fetid air was stifling with the odor of curing hides, drying meat, and unwashed bodies. Knowing they could not show their discomfort, Richard and Flip breathed as lightly as possible.

They followed Naseeka along a compacted dirt aisle past several divided areas where people were sitting and lying about. When they came to three women at work around the ashes of a small fire used to ward off the morning chill, they halted. The women looked up momentarily, then continued with their work.

Twenty persons from several families lived in the longhouse. They maintained separate areas within the structure with stacks of wood, food containers, and drying skins. Most families covered a portion of their dirt floor with woven fiber mats or animal skins that had been laid down over a cushion of cornhusks, dried grass and pine needles. The only openings in the building were small doorways at each end covered with hanging deer hides. The smoke from family fires escaped through cracks beneath layers of bark that covered the roof.

"My mother," declared Naseeka with a wave of his hand, indicating the older woman they had seen when they disembarked the day before. "She weaves a mat from swamp reeds."

Flip glanced at two with her. They were young, possibly eighteen or twenty, he judged. Similar in appearance and dress, they were using a rock mortar and pestle to make pemmican from dried meat, nuts, and maple sugar.

"My sister, Matoka." Naseeka pointed to the smooth featured one directly across the fire ring from them. "Really my half sister. This is not her mother."

"And my promised, Lahana," he added, shuffling his feet embarrassingly as he pointed to the other young woman.

She was a fine boned, trimly dressed maiden whose eyes sparkled, even in the dim light, as she looked up at him. Richard recognized it as a sparkle of love. He recalled the special glisten in Elizabeth's eyes when he held her.

Naseeka motioned for them to sit.

The two men squatted on their haunches, grateful to be where the smoke was less dense.

The mother reached over and placed a large leather pouch before them, then rolled back its top. After watching Naseeka, Flip and Richard dipped into the pouch, pressed the granular food into a compact wad with their fingers, and pushed it into their mouths.

"Not bad," Richard noted, running his tongue back and forth across the roof of his mouth before swallowing. "Not bad at all!"

"Damned good," Flip agreed, nodding approval to Naseeka. Then, turning to Richard, he said, "What I got from the Senecas was just meat and fat. Didn't swallow easy."

While they ate, Naseeka told the women of his rescue and return to the village. Flip watched the expression on their faces. Matoka looked at him and smiled admiringly. He winked at her.

Richard looked around to see what others in the longhouse were doing. He saw shadows of people moving about, but the smoky haze and general clutter of things made it difficult. He assumed they were women, children, and elderly. Flip had said the able-bodied males formed a closely knit association of hunters, fishermen, warriors, and overseers. They left menial tasks to others so they could tend the higher order of things.

He looked at the supply of food Naseeka's mother had stored in her family area. There were stacks of multicolored ears of corn, piles of nuts and acorns, several squash, and containers of berries and crab apples. When she saw him looking at strips of venison hanging from the roof ribs, Naseeka's mother pointed proudly and said, "Naseeka."

Naseeka appeared embarrassed. "She says I brought this to her." Then he stood. "We will go outside now."

Flip and Richard got to their feet and thanked the women in French. As they turned to leave, Flip winked at Matoka again. She smiled.

Richard was feeling more comfortable with Naseeka. He had a family like other human beings. When they stepped outside, he asked, "What do Wyandotte men do?"

"Oh, they hunt, fish, and guard the village," Naseeka replied, proudly. "Of course, the older men teach the children." He smiled and added, "And they keep peace among the women."

At the fire pit, three young braves were being praised by a group of women for bringing in a catch of sunfish. Several boys, vying for attention, tossed a dozen frogs onto the slippery pile. The women immediately began cooking the catch by running a willow stick down the throats of the fish and holding them over the fire.

In a few minutes, eager hands plucked them from the sticks and devoured them ravenously. As they ate, the Indians spit out the scales and bones, then tossed the heads and spines to the dogs.

Richard turned to Flip. "I'm going to show them how to do it."

Flip shot a puzzled look at him, then shrugged as his friend walked off.

When Richard returned, he had a skillet from the canoe. He placed it in the hot coals, then selected a large fish from the pile. As he laid it on a rock and began scaling with his knife, the crowd closed in around him to watch.

He cleaned the fish by slitting its belly and severing its head. Then, holding it high enough for them to see, he jerked out its spine and ribs.

Grunts of approval arose from the crowd as they watched him place the fish into the hot pan. Soon, they were eagerly devouring the bite-sized pieces he gave them.

When he backed away, women and boys grabbed fish from the pile. Using a variety of tools and weapons, sometimes preparing the fish on the dusty ground, they scaled and boned them. Most, not able to get to the skillet, skewered or draped the fish on the end of a stick.

Matoka had been watching from a short distance away. She walked up to Flip, holding a fish in her hand. "Will you teach me how?" she asked.

"Yes," he replied with a smile, pulling his knife from its sheath as he directed her to a flat rock nearby.

When she presented him and Richard with a fish she had prepared, he saw that she was watching them intently. They chewed, swallowed, then nodded approval. He detected a warm glow on her face as she smiled happily.

Leaving the confusion at the fire pit, the two men returned to the lodge. They wanted to discuss the remainder of the journey to Detroit. From what Naseeka had told them, Flip assumed the fort was not very far. "If we get an early start," he said, "we should be able to make it in a day."

Richard thought for a moment. "Of course, we'll be fighting the current."

"Yah, but it's not a strong one."

Noting a dimming of the light in the lodge, they looked up to see Matoka standing in the opened entrance. She had the skillet in one hand, Flip's knife in the other. Flip, who was sitting cross-legged on the bearskin he used for a bed, beckoned her to enter. She walked over and knelt before him, then placed the two objects on the bearskin. She had also brought a pair of neatly folded buckskins. They were the ones they had given Naseeka when they found him.

"Thank you," he said in her native tongue.

Then, he placed his hand against her smooth cheek. Looking into the dark eyes that graced her smile, he studied her face for a moment. A thick crop of jet black hair, parted in the middle, was neatly plaited into tight braids. Their ends lay on the points of her small, buckskin-covered breasts. Slender hands, resting in her lap, were small and delicate, but the rough, scratched skin and torn fingernails showed they had been subjected to the harshness of grinding food, skinning animals, and cultivating the village garden.

She hesitated momentarily then, rising to her feet, turned and strode quickly out the door.

Richard pointed to the items she brought. "I didn't think we'd ever get those back," he said.

"I didn't, either," said Flip, slipping the knife into its sheath. "But then again, these people have practically adopted us."

That evening after they had gone to bed, the door flap quietly parted and a human figure appeared. The two men bolted to an upright sitting position, then watched as the silhouette assumed a kneeling pose beside Flip.

"Matoka," a soft, feminine voice whispered, barely loud enough to be heard above the rustle of movement.

Placing an arm around her, Flip drew her closer. "I half expected this," he explained to Richard.

Her clothes and hair smelled of cooked food and smoke from the longhouse, but her slender body was soft and warm. It had been a long time since Flip had been with a woman. He made room for her as she snuggled in beside him. Cradling her neck in one arm, he placed the palm of his other hand against her face and pressed their cheeks together. He lay there for some time watching the outline of her chest rise and fall as she breathed. He wasn't sure what he should do.

He had no intention of marrying her. Nor did he want her to go with them to Detroit. And he did not wish to insult Naseeka or the Wyandottes. With the Senecas, it had been different. The women came to him as they pleased without others of the tribe caring. But Matoka was different. She was the daughter of the chief and the half sister of Naseeka, and Naseeka was an Indian friend he did not wish to lose.

After several minutes of questioning thoughts chasing themselves through his mind, he kissed her cheek. She snuggled closer. He caressed her breast, and her body stiffened. Then, it relaxed again. When he slid his hand beneath her skirt and placed it at the mossy juncture of her thighs, she rose to her knees and removed her dress.

It was early morning, just as the first light of dawn made tree leaves discernible through the smoke hole in the top of lodge, that Flip dismounted for the fourth time. Richard rolled over on his stomach and raised up on his elbows. "Aren't you overdoing it?" he asked, smiling as he shook his head.

"No fear of that," Flip replied, placing his hands behind his head and looking up at the smoke hole. "You know," he continued, as Matoka cuddled close to him, "every time it feels like a bevy of frightened quail leaving me." He paused, then added, "Besides, there's nothing quite like it."

"Like what?"

"Waking up in the morning with the wonderful scent of a loved woman beside you."

Richard laughed, not quite sure what he meant.

Flip kissed her on the cheek and placed his hand in the hollow between the protrusions of her hips. When he rubbed her taut abdomen, she turned her head toward him. He could see the glow of affection in her eyes as she pressed her lips against the tip of his nose. Then, he handed her the dress.

Sitting upright, she slipped it on. She knelt momentarily looking down at him, then rose and quickly disappeared into the dull gray of early dawn.

———————◆———————

They walked about, shaking hands with those who had come to see them depart. Matoka was standing beside Lahana. As he shook her hand, Flip whispered in the Huron dialect, "I will see you again."

"Yes," she replied in English. A smile parted her lips, baring a trim row of white teeth.

When Lahana pressed a pouch of pemmican into Richard's hands, Naseeka thanked his two white friends for rescuing him. "You must come back again," he said. Then, as they pushed off, he shouted, "I will see you at the fort!"

———————◆———————

The warming rays of a rising sun soon absorbed the crispness of the autumn morning as they paddled easily up the river. The water was clear and almost calm, its smooth surface rippled only by an occasional zephyr that glided over the dense foliage to their left and dropped down upon them. The heavy growth, its brightly colored leaves still holding fast, echoed with the calls and cries of crows and jays and the constant scolding of chattering squirrels. High overhead, a wedge of migrating geese honked messages up and down their lines. They were heading south, following waterways that had guided generations before them.

By midmorning, they had reached a narrow point in the river where its waters were tinted with the red flow from a tributary. Beyond the colored outpouring they could see that the land on the western bank had been cleared. Houses, set back a short distance from the low bluff, appeared spaced at hundred yard intervals.

As they passed the first house, a rooster crowed and a dog came to the bank and barked at them. "First rooster I've heard since Fort Pitt," Richard called out joyfully over his shoulder.

146

"Sure sounds like civilization, again," replied Flip with a smile.

As they passed house after house, they noticed that some had been painted white with lime, but most were the dull, gray-brown of raw mud. Occasionally, they saw a man or woman working in a field who waved or shouted a greeting in French.

The farms, laid out by the French, appeared two to five hundred feet wide and very deep, giving each farmer a wharf and a place to get water and, being close to the river, a means of escape from a sudden attack.

The houses had their backyards to the river and faced a narrow road that led to the fort at Detroit. They contained one or two rooms and were made of notched logs or woven sticks and straw that had been plastered with clay mud. Their roofs were covered with bark, wood slabs, or reed thatch. Each had a rock and mud fireplace from which smoke curled lazily upward.

They rounded a slight curve in the river, and the fort suddenly came into sight. Its corner blockhouses dominated a nearly treeless flatland around it. With the exception of the brown steeple of Ste. Anne's Church, which made a striking contrast against the white clouds behind it, they could see little within the fifteen foot palisade of pointed logs.

From a pole in the center, the bright colors of the flag of St. George fluttered in the breeze. It gave the two men a feeling of security and protection.

A British soldier standing guard on the nearest corner blockhouse directed them up the Savoyard River so they could tie up among the boats, canoes, and rafts in the marshy mooring at the rear of the fort. Stepping ashore, they stretched and looked out across the grass-covered common. A few men were walking about, but showed no interest in their arrival.

Although they had lost track of the day of the week and were no longer sure of the month, they felt elated to be among white people under the protection of a British garrison.

Chapter 7

Wilderness Winter

The fort at Detroit was a massive rectangular structure, having been remodeled and enlarged over the years to accommodate a growing population and to intimidate by its awesomeness any Indians harboring thoughts of hostility. The logs, large in diameter and twenty-one feet long, had been peeled, sharpened to points on their smaller ends, and inserted tightly together, side by side, in a trench six feet deep. Care was taken to place any holes, knots, or bumps toward the inside of the compound lest they afford holding places for enemy hands or ropes during an attack. Large, protruding blockhouses, overhanging each of the four corners of the fort, were constructed in such a manner as to give the sentry an unobstructed view along the length of two walls and to see the blockhouses of two adjacent corners. There was a wide, wooden walkway five feet below the top of the inside wall around the perimeter of the fort, enabling guards to readily walk their assigned beats and to offer a protected firing platform for defenders.

The front of the fort was on the bank of the Detroit River, with the three remaining sides looking out over an area that had been cleared of trees to permit a view of the surrounding land. It also gave the fort a position of dominance over the region so that all distances and locations were given in relation to it. A farmer's house, the mills, the lime kilns, and the Jesuit mission were all indicated as above or below the fort or across the river from it. At the rear was a grassy common extending several hundred feet to the edge of a marshy area drained by the Savoyard River. It was this common that Richard and Flip had to walk across to enter the fort after leaving their canoe tied to a stake.

As the two men approached the massive open gates that hung heavily on large pivot pickets, they saw they were being carefully scrutinized by several Indians loitering at the entrance.

With muskets balanced in their right hands and a determined look on their tight-jawed faces, they brushed past three of the red men who tried to intercept them.

It reminded Richard of what he had seen at Fort Cumberland. Still, it made him nervous. "What did they want?" Richard asked, after they had reached the compacted gravel of the entrance.

"Drink, or something to buy it with," Flip replied. "Ya do 'em no favor giving them anything."

They looked down Rue St. Jacques. A few people were moving about, but the village of Detroit was quiet compared to Fort Pitt.

"Not much happening," ventured Richard, his voice sounding subdued.

"Well," said Flip, watching a soldier walking toward them, "the farmers are busy with the harvest." He wanted to mention the gathering of wood for a cold winter and the presence of British troops, but decided not to. "Besides, there's not that many people around here."

"Where's the trading post?" he called out to the soldier.

"Aye," the soldier responded, holding his musket in one hand as he looked them over. "Right there." He pointed to a weathered clapboard structure a short distance up the street. He started to walk off, then stopped. "Owned by a French chap. But 'e's all right." He wheeled about and hurried toward the blockhouse.

Richard paused to look at the weathered sign, then looked at Flip.

"*Comptoir Grillon*," Flip said, placing his hand against the door. "Means *Cricket Trading Post*. S'posed 'ta be lucky."

Inside, they stopped to let their eyes adjust to the dim light.

Dusty merchandise hung from pegs along the walls. Farther back, a short, bald man with a large, black mustache shuffled about a table, rearranging stacks of tools and clothing. He had a nervous twitch that made his dark eyes close frequently.

Flip approached him and introduced himself. The man nodded, but said nothing.

Flip wondered if they were going to have trouble. "We are trappers. Do you have supplies we can buy?" His voice was stern.

"Yes," the man replied in French. "I have everything you need."

The Frenchman seemed unfriendly for a shopkeeper, but Flip figured he might just as well get things settled. "And we have some things we can't take with us."

The proprietor smiled. "My friends, you have come to the right place." He blinked his eyes several times. "You may leave what you wish in my back room."

Flip was pleased with the friendly response. "Where is the trapping good?"

"It is very good all around here, but the best is fifty miles to the northwest." The Frenchman blinked his eyes several more times, then added, "It gets very cold. You must be well prepared."

"And Indians?"

"No problem. They are friendly."

"Can we get there by canoe?"

"Canoe would be difficult this time of the year. Low water." He thought momentarily, rubbing his bald pate with an open palm. "Probably best to walk the trails."

He led them through cluttered stacks of reed baskets, hoes, broadaxes, and shriveled cowhides that had been heaped on the rough plank floor. Opening the door to a small, musty anteroom, he pointed to several piles and bundles. "This is where I store things for people."

Flip and Richard peered into the dimly lighted room. The Frenchman pointed to a tied bundle in one corner. "Been here over two years." He shook his head. "Something must have happened to him."

After placing three canvas-wrapped packs in the storage room of the Comptoir Grillon, they shook hands with the proprietor. "We'll be back in two days," Flip told him.

As they walked east on Rue St. Jacques, Richard watched two wagons cross at an intersection ahead. "Do you trust him?" he asked.

"Yah, I suppose so. I think he'll expect us to bring our pelts to him, though," Flip replied. He spit onto the dusty street as he thought about the Frenchman. "Besides, we might not have a choice."

When they reached Rue Ste. Anne, they were surprised to find such a large number of people walking it. Looking south past the open gate, they saw where the river road crossed over the wooden Savoyard Bridge they had just passed beneath with the canoe. Flip turned and squinted at the north gate in the distance. To his surprise, it was not closed. "This place is wide open," he observed, his voice registering concern as he looked about. Not wanting to alarm his friend, however, he would say no more. But he was not one to trust the wily red man. He knew that the few Indians wandering the streets were enough to hold one of the gates open long enough to admit a war party that could be concealed in the nearby forest.

Richard, noting that only a few people carried weapons, shrugged. "Probably feel secure," he said.

Trying to avoid fresh animal droppings, they threaded their way through the wagons, carts and foot traffic on the busy street. Rue Ste. Anne housed most shops and storehouses. It also had the blacksmith and livery stable. At its midpoint, set back a short distance on each side, the imposing structures of the council house and Ste. Anne's Church faced each other across tree-shaded lawns.

They halted in front of a log building with a wrought iron sign projecting above its entrance identifying it as the Black Swan Tavern. The door was ajar, so Flip peered in. Turning to Richard, he said, "Must be British."

Richard pushed the door open, and they stepped inside. He scanned the room with a sweep of his eyes. Forgotten hats, coats and powder horns, heavy with dust, hung from deer antlers attached to the dark walls. In one corner, four uniformed soldiers were clustered about the bar talking with the innkeeper and drinking warm ale from copper tankards.

As the two men sauntered toward them, the military men halted their conversation and turned to look at them. The tavernkeeper, in dark blue trousers and a black and white checkered shirt, stepped over to face them across the dark, polished bar.

"Ale," said Flip, placing his two hands on the bar.

Richard nodded his head that he wanted the same. The redcoats resumed their conversation.

"Newcomers?" the tavernkeeper asked, looking them over as he placed the tankards before them.

"Yes," Richard replied. "I'm Richard Locke." He pointed to Flip. "My partner, Flip Wade."

"Henry," the robust proprietor smiled, extending a hand. "Henry Hawke."

"Just passin' through," said Flip, taking a sip from his drink. "Goin' north ta do some trappin'."

"Aye," Henry began. "New m'self. Bought this place cheap from a Frenchman that wanted to leave with 'is troops." He turned, put the coins they had given him in a small box on a shelf behind him, then faced them again. "Good ta 'ave more Britishers in the territory."

They took their drinks to a table near an open window so they could watch the traffic on Rue Ste. Anne. Across the room the four soldiers were engaged in a rambling, boisterous conversation occasionally punctuated with loud laughs and foot stamping. Flip liked that. It meant the military was not tense or fearful. But at the same time, he wondered.

Sometimes the noise of a passing horse or wagon caught their attention, but mostly they sat, slowly sipping their drinks and talking about the trapping they planned to do. Flip shoved a list to Richard that he had compiled. "I think we can pick these up tomorrow and get movin'."

Richard studied the paper, then shrugged. "I'm ready," he replied, pushing his tankard toward the center of the table.

Flip watched as two soldiers walked out the door. He downed the rest of his drink, then pushed back from the table. "Let's see if we can find a place to sleep."

They walked over to the proprietor. "Have a room we could use for the night?" Flip inquired.

"Aye," replied Henry. He unlatched a narrow door that opened into a small room at the rear of the tavern. "Not fancy, but I 'ope ta make it better in the future."

Richard peered into the dim light of the log lean-to. The walls were poorly chinked, and it had a floor of logs hewn flat on the top surface. Six cots made of skinned poplar poles were side by side along one wall. There was a small window covered by a latticework of wooden slats. "And the price?" he asked, turning to look at Henry.

"A shillin' fer the two of ye." He paused as Richard looked back into the room. "Of course, ye'll 'ave ta furnish yer own beddin'."

Richard looked at Flip, then nodded. "We'll take it."

Before retiring, Richard penned a note to his father. He wanted to let him know he had arrived at Detroit and that he and Flip planned to spend the winter trapping. He thought of mentioning Naseeka, but decided not to. It would worry his father to know that he was that close to Indians.

Before sealing it with brittle wax, he added a postscript requesting Elizabeth be informed of his whereabouts and plans.

When he went to bed, he sensed a strong feeling of apprehension, a type of anxiety he had not experienced before. They were on the threshold of an untamed, savage wilderness. Tomorrow, they would enter it. He'd tingled with similar thoughts when they left Fort Pitt, but there was the knowledge that Detroit was ahead of them. Now, the only remnants of civilization remaining were the isolated missionary outposts that relied on faith for protection.

He looked over at the curled up form of Flip rising and falling with the heavy breathing of deep sleep. Turning, he pulled the blanket over his head to shut out any sounds that might keep him awake.

◆

The sun, a great yellow ball, was just clearing the east wall of the fort as the two men strode briskly along the glistening, frost-covered street on their way to the Comptoir Grillon. They encountered several men whose heads and necks were drawn deeply into the collars of their coarsely woven coats, their steaming breath rising up and trailing back over their caps. From white powder caked on their shoes and trousers, Flip assumed they were going to work at the lime kilns just north of the fort. As they passed, each nodded and mumbled a greeting, usually in French.

The slab door of the trading post pushed open easily on its hammered iron hinges. Inside, wood smoke from a newly started fire irritated their nostrils. Through the dim light they could see two men standing next to a small, potbellied stove.

"Naseeka!" Richard called out, recognizing the one dressed in buckskins with a blanket draped over his shoulders.

Naseeka watched them approach, then calmly shook hands with the two surprised men. "I come to help you," he explained in halting English.

"How did you know where to find us?" Flip asked, a weak smile breaking across his face.

"All trappers must come to the Comptoir Grillon."

Naseeka explained that he wished to act as their guide and to carry some of their supplies. The Frenchman, whom he had known many years, had told him of their plans, and he, Naseeka, wanted to lead them to good trapping territory.

"Damned good!" Flip beamed, nodding emphatically to Richard. "Maybe we'll be able to last the whole season without coming back for more supplies."

"What the hell," Richard added, "we can sure use the help." He was elated. Going north of the fort with Naseeka would make it much safer.

It took nearly an hour for them to bundle their equipment, along with the flour, salt, and beans they bought from the Frenchman, into three manageable backpacks. Flip stood and shouldered one of the packs. "Feels good," he said, walking in a tight circle. "But ya know, we could have got most of this stuff right here instead of draggin' it clear across the country."

"Maybe so," Richard agreed, "But how the hell could we be sure?"

◆

North of the fort, the river road ran alongside the Detroit River. The well-kept farms along it were owned by French elite who had come from Quebec and carved out a comfortable life for themselves. Although they resented British occupation, they would try to live with it rather than abandon what they had worked so hard to create. Someday, they were sure, the British would be forced to leave. Then, once again, they would live under French rule.

A large island in the channel, sparsely covered with ash, poplar, and sycamore, split the flow of the great river. Richard slowed from the brisk pace Naseeka had set to observe the contrast between the brilliantly colored leaves and the swiftly flowing blue-green water.

Naseeka saw what was happening out of the corner of his eye. "*Isle de Cochons*," he called out, scarcely turning his head as he pointed to the island.

"Pig Island," Flip translated, wincing under the weight of the pack on his shoulders. He shook his head and adjusted its position. "That damned Indian is like a racehorse," he complained.

After crossing a weathered wooden bridge spanning a sluggish creek, Naseeka made an abrupt left turn onto a footpath leading into the dense woods. To Richard it looked foreboding, but the ground felt moist and spongy beneath a layer of leathery leaves. It offered a welcome cushion to his burdened feet.

The forest floor was carpeted with a generous layer of red, yellow and gold leaves, and although there was no wind, they continued to flutter down like giant colored snowflakes. Recent frosts had killed the small insects, and the warm sun, filtering through the thinning foliage, intensified the sweet scent that permeated the air. Occasionally, sheets of glare struck the travelers in the face as they made their way along the edge of a pond or the bank of a lake where otter, beaver, and muskrat hurried with final preparations for the long winter. Overhead, birds chirruped, scolded, and flitted about, while curious squirrels chattered nervously and flicked their bushy tails at the intruders.

Periodically, Naseeka allowed the two men to rest by sitting on a creek bank or a fallen tree trunk, but such respites were brief. After a few minutes he urged them on again, warning repeatedly of the overdue *white blanket* that would soon cover everything. "Must go! Must go!" he exhorted as he slipped into his pack straps and paced about.

156

"Sure as hell has a wild hair in his ass!" Flip remarked as he slowly got to his feet after a stop.

They waded through streams, jumped across small creeks, circumvented swamps and bogs, and pushed their way through head-high cattail swales, sometimes using a beaver dam as a footbridge. The fall season was the dry period in this area of lakes, swamps, and rivers. It made travel easier. The land was covered by a dense growth of deciduous trees interspersed with scatterings of pine and spruce. It was crisscrossed by foot trails, some new and heavily used, others old, overgrown and abandoned. The confusion created by nature's obstacles and the meandering paths would have confused many travelers, but Naseeka's unfailing sense of direction always brought them to the proper northwest heading.

Late in the afternoon, Naseeka concluded they had covered enough ground for the first day. He selected a place beside a small stream to camp. Then he sat down against a tree to watch his white friends make their beds and cook supper.

As the sun eased itself down in the western sky, the air became chilly. Flip and Richard slipped on their capotes and Naseeka draped his shoulders with a blanket. Sitting beside their small fire, Richard turned to Naseeka. "How much farther do we go?" he asked.

"Three more days," came the quick reply.

"Each day we travel this far?" Richard was concerned about being so far from the protection of the fort.

"Yes. There will be many beaver there. And the fox and wolf are plentiful." Naseeka paused briefly to throw some pine knots he had taken from a decayed log onto the fire. "It is by the land of the Chippewa. They are friends of the Wyandotte, and the white man has not hunted there."

As they traveled, the forest changed. The trail led them into the great evergreen forest with trees so tall and close together that little sunlight reached the ground. It was an area laced with slow moving streams and rivers and was generously dotted with small lakes and ponds.

Approaching a clearing, Naseeka suddenly raised his hand for them to halt. Crouching low, he crept forward a short distance and peered cautiously through the trees. On a tabular strip of land between two lakes were the wigwams of an Indian village. Several smoke plumes rose lazily upward, and women and children could be seen walking about.

He studied the activity for several minutes, then waved for Flip and Richard to join him.

"Ottawas," he said, sitting on his haunches. "They camp here for the winter."

Turning, he led them on a discreet detour through the forest around the lakes.

After they were a safe distance from the village, Flip asked, "Aren't the Ottawas friendly?"

Naseeka stopped and turned to face him, his eyes glistening with fire. "They make trouble!" he snapped. "And Naseeka will tell you more." He pointed to the north. "Two, maybe three days, there is a village of Black Chippewas. It is on the shore of Big Water. They are very bad!" He drew his finger across his throat.

"But you said we will trap in the land of the Chippewa."

"Yes. They are the good Chippewa. They are many villages and are friends of Naseeka. They do not like the Black Chippewa on the Big Water." He took a step closer to Flip and Richard. "You are my friends, my brothers. Naseeka will see that you hunt in peace."

Naseeka was an Indian first, but knew the white man was here to stay and would come in increasing numbers. He realized that fighting a superior force with primitive weapons would only bring further decimation and additional sorrow to his people. Besides, there were certain things the white man had and pleasures he enjoyed that appealed to him. He liked the warm homes that gave protection from the icy blasts of winter, appreciated an ample supply of food all year long, and marveled at the ease with which a deer or rabbit could be struck down by the long reach of a fire stick. He wanted to learn more about these things from his trusted white brothers so he could teach his people.

◆

On the third day, the wind shifted from west to north bringing a crisp chill that spurred them on. When, by evening, it had come around to the northeast Flip knew that rain or snow was on the way. After supper, he stretched a lean-to canvas shelter between trees and hoped the storm would be delayed.

The next morning when Richard awoke, the muscles of his body ached, and his cold feet were swollen and sore. He peered out from beneath his shelter and saw that a freezing rain was falling. A short distance away, Naseeka sat with his back propped against a large spruce, its thick, low-hanging boughs sheltering him from the cold drizzle.

He thought about the comforts of Fredericksburg and hoped the trapping would be worth the misery he felt. Then he wondered how safe it was to be so near the Ottawas and Black Chippewas. He decided to push it from his mind and trust the judgment of Flip and Naseeka.

Flip sat up and stretched. He looked over at Richard and noted his friend's lack of zest. Action, he thought, was needed to revive his circulation and generate enthusiasm. "Let's get moving!" he called out, rising to his knees and clapping his hands.

Richard looked at him, then nodded and smiled. He pulled on his wet moccasins and slowly rose to his feet.

They ate some cold, leftover rabbit, made up their packs as best they could, then started out on the slippery trail. There was a weather induced quietness in the forest. The foliage did not rustle or murmur, and the birds and animals remained in their shelters, resting until the weather improved or hunger forced them to search for food.

"Rain will stop soon," Naseeka said, walking carefully to avoid slipping on the ice-encrusted path.

Richard snapped his head left and right to shake an accumulation of water from the hood of his capote. "How do you know?" he asked.

"Birds and squirrels hide," Naseeka called back over his shoulder. "When rain is to stay, they come out like always."

By noon the wind had shifted back to the west, the sky became clear, and the temperature rose enough to melt the ice. Their clothing soon dried and felt more comfortable on their bodies. Their moccasins, however, continued to be saturated from heavy layers of wet leaves in the few hardwood groves they passed through as they continued to penetrate the thickening forest of evergreens.

◆

It was early afternoon when Naseeka led them through a dense thicket to the bank of a meandering river. Flip looked at the black, leaf-dotted water as it flowed steadily past the clump of roots where they stood. It would be a good place for beaver and muskrat, he thought, and the surrounding area should be teeming with other animals.

On the opposite bank, a fallen spruce created a quiet pool where a fish lunged at a water spider caught in an eddy current. Overhead, a curious fox squirrel stared at the invaders as it clung precariously to the swaying tip of a pine bough.

"On this river the Chippewa see a light they do not understand," Naseeka declared, pointing to the wide ribbon of smooth water. "They call it the *Tittabawassee*. This is a good place for you. Many streams come here. Many beaver live here."

The mention of a strange light intrigued Richard. He wondered if it was the will-o'-the-wisp that old John said had led many a man to his demise.

◆

To build a shelter, they chose a site at the base of a hillock located beneath the protective limbs of a group of mature pines fifty yards from the river's edge. Using the only tools they had, an axe, small shovel, and hunting knives, they cleared the area of underbrush and low-hanging limbs, then dug a shallow cave into the sandy clay soil. They lined it with six-inch poles and continued the structure so it extended several feet into the open. The front faced south to take advantage of any sunshine that might penetrate the overhead foliage. And Richard, calling upon his Virginia experience, built a mud and rock fireplace in one corner. Finally, they covered the protruding flat roof with a layer of cedar boughs and earth.

Except for helping with the hill excavation, Naseeka left construction to his two white friends. To assist, however, he caught small game and cooked it for them, accumulated a large stack of dry firewood, and gathered a quantity of moss for chinking and bed cushions.

He stayed with them a day beyond the two it took to build the crude cabin. When he was ready to leave, he reached inside the neck of his loose fitting buckskin blouse, grasped a small doeskin pouch, and slipped its leather thong up over his head. Then he walked over to Flip.

Flip removed his fur hat and allowed Naseeka to pass the leather loop over his head.

Placing his two hands on the shoulders of the trapper, Naseeka looked into his face. "This will take care of you, my brother."

"I will wear it always," Flip vowed, looking down at the small, bulging bag resting against his chest.

Naseeka repeated the formality with Richard.

"My sister, Matoka, made these for my brothers. She chewed them with her teeth to make them soft, and painted this on them." He grasped the pouch hanging from Richard's neck and pointed to a red arrow aimed skyward. "It is the Wyandotte symbol for fast escape from harm."

Then he squeezed the pouch between his thumb and forefinger. "Inside, she has placed an eagle talon that has been wrapped in the white fur of a rabbit's tail. When you wear this, you will catch many animals in your traps."

He stepped back and looked at them soberly. "If you need help, a Chippewa village is half a day." He pointed to the north.

"They don't know we are here," Flip said with a shrug. He was sure they did, but wanted Naseeka to take him and Richard there. If the village chief was a friend of Naseeka, it would be better that way.

Naseeka smiled. "They know," he said, assuringly.

He shook their hands, looking each in the face as he did, then turned and trotted off.

During the next two weeks they scouted the area, mapping the location of streams, ponds, swamps, beaver dams, and animal trails. At the cabin, they constructed a table and two chairs. Flip would have been satisfied to merely bind a few poles together, but Richard insisted the poles be peeled, notched, and properly fitted.

Using a slab of granite stone, he honed a razor-sharp edge on the axe, then carefully hewed the top of the table and seats of the chairs to a flat, level surface. When he finished, he stood back and eyed his work. "There, that ought to take us through the winter."

Flip detected a sound of pride in his voice. "Damn nice!" he said, sitting down in one of the chairs.

"Tomorrow, we'll make the beds."

The weather grew cold, the ground froze, and the snow no longer melted. They checked their steel traps, made several thong snares, and constructed two dozen hickory hoops for stretching pelts.

One morning they stood at the edge of a snow-covered swale, looking at the myriad of tracks crisscrossing the area. Flip shook his head. "That damned Naseeka. He sure knew where to take us." He thought for a moment. "Been cold enough. We can set our traps in a couple of days."

As they turned to walk away, he stopped. "Know what we'd better do? Visit that Chippewa camp ta let 'em know we're friendly."

———————◆———————

A light snow that had fallen during the night glistened in the morning sun as they picked their way through a maze of animal trails. Timid cottontail rabbits, having left the security of improvised shelters in clumps of dead grass, bounded back and forth before them. Playful spike-horn bucks darted from thickets, gamboled about for a few moments, then raced away to disappear from sight. And a nasty-tempered wolverine, resting in the lower branches of a large pine, snarled a warning.

Flip wanted to travel north along the thicket-lined Tittabawassee until he found some sign of human life. He had made sure their muskets were ready for action and carried a packet containing colored glass beads, oyster shell buttons, and two small, bone-handle hunting knives. He felt slightly apprehensive, but always did when going to an Indian village. This time, at least, he had Naseeka's assurance it was friendly.

After walking for two miles, changing from one small trail to another to maintain proper heading, they came upon a plainly marked footpath leading from a shallow crossing of the river.

Flip walked beside it for several feet. "This is what we've been looking for," he declared. Squinting, he sighted up the narrow lane that faded from view among the low hanging branches a short distance ahead.

An hour later, after encountering several more trails that joined the one they were following, they topped a rise and looked down on a small, slightly tilted valley floor sparsely dotted by a grove of leafless hardwoods. Interspersed among the dormant oaks, maples, and beeches, were thirty or forty bark huts and hide tepees.

Shielding their eyes from the glare, the two men studied the village for several minutes.

"Seems to be plenty of activity," Richard said, his voice almost inaudible. He could feel the tension building in his body and wondered if they really needed to visit the village.

"Probably squaws doing their chores," Flip said, continuing to watch the activity. "Let's go down and see what we find."

Richard dropped in behind Flip as they started along the gently descending path. "I hope that damn Naseeka knows what he's talking about this time," he said, chuckling nervously.

Following a few steps behind his trusted friend, Richard looked down at the trail. The warmth of the sun had made the snow heavy, so it compacted beneath Flips buckskin shoepacks leaving detailed impressions of his tracks. Richard's thoughts wandered, asking the question he had asked so many times before. *Why am I here?* He searched his mind for an answer.

He enjoyed being with Flip. It was an exciting adventure most people would never have the opportunity to experience. And, in addition to earning a lot of money, it would give him the chance to prove he could make his way in an untamed wilderness where man was pitted against the elements, the animals, and the savages. But, how safe was it? He wondered if they wouldn't be better off remaining isolated in the cabin, tending the trap lines and letting the Indians, if they wished, come to them.

Flip, he realized, was more aggressive, confident he could out-fight, outfox, or outmaneuver any man or animal. That is, if he wasn't taken by surprise. He had mentioned that it was better to talk and trade with the red man than fight him. Richard was glad of that. To do so, Flip felt it necessary to know the terrain and its occupants for some distance from the cabin.

Richard concluded this made sense, but it would be some time before he had the confidence and skill of his partner in dealing with Indians. He, however, would make a determined effort to acquire it.

White smoke, escaping beneath the eaves of the bark wigwams and from the tepee smoke holes, curled lazily upward, gathering into a thin cloud before being carried off to the east. Several women, their movements restricted by heavy winter clothing, waddled about, fetching armloads of firewood and carrying leather-lined baskets of water from a small, ice-encrusted creek that flowed through the valley.

As the two men entered the village, several dogs, their ribs showing through their shaggy coats, stood back and barked at them. From the corner of their eyes, they could see a number of curious children peeking from the entrances of the wigwams.

"We sure don't impress 'em," Richard whispered, placing his musket on his shoulder as he walked beside Flip.

"Just keep walkin'. Something will happen afore long."

They continued on at a slow, measured gait until they were near the center of the camp. There, a group of young men were gathered around the base of a massive oak tree. As they approached, they saw a six-point buck hanging by its rear legs from the bottom limb. Up the hill to the right lay a freshly scoured path in the snow showing where the fat young animal had been dragged from the thick pine forest that ringed the little valley. The young warriors were chatting and laughing while stuffing their mouths with bits and pieces of organs taken from a pile of steaming entrails resting on the ground where they had fallen from the animal's opened belly. Two women, holding steel skinning knives in their blood-covered hands, were busily removing the hide from the well-fed carcass.

The two men halted ten feet from the Indians and looked at them with unsmiling faces. Richard was certain Flip had done this many times before, but for him it was a new, exciting experience. He scanned the group, sternly noting the same diverse, motley type of dress he had seen before, and his nostrils detected the smokey body odor they all seemed to emit. Some of the skins they wore still bore thin segments of shriveled flesh and rancid fat.

The one nearest to them turned and stared questioningly with his deep-set, flashing eyes. He wore a skunkskin hat, and his hands, face, and clothing were smeared with fresh blood. Suddenly, he barked two words in his native tongue.

Flip, certain French trappers and traders had been here before, responded. "*Chef!*" he snapped. His eyes searched each of theirs for a reaction.

The one in the skunkskin hat wheeled, extended his arm with a quick flip, and pointed to a round, bark-covered wigwam. As they walked off, Richard looked back. The warriors were again searching through the pile of entrails. They were fifty feet from the chief's lodge, a nondescript, bark-covered wigwam distinguished only by a plume-decorated pole at its entrance, when a bearskin flap was pushed aside and two red men emerged to greet them. One appeared to be in his twenties, the other in his thirties. Similar in build and appearance, they had jet black hair parted in the middle and hanging in neat braids across their broad chests. They were dressed in dirt-stained buckskins topped with highly decorated deerskin capes. Their black eyes, spaced far apart, were accented by dark bronze skin drawn tightly over high cheek bones.

Once inside, Flip and Richard were ordered to sit on the skin-covered floor across the fire ring from where the Indians had their slightly elevated seats. The lodge, lined with skins and pelts decorated with spears, bows, quivers of arrows, and leather shields, was heated by a small fire that blazed before them.

Richard looked around and licked his dry lips with a raspy tongue. His heart beat faster, and his eyes smarted from the smoke. If Naseeka was with them now, he would feel much better. He looked up at the hole in the center of the bark roof and saw the blue sky. Perhaps it wasn't as stifling inside as he first thought.

By using French and sign language to supplement the Huron words he knew, Flip was able to exchange information. In a few minutes they were nibbling on jerked venison and toasted pine nuts. It seemed to ease Richard's fear, and he joined in the conversation.

They were told that the two Indians were brothers. The older, Sacco, was chief of the village. He was assisted by his brother, Naghee, the war chief. Since there were many Chippewa villages, there was a great chief of all Chippewas. He lived two days walk to the northwest. "He is all powerful," Sacco informed them, a serious look showing in his piercing eyes.

During the two hours they talked, the white men were told that the Chippewa knew of their cabin and of their intention to trap. A Wyandotte runner had told them. The Chippewas were hopeful all would benefit from the arrangement.

Richard was becoming restless, having sat cross-legged for the long period of time. He flicked a glance at Flip who appeared to be enjoying himself eating pine nuts and tossing the husks into the fire. "Can we give 'em the presents?" he asked impatiently. "We've got a long walk back. "

Flip nodded. He reached into a leather pouch he carried at his side and removed the doeskin packet. Standing so he could reach around the fire ring, he placed the opened packet before the two red men. The beads and buttons glowed warmly in the firelight.

The Indians grunted acceptance and started to rise. Before they could get to their feet, however, Richard placed a knife on either side of the packet.

There was a slight, almost imperceptible smile on Sacco's lips as he and Naghee rose to shake hands. "The Chippewa will visit you," he said, firmly setting his jaw.

"You can bet they will," Flip stated quietly as they left the lodge.

———————————◆———————————

As winter set in, it brought an abundance of snow that never seemed to melt, only accumulate. This fascinated Richard. Each morning when he awoke, he opened the cabin door a small amount to see if more had fallen during the night. To him, it seemed miraculous that such a large quantity of something could fall out of the sky without making a sound. And it was useful. It insulated the cabin from the bone-chilling cold that rode in on the north wind, it provided water for drinking and cooking, and it made tracking animals easy.

They set four trap lines, each a loop extending a mile from the cabin. Working as a team, they covered two each day, collecting the animals and resetting the traps and snares. They also shot larger animals, mostly deer. Their harvest quickly became so great they had to skip an occasional day on the trap line to catch up on the skinning and stretching of hides and pelts.

Then, disposing of skinned carcasses became a problem. Tossed a short distance from the cabin, they attracted a variety of other animals. Although it provided the opportunity to kill two timber wolves, the foxes, weasels, and bobcats were appearing in increasing numbers, frequently rending the night air with the cries and growls of their fighting and bickering. When, during the course of an evening of beaver skinning, Richard stepped outside the cabin to relieve himself and was challenged by a pair of prowling wolverines determined to get at fresher carcasses inside, the two men decided the frozen pile would have to be taken farther away.

The next day, after a lunch of rabbit and pemmican, they made a carrier of deerskin and poles. They loaded it with frozen carcasses from the scattered pile, then shouldered their muskets and headed in a northerly direction through the fluffy, knee-deep snow.

"Who's idea of a good time is this?" Richard teased, the vapor from his breath shooting out before him as they struggled to work their way around an outgrowth of witch hazel.

"You'll think it fun," Flip replied, breathing heavily, "if ya wake up some morning with a bobcat lookin' ya in the eye."

"I'd play dead."

"Well, I'd shoot the sonofabitch on the spot!" Flip chuckled.

A half mile from the cabin, they tipped the load into the snow.

They leaned against a pair of evergreens to rest a few minutes before returning. Several cardinals were hopping about the drooping, snow-laden limbs. Occasionally, the birds bent a branch enough to send a plume of white flakes filtering down through the lower foliage. Suddenly, Richard signaled for silence. Both men held their breath and listened intently. There was a sound of activity somewhere ahead of them.

Unshouldering their muskets, they squatted down and maneuvered for a better view, their eyes searching the tree trunks and low hanging branches for some sign of movement. Then, not more than a hundred yards before them, three forms loomed into view.

Richard recognized the three as Indians, a pathetic sight of ill-fitting clothing and blanket-wrapped heads. He glanced at Flip standing a few feet from him. This time he felt no fear.

When the trio were even with them, they straightened and took a few steps for a clear stance, their muskets at the ready. The lead Indian halted, uncovered his head and stared at them.

"Naghee!" Richard shouted, recognizing the Chippewa war chief.

Relieved, the two men walked over to him with extended hands.

"Friends," Naghee uttered, maintaining a stern, unsmiling face.

He carried a short-barreled flintlock under his blanket. Behind him were a hatchet-faced brave and a fat, young woman.

"Naghee comes to visit," he stated, ignoring the two behind him. His eyes roved the tracks made by Flip and Richard, searching for a clue to their activity.

Sensing his curiosity, Flip told him what he and Richard were doing.

Naghee walked toward the pile of carcasses. When he returned, he said, "I take them to the village to eat."

Flip and Richard nodded.

Flip looked at the brave and woman. They were wretchedly cold. He understood their stoic refusal to show or acknowledge their misery, but it bothered him. "Let's go," he said, beckoning them to follow.

The cabin was crammed with cured and drying pelts, but the tight quarters did not bother the Indians. As Flip fueled the fire and Richard made a large pot of tea, Naghee sat in a chair. He slid about in the seat and slapped the arms, then ordered the young warrior into the other chair. Pointing to the woman, he barked a stern command. She immediately sat on the floor.

Richard walked over to his bed and motioned for her to sit on it.

"*Non!*" Naghee snapped.

The woman remained seated, a blanket still draped over her head. Richard shrugged, then went back to get the tea.

Flip gave each of the Indians a handful of the pemmican he had gotten from Matoka. "Damn!" he exclaimed, chewing on some he had taken. "Those Wyandottes sure know how to make pemmican." Turning to Naghee, he nodded. "*Bon!*"

Naghee nodded agreement. "*Bon!*" he replied, checking his leather headband to be certain it was centered on his forehead. Then his face grew serious. "Why do you take the carcasses so far from the lodge?"

"It draws bad cats and wolves."

The war chief frowned and moved his head slowly from side to side. "This is the land of plenty," he stated huskily. "But the red man never takes more than he needs."

"There are many white men where the sun rises," Flip began, hoping Naghee would accept his explanation. "They need the skin of the beaver. We bring it to them."

Naghee looked at Flip, then at Richard. Getting to his feet, he raised his hand. "The visit is at an end." Everyone rose to their feet except the woman. "She," he grunted, pointing to the woman, "is Soho! She is for you!" He jabbed an index finger toward Flip.

Flip was stunned. He looked at the round, expressionless face and saw her soft, brown eyes blink slowly as she looked up at him.

Richard had noted Naghee's displeasure of killing animals for only their skins, and now they were being presented with a woman. He knew that it would be an insult to refuse a gift, but they didn't need any help and neither he nor Flip would consider her for a wife. Naghee's jaw was hard set, and Flip still had a startled expression frozen on his face.

Richard looked down at the emotionless appearance of the bulkily dressed woman. Something had to be done to break the silence. He turned to Naghee, remembering Flip had said that a smile during serious discussion meant deceit or ridicule to an Indian. "We will treat her like a sister," he said bluntly. Then he extended his open hand.

Naghee grasped the hand firmly, gave it one strong shake, then released it.

Richard's action shocked Flip from his bewildered state. "Yes, she will be our sister," he blurted, extending his hand. "We will take good care of her."

"Agreed!" Naghee exclaimed, motioning for the warrior to follow him out the door.

Flip shook his head. He hoped they had used the proper word for sister.

———————◆———————

Activity in the isolated winter encampment became one of busy routine. Each chilly morning the two men arose to the warmth of a blazing fire rekindled by Soho. She rose early from the pallet Richard made for her and had hot tea ready for their breakfast of meat and unleavened biscuits taken from a supply prepared once each week.

Bundled in sweaters and capotes to ward off the cold, Flip and Richard shouldered their muskets to tend the trap lines. Tracks they had made previously made walking easier, even when covered with a heavy layer of newly fallen snow. On occasion, however, they had to wear the snowshoes Soho made after she saw them return exhausted from struggling through knee-deep snow that had been covered with an icy glaze. As they traversed the frigid white land where silence was broken only by squeaking snow beneath their shoepacks, they inventoried the tracks that laced the area, occasionally stopping to probe the breathing hole of an occupied den with a limber stick cut from a hickory sapling.

A more productive segment of their trap lines ran along the edge of a large lake. Its smooth, black ice, frozen to a depth of several feet, was kept clear of snow by gusts of cold north wind that dipped down as it raced across the tops of the surrounding evergreens. The two men ran and slid on its slippery surface, following trails of frozen air bubbles that marked the beaver and muskrat runs. A sunfish, frozen into the ice, caught their attention. Flip studied it for a moment. "He'll wake up when the spring thaw comes," he said.

Richard looked at Flip, but said nothing. The fish seemed so dead he wondered if his friend knew what he was talking about.

In contrast to the silence of the forest, there was a thunderous rumbling from the lake. It reverberated from broad cracks that zipped across the expanding ice. The spectacle awed Richard until, while standing well out from shore, a crack opened beneath his feet with the snap of a lightning bolt. Seeing water spurting from the new fissure, he began to run for safety, but halted when it immediately sealed itself by freezing. Puzzled, he looked at Flip who was standing a short distance away.

Flip laughed. "There's no danger out here at all," he said assuringly.

◆

Shyness precluded Soho from volunteering information about herself, but by piecing together answers she gave over a period of time, Richard learned that this was the twenty-second winter of her life. In addition to a mother and father, she had two sisters and a brother. Accustomed to working as a Chippewa woman at routine tasks without praise, she seldom uttered a sound in the presence of the men, but a slight grin of satisfaction graced her smooth, round face when she noted something she had done pleased them.

She was short in stature, under five feet Richard surmised, was blockily built and, although she moved slowly, never seemed to tire. He thought she was probably lonely, but could not be sure because she showed so few signs of emotion. Twice when he and Flip returned from the trap line, he heard her in a low, almost muted voice, chanting a song about her people. As soon as she sensed their presence however, she became quiet and continued her work in silence.

In spite of his initial disapproval, Flip came to realize that she was an asset to their operation. She cooked most of their meals, caught fish from the Tittabawassee, repaired their clothing, maintained the fire and, after Flip had taught her, assisted with the skinning task. She also kept a full kettle of stew and a pot of tea water over the fire.

Although it didn't bother him, it annoyed Richard when she washed clothing in the same kettle she used for cooking. He looked on with amusement as Richard carefully explained to her that the kettles should not be interchanged. Soho, her eyes blinking slowly, watched intently as he placed the kettles apart and indicated they must be kept that way.

A while later, she ladled bowls of soup from a pot she had washed clothes in a short time before.

Richard turned to Flip, his eyes blazing. "Ya know," he said, "she'll stand there and agree with everything I say." He shook his head. "But she doesn't have the slightest notion what the hell I'm talking about!"

Flip smiled. "Maybe she does and figures you don't know what the hell you're talking about."

"Probably used the same damn water," Richard grumbled as he tasted his soup.

To help her people as well as the trappers, Soho fashioned a travois so she could transport the carcasses to the designated pickup point where she hung them from a tree out of reach of predatory animals. Each time she made the trip she was gratified to see the frozen carcasses gone and the tie lines still hanging for her to use again. Sometimes she lingered a few minutes, standing motionless, her solemn gaze staring at the point where the tracks of the retrievers disappeared from view, but she knew she could not return to her village until Sacco or Naghee gave the order.

In the Chippewa wigwam it was the woman's duty to clean and tan the hides. Certain ones were then softened by chewing, giving the woman strong jaws and badly worn teeth. To occupy Soho during the long, quiet evenings in the dimly lit cabin, Flip gave her four deerskins and a pouch of glass beads. After meticulously preparing the hides, she spent many hours making headbands, armbands, and pouches. There were times however, when she went directly to her pallet after supper. Sometimes she went to sleep immediately, but more often she lay there, looking up at the ceiling or into the blazing fire. Since she didn't appear ill, Flip assumed she was homesick, thinking of her family and her village.

Richard, too, often thought of his home in Virginia. As he watched Soho work with leather, he decided to carve a series of miniature wild animals to present to Elizabeth when he returned.

After several days of trying, he completed a cottontail rabbit from hard maple, giving it a final smoothing with a small piece of sandstone.

He handed it to Flip, who was sitting across the table quietly smoking his pipe. Flip looked it over carefully, then handed it back. "Nice," he said with a nod.

Then he handed it to Soho. She fingered it soberly, then looked up at him and smiled. Assuming it was a present, she tucked it into a cloth bag beside her pallet.

Instead of asking her to return it, he decided to let her keep it.

◆

Richard tossed a log onto the fire, then looked around the cabin at the accumulating piles of hides and pelts. The ever diminishing living space made him restless. For several minutes he observed Flip rubbing salt into the flesh side of a prime timber wolf pelt. "How much more curing will it take?" he asked.

"About three more days," Flip replied, halting to look up at him. "Then it'll be fit for a king."

"Anyone in mind?"

"No. I just try ta keep something handy. You never know when ya might need it." He slapped the pelt with his open palm. "And timber wolf can't be beat."

Richard shot a glance at Soho sitting on the floor softening a deer hide, then turned back to Flip. He was anxious for a period of solitude, some time by himself away from the cabin, but he didn't want Flip to feel he didn't want him along. "Bright moon out," he began. "Think I'll go out and look around. Want to come along?"

Flip looked at him thoughtfully. He'd really have liked to go, but wanted to finish work on the pelt. "Another time," he said.

A short distance from the cabin, Richard stopped and looked around. He liked the cold, still nights when a full moon was directly overhead. It bathed the glittering snow in an eerie blue-white light and held the contrasting black shadows close to the bases of the trees. Such moments permitted him to sense the majesty of the remote forested wilderness.

Walking to the center of a pond, he gazed at the deep purple sky sparkling with thousands of fiery stars and marveled at a crystal halo that formed the large milky ring around a stark, white moon. Standing perfectly still so his shoepacks would not squeak in the powdery snow, he watched as hundreds of rabbits frolicked and romped among the shrubs, reeds, and grass clumps at the shadowy edge of the pond. Suddenly, their play was interrupted by the skillful stalking of a hungry fox. It resumed again as soon as the predator had seized its squealing prey and trotted off to the seclusion of the dark forest.

After half an hour, with chill seeping through his clothing, he returned to the cabin. There, he sat in a chair before the blazing fireplace and basked in the spiritual uplift he had received. He was, indeed, acquiring a love, appreciation, and respect for the wilderness.

◆

One evening, after several days of a mild, south wind that reduced the snowpack to half of its three foot depth, the air suddenly went calm. A dense fog, which seemed to rise from the ground like a ghostly specter, enveloped the area. Then during the night, with the same placid stealth, a bitter cold descended that awakened Soho and made her rekindle the fire twice before daybreak to keep the cabin warm.

When Richard and Flip stepped out into the early dawn to tend their trap lines, they saw a sight neither had seen before. A thick coating of bristling hoarfrost covered everything. Every stick, every twig, every reed and blade of dried grass glistened in the dull morning light with a hairy coating of long, gray-white crystals. Even the cabin, except for the warmed roof, looked like a crystalline fantasy. It reminded Richard of the sugar house he had seen in a book of fairy tales his mother read to him in Weymouth. Turning slowly, he looked at the eerie scene that surrounded him. "What has happened?" he asked in a hushed voice.

Flip did not answer immediately. He strained to hear a sound, but there was none. "The goddamnedest thing I've ever seen!" he said.

174

Later, as they walked the trap line, they remained in a silence that was total and complete. There was not a bird, squirrel, or rabbit in sight. Even the sound of their walking was dulled and muted by the bristling landscape.

When they returned to the cabin, Soho was sitting cross-legged on a deerskin mat she had placed on the table. With outstretched arms and upraised face, she wailed a soulful chant, completely oblivious to their presence. Flip knew she was pleading to the spirits for help. Out of respect, he motioned for Richard to remain silent and indicated they should sit in their chairs until she had finished.

When she got down from the table and rolled up the mat, he asked, "What is wrong, Soho?"

She looked up at him, a grave expression covering her face.

"Soho asked the Great Spirit not to claim the earth and take it away."

Noting the puzzled look on Flip's face, she continued. "The earth turns gray like the old Chippewas when its time has come to die and return to the land of the Great Spirit. If all creatures, man and animal, stay in their shelters and plead to the Almighty One, it will be saved and allowed to remain for a while longer."

The next day when the frost had disappeared, she walked up to Flip. Her face was relaxed, and her eyes shone clear and warm. "The Great Spirit heard and has granted our wish," she said. "Now, all creatures can come out again, and the earth will nurture them."

◆

By mid-January, Richard was experiencing an intense feeling of restless agitation. He liked the wilderness, but total isolation from civilization bothered him. For weeks he had been confined to a cabin that was steadily diminishing in size with growing stacks of smelly hides and pelts. What was needed, he thought, was a respite from the routine of eating, sleeping, skinning, and running trap lines. He searched his mind for a reason to make a trip to the fort at Detroit. Noting that their supply of flour, salt, and beans was running low, perhaps he could convince Flip to take a few days off for a visit to the fort.

As the two of them leaned back in their chairs before the fireplace, Richard looked up at the ceiling and calmly said, "Maybe we should make a trip to Detroit to pick up a few things." He held his breath and looked out of the corner of his eye for Flip's reaction.

Flip stared at the fire briefly before responding. "Might not be a bad idea." He thought for a moment, then said, "Trappin's been especially good here. We can afford to take a few days off."

Richard sat upright and looked at Flip. "I hope we can find our way out of here," he said eagerly. "Do you realize that not a damned soul has come around since we got here?"

"Well, hell," Flip countered, "that's what we wanted. We wanted to trap—just trap. No interference. We'll have a helluva pile o' skins by spring, not countin' them we can get from the Chippewa."

"Oh, I'm not complaining about that," Richard assured him. "This is the best as far as trapping is concerned, but it's sure out of the way."

"That's what's so good about it," Flip grinned. "As fer Detroit, we just go southeast. Can't miss. Just keep the sun lined up right and it's got ta show up." He picked up his clay pipe from the table and began to pack it with crumbled tobacco from a small doeskin pouch. "I'm pretty good at directions. Besides, with the rivers and lakes froze, it should be easy."

"Maybe," Richard conceded. "But we've got snow to contend with."

Flip walked over to the fireplace and lit his pipe with a slender firebrand. "Shouldn't be bad," he said, shaking his head. "Some of those trails should be well used."

◆

They brought in a spike-horn buck for Soho's meat supply and told her they would return by the next full moon. Early the next morning they left, confident they could find their way. Each carried a fifty pound pack of beaver pelts and ten deerskins, a small portion of that stored in the cabin. In spite of the depth of snow, travel was relatively easy on the heavily used animal trails that paralleled the Tittabawassee.

When they reached a juncture of rivers where all the waters gathered and flowed north, they found the broad trail they had traveled with Naseeka. Although covered with many freshly made animal and bird tracks, the footprints on it had received a light dusting of snow.

Flip looked them over carefully. "That's good," he said quietly. "Nobody's been here today."

The two men lengthened their stride and stepped up their cadence in the fading light of late afternoon. To avoid being tracked, they continued well into the night before seeking shelter beneath the low-hanging branches of an evergreen a hundred yards off the trail. They were very tired, but felt the most difficult part of the trip was behind them.

By getting under way early each day, sometimes before dawn, and continuing to press on until well after dark, they reached Detroit on the fourth day. Although they had seen no one along the route until reaching the river road above the fort, they had come upon tracks of Ottawa hunting parties, some accompanied by blood-stained paths of slain deer being dragged to their village.

◆

"Told ya I could find it," Flip boasted as they passed through the gates of the fort shortly before the sentry closed them for the night.

"Never doubted it a minute," Richard replied, creases of weariness showing through the stubble of his beard. He was surprised how easy it had been.

Pleased at the sight of white men and women, Richard smiled, nodded, and spoke a word of greeting to each person they met. Some acknowledged him, but most just looked at the shabbily attired strangers and kept going.

"Sure nice to be back among people," Richard smiled, inhaling the odor of wood smoke that filled the air.

"They'll talk more when we get rid of these hides and clean up a bit," Flip replied, he voice reflecting the strain of their journey.

The accumulation of snow had been shoveled clear of most doors and some walkways, but the major portion of it had been allowed to remain where it fell, collecting to a depth of two feet. The heavily traveled streets were covered with a compacted icy coating, their slick surfaces coated in some places with a scattering of ashes.

The two men trudged along, making their way past the church and council house. At the Black Swan, they stopped to admire the fancy, snow-dusted sign that still hung in stark contrast to the plain wooden ones of the nearby bakery and harness shop. "We'll come back here," Flip said, pointing to the closed plank door of the tavern. "Hope ta hell they have a supply of ale."

Richard smiled. "Well," he said, as they continued on, "wherever you find man, you'll find he has brought with him the fermented juice!"

Entering the dimly lighted Comptoir Grillon, they inhaled its familiar musty odor. The Frenchman was about to close for the day. He looked up, squinting to see them. "*Mon amis! Mon amis!*" he shouted, rushing toward them with outstretched arms.

Richard stamped the snow from his shoepacks. He wondered if the proprietor was really pleased to see them, or whether his enthusiasm was caused by the packs he saw on their backs.

"Bon!" the little man uttered, exhaling a long, low-pitched whistle as he fanned the bundles of pelts they placed on the cluttered counter. "*Si bon!*"

"We need money for tonight," Flip explained as the Frenchman looked into his tired eyes. "So give us some now, and we'll come back tomorrow for the rest."

Squatting down so he could reach deep into a cabinet beneath the counter, the short proprietor withdrew ten one-pound notes and spread them out before the two men. Flip took five and handed the other five to Richard. "We'll be back tomorrow morning," he said assuredly.

———————◆———————

There were two dozen men in the Black Swan who had eaten supper and finished chores at their homes, but were unable to entertain themselves during the long winter nights. They frequently went to the tavern to break the boredom.

Several tallow-candle lanterns, fastened to the walls and backed by reflector mirrors, furnished a hazy light barely able to penetrate the turbid, smoke-filled air that stung the noses and smarted the eyes of Flip and Richard as they approached the bar.

"Hello, Henry!" the two of them called out in unison.

"Aye!" Henry replied, raising an open palm as his mind flashed back to recall their names. "Never forget a face," he continued. "Let's see. Flip and Richard, I believe."

"Right you are!" Richard exclaimed as they shook hands. Surprised and pleased that Henry had remembered, it made him feel comfortable.

"Do ya have any ale?" Flip inquired, looking about at the drinks of others.

"None a'tall," Henry replied. He shook his head sadly. "Been out two months. Rum and brandy's all."

"Rum," Flip said, placing his hands flat on the bar.

Richard nodded that he would take the same.

After taking a sip front his cup, Richard asked, "How about a room?"

Henry waited to answer until he had finished drawing a glass of brandy from a small barrel behind him. "By all means," he replied, "And I've fixed things a bit since ye were 'ere before. I'll go right now and start the fire so it'll be warm."

Richard detected a sense of pride in his voice.

When they turned in, they found that the room had, indeed, been upgraded. It was lighted by a copper lantern, like those Richard had seen his father make in England, that was suspended from a ceiling beam by a short iron chain. Along one wall, opposite a small, vigorously burning fireplace, were four beds constructed of sassafras poles that had been fitted with new cornhusk mattresses and woolen blankets. Between the center pair of beds, a deeply scarred, maple table held an earthenware pitcher of water, a copper basin, and a mirror.

"By George!" Flip declared in amazement. "This *is* class. Haven't seen anything like it since Boston."

"It's sure nice," Richard agreed. "Wonder where he got the stuff?"

"Beats me. But I'm sure gonna enjoy it."

The next morning, after rekindling the fireplace from the stack of split wood beside it, they washed and shaved.

"Feel a lot better," Richard stated. Then, looking down at his clothing, he added, "But these buckskins sure aren't much anymore."

They stepped out into the brisk chill of dawn to see the same scurry of people and clatter of horse drawn carts they had seen when they were here before. Bundled in winter clothing, the people now walked stiffly on the slippery streets and exhaled little puffs of steam that formed ice crystals on their beards and mufflers. The long, blue-gray shadows still covered most of the street, but the clear eastern sky was bright with a rising sun, already warming the brown fronts of stores and houses facing it.

Walking south on Rue Ste. Anne, they stopped at the tailor shop. Inside the small, log building was a long rack of cloth coats and trousers. Beside it was a narrow table piled with capes, blankets, and sweaters.

Richard searched through a stack of ruffled shirts, carefully scrutinizing a white one with a lacy, gathered front and long sleeves. He really didn't have any need for it, but had often wondered what it would be like to wear one. "How much?" he asked the proprietor.

The tailor, a short, ruddy-faced man with a slicked-down head of hair neatly parted in the middle, come over to him. He felt a sleeve of the shirt, then replied, "For you, four bucks." He spoke in English with a heavy French accent.

Flip saw the puzzled expression on Richard's face. "That's four deerskins—buckskins," he said,

"Oh, sure," Richard replied, inferring he knew.

After telling the tailor they would be back later in the day, they left the shop.

"Sure a nice day," Richard said, noting the icicles had begun to drip in the warm sun. He felt good about himself. His growing confidence to manage on the frontier had reached a point where he was certain he could hold his own in dealings with the white man. He would have to learn the market value of some commodities, but that would come with time. And he needed more experience dealing with Indians before he could approach them in the same fearless manner as Flip. But he was no longer afraid.

"Still cold enough ta freeze yer ass," Flip said, closing the flap of his collar. "Summer's still a long way off."

"Want to go to military headquarters," Richard said as they approached Rue St. Jacques. "Maybe there's a letter from home."

"If we turn left here, I think we will find it."

The headquarters building was easy to find, standing in front of two long troop barracks. They walked up to the lone sentry standing in the tiny guardhouse beside the entrance. "We want to see if we have any letters," Richard stated matter-of-factly.

The red-nosed guard stopped tapping his feet and extended an arm from beneath his red cape. "Go inside," he said, pointing toward the door.

"Thank you," Richard said gratefully, watching the young soldier wipe his wet nose with the back of his hand before dropping his arm to his side beneath the cape.

When Richard neared the rough-hewn, slab door, his pulse quickened and a chill raced up his spine. Inside he hoped to find a letter from home, preferably from Elizabeth, telling him everything was well and reaffirming her love for him. He hesitated momentarily to read the eye-level plaque. *Major Robert Rogers, Commandant* had been burned into the pine board. Then he lifted the wrought iron latch, and the two of them entered.

Sliding the capote hoods back from their heads, they approached the orderly sitting behind a small desk in the center of the little anteroom. Richard, feeling they were there at his behest, took the initiative. "I'm Richard Locke, and this is Flip Wade. We want to know if there's any letters for us."

The neatly dressed orderly rose slowly from his chair and pulled himself to his full height. Turning, he strutted with a deliberate cadence to a table in one corner of the room piled with several stacks of papers.

"Hell, there's nothing fer me," Flip mumbled.

The orderly returned and stood behind his chair, a small bundle of letters in his hand. Slowly, he shuffled through them, halted and looked up at Richard. "Richard Locke, ye say?"

"Yessir!" Richard replied, his face beaming with a broad smile as he reached for the folded paper.

Not wanting to break the seal until he and Flip were alone, he examined its exterior as the orderly continued through the stack. It was Elizabeth's handwriting, he was sure. He directed his eyes back to the orderly again. The young soldier seemed to be having difficulty reading some of the names. Richard was hoping for a letter from his father, also.

"Flip, ye say? Flip Wade?"

"Yah," Flip replied, looking at the orderly questioningly.

"None for Flip Wade. But 'ere's one for Flip the Trapper."

Flip appeared stunned. "Good God!" he gasped, catching his breath. "Who in the bloomin' hell'd write me?" He fingered the letter for a moment, then turned to Richard. "You look at it."

"Are ye sure it's 'is?" the orderly asked.

"Must be," Richard replied, carefully examining the soiled paper. "Let's have a look."

He popped the seal loose, scanned the writing, then turned to Flip. "It's from old John," he said with a smile.

"That old codger? Hell, he can't read or write."

"It's from John, all right," Richard assured him. "It's in a woman's hand, though. Probably his wife's."

Flip took the letter from Richard and looked it over briefly before stuffing it into his pocket. "Well, sure s'prised me."

◆

The little proprietor of the Comptoir Grillon was waiting when they arrived. "Mon amis!" he welcomed from behind his counter when they stepped through the doorway.

"Hello, Frenchy!" Flip called out. Turning to Richard, he said softly, "I think we'll start calling him Frenchy."

"Hallo!" the Frenchman answered with a broad grin. "I speak English, you see!"

"You sure do," Richard said, reaching out to shake his hand.

After looking through stacks, bins, and barrels of merchandise, they put on new buckskins and shoepacks and set aside sacks of flour, salt, and beans.

"I'd like some cloth for Soho," Richard said, standing beside a table with several bolts piled on one end. "I'm sure she could use it."

"Just don't give her anything red," Flip warned.

"Why not?"

"Usually means ya want ta marry her."

"Oh, Lord!" Richard exclaimed. He thought for a few seconds. "Let's get her two yards of blue."

"I sure as hell don't plan ta marry her," Flip said emphatically, helping Richard dig out a bolt of blue satin that was buried in the pile.

"What are you going to do when Naghee comes around again?"

"I don't know. Probably send her back with him. Remember, I said we'd treat her like a sister."

"Did he understand?"

"Sure as hell hope so."

After deducting for their supplies and setting aside ten deerskins Richard wanted to keep for barter with the tailor, Frenchy gave them forty pounds in British New York currency.

"Hell, he'll take money," Flip said, impatiently looking at Richard rolling the skins into a bundle.

"I know," Richard replied, "but he's got prices marked in buck-skins, and I think I'll get a better deal this way."

"Suit yerself," Flip sighed. Then turning to the proprietor, he said, "Frenchy, we'll be back tomorrow to pick up our things."

"*Oui, oui.* That will be good," came the labored reply as he and Richard started for the door.

When the two men entered his shop, the tailor set aside the military uniforms he was mending and rose to his feet.

Richard went directly to the ruffled shirts and looked through them for several minutes. After holding one to his chest, he shook his head and placed it back on the pile. Someday he would wear one, but not for a while. Then he selected a blue and white knitted shawl and asked the price.

"Two bucks," the tailor replied.

"And the blanket?"

"Four bucks."

"I'll take them," Richard said, handing the two items to the little man.

Richard unrolled the deerskins and placed six of them on the tailor's mending table.

Noting the remaining four, the tailor inquired, "You want shirt?"

"No," Richard answered. "Not today."

They returned to the Black Swan, ordered meat pie and rum, then sat at a table where they could read their letters. Richard rapidly read his to quickly assess the contents, then slowly reread it to relish Elizabeth's words.

She wrote that his father and her parents were in good health, that some new families had moved into Fredericksburg, and she was, with the help of her mother, making two patchwork quilts for her hope chest. "I just know you'll like them," she wrote, "especially the wedding ring pattern. We'll put it on our bed and use the other one, the daisy pattern, for our guest room." She concluded by stating how much she missed him and wanted him to return as soon as possible. "My love for you grows with each passing day, especially when I think of the time we became totally committed to each other. Remember?" she signed it, "Forever, totally and completely yours, Elizabeth."

He could feel the blood surging through his temples and the quivering tingle in his loins. He looked across the table at Flip. Flip was squinting, trying to decipher the letter from John. "Hard to read, Flip?" he asked.

"Well, I guess I'm not too good at it," Flip replied, slowly dragging his words in hesitation. "Outta practice, I guess." He could read printed words, but always had trouble with handwriting. Handing it to Richard, he said, "Here, you read it."

The letter was short, but written by someone well versed in the English language. Richard suddenly realized that Flip could read and write with only limited ability. This surprised him since Flip had told him how his aunts made him go to school. However, it would have no bearing on the respect and admiration he had for his closest friend. He regarded Flip as an outstanding person. Without hesitation, he began reading slowly and deliberately in a low voice.

The letter was written as if it was from John, but Flip and Richard was certain it was done by his wife. It stated that he was doing well at farming and enjoying the life of a settled, married man. "That cow Richard saved," the letter went on, "is about to have a calf. I'm grateful for the help in giving her a new cud plus all the other help you two gave me. Be sure to stop in on your way back." It was signed, "Your friend, John."

"Yah, grateful," Flip grinned. "That sinnin' sonofabitch. We saved his ass." He paused, then added, "Wonder what'll happen if we show our faces at Fort Pitt again?"

"I don't know. Hope they forget it. I'm sure she doesn't know about the ruckus he started."

Richard wrote a short letter to Elizabeth assuring her he would return in the summer and *take steps* to settle their future. His wording was purposely ambiguous. Although he wanted her for his wife, he wasn't sure he should marry this summer. Perhaps it would be better to spend another year trapping to make more money. Anyway, that question could be settled after he found out what this year's take amounted to.

He looked up at Flip who was slowly reading John's letter. "Know what date this is?" he asked.

"Hell, no," Flip replied. "Lost track long time ago."

"Henry," he called out to the proprietor. "What's the date today?"

"Aye," came the stiff response. " 'Tis Wednesday, January 14th, in the year of our Lord, one thousand seven hundred and sixty-one."

"There, Wednesday, January 14th," Richard repeated as he wrote it down. "We'll have to remember that."

"Maybe," Flip replied nonchalantly. "Don't see what difference it makes."

"You may be right. But I'll keep track just the same."

As they walked up Rue Ste. Anne to post Richard's letter, they saw a heavily clothed figure trotting toward them through the south gate. At first it seemed vaguely familiar, but as the distance closed they recognized their Wyandotte brother.

"Naseeka!" the two men called out as the Indian took the last few steps before halting in front of them.

"We didn't expect to see you," Richard said, placing an arm on the red man's shoulder.

"Yes," said Flip, shaking Naseeka's hand. "We came in to get supplies. Will leave in the morning."

"When my brothers are here, I know I must see them," Naseeka explained, still breathing heavily.

Richard looked at the tailless coonskin hat and shaggy rabbitskin cape Naseeka wore. "How did you know we were here?"

"There is much travel and much talk on the river road. Wyandotte people know about the fort, always."

Richard concluded it was too cold to stand and talk. "Come," he beckoned, pointing to Rue St. Jacques. "We must go down here."

Richard gave his letter to the same orderly they had seen before. As the young soldier returned to his desk after placing the letter in a basket on the table at the rear of the room, Richard noticed he was eyeing Naseeka suspiciously. Naseeka, standing ramrod straight with arms folded, merely stared back at the orderly with his cold, dark eyes.

It made Richard feel uncomfortable. He cleared his throat. "This is Naseeka," he said quietly, "son of the Wyandotte chief, Nasingah."

This seemed to ignite a spark of recognition in the mind of the orderly. "Why, yes," he stammered. "Right. The Wyandotte. 'e was in some weeks back"

"He's a friend of the white man," Flip assured the soldier.

"Aye," the redcoat replied, relaxing somewhat. " 'Tis what 'e said afore. His people are our friends, 'e said."

"Yes!" confirmed Naseeka, snapping his head emphatically. He was proud he could respond in English. "I speak to Major Rogers." His words were slow and deliberate.

The soldier nodded nervously. He hoped this Indian was a friend. He'd hate to face him as an enemy.

◆

Frenchy had just poured himself a cup of hot tea when the door of his trading post opened and the three men entered. "Welcome, my friends!" he shouted, motioning for them to join him.

He took three dusty porcelain cups from a ledge on the wall behind the counter and filled them with the steaming liquid.

Naseeka hopped upon a molasses hogshead and sat with his legs crossed, legs which appeared oversize from the dry grass insulation he had stuffed into his high moccasins. As the Indian sipped the hot tea and talked with Frenchy, Richard squatted on a stool beside the stove. He quietly studied the red man for several minutes, noting the bristling coonskin hat and shabby, moth-eaten cape hung with dozens of fur strips and the remains of legs and tails of rabbits and squirrels. How unregal, he thought, this son of a chief, this next leader of the Wyandottes. Type or style of dress appeared of little interest to the Indian, who seemed to make do with whatever was available at the time he needed it. But he admired Naseeka for the loyal, intelligent human being he was, and felt a complete trust in him. He looked down at the dark stains in his cup and sensed a sudden uneasiness deep within telling him that someday he and Naseeka would be in dire need of each other.

Flip, speaking in French, asked Naseeka if the cold weather had affected the Wyandotte food supply.

Naseeka replied that the food supply in the Wyandotte village was adequate, but it was due to planning on the part of its leaders. He nodded his head proudly. "Plenty of corn, beans, dried cranberries, and smoked fish," he said. "And," he added, extending an arm, "we can always catch deer."

There was a silence for several minutes as Naseeka appeared consumed in thought. Then, he shook his head in a negative manner and said, "Potawatomi will be hungry. Do not work in summer. Lazy!"

"And the Ottawa?" Flip asked, trying to learn about the largest tribe.

"Good!" Naseeka assured him. "They have strong chief!" Then he turned to look Flip squarely in the eye. "Did you visit the Chippewa?"

"Yes," confirmed Flip, at the same time noting a smile growing on Richard's face. "We saw their chief, Sacco, and Naghee, the leader of their warriors."

"Did they treat you well?"

"Yes."

Naseeka nodded his head with a snap, indicating he was pleased with what he had done for his two white brothers.

There was a brief lull in the conversation; then Richard turned to Naseeka. "How is Lahana and Matoka?" he asked in halting French.

"They good!" Naseeka replied in English, pleased that someone was showing interest in his family. "They speak of you. Someday you must see them."

"We will," Flip declared earnestly. "But now we must go back to the land of the Chippewa."

Naseeka grunted concurrence, then jumped down from the hogshead. He watched as their provisions were placed in a heavy cloth sack and noted that Richard was given a British pound for the four deerskins he brought back from the tailor.

While Richard picked up his money, Frenchy tossed several silver coins onto the counter. The young Virginian studied them for a moment, then looked up questioningly.

"*Livre*," Frenchy replied, arching his eyebrows and gesturing with upturned palms. "*Francais*. Now, no good!"

He tossed them into a container beneath the counter, then turned and placed the empty teacups back on the ledge. "For your tea when you come back with more furs," he said.

At the intersection of Rue St. Jacques and Rue Ste. Anne, Richard and Flip bid farewell to Naseeka. Both men were pained to see him leave.

As an expression of brotherhood, he volunteered to go with them to be of whatever service he could. It was declined, as he knew it would be, because he was needed at the village. He shook their hands. "I will see you here, my brothers, when the white blanket has gone into the earth."

Flip and Richard nodded.

Then he turned and trotted off toward the big gate, pausing once to look back and wave as his two white friends stood and watched.

At the Black Swan they asked Henry how they might get their furs to Detroit in the spring.

"I've 'eard 'em tell 'ow they canoe 'em down the Saginaw 'ere." He pointed his stubby finger at a crude map he had unrolled on the bar. "Then travel around the lakeshore, 'ere." He sighed. "But 'tis terribly unhandy."

Two soldiers who had been drinking rum at a table came over to look at the map.

Henry continued, "So I think yer best bet'd be ta let the 'udson's Bay Company 'elp ye."

"Didn't know Hudson's Bay was here," Flip said, looking surprised.

"Aye. Takin' over the old French fur warehouse. Should be open soon."

Flip and Richard stared at him, still not convinced.

"Tell ye what," Henry said. "When yer ready ta 'ave yer furs 'auled, come back and talk to 'em. They'll probably furnish ye with packhorses."

Flip and Richard looked at the two soldiers.

They nodded agreement. "Aye. 'Tis what we've been told," one of them asserted in a raspy voice.

"By God, we'll do it!" Flip shouted, pounding a fist on the bar. "Some rum, Henry!"

"And some rum for the two gentlemen in the king's service!" Richard added, extending a hand in their direction.

<hr>

Ten miles from the cabin, as they plodded through deep snow, Richard looked back and saw a pack of eight wolves following a hundred yards behind.

Flip stopped to watch. "They're sniffin' our tracks, all right," he said. "We'll just keep movin'. They should drop off in a little while."

Two hours later, the wolves were fifty yards to their left and moving parallel with them.

"They're gonna circle us, by God!" Flip declared, concern showing on his face.

"They can't be hungry." Richard said, struggling to keep close to Flip. "Plenty for them to eat out there."

"Maybe so, but they smell something on us they want. Maybe we can reach the cabin before they make their move."

"If not?"

"We'll have to fight 'em."

Just then Flip saw a deer browsing on some twigs a short distance ahead of the wolves. He dropped his pack, took careful aim, and felled the deer.

The startled wolf pack froze in their tracks and stared at the two men. Suddenly, their attention was diverted to the deer when it took a half dozen steps before falling. They ran to it and quickly began to feed.

As they approached the cabin, it appeared to be abandoned. No smoke came from the chimney, and the few footprints about the door did not appear fresh.

Both men dropped their packs. Richard motioned for Flip to stay back as a rearguard while he went up to investigate. Musket at the ready, he scanned the trees above as well as to his left and right, then silently tiptoed to the door. One set of tracks made by loose-fitting moccasins, fresh enough to have been made that day, led from the door toward the river and returned.

He sensed a dryness in his throat and could feel his pulse quicken. He knew someone was inside. Looking at Flip, he pointed to the door and nodded his head. Flip nodded to acknowledge he understood.

Richard stood at the side of the doorway, pulled the latchstring, then gently nudged the door open with the barrel of his musket. Squinting to see inside the darkened structure, he saw Soho rising up from her pallet, surprised and frightened, vapor issuing from her opened mouth into the cold air.

When his eyes became accustomed to the dim light and he was satisfied no one else was inside, he motioned to Flip, who was already running toward him.

As Flip questioned Soho, Richard quickly looked around the cabin. Everything appeared intact. He took out his tinderbox and flint and started a fire.

In less than an hour they were unpacking the supplies they had brought from Detroit, and Soho was making stew from two rabbits Richard had shot behind the cabin.

It took most of the evening for Flip to get details from Soho as to what had happened. Four days before, Naghee had come to the cabin. His concern had been aroused when the food hunters reported that carcasses no longer appeared at the pickup point. He led a small party of warriors to the cabin. Soho refused to return to the village with him because her white protectors expected her to be here when they returned with more supplies. Naghee ordered her to be taken forcibly, along with the remaining supply of meat and tobacco. He remembered other white men, not accustomed to the long, cold winters of lonely isolation, who abandoned their camp and ran off to the warmth and companionship of Detroit or Fort Baude at Michilimackinac, never to return again.

Soho, loyal to her belief, slipped out of the village early the next morning and returned to the cabin, but its door had been left open and fire was out. Her search of the ashes for a hot ember was fruitless, so she decided to wait in the cold cabin for her keepers to return.

To sustain herself, she chewed mouthfuls of snow and ate raw fish she caught through a hole in the ice of the Tittabawassee using a bone fishhook she made, and now that faith in her protectors had been confirmed. She was warm and contented, satisfied she was wanted and needed.

That evening, Richard gave Soho the two yards of satin he'd bought for her. Holding it in her outstretched hand, she looked up at him and wondered what he wanted her to do with it. She had never been given anything for herself before, so she thought he wanted her to make something for him.

After Flip convinced her that it was a gift for her, and her alone, her eyes brightened. She unfolded it and wrapped it around her body. Not satisfied with that, she held it in front like an apron. Finally, after checking its length and width, she put it over her head like a shawl.

The glowing fireplace highlighted the creased squares in the shiny material as she stood back and looked up admiringly at Richard. He smiled and handed her the knitted shawl. She unfolded it, put it over the satin, then looked up at him again. This time he saw tears well up in the corners of her almond eyes, then run down her chubby cheeks and make dark stains on the blue satin where it draped over her bosom.

———————◆———————

Clearing the trap lines after they had been unattended for several days was a tedious, time-consuming task. The fallen snow had nearly obliterated the trail, making it difficult to locate the settings.

Although nearly every trap held a beaver, muskrat, or otter, many had to be chopped from ice that had formed around them, and to transport the heavy take, the two men had to hang them from a pole they carried on their shoulders. Then the animals had to be thawed in the cabin before they could be skinned.

When the Chippewas did not collect the carcasses, Flip and Richard visited Sacco and Naghee. They were received warmly by Sacco, but Naghee treated them with a cool aloofness. On the way back to the cabin, Richard voiced his concern. "That Naghee doesn't seem very friendly," he said.

"That sonofabitch is just another Indian hothead," Flip replied, turning his head sideways so Richard, who was following his footsteps, could hear. "He thinks he knows how to run the village better'n Sacco."

"Do you think he knows how to lead his braves?"

"Oh, hell yes! That kind always does. He's a natural born troublemaker, always looking fer some kind of a fight just so he can wear another feather in his hair." Stopping to catch his breath, Flip turned to face Richard. "And," he continued, "ya can bet he has a few others that's willin' ta pitch in with him. Hell, he's the kind that'd lead a party of raiders ta kill somebody just fer the fun of it."

"What would Sacco say to that?" Richard asked, troubled by the thought.

"The thing is, Sacco wouldn't know about it until the renegade came back to the village with some bloody scalps hangin' from his belt. Then it's too late."

"Think he'd raid us?"

"Probably not. We've done too much fer his village."

"Maybe we should keep up our guard."

"Oh, we will. Ya can bet on that." Flip patted his musket. "Just always keep this ready and with ya."

◆

The harvest of prime furs was so bountiful that space in the cabin was reduced to one T-shaped aisle. The table had been moved outside, forcing them to sit on their bunks to eat, and furs were stacked beneath Soho's pallet until it neared the ceiling.

To placate her, they gave her three deer hides so she could make a new skirt, blouse, and moccasins. She adorned them with a generous quantity of colored beads, making her look like a robust princess-in-waiting. Her most prized possessions, however, remained the piece of satin and knitted shawl. She wore them continuously.

Richard stood with his hands on his hips, looking at the stacks of furs. "Isn't this something," he chuckled.

"Couple of years like this will make ya rich," Flip asserted. "Rich as hell."

"Sure smells rich, too," Richard retorted with a smile.

The first week in April brought a warm south wind that melted the snow and thawed the ground enough to soften it to a depth of several inches. Water levels rose in the ponds, lakes, and streams, and the Tittabawassee overflowed its banks creating a wide, moving sea of water that came within a few feet of the cabin before it began to recede. For several days the men could get to only a few of their traps, and when the water level dropped so others could be reached, many had disappeared. The trapping season had come to an end.

Flip prepared for a trip to Detroit to contact Hudson's Bay Company. Before leaving, he cautioned Richard to stay near the cabin. "Keep your musket always ready to fire, and have plenty of powder and lead handy. And," he looked around the cabin, "be sure ta have enough water inside in case ya have ta hole up for a day or two."

He walked over to the door. "Most of all," he warned, "don't let anyone, especially strangers, come inside the cabin."

"Don't worry," Richard replied convincingly. "After working all winter in this place, nobody's going to take our furs." Then he added, "And you won't find my hide tacked to the wall by Naghee, either, by God!"

Flip liked the sound of Richard's determination. "There shouldn't be any trouble," he said. "I'll see if Hudson's Bay has any horses we can use." He rubbed his chin. "Even if they do, we still ought ta sell some ta Frenchy."

"I think so, too," Richard agreed. "He's been damn good to us."

◆

After seven days, Flip returned with three skinny horses, a dapple gray and two sorrels. They had no bridles, only ropes around their necks, and their protruding ribs and dull, shaggy coats indicated they had endured a cold winter with a minimum of care.

Richard, remembering the horses on his father's farm, petted their velvet noses and ran his hands over the matted hair on their necks. It troubled him to see horses in this condition. "My God!" he said, looking into Flip's eyes, "they're half starved!"

"It's not that bad," Flip replied, patting the gray's rump. "But they could have been fed better. They had ten of 'em. None of 'em very fat."

"Must have been outside all winter, too."

"They were in a shed, but it wasn't too tight. Left a lot of cold in on them."

"They're sure skinny," Richard said, shaking his head.

"My backside knows about that," Flip sighed.

Soho had been watching from the cabin doorway. She walked up to the horses and patted the nose of a sorrel. It nibbled at the fringe of her buckskin blouse.

Richard led the horses to a nearby pond and tethered them so they could eat from the abundant dead grass that grew at its edge. Late in the afternoon, after they had eaten their fill, he tied them outside the cabin door. He would protect them from predators during the night.

The next morning, Flip told Soho the time had come for her to return to her village. Believing she had been permanently assigned to work for them, she told him she would either stay at the cabin or accompany them to Detroit.

"Let's leave her at the cabin," Richard said with a shrug.

"Can't do that," Flip asserted. "If the Ottawas get their hands on her, she'll be in trouble. She'd probably never get back home, even if they let her live." He thought for a moment, then shook his head. "And the Mackinaw Trail is only a mile away. Lot of white rogues on it in the summer. Might wander over here and work her over."

Flip pleaded with her for another half hour, but she stood defiantly with her back against a stack of furs at the back of the cabin, stating repeatedly that she would stay and work for them.

"To hell with her!" he snapped, incensed that she would defy his order to leave. "Let 'er stay!"

Although considered a lowly squaw woman by most men, Flip and Richard had grown to admire and respect her. The fondness was even more pronounced in Richard, for he harbored a greater compassion for his fellow man. Of course, he had never witnessed the savagery that Flip had, and his religious upbringing and devotion to his mother and Elizabeth may have influenced him. At any rate, he refused to abandon her to the perils of the wilderness. He walked up to her, and, as best he could, pleaded with her to return to her village.

She stared at the floor and shook her head slowly from side to side.

After a few minutes, he turned on his heels and said to Flip, "Let's get Naghee."

"Just let her here!"

"No! We can't do that!" Richard insisted.

Frustrated to the point of desperation, Flip grabbed his musket. "Wait here," he called, walking off in the direction of the Chippewa village.

He returned at nightfall. "Naghee will be here in the morning," he said, slumping in his chair.

———————◆———————

It was mid-morning when the Chippewa war chief, accompanied by three braves, arrived. Flip and Richard had tied the furs and hides into bundles and loaded most of them onto the horses. As they tossed on a few supplies, Naghee presented them with thirty beaver pelts as a token of his people's appreciation for the carcasses. Then, he requested they sit down for a talk.

Flip refused, saying they had been delayed long enough and wanted to leave.

The refusal visibly irritated Naghee. He looked sternly into the eyes of the trappers, then glanced at the burdened horses. Finally, he fixed his stare on the opened cabin door.

Flip and Richard, their faces mirroring concern, stood with muskets in hand and watched as the Indian told his braves to remain where they were. He took several long strides to the door, then halted to peer inside. When he barked a one syllable command, Soho, dressed like a queen in her new buckskins and shawls, emerged and trotted off through the trees in the direction of the Chippewa village.

Naghee disappeared into the cabin, then reappeared holding up a sack containing the remains of the flour supply. He looked questioningly at Flip and Richard, and when they nodded approval, handed it to one of his braves. The two trappers then joined him inside and informed him he could take what he wanted. He nodded and grunted satisfaction. Then, he asked for gunpowder and lead.

Richard and Flip shook their heads and told him they had very little left and needed it themselves. Naghee placed his hands on the barrel of Richard's musket, and Richard quickly withdrew. Flip retreated and stood beside the horses.

Naghee, seeing the bargaining was over, asked if they would be back next winter.

"*Oui*," Flip replied.

"*Au revoir*," Naghee snorted.

As the two trappers departed, Flip leading the string of horses and Richard trailing behind, Naghee and his braves began to clear the cabin of the supplies they could carry.

Before the cabin disappeared from view, Richard looked back. He could see the Indians tossing things about and hear their deep guttural shouts and grunts as they rummaged through the remaining clothing, utensils and food supplies.

For Flip, the cabin had been just another winter camp, one of many he had lived in over the years, but to Richard, it represented a more personal experience, a reminder of the log house he had watched his parents build when they settled on the Rappahannock.

It had also been a shelter from the raging blizzards and the coldest temperature he had ever experienced and a snug haven in a quiet, remote wilderness, a wonderland he didn't know existed. He had learned to survive on the frontier and live among the animals and Indians. It gave him the experience and confidence needed to be a successful trapper and trader.

"Sure glad to go, but I'm going to miss that place," he muttered, turning to get in line behind the last horse.

Flip looked back at him. "We're leaving just in time. That red bastard's no friend of the white man. I felt it coming on. He's acting different now—showing his true colors. The people at the fort had better wake up. There's trouble brewing."

Chapter 8

Decision

Richard shifted his musket to his left hand and pulled a hard biscuit from the leather pouch hanging at his side. He was enjoying the pleasant warmth of a balmy spring day as he walked a short distance behind the rear packhorse.

Along the trail, vigorous new life was apparent everywhere. Pine branches heavy with an abundance of sap were pushing forth buds of new, light-colored growth from their finger-like tips, and small, fragile leaves, only a few days out of their sprouts, were growing rapidly in an attempt to quickly hide the gray nakedness of deciduous trees. Occasionally, bright flowers of dogwood or chokecherry glared out in welcome relief from the tone on tone green that smothered the traveler on all sides. From time to time, an outcropping of violets or marsh marigolds appeared in the saturated, spongy black soil or among reeds in a water-filled bog.

Young animals that had been born the previous summer raced, gamboled, and frolicked, ofttimes to the dismay and annoyance of their elders. They were delighted to be free from the winter confinement of their dens and burrows. And in addition to the usual chattering of squirrels and chirruping and singing of birds, frogs in large numbers provided a continuous, multipitched chorus that varied little in volume regardless of time of day or amount of noise on the trail.

In contrast to the low water level he and Flip had encountered in the fall, swollen rivers and streams were filled bank to bank and ran with greater speed. On three occasions their depths necessitated unloading the horses, building rafts of poplar poles, and ferrying the loads of pelts across the heavy flow.

The two men found that evenings, before darkness descended, were delightful along the trail. On the second night out, after unloading the horses, they ate supper and spread their beds beside a pond a short distance off the trail. Propping themselves against a bush of pussy willows covered with silky gray catkins, they watched the hobbled horses forage at the water's edge. Flip lit his battered clay pipe, now bound together with a leather thong, while Richard sat quietly with his arms wrapped about his doubled-up knees.

The dark water was like a mirror, clearly reflecting the surrounding trees. Suddenly the glassy surface was rippled by a frog that had ceased croaking and leaped from a lily pad into the murky depths. As it dug into the muddy bottom, several redwing blackbirds chirruped their song while swaying precariously on a cluster of cattails. Keeping an eye on the motionless men, the birds watched a colony of water striders darting about on the shiny liquid surface beneath them.

When darkness came, the warm, humid air buzzed with only a few mosquitoes. It was early in the year, and water was moving too rapidly for them to breed in great numbers. Fireflies, however, had emerged, their flickering sparks reflecting from the mirror-like surface of the pond.

Richard interrupted the spell. "Certainly restful here," he said, speaking loud enough for Flip to hear above the din of croaking frogs.

"Yea," Flip agreed, shoving the still warm pipe into his pocket. "This is a nice time of day. Nothin' like it in Boston or Philadelphia."

They rested and early the next morning continued their journey.

Just as the fort's sturdy palisade loomed into view, they encountered six soldiers and a dozen neatly dressed civilian men on their way to the mission at St. Joseph. When the group learned the two bewhiskered trappers had just traveled the trail from the Tittabawassee, they halted. "Any trouble?" the lead soldier asked.

"High water in a few places," Flip replied. "Saw a small Ottawa hunting party a ways off. Seemed friendly, though."

"How long did it take ya?" the soldier inquired. He was pleased the first part of his journey would pose no serious problem.

"Left four and a half days ago," Flip replied, looking at Richard to confirm it.

Richard nodded.

◆

They deposited two loads of furs at the Hudson's Bay Company, then led the third horse to the Comptoir Grillon.

When Frenchy saw the load of pelts, his face beamed. "Welcome, my good friends!" he said, embracing each of them.

As they carried the furs inside, the Frenchman explained that very few trappers brought their catch to him. "The men from Hudson's Bay come," he said with a sigh, shaking his head. "They have much money. Take all the business." He paused, then added, "Detroit, she has changed."

He showed them two stacks of beaver pelts on a table in the storage room. "For you." he said. "From Naseeka." A sly smile twisted his mouth as he watched the surprised expression grow on their faces.

Flip leafed through the superbly stretched skins, then gave a low whistle. "Mighty fine furs!" he exclaimed. "A lot better than we got from the Chippewa."

"Didn't think we'd really get them," Richard stated frankly, walking over beside his partner. "Thought they'd just forget them."

"Oh, no," Flip countered, turning his head to reply. "An Indian never forgets." He paused, then said, "And Naseeka's a damn good friend."

Frenchy, who had learned to understand English, nodded agreement, his face twitching as it had when they first met.

The two men bought new buckskins and replenished their supply of powder and shot. Then they departed.

"Thank you, my friends!" Frenchy called out as he watched them lead the horse down the street.

At the military headquarters Flip waited while Richard went in to see about mail. There were two letters, both from Elizabeth. Richard scanned them quickly. They were warm and intimate, reminding him she loved him very much and could hardly wait for his return.

"From Elizabeth?" Flip asked, as Richard, pushing the letters into his pocket, walked up beside him. Although his friend was tired, he could see his face was much brighter.

"Yes," Richard said with a smile.

A weathered notice was tacked to the door of the Hudson's Bay Company. Before entering, Richard stopped to examine it. *Trappers Ball*, it read. *Saturday Night, May 2, 1761. Join us for fun and entertainment. Cyrus Treadwell, Agent.* He turned to Flip standing beside him. "Trappers Ball," he said enthusiastically. "May 2nd. That's tonight, isn't it?"

Flip shrugged. He wasn't sure about the date. "Let's find out," he said, pulling the door open.

When they reached the Black Swan, Richard and Flip learned that there had, indeed, been changes at the fort. The British, determined to explore, inhabit, and establish a perimeter of permanent population centers along the new frontier, were offering immigrants land, an ax, spade, plow, cow, pig, and wagon. This brought new families to the area. But it also brought renegades and misfits.

Hudson's Bay Company came to take over the rich fur trade the French had established. The French had developed a friendly relationship with the Indians, even intermarrying with them, and when the British came, the natives were pleased. An agent told them the English would treat them even better than the French.

To maintain a line of communication an armed sailing ship, *Michigan*, would make a round trip every three weeks, carrying passengers, mail, and supplies between Detroit and Fort Niagara. A second ship, *Huron*, was being outfitted to assist and would be in service shortly.

The *Michigan* had made its initial trip bringing a large quantity of salable goods, supplies, and ammunition, and had sailed again for Niagara taking a load of furs and several French families who wished to return to France. Among the two dozen passengers it brought to Detroit were three agents of the Hudson's Bay Company carrying a large quantity of money. They were eager to establish a reputation of paying top prices for furs and pelts to all white men who delivered them.

———◆———

It was well after sundown when Richard and Flip, having dozed off while resting in their room at the Black Swan, walked through the broad, open warehouse doorway amid the strains of an Irish jig. It was an expansive structure that had been built near the council house ten years before. With outer walls of oak logs standing vertically, it had a number of posts within to support the large board roof. The rear half contained stacks of furs waiting for shipment to Niagara.

Numerous lanterns, backed by reflectors to intensify the feeble light of tallow candles, hung from the walls and posts. At the center, three fiddlers provided music for dancing on a hewn log floor that had been sprinkled with cornmeal to enhance its surface, and along one wall several barrels of brandy, rum, and ale had been tapped for the men and a large caldron of tea steeped for the ladies.

The agent who had supervised the grading and pricing of their furs earlier in the day greeted them. He decided they were the type of trappers Hudson's Bay wished to cultivate. "Come in, me lads," he welcomed. Perspiration was beginning to show at the roots of his sparse hair. "Locke and Wade, I believe."

Richard eyed him momentarily, noting that his new blue suit and white shirt had already been food stained.

"Right!" Flip replied.

"Treadwell," the agent said with a smile. "Cyrus Treadwell." He extended his hand.

Treadwell pointed to the long counter. "There's a bit o' drink fer ye."

With a sweep of his eyes, Richard surveyed the crowd in the dim, hazy light as he and Flip made their way to the counter. There were, he judged, a hundred people present, mostly trappers. A few women, probably wives of farmers, merchants, or the military, sat on benches that had been placed along the wall. In addition to those dancing, several clusters of men stood near the bar chatting and watching while sipping their drinks.

"Far cry from that bunch at Fort Pitt," Flip stated as he withdrew the wooden cup from his lips after taking a drink of rum.

"Yes," Richard agreed. "That was a bunch of roughnecks."

"I'm sure there's some here, too," Flip asserted with an air of authority. "But those Irish loggers'll keep 'em in tow." He pointed to two burly men serving drinks from behind the bar who volunteered to arm wrestle anyone who challenged them.

Their attention was diverted by loud talk coming from a group of men standing nearby. "Rassle? Hell, I rassle any sonofabitch that's walked the pike!" a drunken trapper yelled. "And I'll win!"

"Yessiree!" his inebriated friend shouted, pressing his hand against his partner's back as they elbowed their way toward the bar. "Ain't no Detroit bastard can whip ol' Jake!"

One of the bartenders came from behind the counter, grabbed each of the cussing men by the scruff of the neck and knocked their heads violently together. Holding them by their collars, he turned toward the door. Then he pushed and dragged the protesting troublemakers along a parting pathway made through the awed spectators. Pitching them through the doorway into the darkened street, he shouted so all could hear, "And don't come back 'til ye've washed yer stinkin' carcasses as well as yer foul tongues!"

A cheer arose as he made his way back to the bar among the backslapping crowd.

A few minutes later, a fuzzy-faced young ruffian dressed in tattered clothing came up to the bar beside Richard. "Step aside, son," he said, waving his hand in an unsteady manner, "and give a man some elbow room ta drink!"

Seeing ample space for the stranger, Richard ignored him.

"I said, give me some room!" the man demanded, tapping Richard on the arm. "Or I'll give ye some punishment!"

The young Virginian drew himself to his full height and slowly turned to face the stranger. His blue eyes flashed as he said in a low, firm voice, "You bother me once more and your nose will hang from the back of your head!"

The agitator looked up at Richard, who stood a full six inches above him, then glanced around the crowd. Noticeably cowed, he picked up his drink and slinked away, muttering to himself.

"You said that like you meant it," Flip said, walking up to his partner.

"I did," Richard assured him. He thought for a moment, then said, "I thought you said this was a quiet crowd."

Flip shook his head. "Never can tell, I guess."

Shortly after midnight, Richard and Flip decided to leave. They were met at the door by Cyrus Treadwell. He appeared haggard and tired. "Pleased ta 'ave ye," he said, a broad smile being forced to stretch across his face. "Ye must avail yerself o' the next one in October."

"We will," Flip assured him.

The party had accomplished what Treadwell wanted by creating an atmosphere of company goodwill. It attracted a fair number of local residents as well as itinerant trappers and hunters who were certain to spread the word. Although Major Rogers did not attend, several of his men did and were noticeably well behaved. Women were in short supply, only six were present, but Treadwell was certain more would show in the fall.

◆

Although Richard was very tired, he slept fitfully. His mind was occupied with the trip home. On several occasions he looked over at Flip regenerating his weary body by sleeping soundly. Of course, Flip had no family concerns and planned to remain to scout another trapping site for the next season. And Fredericksburg was a great distance away.

Early the next morning in front of the Black Swan, the two men agreed to meet at the tavern in the fall. "Take care of your money," Richard advised, patting the doeskin belt next to his skin into which he had sewn 650 pounds of British New York currency.

"Rest assured," Flip vowed with a nod. Then his brow wrinkled. "Still got some at Fort Pitt I'll have ta dig up some day."

When Richard walked through the south gate and crossed over the Savoyard bridge, a feeling of apprehension swept over him. He was traveling alone on a trail that was not well established. When he halted to take a last look at the huge structure, a sentry walking its upper perimeter waved. Richard raised his hand, then spun around and walked off down the river trail at a brisk pace. A feeling of confidence rose within him. He was sure he could traverse the frontier as well as anyone. Better than most.

He had topped his backpack with a roll of two prime timber wolf furs he wanted to take home. The warm sun and high humidity made them weigh heavily on his shoulders. It would have been easier in the canoe, but the winter had opened its seams and rotted the frame. Besides, he'd have to abandon it at the mouth of the Cuyahoga anyway.

During the first hour he passed many farms, their houses, barns, and sheds built between the road and the river. On his right, stump-dotted orchards, pasture fields, and freshly tilled, newly planted tracts stretched westward for a great distance.

Several farms were unoccupied, abandoned by Frenchmen who chose to leave when the British arrived. Although their fields lay fallow, the buildings remained closed and secure, protected by neighbors hoping for new families to bolster the number of able bodied settlers. As he passed, Richard wondered what it would be like to work a piece of land here. When his father staked the farm on the Rappahannock, the area was more settled, more civilized, but Mr. Locke still had to hack his farm from raw land. Here, it had already been cleared.

Frequently, farmers waved and halted their work to watch as the young Virginian made his way down the rutted road. Richard was certain a few wished he would stop and talk. But Fredericksburg was a long way off, so he kept moving.

After crossing the narrow, shaky bridge that spanned the muddy, red water of the Rouge River, he entered the forest. Although shaded from the sun, his vision was restricted. Looking ahead, he saw a red man standing on the trail. It was Naseeka, dressed in a breechclout, buckskin vest, and low cut moccasins. The red man's hair was plaited into two long braids and adorned with several feathers of the red-tailed hawk. He looked much better to Richard than he had last winter in his motley garb.

"Naseeka!" Richard greeted, extending his hand. He was pleased to see that it was his friend.

"Naseeka is hunting," the Indian explained, grasping Richard's hand warmly. "Today I learned you were at the fort."

Richard could see the warmth in his eyes and feel the respect that radiated from the small smile that parted his lips. "Yes, we came yesterday with many furs from the land of the Chippewa." Then he remembered the beaver pelts from the Wyandottes. "And those from our friend, Nasingah, pleased us very much."

Naseeka walked to the side of the trail and picked up two rabbits and a pheasant. Then he slipped his bow over his shoulder.

"You use bow and arrow," Richard observed as the two of them walked down the trail.

"It is a good way for small animals," Naseeka said. "For the deer and bear, the fire stick is better." He thought for a moment, then shook his head. "We get no gunpowder from the English. That is bad."

Richard knew the English had a policy of not selling gunpowder to the Indians, but he did not wish to discuss it with his friend.

"The English tell the red man they make life good for him," Naseeka continued. "Rivers will run red with rum, and the white chief across the big water will send many presents. All English things will be plentiful, so a fine blanket will cost only two beaver skins." He looked at Richard for a response.

Richard placed his hand on his chest. "I do not know about this," he said, hoping to drop the matter. "But maybe Flip can find out."

Naseeka grunted and nodded that he understood. He was pleased he had two white friends who respected his knowledge and judgment. With the continuing intrusion of settlers, his people needed someone from the world of the white man to speak on their behalf.

"Flip? Your friend, Flip? Is he with you?" Naseeka asked.

"No. He will stay by the fort. He will visit you soon."

Again, Naseeka grunted and nodded. Then he asked if he could carry Richard's musket. Richard hesitated, then handed the weapon to him.

Naseeka placed the musket on his shoulder and took a dozen snappy steps. "Just like English soldier!" he called back, turning his head to see Richard's reaction.

"Just like English soldier," Richard agreed.

♦

As Richard entered the Wyandotte village with Naseeka, it appeared to be idle and sluggish. Although Chief Nasingah was the ultimate authority, he discovered it was a beehive of activity supervised by a matriarchal hierarchy of older women. A large contingent of braves was away hunting and fishing, but some remained to make weapons. And the elder men taught young children tribal lore and the ways of their people.

Older children and the remainder of the women, including those heavy with child, were working at communal tasks of the tribe. They were planting seeds in shallow furrows cut into soil around the dead, ringed trees of the planting area, slabs of bark were being placed over holes winter had made in walls and roofs, fishing nets were being woven, canoes were being repaired. And in the center of the village, the same large caldron Richard had seen before was boiling with sap carried in by older boys in leather lined reed baskets.

Naseeka was proud of his white friend and strutted with an air of dignity as he led him through the village to the tepee of Nasingah. The chief was sitting on his throne-like stump enjoying the warm freshness of a spring afternoon. Remaining seated with an expressionless face, the elderly leader grasped Richard's hand firmly and gave it one strong shake. He uttered no sound but nodded his head to note recognition.

Although Richard had told Naseeka about the beaver skins, he wanted to let Nasingah know they were appreciated. Speaking slowly in French and using words he hoped the chief understood, he said, "The beaver skins from your people were very good. Very good! Flip and I liked them very much."

Naseeka quickly translated and Nasingah nodded.

Having duly notified his father of their white friend's presence, Naseeka led Richard to a sitting log a short distance away.

"You stay in Wyandotte village tonight," the red man stated in a voice that half suggested and half commanded.

Richard knew he was welcome and Naseeka would feel a sense of pride if he stayed, but there was something he felt since entering the village telling him that, although he was looked upon as a friend by most, others were not convinced. He was a white man, and a white man could not be trusted.

"I can travel more today before the sun goes down," Richard countered weakly, not wanting to damage Naseeka's esteem among his people.

"You stay here tonight! Tomorrow you go fast with Wyandotte canoe!"

"But I cannot return the canoe. I must leave it when I leave the Big Water."

"That is good!" Naseeka concluded, bringing the matter to a close.

On their way to the guest tepee, they encountered Matoka and Lahana. The young women beamed as Richard shook their hands.

"Lahana, she catches fish," Naseeka explained, pointing toward the shoreline. "My sister, she plants seeds," He pointed to the planting area.

Matoka wiped her earth-stained hands on her soiled buckskin dress as she asked Naseeka a question. Naseeka responded, then turned to Richard. "She asks about Flip. I tell her he visit soon."

Richard reached into the opening of his blouse and lifted out the small doeskin pouch that hung from his neck. The women recognized it immediately as one they had made.

"Bon! Si bon!" he said, watching a wide smile stretch across their faces.

◆

Richard and Naseeka were fed passenger pigeon and wild turkey at the family space in the longhouse. After eating they went outside so the women could eat, as was the custom. Sitting on a log, the young Wyandotte complained bitterly about the lack of powder and shot. "Deer not plentiful now. White man take too many." His face looked grim. "When white blanket is here, we have much trouble."

"But you have deer meat in the lodges now," Richard pointed out, trying to act sympathetic. At the same time he wanted to show the hardship was not all that severe.

"But we must get powder from our French friends!" Naseeka spit back. "When the French no longer give us powder, it will be bad!"

Noting the rising temper of his friend, Richard changed the subject to that of his trip home. He expressed his appreciation for the canoe, explaining he would make better time because following the trail would mean crossing many swollen streams. He tried to tell him about the hilly terrain and distance of travel, but doubted Naseeka understood since the Indian had traveled only short distances on flat land.

Soon after Richard went to bed in the guest tepee, Matoka entered as she had on his prior visit. She was wearing a new buckskin dress and smelled of juniper. He watched her dim outline in the darkness as she removed the dress and crawled in beside him.

He permitted her to remain, but to her surprise, did not make love to her. To him, Indian women were for Indians. And Elizabeth was the only woman for him.

She remained the night, cuddled against him, and left as she had previously, just before dawn.

With a large pouch of dried meat and maple sugar pemmican tucked into the prow of a small canoe, he paddled out from the Wyandotte village. Many inhabitants of the village stood at the water's edge to bid him safe voyage. Naseeka's mother waved with tear filled eyes. Above the chatter, he heard Naseeka's resonant voice, "Come back when the geese fly that way!" He pointed to the south.

Richard nodded and waved. "When the geese fly that way!" he repeated.

◆

Although she tried to hide it, Elizabeth was hurt and disappointed when Richard had departed for the wilderness. She knew he wanted to make enough money to begin their life together in better fashion than if he worked for wages. Still, she felt that, if he really loved her as much as he said, they could get married and, in a few years, reach the same goal with more stability and considerably less risk.

For several days she spent long hours in her room crying, pouting, and brooding. Then, with a strength and determination she possessed but seldom displayed, she decided to carry on, hopeful he would return and they would get married. Nevertheless, deep inside she harbored the thought that, if another good prospect appeared, she would consider him.

The idea lasted less than a week. Her love for Richard was so profound and overwhelming there was no way she could picture herself married to anyone else. Perhaps if she kept busy, the time would pass more quickly. She began doing more work around the house. She did all of the washing, ironing, and mending, as well as most of the sweeping, dusting, and mopping. Her mother, however, insisted on doing the cooking and baking. She did not like to see her daughter perspiring heavily around the hot stove during the sweltering days of summer.

But when it was time for canning and preserving, Mrs. Locke accepted her daughter's assistance. "Good practice," she informed Elizabeth, as the two of them worked over the steaming kettles. "Next year you'll be doing it for yourself."

Elizabeth continued to complete her hope chest. She made muslin sheets and pillow cases, embroidering an L on each, and hemmed dish towels from cotton squares, afterwards sewing bright little figures on their corners. Sometimes as she sewed, she fantasized her role as the wife of Richard Locke, a prosperous farmer. She quietly called out her name in different ways to see how it sounded. "Elizabeth Locke... Mrs. Elizabeth Locke... Mrs. Elizabeth M. Locke." She paused after each to sense its imagined impact.

After the harvest had been completed, the social aspects of life in Fredericksburg took an upturn. There were dances, husking bees, and box socials with cider, apples, and popcorn. There also were hayrides, but Elizabeth was discouraged from participating in them. "Young ladies, especially those who are promised, don't attend such boisterous, risque events," her mother reminded her.

"But, Mother," Elizabeth protested, "they are chaperoned."

"Yes, so was that husking bee," her mother countered. "Tongues are still wagging about you getting kissed twice by the young rogues who husked those red ears. Flannel-mouths said you enjoyed it." She paused and shook her head. "I think those ears were sneaked in."

Shortly after Easter, Mrs. Wright's school held a box social to raise money for a new blackboard and some reference books. All students and alumni were urged to attend this worthwhile project.

A handsome, well dressed man from Philadelphia, passing through town on his way to Richmond, was obliged to spend the night. When the innkeeper informed him of the box social, he decided to attend.

He took a seat at the rear of the classroom amid a group of neatly dressed schoolgirls. Elizabeth, sitting near the front of the room clad in a yellow chiffon and organdy dress and with long streamers hanging from a yellow ribbon that graced the back of her curled hair, caught his eye. Seeing her as a lady of class, he promised himself he would buy her box. Turning to one of the girls next to him, he inquired, "Do you know that lady over there?"

"Sure," came the whispered reply. "That's Elizabeth. Elizabeth Harrington."

"Does she have a box here tonight?"

"I think so."

The girl consulted her friends. "Yes," she said, turning back to him.

"Which one is it?" he asked, continuing to probe.

"I don't know," the girl answered.

"We're not supposed to tell," replied another.

"Oh, you can tell me," he assured them as he smiled and winked.

After a brief, whispered discussion, the girls faces brightened. "It's the one tied with the yellow ribbon," one of them informed him.

"Thank you," he said, again winking to reassure them he would not violate their confidence.

The boxes were sold for five to fifteen shillings. Occasionally, one was auctioned for a guinea when a young man wished to impress a girl by having a friend raise his bid a predetermined amount. Elizabeth's box, held aloft by a lady assistant of the auctioneer, faltered at twelve shillings. Suddenly, the bold voiced stranger at the back of the room called out, "Three guineas!"

Everyone in the room turned to watch as the box was delivered to him. Out of the corner of his eye, he saw a slight flush ascend the white skin of Elizabeth's neck and face. Not wanting to let on he knew who owned the box, he pretended to focus his attention on the continuing auction.

Elizabeth tried to enjoy eating and conversing with the young man, but she felt miserable. She was not impressed by his big city mannerisms. And when she looked around the room, numerous eyes were watching her. It made her uneasy.

His name was Rolf Talbot, and he worked as a bookkeeper in his father's shipping firm. He was well dressed and behaved properly, but talked incessantly. As Elizabeth listened, she thought he used the pronouns *I*, *me*, and *my* too often.

When they finished eating, he asked to escort her home.

"I think not," she replied. "I have some work to do here."

He looked at her and was about to say something else, but she interrupted. "Besides, I'm betrothed."

◆

When Elizabeth received a letter from Richard she prized it very much, not only because she loved him but because she knew it had come by a long and circuitous route. Written correspondence between larger cities was carried by coach lines that ran regular schedules. Disseminating it to towns and villages was left to couriers, draymen, or trusted citizens traveling through the area. But for frontier settlements, it was carried by supply trains and military messengers.

She carefully read and reread each letter, then tucked it into a bundle tied with a blue ribbon she kept in her bureau drawer. Many times during the long winter evenings she took them out and read them again to see if there was an interpretation she had overlooked. When spring arrived, her feelings intensified until she found it nearly impossible to wait for him to arrive. Reflecting back to last summer, she remembered the thought of considering someone else. It bothered her. There was no one in the world for her but Richard, her Richard.

Frequently, after going to bed in the evenings, she closed her eyes and relived her experiences with him. When she thought of the more intimate moments, a tingling sensation developed in her breasts and abdomen. In spite of the childhood counseling she remembered from her mother, she found her right hand slowly descending past her stomach to the hair-covered mound at the juncture of her thighs. It released the tension that accumulated with increasing intensity as his arrival time drew near.

When her friend, Mary Moore, asked about Richard the first week in June, Elizabeth brushed a lock of hair from her forehead and replied, "He's on his way home. Should be here in a week or two."

Although Mary was not engaged, she had been courted on several occasions by Lewis Mercer, an Episcopal deacon from Woodbridge. Elizabeth got the impression Mary thought Lewis was of a higher order than Richard, but still she was Elizabeth's closest friend.

"It'll be nice to have him back again," Mary said, trying to ease the concern she knew was on Elizabeth's mind. She wondered, however, if Richard would return. Perhaps he had been killed by Indians. Or maybe, he found life was more exciting in New York or Philadelphia.

"Can hardly wait," Elizabeth said, excitement showing on her face. She was certain he would come back. Her big hope was that he would want to get married this summer instead of waiting another year.

◆

In the early afternoon of June 11th while sitting in a parlor rocker, Elizabeth heard the tread of heavy shoes on the front steps. She looked out the curtained window of the front door and saw a young man, neatly dressed in a white shirt and brown suit with vest, walking up to the door. Leaping to her feet, she raced to the door and jerked it open just as he was raising his hand to the knocker.

"Richard!" she gasped, placing her arms about his waist and pressing the side of her face against his chest.

Pushing her gently backwards into the room, he closed the door. "Your mother?" he asked, brushing his lips against her cheek.

"Out back," she answered, her eyes closed and head tilted back.

214

She felt the spreading fingers of one of his strong hands between her shoulder blades and the other at the small of her back, drawing her tightly against him until her breasts flattened and stomach pressed hard against him. His lips sought hers, plied them apart, and kissed them bruisingly as the blood raced through her temples. Just as she felt his love rising, there was a squeak at the back door. Separating, they walked into the kitchen.

"We have a visitor," Elizabeth called out cheerfully.

Mrs. Harrington, sensing the excitement in her daughter's voice, looked up, knowing who the visitor was before her eyes focused on him. She grasped his hands and greeted him warmly. "So nice to have you back."

"Nice to be back," he replied, squeezing Elizabeth's hand.

"You look a bit thin, though," Mrs. Harrington observed. "Must be tired after such a long trip." Then, turning to Elizabeth, she added, "You two go to the parlor. I'll get some tea and cookies."

The three of them talked for well over an hour. Richard explained that the frontier was not the dangerous place pictured by many where a raging, hide-and-seek battle was going on at all times in a forest crawling with bloodthirsty savages. Elizabeth and her mother were intrigued by the story of his Wyandotte friend and amused at the design of Richard's buckskins. They thought it would be exciting to visit an Indian village.

When the conversation turned to Fredericksburg, he was pleased to learn his father had regained his stamina and cheerful outlook and was farming effectively with seasonal hired help. Twice as they talked, Mrs. Harrington alluded to their wedding, indicating most of Elizabeth's friends expected it to take place soon. This troubled Richard, and although he tried to hide it, his concern was noticed by Elizabeth.

The sun was dropping below the horizon when Richard started up the Locke driveway covering the last hundred yards of his long journey. His father had just finished eating and was coming outside to sit on a bench in front of the little house where he could enjoy the tranquility of a warm evening. Sam studied the form approaching him, squinting to concentrate the sight of eyes that were becoming harder to focus.

Richard remembered his father's past seizure and waited until he was a few feet away before calling out. "Hello, Father!" he said in a voice confirming the elder Locke's deduction his son had come home.

"My son!" Sam declared, taking a few steps forward to grasp Richard's outstretched hand.

Richard dropped his pack to the ground. Then the two men embraced for a long moment before stepping back to look at one another and note the tears that had welled up in each other's eyes.

"Sure glad to see ya, Son," Mr. Locke confessed. "I knew you could handle yourself. But there's a lot of untamed country out there."

"It really wasn't bad," Richard said convincingly. "But it's nice to be back."

Sam was pleased to hear that. Maybe now, his son would stay put. "How about something to eat?" he asked.

"I ate in town, but could stand a little more."

"Come on in," Sam beckoned, opening the door to the little log building. "Got some pork and beans that must still be warm. We can make up some tea, too."

Nothing inside the cabin had changed since Richard had last seen it, and he was impressed how neat his father kept it. He sensed the loneliness isolated living brought, but knew his father had the ability to adapt to adversity. Besides, recalling how devoted his parents were to each other, he knew Sam would never entertain the notion of remarrying.

It was the time of year between heavy work periods on the farm. Crops had been planted but were not high enough to weed, and hay was still two weeks from mowing. Richard assisted with the few daily chores and helped to mend fences and refasten loose boards on the buildings. He liked doing these tasks, sometimes halting to recall events of the past that had changed the land from a wild, wooded area to a fine, productive farm and to enjoy the nostalgia that swept over him. Occasionally, when he mentioned an episode to his father, they discussed it briefly and chuckled as it was reviewed in retrospect. And when he walked out to the large oak where he and Linda had experimented with each other's body, he looked at the dead, flattened grass and wondered where she was and if she remembered. It all seemed so long ago.

He spent long periods with his father, discussing the Braddock Road, Fort Pitt, and Detroit. The elder Locke was impressed with the accomplishments of his son, and when Richard presented him with a wolf skin, he fastened it to the wall so it would be readily seen by everyone who entered. It made Richard feel proud of what he had done.

Sam was grateful Richard had been befriended by such a capable frontiersman as Flip, but expressed concern about Naseeka and the Wyandottes. Except for the few Indians who lived near Fredericksburg, he had never met any, and since they were not part of an organized tribe, he didn't have to deal with them. He formed the impression, however, that they were savages who, regardless of how friendly they became, could revert back to their wild, lawless state.

On Saturday evening, Richard sat on the bench in front of the house with his father enjoying the last rays of a setting sun. The thought of getting married troubled him. It would disrupt the time schedule he wished to follow, but remembering the tearful farewell of last summer, he was afraid Elizabeth would not wait another year. "You know," he began, "Elizabeth wants to get married this summer."

His father did not appear surprised or concerned, but continued to look straight ahead at a large heron flying up the Rappahannock. He had heard it mentioned in town, but decided to wait for his son to tell him. "So I've heard," he said calmly. "Nice girl. She'll make a good wife."

"Well," said Richard, speaking hesitantly, "I'm not sure I'm ready."

"Would work out real good," Mr. Locke continued, as Richard sensed a repressed enthusiasm in his voice. "We got time to build a nice house the other side of the barn afore winter. We could work the farm together and split the take right down the middle." He paused a moment, then added, "And later on, the whole thing would be yours."

Although Richard enjoyed the safety of life on his father's farm and appreciated sleeping in a bed and shaving with a razor instead of a hunting knife, there was something about the frontier that beckoned him. He still remembered the satisfaction he and his father felt when they cleared a piece of land and harvested its first crop. He yearned to do the same thing himself, to relish the gratification of taming a plot of wild, unharnessed land and making it produce for him. Detroit offered such an opportunity, and he was certain he could do it. He wanted to be sure, however, he had enough money to buy seed and equipment for a good start.

He slept better that night, having shared the concern he felt. The next morning, in the little chapel he'd attended as a boy, he went to services with his father to seek spiritual guidance in the decision he had to make. In the afternoon he took a buggy to town, stopping several times to chat with friends he hadn't seen for some time. One of them informed him of the attention Elizabeth received from the handsome Philadelphian at the box social.

Elizabeth had been waiting each day since he'd left her on Thursday. She thought he would return in a day or two. When he hadn't appeared by Saturday evening, she became very distressed and cried most of the night, but when he arrived Sunday afternoon, she felt certain it was in answer to a prayerful appeal she'd made in church that morning. So eager was she to see him, she ran out onto the porch instead of waiting coyly, as she had in the past, until he came to the door.

They drove slowly through heavy traffic, passing several new houses as they made their way up to the overlook. Hitching the horse to a sapling, they walked a short distance through the trees and sat on a log. Elizabeth knew Richard's moods very well and sensed he was troubled. She took his hand in hers and held it in her lap. The sun was shining and the air calm, but north of town a storm was gathering. Streaks of lightning were stabbing out from the black, churning clouds, and she could hear the distant rumble of thunder. "Looks like a storm coming," she said to get a conversation started.

"Won't come here. They always go east," Richard stated confidently, maintaining an attitude of coolness as he watched the lightning flashes.

Elizabeth was puzzled and dismayed. She knew the matter of their wedding date bothered him because she had noticed his reaction when it was mentioned Thursday, but it was not a problem that couldn't be settled between two people who knew each other as well as they did. Pulling his hand to her bosom so he faced her, she looked directly into his eyes. "I love you, Richard," she said tenderly. "I want you for my husband."

"Even if I'm not a classy dresser from Philadelphia?" he questioned aloofly.

"Oh, that," she said, exhaling a sigh of relief. "He was a nobody and meant absolutely nothing to me." She paused, then said, "Besides, he thought he was a godsend to the women."

A tight smile broke across Richard's face. "I love you, my darling. I want to marry you."

She sighed, smiled, and held his hand even closer. Since his love appeared as strong as ever, she pressed on. "Well then, should we set a date?"

He looked off to the north again. "That would be all right, but let's set it for next year."

"Why next year?" she asked, elation draining from her voice as wrinkles of disappointment gathered on her forehead. "I love you! I need you! I want you now!"

He looked at her again. "I think I should earn more money. One more season like the last and I'll have enough to give us a good start."

"I don't care about a good start!" she said, rearing back to demonstrate the sincerity of her protest. "I'm not proud. I'm not afraid to work or to bear your children. I'll help you earn anything you want. We can do it together and take whatever God grants us. I just want to be with you wherever you are!"

"My father said we could build a house on his farm and work it with him," Richard said, his voice showing relief as he pulled her to her feet and placed his arms about her shoulders.

Putting her arms around his waist, she looked up at him and said softly, "Your father's farm, Detroit, farming, trapping—I don't care. Do anything you want. Just take me with you, and we can do it together."

"All right," Richard agreed, kissing her on the nose. "Let me figure out what's best, and we'll get married and do it."

Tears filled her eyes and spilled down her cheeks as he vigorously kissed and embraced her. Her lips were being bruised and she could hardly breathe, but it didn't matter. When she felt his passion rising, she whispered, "Do you want to take pleasure with me now?"

"Let's save that until after the wedding," he replied, kissing her again. "We don't want any worries beforehand."

She placed her head against his arm as he turned to walk her back to the buggy.

———————◆———————

Sam Locke would have liked to see his son marry and reside on the farm the two of them had worked so hard to carve from the raw countryside, but he also understood the young man's innate pride and desire to build a life of his own. And Richard was aware of his father's expectation and appreciated the elder Locke's discretion in not applying undue influence toward the decision.

Since he would always be welcome to return to his father's farm, Richard decided he would try to establish himself at Detroit. He was certain he could do it, especially if he obtained one of the farms abandoned by the French, and he could also supplement his income by trapping. Besides, if he didn't try it now, he would never have the opportunity to do it.

"But how safe is it?" his father questioned. "Heard terrible things the French and Indians did to English families."

"The British are in complete control now," Richard said. "They have a string of forts that guarantee protection to all the king's subjects." He paused. "And don't forget, Flip and I spent the winter living in the forest among them."

The Harringtons were reluctant to have their only daughter, whom they'd carefully raised, groomed, and educated, leave, and she was not *just* leaving Fredericksburg, but civilization. However, she would have it no other way, and when Richard assured them he would take good care of her, they consented to let her go. Nevertheless, in the back of their minds they hoped that, after enduring frontier hardships for a year or two, the young couple would return to Fredericksburg and settle down to a pleasant life in Virginia.

———————◆———————

Elizabeth Mary Harrington and Richard Edward Locke were married at two o'clock on the afternoon of Wednesday, July 8th, 1761, before seventy persons in the little white Congregational church of

Fredericksburg. They spoke their vows before the Reverend Alvin Sawyer, who afterwards would duly record the event in the church annals. It was a brief ceremony attended by family and close friends who had known them for many years.

Sarah Harrington sat in the front pew beside her husband, occasionally dabbing her eyes with a lace-edged handkerchief. Elizabeth was her only child and she would miss her, but she was proud of how striking the young lady looked in the white satin dress she'd made for her. It was designed from one she'd remembered seeing in Philadelphia. It had a floor-length flared skirt, slit front neck, and standing collar tied with a long, soft bow. She'd made it with long, cuffed sleeves, a fitted bodice, and a narrow belt to accent Elizabeth's tiny waist.

Although Richard was raised on a farm, Sarah was pleased with the way he was dressed. She thought his white shirt, with ruffles on the sleeves and front, contrasted nicely with his brown oxford cloth vested suit. He also wore a large brown tie, tan stockings, and dark brown, leather shoes.

When Richard reached into his pocket for the wedding ring, Sarah looked over at Sam Locke who had been soberly watching the ceremony from the far end of the pew. His face suddenly lit up when he saw the gold band he had hammered and carved from two newly minted guineas. After his son slipped it onto Elizabeth's finger, Sarah noted he was still smiling and his eyes glistened. Now she was sure he felt glad about the marriage.

Elizabeth was a picture of happiness as she held the arm of her husband while they made their way to the reception in the tree shaded backyard of the church. She was completely at ease, enjoying the excitement of the event. Richard, however, was nervous, feeling slightly embarrassed by the procedure. He was especially abashed when a matron cautioned, "Be gentle with her," and later, when a man with a sly smile winked and said, "May you have a long and fruitful marriage."

For the rest of the week they lived with the Harringtons. Each day, while Elizabeth packed the necessities they planned to take to Detroit, Richard rode out to the farm to assist his father. He felt it was better than sitting idly about the Harringtons' house.

Although Sam Locke was disappointed Richard was going away, he was proud to have reared a son with the initiative and foresight to know what he wanted to do, where he wanted to go, and how he planned to get there. Besides, he, like the Harringtons, thought that, after expending some his youthful energy on the rugged frontier, Richard would return and take up residence on his farm.

Richard was certain he could establish himself near Detroit and take advantage of the unlimited opportunities that existed there, but when he thought of Elizabeth living with him, he was concerned about her. She had never worked on a farm and had not engaged in hard, manual labor. Although she expressed her determination to stand by his side, he wondered if she realized what she faced.

Chapter 9

Mohawk Trail

Sunday dawn broke early with the fiery rays of a brilliant sun shooting upward from a tree-crested horizon to probe the cloudless sky and signal the beginning of another hot, humid day. Mr. Harrington had awakened an hour before when several roosters began crowing and mockingbirds started their noisy chattering. Still drowsy, he descended the back steps and slowly made his way to the brick oven, digging for the tinderbox in his pocket as he went. He'd built the oven the second year they were in the house so his wife would not have to do her baking in the hot kitchen during the warm summer months. Sheltered in the shade of a large, stately elm, it was constructed with a fancy cast iron door that had been shipped all the way from Philadelphia.

Mrs. Harrington, wearing a starched, neatly ironed, blue apron, joined him shortly after he severed the head from a large goose purchased from a neighbor two days before. Not wanting to soil its clean gray and white feathers, she waited as he held it at arm's length until the thrashing and bleeding subsided. When he tied off its neck and hung it from a clothesline pole, she began plucking it.

First, she selected six large, stiff feathers to save for writing quills. Then she removed the rest, along with the down, and stuffed them into linen bags to keep for pillows, quilts and comforters. After a quick singeing with a firebrand, she placed the heavy bird on a table to remove its entrails and complete the cleaning process so it could be stuffed with apples, grapes, and bread.

She put it into a large pan, covered it with a butter-soaked cloth, and slid it into the heated oven. Grabbing the sacks of down and feathers and picking up a pan filled with fat cut from the goose, she returned to the house. The sacks would be stored in the garret, and she would render the fat and add it to the crock she had been saving for Elizabeth. Young wives, she knew, used a lot of it during the first year they were married. Besides, she wasn't sure how many ducks and geese were available at Detroit.

◆

Sam Locke arrived at the church a few minutes early and was standing beside his buggy in the shade of a large sycamore when Richard, holding Elizabeth's hand, approached. Sam was wearing the dark blue suit, black tricorn hat, and white stockings he'd bought for the wedding. Although his clean-shaven, weathered face was beginning to crease and his brown hair was graying at the temples, his body was still lean, wiry, and ramrod straight.

"Hello, Father," Richard began, his face beaming. He was proud of his father, not only because he was trim and handsome, but because of his even temper, keen judgment, and seasoned wisdom. After his experience on the frontier and their discussions during the past weeks, he appreciated his father more than ever, and he understood the courage it had taken for him to leave England, never to see friends and relatives again. Looking back, he remembered it as a hard life, but also a good life, and he felt his father had given him the necessary spirit to go to Detroit.

"Hello, Son," his father replied, tipping the ashes from his pipe before tucking it into his pocket. "And Elizabeth," he continued, lifting his hat and nodding to his new daughter-in-law. Although he was not well acquainted with her, he had known her family for years and admired her femininity and beauty.

"Hello, Mr. Locke," Elizabeth replied. Her mother had taught her a man must initiate conversation on such occasions. She was pleased he came, even though he was reluctant to do so. On this last Sunday in Fredericksburg, she wanted all the family to attend services before going to the Locke farm for the outdoor dinner.

Arthur and Sarah Harrington walked up, greeted the three with a handshake, and spoke briefly of the nice weather for the planned outing. Then they led them to the family pew not far from the altar.

Reverend Sawyer began his sermon, "Will You Be Ready When the Lord Calls," in a very vigorous and demonstrative manner. Soon the heat and humidity made him perspire profusely, so he reduced the forcefulness of his delivery. Still, the task was too much to endure. Sarah noticed that the congregation was noticeably relieved when he cut his message short and promised to present the last half at a later date.

After leaving the church, the congregation stood in small clusters exchanging greetings and engaging in discussions with those they had not seen since the previous Sunday. Their attention focused on Richard and Elizabeth. Most had known them for years, many had attended their wedding, and all but a few knew of their upcoming trip. Several expressed an interest, some a desire, to go with them to Detroit.

"Come along," Richard urged, certain none were willing to start over again somewhere else.

Several responded by saying, "Sure sounds good," or "I would've fifteen yar ago," or "If 'tweren't fer the kids, I'd be right with ye."

As each moved on, Richard, with Elizabeth clinging to his arm, nodded he understood. Afterwards, he turned to Elizabeth and quietly said, "Wishful thinkers."

Reverend Sawyer, his threadbare, broad white collar contrasting with his black suit in the bright sunlight, came over to wish them well and give them his blessing for a safe journey and a bountiful new life. "We'll keep track o' ye through yer parents, and we'll all be a-prayin' fer ye," he concluded, shaking their hands with both of his.

Richard and Elizabeth climbed into Mr. Locke's buggy, and the three of them started for the farm. The Harringtons waved and called out, "We'll see you in an hour!"

Elizabeth smiled and nodded.

Feeling strange in the Locke kitchen, Elizabeth, still dressed in the red and white flowered dress she wore to church, was assisted by Richard. He lit the fireplace, then found a kettle for the corn Mr. Locke was picking in the field. She felt more relaxed after being kissed on the nose and shown the location of other items needed to prepare the vegetables her mother had instructed her to cook. "Help yourself to anything you need," Richard stated, patting her on the seat. "And if you can't find it, let me know."

She blushed and slapped him playfully on the arm.

Sam Locke stared at the plank table before covering it with a checked cotton cloth. Over the years it had been used for everything from checker playing to hog butchering. Two days before, looking forward to the outdoor dinner, he'd scrubbed it with soap and water and placed it beneath a tree in the apple orchard not far from the house. Then he examined the benches to be certain there were no loose slivers to injure his guests.

He spread the cloth and placed a blue milk glass vase filled with irises and roses at its center. Then he sat down on a bench with his back against the table. For several minutes he looked out over the fields of growing corn and wheat, thinking about his situation in life. Although he was not happy about his son leaving the safety of Fredericksburg for the dangers of the frontier, he was pleased by Richard's selection of a stable, intelligent wife. He knew she would have much to learn about the rigors of living in the wilderness but felt confident she, guided by his strong and determined son, could manage. He had trained his son well, reared him to be independent and self sufficient, and he had taught him the necessary phases of farming from the clearing of land to harvesting the crop.

As he sat, he reviewed the traits in his son that he himself possessed. Smiling, he rose to his feet and said, "By God, that's my boy all right."

Feeling underfoot in the kitchen, Richard picked up the wooden bucket from the little worktable beside the fireplace and went outside to fill it with water. Walking toward the well, he was joined by his father.

"Sure good water," his father said, lifting the hinged wooden cover from the rock-lined hole.

"Never tasted better," Richard agreed, hanging the wire handle over a forked hook at the end of a long, slender pole. He lowered it into the well and, with a snap of his wrists, made the bucket tip and scoop itself full.

"I look at these things and can hardly believe we did them so well," his father said, lowering the cover. "Hell, this thing'll last a hundred years." As they started toward the house, he added, "That's one of the last things we worked on together afore you went to work in town."

"Yah," Richard agreed, feeling a tinge of guilt about leaving his father alone.

They took a seat on the bench outside the front door to await the Harringtons and talk about the trip to Detroit. Initially, Richard had planned to go by way of Fort Pitt, but several days earlier after discussing it with his father, he decided the longer Mohawk Trail was safer. Besides, there was no road beyond Fort Pitt for the horse and wagon Sam was giving him.

"You catch the Mohawk Trail at Albany," Sam said. "Good roads that far. And the trail's supposed to be safe. Takes you right to Fort Niagara."

Richard nodded. "They have ships going from there to Detroit." The thought of the *Huron* and *Michigan* excited him.

"I've put a few little sacks of starter seed in your wagon," Mr. Locke said, remembering how he'd borrowed from the neighbors when he first came from England.

"Thanks, Father," Richard said gratefully. "They'll help." He thought for a moment, then said, "I think I can buy most things at Detroit. The British are trying to get people to settle there. Going to give me some equipment."

When Sam heard the mention of buying, he interrupted. "And another thing," he said, turning to face his son. "Get rid of that paper money as soon as you can. The only sure money is hard coin." He jerked his head to emphasize the point. "Go to a bank in New York and change it for silver crowns and gold guineas."

"I will," Richard assured him.

Just then the Harringtons turned into the driveway and slowed their filly to a brisk walk.

Richard called out so Elizabeth could hear, "Your mother and father's here!"

Elizabeth, wearing an apron, came outside and stood between the two men. Her face registered a broad smile.

After the men carried the food inside from the buggy, Mrs. Harrington joined her daughter in the kitchen. Her presence contributed an air of authority that gave Elizabeth more confidence. It was not that Elizabeth lacked skill or knowledge, but the presence of her mother, with her experience in similar preparations for the church and school, made the young Mrs. Locke feel everything was going according to plan.

The three men walked into a field of chest-high corn. "Gonna be a good crop," Richard said, kicking a clod of dark gray soil that had been lifted by a recent cultivating.

"Yes, the Lord has looked favorably upon it," his father agreed, reluctant to accept credit for it.

Mr. Harrington looked at the lush leaves that were being slowly rippled by a light breeze. "Well, the Lord may be entitled to some of the honor, Sam," he said, looking Mr. Locke in the eye as he patted him on the back, "but it was your grit and sweat that changed a tangled woods into this."

Sam smiled and nodded. "Thanks, Arthur," he replied, placing a hand on Richard's shoulder. "I guess we did do a lot o' work."

Richard said nothing, but enjoyed the warm feeling of recognition for the years of toil he'd put into the transformation. He knew his father appreciated his help even though compliments and praise were given sparingly. Looking off into the distance, he saw the large oak at the far end of the field, and again, he wondered what had become of Linda.

His thoughts were suddenly interrupted by the sound of Mrs. Harrington's voice. "Time to eat!" she called.

At the table, Elizabeth and Richard sat on one side, their parents on the other. With heads bowed, they held hands as Arthur gave the blessing. It was long, thanking the Almighty for the food, love, friendship, and bountiful conditions in which they lived. He concluded with, "May we beseech thee to grant us the opportunity to gather together again in the not too distant future. Amen."

"Amen!" the others responded.

When the bowed heads were raised, Richard noted tears in the eyes of the women.

"Well," said Mrs. Harrington, trying to draw attention to the food as she lifted the net-covered fly protectors from the dishes. "Let's not allow things to get cold."

Elizabeth, still holding Richard's hand, squeezed it before letting go to pass the corn. She had removed her apron and tried to appear fresh and cool, but the hot kitchen had moistened her hair at the temples.

Richard looked at her admiringly. She appeared so feminine and beautiful, he thought.

"These fly covers were made by Elizabeth," Mrs. Harrington said, wanting to impress Mr. Locke with her daughter's abilities. "Made them for my birthday."

"She knows a lot about housekeeping," Sam replied, smiling as he looked from Sarah to Elizabeth. Then he turned to Richard, "Son, you've got a mighty fine wife here."

"She sure is," Richard agreed, patting Elizabeth on the back.

The attention caused Elizabeth's face to redden.

After a dessert of blackberry pie and tea, Mrs. Harrington told Richard to take Elizabeth for a walk while she cleared the table and stored the leftover food in the house. "Your father will have enough to last a few days," she told Richard as he helped Elizabeth to her feet.

Taking Elizabeth by the hand, Richard led her from the orchard to a pasture field behind the barn, tactfully staying upwind from the outhouse hidden behind a large lilac bush. He lifted the hickory loop from a pole gate, and they walked across a bumpy field covered with grass that had been cropped short by foraging animals.

"I like your father," Elizabeth said, stepping gingerly around some animal droppings.

"Yes," Richard agreed. "He's a nice person. Has a big heart."

She stopped and looked around. "Where's the cows?" she asked. She wanted to learn about farming.

"Back near the woods where it's cooler. They return around milking time."

Elizabeth halted suddenly, then squatted down to look at three speckled eggs in an unprotected killdeer nest. "May I touch them?" she asked, looking up at Richard.

"You shouldn't. Sometimes the mother will abandon it."

"Do you think she's around?"

"Certainly. She's watching us now. Probably not far away."

Elizabeth rose to her feet and looked around. She was impressed with the farm. It was so serene, and it gave her a much closer feeling to nature than she had experienced before. She was glad she'd married a farmer.

They sauntered back toward the house and walked up the narrow footpath to the feathery-leafed locust sheltering the graves of Martha and Mrs. Locke. Holding hands, they stood motionless with heads bowed and looked down at the marble headstones. Neatly trimmed grass grew around and between the graves, but the recently raked mounds looked as if the burials had occurred but a few hours before. Small, blooming geraniums, white for Martha, red for Fanny, grew at the base of the markers. The inscriptions gave their names and dates of birth and death.

Richard broke the silence. "It doesn't seem that long ago," he said quietly, still looking down at the graves.

Elizabeth leaned her head against his arm. She had not experienced the death of a loved one, but her feeling for Richard made her heart ache so painfully that she pressed her hand against her chest. "They may have left us for now, but we will all be together again some day," she said, her voice cracking with the last words.

Richard remembered how his father had led him and his grieving mother away when they buried Martha. He turned Elizabeth around, placed an arm about her shoulder, and started down the path. Tears were flowing across her cheeks and soaking into the bosom of her dress.

◆

Richard's father had tied a sleek bay horse to a tree near the table where he and the Harringtons sat waiting for the young couple to return. The brown, mixed breed filly was plump, neatly groomed, and newly shod. She was attached to a lightweight, covered wagon which had black thills and wheels and a dark green box trimmed with yellow pinstriping. It still smelled of fresh paint and new canvas. He had purchased it two weeks before but had not picked it up until the previous evening.

When Richard and Elizabeth saw the wagon, they both gasped. They knew Mr. Locke planned to give them a horse and wagon, but did not think the wagon would be new or the horse of such fine quality. Standing beside the table, they looked first at Mr. Locke, then at the rig.

"The Briggs Wagon Works, Newark, New Jersey," Richard read aloud, eyeing the circular emblem on the side of the wagon box.

He peered into the rear opening and looked at the ash bows supporting the cover, then glanced at the spring mounted seat at the far end. His father walked up beside him and pointed to several sacks along one side. "Them two big ones is oats for the horse," he said. "The others is starter seed. Grain and corn." He hesitated for a moment, then pointed again. "Except the far one. That's salt."

"You didn't have to do all that," Richard said as he walked around to examine the horse.

"I wanted to," his father said determinedly. "Can you use it?"

"Oh, sure. Actually, it's much better than I would've got myself."

"Take the best, Son. Take the best," the father warned. "It could mean the difference someday."

He slapped Richard on the back and turned to walk away. Elizabeth grabbed his arm and kissed him on the cheek. He looked over at the Harringtons and smiled.

◆

It was nearly ten o clock when Richard drove the loaded rig up to the ferry ramp. Insisting the weight be kept to a minimum, the only furniture he had packed was Elizabeth's bed and chest of drawers. They were taking a large quantity of bedding and clothing Elizabeth and her mother had made over the years and a small maple rocking chair Mr. Harrington had given her on her third birthday. The heaviest item was a box filled with dishes and utensils placed directly over the rear axle. In it he had hidden their money, except for a small amount carried on his person. Beneath the seat, which Sarah had padded and covered with a woolen coach blanket, they'd positioned boxes of food, shot, powder, and the cooking and eating utensils to use along the way.

The Harringtons followed the wagon in their buggy and drew up to a small tree. Arthur looped the reins over a limb, then told Sarah to stand where Sam Locke was waiting. He checked the ferry ramp, then directed Richard to drive aboard.

When Richard drove off on the other shore and halted the rig on the gravel road leading north, Elizabeth, sitting beside him, quivered noticeably. She had been looking forward to this moment for weeks, but the sudden realization that the moment of parting had arrived frightened her. For the first time in her life, she would be separated from her parents. They would no longer be available to direct, protect, and advise. Terrible thoughts of loneliness and fear raced through her mind.

By the time Richard stood waiting to assist her to the ground, however, she had regained the strength and determination to carry on. She no longer needed the care and protection of her parents, she reasoned, for she was a capable, able-bodied adult and was married to a strong, experienced man.

They gathered in a small circle for a final farewell. Richard kissed Mrs. Harrington on the cheek. She threw her arms about his shoulders and, as tears streamed down her face, drew him close and spoke into his ear. "Take good care of her. She's all we've got."

"I will," he promised. "I love her, too."

He shook the hand of Mr. Harrington who, with tear-filled eyes, managed to force a smile but could not speak.

His father stepped forward and grasped his hand firmly. Looking his son squarely in the eyes, he said, "Goodbye, Son. Good luck. I hope you'll come back to live with us again."

Richard looked at his father's face, a face that was furrowed by experience, age, and sorrow, but one that radiated strength and confidence. "We just might do that," he replied.

Elizabeth was embraced and kissed by the men, then she turned to her mother. After waiting momentarily, they threw their arms around each other and convulsed with audible sobs as tears streamed down their faces.

Richard looked at his father and shook his head. He gently pulled the women apart, then firmly led his wife to the wagon and helped her climb aboard. Placing one foot on the wheel hub, he looked back at his father. His father nodded.

Forcing themselves to look straight ahead until the wagon had rolled forward a hundred yards, Elizabeth and Richard turned their heads to look back. Framed in the arched rear opening of the wagon stood the three parents. Mrs. Harrington was twisting a moist, white handkerchief in her hands, while the arms of the men hung limply at their sides. All five raised their hands for a final farewell. Then Elizabeth and Richard looked at each other and smiled. Although her cheeks were still damp, Elizabeth's tears had stopped flowing. Richard kissed her warmly on the mouth. He knew his wife was ready to begin the long journey.

Elizabeth looked back again and saw her mother still standing, waving the handkerchief. The men were walking slowly toward the ferry.

◆

Late in the afternoon, Richard drove the wagon into a grove of butternut trees fifteen miles north of Fredericksburg. "Are you sure you don't want to stay at an inn?" he asked, looking questioningly at Elizabeth. He had asked before as they passed taverns along the way.

"No," Elizabeth replied, grasping his arm firmly and pressing her cheek against his shoulder. "This is the first chance I've had to spend a night with you with nobody else around. Besides, how am I ever going to learn to camp out if we don't get started at it?"

"That's fine with me," Richard agreed, smiling at her determination. He was elated at the thought of them being alone.

"And another thing," she grinned. "We've got to use up that stew and smoked meat mother gave us."

"And the hardboiled eggs and bread," he added, recalling bags of buns, cookies, and jam Mrs. Harrington had prepared for them.

As Richard let the horse drink from a little stream, he wondered about bandits. He had heard of them but never met anyone who'd encountered them. He'd be careful.

He hobbled the horse so it could graze, then assembled a ring of stones. "Wait until the fire dies down all the way," he cautioned as Elizabeth got the stew and bread from the wagon. "Then you won't burn yourself and the kettle won't get smoked up."

Richard was pleased with his bride's eagerness to learn. He showed her things he'd learned from Flip—to wipe dishes with dead grass before washing them in a stream and to dispose of leftover food so wild animals would not be attracted to the campsite.

She watched as he loaded the musket with fresh powder, then walked beside him as he got the horse and tied it to a tree.

"Must be near enough to hear its breathing during the night," he explained. "We'll know if she's being bothered by anything."

They sat down on a short log beside the ash-coated remains of the fire. Richard placed his arm around her shoulders, drawing her near so her head was cradled against his chest. He kissed the back of her neck and smelled the fragrance of her hair. For some time they sat cuddled together, staring at the little blue tongues of flame that still issued from the dying embers. Crickets chirruped, a fox barked, and the call of a whippoorwill became loud, then faded into the distance.

Elizabeth broke the silence. "What time do you go to bed on the trail?" she asked, without looking up.

"Quite early," Richard replied, the action of his chin causing movement among the waves of her hair. "It makes for an early start in the morning so we don't have to press so hard to get our distance."

"How far will we go tomorrow?" she asked, looking at him.

"Probably thirty miles along here. Road is good." He stroked her hair with his hand. "Best we make it while we can."

"Maybe we'd better go to bed, then," Elizabeth said, nestling against him.

"You go ahead. I'll join you in a little while."

Elizabeth lingered a few minutes, enjoying the warm, secure feeling she felt. The thought of her parents and home flashed through her mind, but at the moment she was too enthused about her new life to let it bother her. She would be a capable partner and helpful frontier wife.

Wanting this first night away from home to be special, she had prepared for it for several days. After removing her clothing and carefully folding each item in the dark wagon, she slipped into a pink flannel, ankle-length nightgown that had been packed in a box containing lavender sachet. Then she brushed her hair and quickly braided it.

Lying back, she scooped a dab of goose grease and inserted it, making certain it was evenly distributed. Although she wanted children, she didn't want to conceive the first year if she could avoid it. It would be a difficult period, and she wanted to devote her time and strength toward helping Richard get established.

As she lay quietly waiting for the lavender to hide the odor of goose grease, she could hear the soft shuffling of footsteps. Richard had explained the precautions that had to be taken on the trail, so as she listened she visualized each task. He made sure the horse was properly tethered, scooped a ring of sand around the fire, and blocked a wheel so a gust of wind would not move the wagon.

Although she sensed a tinge of anxiety about going to the frontier, she felt a confidence building that should allay any fear by the time they reached Detroit. Anyway, at the moment she was cozy and secure.

"Are you settled?" Richard asked, pushing aside the flap.

"Ready," she replied, sitting up. She could feel her breasts firm and her nipples extend and tingle as they rubbed against the fabric of her gown.

◆

When they entered the outskirts of New York, the overcast sky that had hidden the sun most of the day darkened and a light drizzle began to fall. It was a warm rain, being driven by a mild, southeast wind against the rear of the wagon. The canvas top, extending over the seat, kept them from getting wet.

The filly, which Elizabeth named Molly after a horse owned by a family friend, didn't seem to mind the rain that soaked her sleek, rounded back turning it a dark brown. She walked proudly at a brisk cadence holding her head high and ears perkily upright, occasionally splashing water from one of the many depressions dotting the gravel road. She appeared to sense that the spacious grounds and fine homes she was passing signaled the approach to a busy city of people, dogs, and horses.

"We'll find a roadhouse for the night," Richard said, squinting as he looked up the tree lined road at an approaching buggy. "Maybe they'll have a stable for Molly, too."

"You don't have to," Elizabeth replied, watching the buggy, now only a few yards away. "We can make do." She would have liked to get inside for the night, since making a meal inside the wagon would be a problem, but she knew there would be times when she had to, and was prepared to accept it. However, the shelter and warmth of an inn seemed very inviting. And there was Molly. She was growing fond of the horse and didn't want her to spend the night in the rain on a short tether.

Richard waved his arm to flag down the buggy. Its lone occupant, a well dressed, robust gentleman with puffy, rose-colored cheeks and reddened eyes, squinted at them. "Is there an inn ahead?" Richard shouted as the man reined to a halt.

"Bout half mile," the man replied stiffly. "The Eddystone Roadhouse, 'tis called."

"Thank ye," Richard said, nodding his head gratefully as he flipped the reins on Molly's back.

The man tipped his gray beaver hat without replying, then drove off.

"We've been on the road nigh on ten days without gettin' under cover," Richard said firmly, indicating his mind was made up. "It'll be good for us to get in a bed again."

"If you want," Elizabeth acquiesced. "But we could manage."

A heavy rain was falling when Richard turned Molly into the graveled driveway and reined to a halt at the entrance of the large, two story, half-timbered building. Gusts of wind whipped the branches back and forth on the huge oaks and maples that surrounded the stately structure.

"Hold the lines," he directed Elizabeth, handing her the reins. "I'll go in and see what they have."

236

Opening the thick, varnished oak door, he stepped inside and quickly surveyed the room. Several gentlemen were sitting at tables near windows drinking from tankards and watching the rain beat against multicolored panes in the leaded frames. Their conversation halted briefly as they turned to see who had entered. When they saw Richard walk toward the man behind the bar, they resumed talking.

"Have you a room for my wife and myself?" Richard inquired, placing his hands on the smooth surface of the walnut bar.

The tavern section was large, occupying the front half of the lower floor, its dark, paneled walls decorated with pictures of hunting scenes and hung with antlers and animal heads. Several reflector lamps were burning in the storm darkened section of the room.

The bartender, a short, middle-aged, balding man with a pale complexion and long sideburns, was dressed in a dark vested suit and an open collar shirt. He eyed Richard sternly, then replied, "See the lady over there." He pointed toward an alcove containing tables covered with linen cloth and set with dishes.

Richard turned the corner in the alcove and was met by a slender, plainly dressed woman. She had dark, penetrating eyes, a long, pointed nose, and a chisel-shaped chin. They appeared held together by a tight-jawed determination that created pucker creases around her thin, pale lips. Her braided, graying hair was brushed severely upward and wound into a tight coil on the top of her head. "You want a room?" she asked coldly, her eyes searching him from head to toe.

"Yes, ma'am. For me and my missus," Richard replied, nodding politely. He was thinking she must be one of those tight-assed blue noses Flip had told him about.

Turning to look up the carpeted stairway behind her, she statedly flatly, "I think we 'ave a room upstairs for ye."

"Thank you. I'll fetch my wife," Richard said, turning toward the front door.

"Guests use the side door!" the woman snapped, pointing to the far side of the alcove.

Elizabeth, having placed their overnight needs in a carpetbag, was brought in and introduced to the proprietress. The woman looked her up and down as she had Richard, then directed her toward the room. "We eat supper promptly at six and breakfast promptly at seven," the woman called out. "You'll 'ear the bell."

Richard went outside to tend the horse and wagon. He was met by a colored stableboy who was leading Molly to the shelter of an adjacent building.

"Have room for the wagon inside, too?" Richard asked.

"Yes'm," the boy replied. "Can set da wagon back o' da horses."

After they stabled Molly and positioned the wagon close to the rear wall, the boy began drying and brushing the horse. The care pleased Richard.

After donning a clean dress, Elizabeth combed and brushed her hair. The humid air had tightened the natural waves, so she made gentle curls like those she wore on special occasions.

Richard had been watching from behind. He spun her around, seized her about the waist, and lifted her off the floor. She placed her hands on his shoulders and pushed back. Smiling, she looked into his admiring eyes and said, "I love you." Then she kissed him warmly on the lips.

They stood at the window as the rain beat against the glass, and watched a dozen sheep contentedly chewing their cuds in a small shed below. Richard thought he heard the tinkling of a bell. He opened the door a few inches , then said, "Time to put on the oat bag."

"You'd better behave, or that woman won't feed you."

"That old biddy just might not," he replied with a forced grin.

"Richard!" Elizabeth cautioned, drawing out the last half of his name with a forceful exhale.

There were eight guests, four seated on each side of the table. Except for the proprietress, who sat at one end of the table, Elizabeth was the only female. The bartender sat at the other end. The fresh powder on the face of the woman gave her a death mask appearance. It stopped midway down her thin neck, revealing the dark complexion of her skin.

Elizabeth had been schooled in proper etiquette but felt uneasy about proceeding. She would follow her mother's advice and watch the hostess from the corner of her eye.

Richard wanted his behavior to be proper for Elizabeth's sake, so he watched his wife discreetly for guidance. The others were also confused. One man fumbled with his utensils and teacup. Another tucked his napkin into his collar beneath his chin and waited.

The proprietress scanned their faces, then lifted a silver bell from beside her plate and shook it once. Replacing the bell, she clasped her hands in her lap and bowed her head to wait for others, including those in the tavern, to do the same.

Half a minute later, which seemed like an eternity to Richard, the bell rang again, signaling the end of the silent period. Two apron-clad kitchen maids then entered with bowls of steaming food.

One gentleman, after finishing his dessert of tea, milk and bread pudding, slid his chair back so he could leave the table.

"Mr. Hedgecock, we all leave the table together," the sober-faced woman told him. She placed her hands in her lap and, sitting stiffly erect, waited for him to return his chair to its former position.

Flushed with embarrassment, he sat uneasily and fidgeted with his hands until the bell was again sounded to indicate the meal was finished.

"Breakfast will be promptly at seven," the woman said as everyone got to their feet.

Most of the men walked over to the fireplace in the tavern section and sat down in the soft, leather chairs to talk and smoke their pipes. One guest took a seat beside a lamp. He ordered a tankard of ale, then began reading from a small, hardcover book he took from his pocket.

Richard and Elizabeth returned to their room and sat, propped against the pillows on their bed. They talked about settling near Detroit. Richard's description of the Indians he had met intrigued Elizabeth.

"And I want to meet Flip," she said enthusiastically.

"You will," Richard assured her. "He'll come to see us."

Richard and Elizabeth had never seen a city the size of New York, and what they saw enthralled them. They passed through areas of elegant rural estates with great homes set back from the road and rode past clusters of modest wood, brick, and stone houses located on small plots surrounded by whitewashed picket fences.

As they continued toward the center of the city, the houses became smaller and closer together. The streets were narrower and domestic animals pastured on grass-covered commons instead of on the land occupied by the houses. The number of people walking, riding, and driving also increased until Richard had to pay strict attention to his handling of Molly.

"We must be getting close," Richard said when they arrived at a point where firmly set cobblestones covered the streets.

"Hardly wide enough for two wagons," Elizabeth observed, her voice sounding concern.

The brick and stone houses were joined together in what she thought was one continuous building that went on as far as she could see up the winding street. In a few places there was a narrow sidewalk, but mostly the inhabitants stepped from their doorsills onto the street.

The street sloped toward its center forming a shallow trench where slop buckets were emptied. To Elizabeth's sensitive nose the stench of the mid-morning heat on the accumulated swill and sewage was nauseous.

But Richard could not be distracted by it. He was looking for the bank while driving among a throng of walking people and playing children.

The street became wider in the merchant section. It permitted him to stop the wagon in front of the British Bank of New York without blocking passage. Handing the reins to Elizabeth, he took the currency from the box and tucked it into her carpetbag. Then he entered the brick building through its lustrous, black enameled door.

Elizabeth, waiting uneasily for what she thought was a very long time, noted the diversity of people who walked past. Most were of light complexion; English, she assumed, as in Fredericksburg, but there were also some with brown eyes and olive skin she thought were French or Spanish, probably sailors. A few blacks, slaves who walked several steps behind their masters, carried heavy bags in their hands or loaded baskets on their heads and shoulders, and she saw two Indians who appeared lost and confused.

The clothing she saw was as diverse as those who wore it. There was the exquisite, like that seen only on Sunday or holidays in Fredericksburg, and the plain but durable, used by the working class. But the greatest number were poor, dressed in worn, tattered, and patched garments.

She was so occupied watching people on the street that she didn't see Richard emerge from the bank. When suddenly he climbed into the wagon, it startled her. "Everything all right?" she asked, watching him slide the heavy bag under some bedding behind the seat.

"Yes, fine," he assured her, taking the reins and flipping them. "We'll put it in the box when we get out of town."

A few yards up the street, they came upon a man dressed in badly soiled, threadbare clothing sprawled against a building. His distorted, bewhiskered face and matted, dirt-caked hair rested in a pool of vomit and drool.

"The poor man must be ill," Elizabeth stated, turning to Richard with a look of alarm.

Richard realized she had not been exposed to such a level of human dissipation. "He's just drunk," he said matter-of-factly.

When he looked up, he saw two men dressed like sailors staggering toward Molly. One, with a cloth band around his head, grabbed her bridle bringing her to a halt. The other walked up to the wagon. He looked at Richard, then at Elizabeth. "Well," he said, "what do we have here?" He reeked of rum.

Richard's eyes flashed. He picked up his musket and held the muzzle a foot from the man's face. "Off with you!" he warned. "Or I'll put a lead ball in your head!"

The sailor reached up and pulled the brim of his black felt hat low on his brow. "Leave her alone, Alex," he said, turning his head toward his friend. "This man means business." Then he turned back to Richard and smiled weakly. "Just havin' a little fun."

"Get your fun somewhere else!" Richard scolded as he flipped the reins.

Elizabeth was pale and shaking. "Such awful men," she said, dabbing her face with her handkerchief.

"Better be ready for it," Richard said firmly. He was still angry about the incident. "Might run into some others."

Then, seeing two men dressed in buckskins, he pointed to them and smiled. "That's what I'll be wearing in a few days," he said enthusiastically.

As they entered the village of Albany, Richard looked at his wife. He could see the fatigue showing in her face. They had been under way for nearly a month, camping beside the roadway, cooking game over open fires, and washing their bodies and clothes in brooks and streams.

Elizabeth no longer dressed in the frilly attire she wore at the beginning, but donned a plain gray waist and long, flared skirt she stitched from coarse linen cloth brought with her. She planned to make the dresses at Detroit for use on the farm, but after seeing how practical they were for other women on the trail, she cut and sewed one while riding beside Richard. She also restyled her hair into a chignon at the nape of her neck.

Her face and arms were tanned by the sun, and she could feel a new firmness in the muscles of her back and limbs. She was weary, but knew it was not caused by physical work. It came from the bouncing ride on a rutted, hole-filled road and the boredom of traveling a trail that seemed to go on without end. She held out her hands and looked at the dry, chapped skin and broken fingernails. "Like a scullery maid," she said.

Richard placed his arms around her shoulders. "No, my darling. Those are the hands of a frontiersman's lovely wife." He kissed her on the cheek. "My mother's looked just like that most of the time."

She smiled and leaned her head against his shoulder.

Richard went into a store to buy flour and cornmeal and a sack of oats for Molly. "Where's the blacksmith shop?" he asked, handing the proprietor some money.

"Just around the corner," the man replied tersely.

While waiting for Molly to be reshod, Elizabeth watched as Richard greased the wagon wheels. Afterwards, they went to an inn across the street for a bowl of leek soup and corn biscuits.

"Good soup," Elizabeth said as they stepped out into the dusty street. Much of the fatigue had left her body.

"Would be better with some meat in it," Richard complained.

"But that wouldn't be leek soup," Elizabeth said, holding onto his arm as they walked.

A few miles outside of town, they came upon two wagons stopped in a grove of maple trees. Several people were sitting on the ground eating. One of the wagons was a large, heavily laden vehicle hitched to a massive yoke of oxen. A cow and calf tied to the rear of it swished their tails and stamped their feet to fend off a swarm of deer flies.

The other wagon was a light, horse-drawn dray loaded with sacks, kegs, and cartons. To protect it from the weather, it was covered with an undersized sheet of canvas laced down by a crisscross net of small rope.

"Hello there," Richard greeted, reining Molly to a halt.

"Hallo," replied one of the men who rose to his feet and came to the wagon. "Want ta join us?" he asked, still nibbling on a slice of cheese.

Richard turned to Elizabeth. She nodded. "Certainly," he replied. "Why not?"

After maneuvering the wagon so Molly was in the shade, Richard jumped down and assisted Elizabeth to the ground.

"Richard Locke," he said, extending his hand. "And Mrs. Locke."

"Morris. Tad Morris," the man replied, shaking Richard's hand and tipping his tricorn to Elizabeth.

A barefoot boy ran up beside him. "My boy, Jeremy," he added, looking down at his offspring.

The boy removed his broad-brimmed, floppy hat and shook Richard's hand. Then he turned and bowed to Elizabeth. "Howdy, ma'am," he said shyly.

"Pleased to meet you," Elizabeth said with a smile.

The boy forced a weak grin as his freckled face reddened.

"Got a farm up the trail a piece," Tad explained as the four of them walked slowly toward the others. "Been ta town pickin' up supplies."

He halted before a circle of people sitting on the ground drinking a thick gruel from small wooden bowls. "And this is the Coles, the John Coles," he said, turning to Richard.

"How do you do," Richard responded. "Richard and Elizabeth Locke."

A family of eight persons was in the circle. The husband appeared noticeably older than his wife. Among the six small children, one was a toddler without clothes. The man and woman looked up and nodded, then continued to sip noisily from their bowls.

Tad pointed to an open pan located on a rock where he and Jeremy had been sitting. "Got some cold tea and bread ye can 'ave if ye care ta join us," he said. "Cheese is all gone."

"Oh, thanks," Richard replied. "But we have plenty."

Elizabeth spread a cloth on the ground and set it with plates of biscuits, jam, bread, and highly spiced sausage her mother had sent with them. Richard got some water from a stream and made a pot of tea.

When they sat down to eat, the children came over and stood by them. Elizabeth, sensing they were hungry, gave them biscuits spread with jam. They quickly gobbled it up, so she went to the wagon for more.

When Mr. Cole walked over to his wagon, Elizabeth offered some food to the children's mother. The woman, heavy with child, rose slowly to her feet and wearily walked a few steps to sit beside Elizabeth.

"Thank ye," she said gratefully, forcing a smile that revealed a number of missing teeth. "Gettin' kinda tired o' movin'," she confided. "He just never seems ta want ta settle down." She sighed and shook her head. "We stay in a place a year or two and he wants ta go someplace else."

"Where are you from?" Elizabeth inquired, giving her a slice of sausage.

"Massachusetts. And afore that, Rhode Island." She chewed the sausage with difficulty, then added, "And afore that, God only knows."

"You have some nice children," Elizabeth said, trying to brighten her outlook.

"Only six livin'. Five died with lung fever or the pox." She hesitated momentarily, took another bite of sausage, then continued, "Can ye believe it? Thirty-two years old and eleven children."

Elizabeth surmised she was married at a young age to an older man who treated her like a child. Her brown hair was graying, and the tan, wrinkled skin of her face was deeply furrowed. The thread-bare linen dress she wore had been patched several times and showed heavy soil over her low-hanging, pendulous breasts.

When the men walked over to repack the wagons, Elizabeth looked at the woman's bare feet and noted her swollen, varicose ankles. "Where are you going now?" she asked.

"Up the Mohawk Valley somewhere. He don't tell me much. Just tells me what ta do."

The men agreed the three wagons would travel together, led by Tad Morris who lived in nearby Herkimer Valley. "Indians is friendly," he told Richard. "But three or four bucks might try ta scare ya into givin' 'em sunthin' if you're alone. We learned ya give 'em nuthin' unless ya get sunthin' in return. They consider it a sign of weakness if ya do."

The thought of encountering Indians stirred Elizabeth, but she hid her concern until the wagons got under way. "Do you think we'll see some savages along here?" she asked, hugging Richard's arm as she sat on the bobbing seat beside him.

"Oh, I don't know," he replied calmly. "They shouldn't give us any trouble."

Richard was concerned for their safety, but hoped others would join them before the Morris and Cole families turned off. The Mohawk Trail was more primitive than the Cumberland Trail and, from the looks of the roadbed, had less traffic. It was narrow, rutted, filled with mudholes, and frequently overgrown with grass, and the farther they got from Albany, the worse it became. He wished he had brought a second musket.

After supper they sat around a large campfire, secure in numbers and sated by food. John Cole, his steel-gray beard smeared with gravy, lit a corncob pipe, leaned back against the trunk of an oak and, after an audible gastric rumble, let roar a loud belch that echoed through the trees. "Good meal. Damned good meal," he stated, digging the heels of his heavy leather boots into the moist, humus soil.

Elizabeth winced at his crudeness, then gathered up the dishes. As she walked to the creek, she was joined by Mrs. Cole. "My heavens," Mrs. Cole began, "do you always wash yer dishes?"

"Certainly," Elizabeth said emphatically. "That's the only way to get them clean. Besides, it takes the scraps away so as not to draw the wild animals." She was proud Richard had taught her.

"I usually just wipe 'em clean in the grass. Hain't been bothered yet."

After making the parents' bed on the ground beneath the Cole wagon, the two women lifted the children so they could crawl into a pallet of rags on the inside.

Elizabeth was shocked that the children slept in such a small, filthy area that reeked of urine. She would like to have bathed them but was reluctant to offer for fear of offending Mrs. Cole.

"And don't pee the bed tonight, Peter, or I'll flail ya in the mornin'!" Mrs. Cole threatened. Then she turned to Elizabeth. "Just can't seem ta break him of the habit."

"Well, what about the little one?" Elizabeth asked.

"Oh, she does pretty well. I get her up just afore we turn in and again the first thing in the mornin'."

Returning to the fire, the two women sat on a log placed there by Jeremy. "Is this for us?" Elizabeth inquired, hesitating before sitting down.

"Yes'm," Jeremy replied. "I brought it over for you."

"Oh, thank you, Jeremy," Elizabeth said sweetly, carefully selecting a seat to avoid stubs of broken branches. She knew Jeremy was becoming fond of her.

"Woman," John Cole broke in, still puffing intermittently on his pipe. "Tad Morris here says Herkimer Valley's a good place ta settle. Thinks we oughta go there."

"Oh?" Mrs. Cole responded, showing neither surprise nor enthusiasm.

"Yup. Lotsa good land," John said. Then turning to Tad Morris, he added, "Hain't that right, Tad?"

"Well, it's a nice place," Tad assured her. "Six families there now. Some of the land ya might want don't have many trees anymore. Won't be hard ta clear." He drew up his knees and wrapped his arms around them. "And there's some young'uns fer yours ta play with."

"He says the Indians is friendly, too," John chimed in.

"Just treat 'em like Indians, and they'll behave," Tad corrected.

"Well?" John said, raising his voice. "What do ya think, woman?"

Mrs. Cole knew what she thought would have little effect on her husband's actions. "Well, it's all right, I guess," she replied meekly.

The discussion turned to the trip to Detroit. The Coles had never heard of the place. Although Tad Morris knew of it, it was so remote in his mind as to be meaningless. To them, the limit of settlement did not extend beyond the fortified outposts of Niagara and Pitt. Besides, all they wanted was a piece of land to call their own—a place to till the soil, raise animals, and bring up their families, and they didn't have to go that far to get it. These were the things their ancestors yearned for and dreamed about in the old country but were denied because of their lowly status in the social scheme of things.

"Awhile back I heard some talkin' about goin' ta Detroit," Tad said, his forehead wrinkling as he tried to recall the details. "They was taggin' along behind a supply train headed fer Niagara."

"That's what we'd like to do," Elizabeth said, her eyes lighting up as she heard of the supply train.

"But they didn't seem like farmers," Tad added quietly. they was afoot and seemed more like drifters

"Probably trappers," Richard cut in. "There's a lot of furs taken around there." He put down the stick he had been whittling on, then continued, "You see, we plan to farm in the summer. There's some good farms the French left when they moved out. We want to take over one of these, then trap for furs in winter."

This roused the interest of John Cole. "Ya say there's farmin' and good trappin'?"

Elizabeth's heart sank. Now she was afraid he might change his mind and travel to Detroit with them. She didn't care to be around the arrogant boor any longer than necessary, and she didn't think Mrs. Cole, pregnant and with six children, could take the arduous trip.

Richard shared these feelings and sensed her concern by a sudden change in her expression. He tried to downplay the situation. "Well," he said coolly, picking up the stick again to poke at the ground, "trapping's not as good as it used to be. The French were at it for years. And now there's a lot of hunters coming in who kill everything that moves."

"That's the trouble," John conceded. "Just when ya find somethin' good, a batch o' renegades'll come in and ruin it." He turned to Tad. "Herkimer Valley sounds good ta me!"

Elizabeth nodded. She felt better.

◆

Two miles before the Herkimer Valley turnoff, they encountered two parties going east. One was a lone farmer from the Utica settlement going to Albany to trade furs and wheat for staples to get his family through the summer.

The other was a harried looking group. The man, woman, and three children had their possessions in two wagons and were returning to Connecticut from Fort Niagara. "Tried frontier living for a year," the man explained. "Winter was too cold." He paused to look off into the distance, then shook his head. "Wife and kids was even bothered by drunk soldiers and Indians. And wild animals made off with m' calves and chickens."

After they moved on, Tad turned to Richard. "It's not fer everybody. Some can make a go of it, some can't. M'self, I like it, and so does my family."

Tad's words heartened Elizabeth. After hearing the complaints, she had questioned the wisdom of going to Detroit.

Richard, perceiving her fear, was relieved by Tad's statement. "I've got things fairly well laid out," he assured her, "so there shouldn't be a problem for us."

When they reached the lane leading to Herkimer Valley, Tad suggested Richard and Elizabeth camp in his yard and rest for a day or two. At first Richard wanted to do it, thinking someone going to Fort Niagara might come past but, when he considered the distance that lay ahead, declined the offer.

"Suit yourself," Tad said, shaking his hand. "Been nice knowin' ya."

After saying goodbye to Mrs. Cole and the children, Elizabeth turned to find Jeremy waiting for her. He doffed his hat and shook her hand, then withdrew a small, worn deerskin pouch from his pocket. "I want to give you this," he said shyly.

She took it and, smiling gratefully, removed a perfectly shaped flint arrowhead from it. "My, this is nice," she said, looking at his down-turned eyes. It felt warm from being in his pocket. "Are you sure you want me to have it?"

"Yes'm," he replied weakly.

"I shall treasure it always," she assured him, bowing down to kiss him on the cheek.

His face reddened. Then he replaced his hat and trotted off to his wagon.

"This is a fine arrowhead," Richard informed her, rubbing it between his fingers. "It wasn't chipped by hammering. This was heated and had cold water dropped on it. Must have been made for a special cause."

When Richard and Elizabeth moved on, they watched the other wagons for several minutes making their way through the shimmering afternoon heat toward a scattering of buildings in a cleared valley to their left. A short time later they heard the shouts of children and barking of dogs to signal their arrival at the little settlement.

Five miles beyond Herkimer Valley, they looked for a place to camp for the night. Suddenly, six Indians emerged from the dense forest a hundred yards ahead. Two were on horseback, and four were walking. When the savages saw the approaching wagon, they halted, then came slowly toward it.

"Oh, my God!" Elizabeth exclaimed in a low voice.

"Don't get excited," Richard cautioned. "Probably just a friendly Oneida hunting party." He took the musket from behind the seat and stood it upright between him and Elizabeth.

Tad Morris had told them they might encounter the Oneidas and Onondagas. Richard recalled how he was instructed to treat them, and he remembered how he and Flip had conducted themselves. It gave him confidence. He could show Elizabeth how such matters should be handled.

Continuing to look straight ahead, he gave her instructions. "Remember, no smile. Never smile. If you look at them, look 'em in the eye. Probably best just to look ahead up the trail."

In spite of how she had prepared herself, Elizabeth was terrified. Her face turned ash white as the color drained from it. She felt her heart beating in her chest and the pulse throbbing at her temples. She didn't expect to be so frightened, but could not help it. Determined to do what she was taught, she set her jaw and stared icily into the face of the lead Indian sitting bareback astride a black pony. He carried a rusted musket and wore only a breechclout on his blood-smeared body. A small deer was draped over the horse's rump.

The Indian pulled his mount to a halt as if wanting to talk, but Richard, raising the open hand of friendship, looked at him sternly and continued on. Ahead, two of the red men stood across the trail to block it. They had dead rabbits hanging from their belts and were armed with bows, arrows, and fire-tempered wooden spears.

Richard hoped to avoid a confrontation, so he drove Molly between them, forcing room for the wagon. He was grateful they did not try to stop her.

Since leaving Albany, Richard had kept the rear flap of the wagon laced shut to prevent anyone from climbing in unexpectedly. Although he couldn't see the Indians, he was certain they were following close behind. Glancing at Elizabeth, he saw fright showing in her face. She sat rigidly erect, her moist face shining in the soft rays of the sinking sun.

"It's all right, sweetie," he whispered calmly. "Just a hunting party. They'll leave us in a few minutes."

Unblinking, she continued to gaze ahead with a fixed look. "I know," she whispered. "But it scares me."

When the wagon reached the place where the Indians had come onto the road, the hunters stopped and watched the wagon for a few minutes. Then they disappeared into the forest. When Richard looked back and saw they were gone, he grasped Elizabeth by the chin and turned her face toward his. Smiling, he kissed her on the mouth. "They're gone," he said.

An hour later, they camped so they could not be seen from the trail. After they had eaten, Elizabeth sat back and thought about the incident with the Indians. She was pleased with the way she had conducted herself. Everything went the way Richard had said it would, and now she would be less afraid to meet others. She was impressed, however, by the cold harshness of the red man's expression and the piercing stare of his bold, dark eyes. These savages seemed so different from the lethargic ones that occasionally wandered through Fredericksburg.

They made their bed beneath a large spruce with branches drooping to the ground. It seemed like a cave with a small opening to see Molly and the wagon. However, their minds and bodies were so stimulated by the Indian encounter they could not go to sleep. On several occasions Richard, alerted by a noise, rose to his elbows and fingered the trigger of the musket, only to find it was made by a bird or animal.

Shortly before dawn he heard the frightened whinny of Molly. Crawling cautiously from beneath the spruce, he saw a pair of foxes intent on exploring their campsite. After chasing them off, he thought of going back to bed, but the roused forest creatures had begun their ceaseless chirruping, calling, and chattering.

◆

After eating lunch, Richard pulled his hat down over his face and laid back against a small, grassy mound. Suddenly, he realized the forest had become quiet. An alert had been signaled by the birds and animals. Jumping up, he grabbed his musket, took the oat bag from Molly's head, and explained the quietness to Elizabeth.

For several minutes they listened intently, holding their breaths and slowly rotating their heads. Dropping to his knees with a suddenness that startled Elizabeth, Richard placed his ear to the ground. He heard a faint rumble like that he'd heard on the Braddock Road. It was, he was sure, a train of heavy, military supply wagons.

"It's an army supply train!" he said hoarsely, jumping up to throw his arms about Elizabeth. Then, more soberly, he added, "I hope it's going west."

A short time later, sixteen supply wagons appeared on the trail behind them. The train was accompanied by a contingent of British soldiers. Following behind were three civilian wagons and a dozen walking travelers.

The officer in charge reined his horse to a halt. Richard started to introduce himself, but the officer interrupted. "Going west?" he asked.

"Yes. To Fort Niagara and on to Detroit," Richard replied with a smile.

The officer looked at him coldly, then said, "Fall in behind the last wagon."

Richard liked traveling with a supply train. It was more relaxing than being alone. The train traveled at a slow, steady pace from early dawn until sunset, but he did not have to be concerned with selecting a campsite, encountering Indians, or taking the wrong fork on the trail.

The sergeant in charge of the hunting detail, although polite and mannerly, took a liking to Elizabeth. Each evening he gave her meat to cook for supper. Richard was pleased, but others grumbled their jealous dislike for him. Their frowns turned to smiles, however, when the convoy cook prepared enough for everyone to share supper with the troopers.

One evening, after the soldiers had been issued a ration of rum, strong language and bawdy singing echoed through the camp.

Richard thought it too offensive for Elizabeth. "I will complain to the sergeant," he said, getting to his feet.

"Oh, no," Elizabeth said, tugging at his trouser leg. "I've heard about these things."

Richard looked down at her, a surprised expression on his face.

"Besides," she said, a smile showing on her lips, "it's a part of the frontier I have to get used to."

Four supply wagons and one family left the train at Fort Stanwix. The next evening the remainder of the group reached the shoreline trail on Lake Erie. Tied up at a short pier adjacent to a small blockhouse was the *Michigan*. The sight of the vessel made Richard's skin tingle. "There she is!" he shouted. He turned to Elizabeth. "She'll take us right to Detroit!"

Elizabeth stood on her toes and stretched to see the ship from where they stood. She could feel the excitement of those who planned to sail on it.

An army captain gathered the civilian travelers together. "Tomorrow, we go north to Fort Niagara," he told them. "Any o' ye are welcome ta follow." He cleared his throat to be heard above the murmuring voices. "I know some o' ye want ta board the ship. It will sail in two days. Until then, ye'll camp here and stay out o' the way until it's ready."

In addition to Richard and Elizabeth, a family in a wagon and six men planned to take the ship to Detroit.

◆

The *Michigan* revived recollections Richard had of his boyhood passage on the *Scythian*. There was the smell of tar and hemp, the slapping of sails and chafing of ropes, and the singsong creaking of the timbers as the vessel lazily rolled and pitched while being propelled by a gentle wind. He was surprised how much he remembered. Since Elizabeth had never been aboard a ship, he took great pride in showing her the various sections of the vessel and explaining how things worked.

Below deck, they found Molly and the other horse tethered with a short rope. There were also a dozen sheep in a small pen. Molly was nervous and greeted them with a nuzzle and quiet whinny. They petted and stroked her for several minutes, and when she was calmed, they walked over to the sheep.

"I like to feel their wool," Elizabeth said, digging her fingers into their soft, springy coats.

In the passenger quarters they saw a mother and two children getting settled for the crossing. The air reeked of animals, people, and the rancid fat from past cargoes of fur pelts. The children, wrapped in folded blankets on a floor pallet, watched their mother pull a loaf of bread from a bag.

"Going to Detroit?" Richard asked cheerily.

"Yes," the woman replied wearily, handing her children chunks torn from the loaf.

They had spoken to her prior to boarding, but had not introduced themselves. Elizabeth wondered if they could become neighbors at Detroit. "We are, too," she said. "Want to start a farm."

"So does my man," the woman said soberly. "Wants ta get a new start with new soil."

"We're the Lockes," Elizabeth volunteered. "Richard and Elizabeth."

"Pleased ta meetcha," the woman responded. "We're Simons." She did not mention her husband.

Richard sensed she did not wish to talk, so he turned to Elizabeth. "Let's go on deck," he said, pointing to the exit.

The two wagons had been blocked and tied down securely. Richard decided, barring bad weather, they would spend most of their time topside. "We can eat right here at the wagon and sleep in it," he told Elizabeth.

Elizabeth nodded. "That's good," she said. "Don't like the smell down there." She walked over to the rail with Richard and looked at the endless expanse of light swells in the blue water. "We'll sleep with our clothes on, though," she warned.

"Of course," Richard agreed, smiling slyly.

Late in the night Richard was awakened by a flurry of activity on the deck. He peeked out of the canvas flap at the front of the wagon. "What's the trouble, mate?" he asked a passing sailor.

The startled sailor halted and looked at him. "Changin' the set o' the sails," he replied, placing his hands on his hips. "The easterly were good as long as she lasted. But now she's a sou'wester."

"Is that a good wind or a bad one?" Richard's voice showed concern.

"Oh, 'tis good," the sailor replied. " 'Tis the prevailin' wind. Means fair skies." He hesitated momentarily, then added before hurrying off, "But we got some tackin' ta do now."

◆

The *Michigan* pulled alongside the dock at the northern end of the fort at Detroit shortly before noon on Wednesday, the 9th of September. Richard's heart was racing. They had been traveling nearly two months and were just a short distance from the piece of land they would call home. If things went well, he could make a good living working the farm and trapping for furs.

Standing at the ship's rail as the dock crew manned the ropes, Richard and Elizabeth looked out across the countryside. Tall, luxuriant grass sparkled with drops of water in the bright sunshine. The land had been cleansed by a thundershower that passed a short time before, and beyond the grass, a dark green forest stretched to the north as far as they could see.

"It's beautiful!" Elizabeth said, excitement ringing in her voice as she inhaled the fresh scent of pine rosin carried from the forest by the warm air. She drew herself close to Richard's arm. "Simply beautiful!"

"It sure is," Richard agreed. "The farming should be good, too."

After the passengers went ashore, Richard got Molly and led her down the broad gangplank. Trusting her master, she went willingly, but Mr. Simon had to place his coat over his horse's head before she would descend the cleated ramp. Then several of the crew, using ropes to slow the descent, eased the wagons down the same ramp.

Richard drove directly to the military headquarters. "Just hope that farm next to the River Rouge is still there for us," he said, snapping the reins to urge Molly on.

Elizabeth sat quietly beside him, awed by the looks of the primitive village they were in.

A neatly dressed lieutenant placed a plot plan on his desk and ran his finger across it. "Oh, yes, the Cousineau place. Aye, 'tis still open." Hesitating, he looked up at Richard. "Ye wouldn't be the Virginian, would ye?"

"Yes," Richard said, somewhat surprised. "Yes, indeed."

"Aye," the lieutenant responded, nodding his head. "Yer friend, the trapper, was 'ere and said ye'd be a-comin'. Said we should 'old it fer ye."

"Oh, that's right. Glad he did."

"And what might be 'is name? Flip something?"

"Wade. Flip Wade," Richard broke in.

"Aye, Flip Wade," the lieutenant agreed. "A rather nice chap."

Lifting the silver cover on a blown glass inkwell, he wet the end of a quill and wrote *Richard Locke* on the long, slender rectangle.

"Family?" he asked, without looking up.

"A wife, Elizabeth," Richard replied with a broad smile as he reached back and pulled her up beside him.

"And wife," the soldier said, writing it on the map.

Chapter 10

River Rouge

As he passed the last three farms before his, Richard's heart began pumping faster. Anxious to set foot on a plot of ground he owned, he was determined to make his wife pleased with his decision to settle here. Several farmers, eager to have other whites settle in the area, waved as the little wagon went by.

"See how friendly the neighbors are," he said, returning the greeting.

In the distance, he could see the narrow bridge spanning the River Rouge, and there was the tree line on the other side that represented the demarcation line separating the settled area from the forested domain of the Indian. Someday, he thought, that line will move farther south. The red man will again be forced to give way.

Approaching the driveway, Richard's heart sank. The last time he'd seen it was four months earlier when he passed on his return to Virginia. The new spring growth was short then, trim and vibrantly green, and the buildings were tightly closed. But a summer of inattention had taken its toll. The buildings, with open doors and missing windows, were nearly overwhelmed by scrub brush, seed-topped weeds, and overripe grass.

On the west side of the river road, fields that had been used for pasture and the growing of crops were in a dreadful state of neglect. Yellow patches of wild mustard and brown spears of bitter dock floated on a green sea of waving quack grass that extended to the far-off woods. He had forgotten how tall and abundant weeds grew where sod had once been turned.

He reined Molly to a halt a short distance from the house and sat, glumly surveying the situation. As his eyes traced the paths tramped into the weeds from building to building by trespassers, he wondered what Elizabeth thought. "Well, here we are," he said gloomily. "It's not nearly as nice as I remember it."

Elizabeth had watched his enthusiasm wane during the last few minutes. She was not sure what must be done to put the place in order, but knew it would be much easier than hacking a new farm out of the forest as the Simons would have to do.

"Well, come on! Let's look the place over!" she said eagerly, trying to revive her husband's spirit. She wanted to show him she possessed the mettle to see his idea through.

As they walked through the tall growth hand in hand, Richard cautiously led the way while Elizabeth held her skirt up with her free hand. A flurry of mature grasshoppers, clicking loudly as they fled, flew before them, and a dense cloud of pollen from seed-forming sweet clover and waist-high goldenrod wafted in the still air. It clogged their nostrils and dried their throats. Several horseflies, attracted by Molly, buzzed back and forth, still wary of their newly found host.

Approaching the cabin, Richard cautiously pushed against the partially opened door. He stepped inside onto a debris-littered, plank floor and looked around. Satisfied it was safe, he pulled Elizabeth in after him.

He was surprised by its size and condition. The three rooms, two bedrooms and a combination living room-kitchen, were well chinked and coated with whitewash. Its light color amplified the sunshine filtering through small glass panes in the windows. Although the entire sash was missing in the living room, he was not concerned. He could get another at the fort.

The large fireplace with its raised, granite hearthstone caught Elizabeth's eye. She walked over and touched its pothook and andirons. "Look, Richard," she called. "What a lovely fireplace."

"That," he said, eyeing its construction, "took a lot of hard work." He kicked the hearthstone. "Must've had quite a time hauling this thing here."

Although dirt strewn and inhabited by insects and rodents, the buildings were solidly constructed of squared logs that had been carefully fitted. It made Richard's outlook much brighter. "Guess it's a fair start," he said, stepping from the barn.

"I'm anxious to get under way," Elizabeth replied, her enthusiasm building as she tried to picture a blazing log in the fireplace of the furnished cabin.

When they reached the wagon, they saw a man and woman walking down the driveway toward them. The man carried a small, covered, copper kettle. The woman was holding a long, slender loaf of bread and a bottle of wine.

"Bon jour," the man began, doffing his red knitted hat.

The woman adjusted the kerchief on her head and nodded. Then the two of then extended their hands.

The Lockes grasped them cautiously.

The man was short, not more than five feet, Richard estimated. He was slight of build and had dark hair and a thick, black mustache. The legs of his full-cut blue work pants were tucked into badly scuffed leather boots with run down heels, and the gray shirt he wore was accented by an unbuttoned black vest.

The brown eyes of the woman matched her smooth olive skin. Stout and about the same height as the man, she appeared to be in her thirties.

"Bon jour," Richard replied.

Noting the coolness of Richard and Elizabeth, the man offered an introduction. They were Louis and Marie LaCroix, he told them. For the last five years, they had occupied the farm to the north. They had two young children and, although they spoke no English, decided to remain, instead of leaving as so many of their friends had when the British took command of the territory. As a gesture of neighborly friendship, they brought a kettle of hot goat stew and some bread and wine for the Locke's supper.

"You have much grass and weeds to cut," Louis noted, kicking at the waist high sweet clover.

"Yes," Richard agreed. "I'll have to get a scythe to clear the area around the buildings."

"I will loan you mine," Louis volunteered. "And I will help when I can." Then turning to his wife, he said, "And now, woman, we will go so these good people can do what they need to do."

Although Elizabeth didn't speak French, the Latin she had been taught allowed her to understand the conversation.

After the LaCroix departed, she turned to Richard. "I think I'm going to like them," she said with a smile. "They are so friendly."

◆

They worked the next three days clearing the area around the buildings and cleaning the house so they could unload the wagon. Using a flaming pole, Richard cleared the cabin and privy of wasps and spiders. Then he hauled buckets of water from the River Rouge so they could scrub the two buildings.

After digging a new trench for the privy, he and Elizabeth skidded the little structure over it. "Now," Elizabeth said emphatically, the back and underarms of her dress wet with perspiration, "I won't worry about going in there."

Richard was amazed at his wife's eagerness to work at tasks she wouldn't have been asked to do in Fredericksburg. She washed the walls of the cabin and scrubbed the floor on her hands and knees before being satisfied with its condition. Much to his delight, she discovered a loose stone in the base of the fireplace at its juncture with the wall that bared a cavity for secreting valuables.

She also gathered and fitted stones together in the form of a landing platform outside the doorway. It would keep dirt from being tracked inside, she told him

Elizabeth enjoyed what she was doing. Although the work was hard and tiring, it gave her satisfaction to find she had the ability to do such things. Most of all, she liked to watch the progress of her labors on a home of her own, and for the first time, she had the freedom to do something without being concerned about looking proper and ladylike.

She realized, however, that even with a bonnet, the sun and wind was harsh on her skin, and the hard work made blisters and calluses on her hands. But this was her role, and other farm wives bore the same indicators of farm work. She would, however, minimize their effects by protecting her skin from the elements and periodically applying chicken oil to her face, arms, and hands.

In the evening, after bathing in water warmed by the fireplace, she and Richard stretched out on the bed.

"Sure a nice, soft bed," Elizabeth said, looking up at the indistinct color of the board ceiling in the fading light.

"Almost as soft as you are," Richard said, caressing her body.

The next morning they took the cover from the wagon and drove to Detroit, stopping briefly at the LaCroix's to return the scythe. Inside the fort, they went directly to the Comptoir Grillon.

Frenchy greeted Richard with a vigorous embrace. "My friend!" he shouted with a heavy accent. "My friend, Richard!" He stressed the last syllable of Richard's name.

When he saw the shadowy figure of Elizabeth near the door, he suddenly sobered and stared at her.

Richard noticed the direction of his attention. "I want you to meet my wife," he said. "Her name is Elizabeth."

Frenchy walked quickly over to her. He took her extended hand in his and kissed it tenderly. Then, looking into her eyes, he said, "Madam, the pleasure is all mine." It was something he had not done in a long time.

When Elizabeth initially stepped inside the door, she hesitated. She surveyed the dust and disorder in the dim light and sniffed the musty odor. She had never been in a place of business like this, and when Frenchy approached, she reluctantly held out her hand. His clothing was wrinkled and grimy, and he reeked of wood smoke.

"This is Frenchy, the man I told you about," Richard said enthusiastically. "He has some things we need."

"You see how good I speak English?" Frenchy beamed, looking at Richard.

"Yes, it is very good."

"She is a new wife?"

"Yes."

"Have you had a *charivari?*" Frenchy asked, wrinkling his forehead.

"No," Richard replied. "What's that?"

"Oh, a special French party for a man and his new wife."

Richard thought he spotted a gleam of devilish mischief in Frenchy's eyes.

Elizabeth was not pleased with the condition of the merchandise. It was of good quality, but so dusty and disorderly. She turned to Richard. "Will we be going to other stores?" she asked.

"Oh, sure. But if you see something here you want, take it." The way the items were displayed did not concern him.

She shrugged, then walked about and picked up several items. When she placed them on the counter where Richard was talking to Frenchy, her husband pointed to a pair of ornate brass sconces. "What's this?" he asked.

"Going to put them on the living room wall to hold candles," she told him.

Frenchy picked them up. "They are very nice ones," he told Richard. "Made in Spain." He nodded. "Your wife, she has good taste."

Richard smiled. As Elizabeth looked for more items, he continued his conversation with Frenchy.

When he asked about Flip, he was told the trapper had been away for three weeks. "Building a cabin to trap," Frenchy explained.

"Do you know where?"

"I don't know," Frenchy answered, sorting through the stack of kettles, knives, and ladles Elizabeth had brought to the counter.

On Rue Ste. Anne they bought food staples from a general supply store and two dozen candles at the candle shop. When she got back into the wagon, Elizabeth said, "Now, let's stop at the tailor."

"What for?" Richard asked, looking at her questioningly.

"So I can get material to make you some farm clothes."

"But I have clothes."

"Yes," she countered, "dress clothing." She paused for a moment, then said, "And those buckskins. They may be all right for trapping, but they're too hot and smelly around the farm."

Richard shrugged.

While she was at the tailor, Richard ordered the window sash at the glazier, then walked to the Black Swan.

"Ah! Richard, the Virginian!" Henry shouted, his robust face beaming. He extended a hand across the bar. "What'll it be today?"

"Nothing right now, Henry. I came to ask about Flip. You know, my trapping partner."

"Aye," Henry began, placing his hands on the bar. "He was 'ere a month ago. Buildin' a cabin on the Shiawassee, 'e was. Gonna make winter quarters there."

"Will he be back afore winter?"

"Ye can bet on it," Henry assured him. " 'e said you'd be a-comin' back ta settle. 'ave ye now?"

"Yes," Richard answered with a smile. "Took over the old Cousineau place."

"I say," Henry said huskily, raising his eyebrows. "That's the end o' the line. Right next ta the savages."

"It is," Richard agreed. "but I don't mind." He hesitated, then went on, "I've got to go now, but I'll be back again. Be sure to tell Flip I'm here."

"I will," Henry promised. Then, with a twinkle in his eye, he said, "By the way, I 'ear 'e's takin' in an Ottawa chickawee ta warm 'is bed."

"Wouldn't surprise me," Richard called back over his shoulder.

At the military headquarters they posted a letter Elizabeth had written to her parents. It was one of the few sent from the nearly illiterate village. And Richard was handed a requisition for grant items given new settlers.

At the Hudson's Bay Company corral and warehouse, he received a plow, axe, spade, and light wagon. He also was given a non-milking cow and castrated pig he was not ready to take. After being refused permission to leave them until he could get pens ready, he tied the cow to the back of the new wagon, hooked it in tandem to his, then loaded the crated pig into it.

"Looks like a nice cow," Elizabeth said, speaking loud enough to be heard above the squealing pig as they drove along Rue Ste. Anne toward the south gate.

Richard nodded. "Just needs more feed."

"Do we have it?"

"Can pasture 'em now. Have to cut and store some. Maybe have to buy some."

After repairing the barnyard split rail fence for Molly and Bessy, a name Elizabeth gave the cow, they erected a pigsty of sharpened poles to keep out wolves and deter bears.

When the LaCroix came over to help, Elizabeth retreated to the house so she and Marie could organize its sparse furnishings. They hung copper pans on forged nails they found in the barn and drove into the wall with a hatchet.

As gifts, Marie brought a multicolored, braided rug to lay before the fireplace and several crocks of jam made from strawberries and cranberries. She also showed Elizabeth how to make town bread in the outdoor clay oven located a few steps from the cabin door. As they worked, Elizabeth developed a warm, friendly relationship with the French woman and learned the basics of understanding and speaking the language.

◆

A week after the trip to Detroit, Elizabeth was gathering acorns for the pig beneath a red oak near the barn. When she looked up, she saw Marie running toward her. Very unusual, she thought, for the normally slow-moving woman. Sensing an urgency, she lowered the wooden bucket to the ground and ran toward the plump, little figure.

They met at the driveway. Marie, perspiring profusely, tried to talk between gasps for breath. "Charivari tonight!" she exclaimed, puffing heavily. "Charivari tonight!"

Richard, who had been cutting timothy and clover across the road, dropped the sickle and rushed to their side. "What's the matter?" he asked.

"I don't know," Elizabeth said soberly. "I can't understand her. She keeps saying something about tonight."

Richard placed a hand on Marie's shoulder and looked into her face.

"Charivari tonight," she repeated. Her labored breathing had begun to subside. "French custom."

"Oh!" Richard replied, nodding to indicate he understood. Turning to Elizabeth, he explained, "This is that party Frenchy was talking about. Seems it's going to happen tonight."

Marie mopped her brow with a gray handkerchief. "In Detroit I sell eggs. Friend tell me." She glanced at the house, then back at Elizabeth. "You must have something for them to eat and something to drink," she said, holding up a little pot of honey. She grabbed Elizabeth's hand and started for the house.

"Everything will be all right," Elizabeth assured her, showing a calmness not fully understood by the French lady.

Using honey as a sweetener, they made several dozen cookies and prepared a large crock of tea.

"They come tonight," Marie said as they worked, "after you go to bed. They will make much noise, but don't be frightened. It's a celebration."

◆

Seventeen persons, fifteen men and two women led by Flip and Frenchy, left the Comptoir Grillon at sundown for the Locke's farm. They would give the newlyweds a charivari, a proper welcome to this frontier community. Besides, Flip was anxious to see his friend and meet the bride. Although he and Frenchy were the only ones who knew the Virginia couple, the others went along to lend support and enjoy the merrymaking. They rode in wagons and on horseback, carrying pans, muskets, horns, and a drum. Most had been drinking rum and brandy. As darkness settled over them and distance from the fort grew, the exuberance of some faded. Determined to give the Locke's a rousing party, Flip and Frenchy urged them on.

When they arrived at the LaCroix yard and could see the light in the window of Richard's cabin, they quieted and waited for the young couple to go to bed. Marie LaCroix served them water, cider, and cookies as they sat in the grass swatting mosquitoes, listening to crickets, and joking about newlyweds.

When the dim yellow light went out, one of the men jumped up. "Let's go!" he said.

Flip stood. "Let them get settled in bed," he said. "Be even better if they got to sleep."

A short time later, the impatient band slipped quietly through the fields and surrounded the Locke house. After a brief wait to allow everyone to get into position, Flip fired his musket into the air. It signaled the beginning of a tumultuous din of yelling, pan beating, horn tooting, and gunfire.

Richard and Elizabeth were lying on the bed fully dressed to await the group's arrival. They relit the candles and opened the door to invite the boisterous crowd inside. Crocks of tea and dishes of cookies were on the plank dining table Richard had constructed a few days before.

Since Flip was best acquainted with Richard, others waited while he walked through the door into the lighted room.

"Flip!" Richard shouted. "You old son-of-a-gun!"

"What a sight for my tired eyes!" Flip replied as they embraced. "How have you been?"

In a matter of seconds the cabin was filled with the noisy crowd, some still maintaining the clamor by pounding on pans and tooting horns. Others helped themselves to the cookies and tea.

Marie, ignored by the revelers, shuffled about placing more cookies and a crock of cider on the table. When she saw liquid being spilled onto the floor from a man's cup, she rolled up the rug and placed it next to the wall. As she worked, she remembered her charivari in Quebec sixteen years before. Tears welled up in her soft brown eyes and rolled down her plump cheeks.

"You sure got dressed in a hurry!" Flip said with a smile.

"Sure did!" Richard replied, winking at Elizabeth.

Flip was dressed in worn buckskins that were scuffed and mended and had much of the jacket fringe missing. He was clean shaven and his hair, long enough to be tied at the back of his neck with a black ribbon, was held down by a pomade of bear grease and perfume. The flowery scent did not mask the odor that issued from his soiled clothing. Looking at Elizabeth, he smiled and said, "And this must be the little wife." Then, recalling his Boston manners, he bowed and kissed her hand. "Pleased ta make yer acquaintance, ma'am." He looked back at Richard. "You sure got yourself a good looker."

"She's a good woman," Richard declared. Turning to Elizabeth, whose hand was still held by Flip, he said, "This is Flip Wade, my trapping partner."

"Richard told me a lot about you," Elizabeth replied.

"Not too much, I hope."

"Oh, it's all good."

At that moment a young man, exaggerating his state of tipsiness, came up to Flip. Holding a jug up to the trappers face, he said, "Here, try some o' this!"

Flip took a draw from the container and puckered. "Vinegar!" he exclaimed.

"No sir!" the man said, tipping the jug to his lips as he wandered off. "Hard cider! Genuine hard cider!"

"These people friends of yours?" Richard inquired.

"Not really," Flip replied, shouting above the noise. "Had drinks with some o' them at the Black Swan. The others are Frenchy's friends." He paused and surveyed the group. "Good thing they came along, though. Been a damn poor party if we only had the two or three friends I have."

As the two men talked, Marie and Elizabeth circulated among the group. They spoke with some, and watched others spiking the cider with rum or brandy carried in pocket flasks. Louis LaCroix stood quietly with his back against a corner and watched, all the while sipping blackberry wine from a bottle he'd brought from home. Occasionally he responded to a remark directed to him in his native tongue by Frenchy.

When Elizabeth and Marie approached the two young females, the girls stepped forward and introduced themselves as Sarah and Agatha, domestics who worked in and about the fort. As Elizabeth eyed their gaudy clothes, she spotted a fringe of black hair showing beneath Sarah's powdered wig. By their crude mannerisms, she sensed they had been reared in lower-class English families. Their cockney accent seemed harsh to her ear.

"Domestics?" Marie whispered after they walked away. "Ha! Camp followers, if you ask me!"

An hour later, having consumed the tea, cider, and cookies, the revelers departed. As they left, each shook hands with Elizabeth and Richard, welcoming them to the community and wishing them success with the farm. One, a trader who had been under Indian attack at Fort William Henry, sidled up to Richard and said,

"Always have transport ready for a quick dash to the fort should the demented savages stage an uprisin'."

Flip was the last to leave. He kissed Elizabeth on the cheek and shook Richard's hand. "Sure good ta see ya. I'll drop around again in a few days. Maybe we can get together on some hunting."

◆

Richard rested his elbows on the top rail of the barnyard fence. It was mid-October, and the signs of approaching winter were all about. Trees in flaming colors were rapidly dropping their leaves, fox squirrels were hiding small caches of nuts and acorns, and great vees of geese and ducks were honking overhead.

He had accumulated a large stack of hay in the barnyard and banked the house with dirt to keep winter winds from blowing in beneath the floor.

Two or three times a week, he hitched Molly to the wagon and went to the woods at the back of the farm to get logs for the fireplace, a task he did not like. Cutting wood seemed such a waste. After spending time and energy to gather it, it was merely tossed on the fire and burned, but he continued to haul loads of the three-inch trees to the house where he cut them into fireplace lengths with a bow saw.

One warm, balmy day, Elizabeth packed a lunch and rode with him through the stump studded pasture to the edge of the forest. Richard tethered Molly to a large sassafras with a long rope so she could eat grass and nibble at low hanging leaves while he cut the small trees from among the larger ones. As he worked, Elizabeth plucked pitch-soaked knots from the rotted remains of pines that had fallen scores of years before. She liked to use these for boiling water and heating the caldrons because they burned so hot.

As she continued her search, ranging farther and farther from the clearing to fill her buckets, she came to a sharp incline. The abnormality in an otherwise flat land aroused her curiosity. She wanted to climb to its top. Although it was only a hundred yards from the wagon, she was mindful of Richard's warning to stay within earshot of his chopping. She returned and informed him of her find.

"Well," he said, wiping the sweat from his forehead, "we'll go have a look as soon as I finish loading these last two logs."

He grabbed the musket, and she slipped the handle of the basket over her arm as they headed into the woods. The ground was covered with leaves and the air filled with a spicy tang of fall. They climbed to the crest of the little hill, an elongated mound of uplifted soil sparsely covered with trees, then squatted so they could look beneath the low-hanging branches.

At the base of a gentle slope, the glossy surface of a small pond reflected the glittering rays of the noon sun. After watching for several minutes to be certain they were alone, they walked down the hill to an unobstructed view of the quiet little body of water.

The pond was oval shaped, half an acre Richard estimated. Its surface was free of vegetation except for a cluster of lily pads, reeds, and cattails at one end camouflaging a large muskrat hut. A few water striders darted about on its smooth, black surface, and a lone marsh wren swayed precariously on the fuzzy tip of disintegrating cattail.

"This is a nice place," Richard said, sitting down in the filtered shade twenty feet from the water's edge.

"I like it," Elizabeth agreed as she took some bread and baked sturgeon from the basket. "Just like the hill at home." A surge of warmth raced through her body, and she leaned her head against Richard's arm.

He looked at her and smiled. "Just like the Rappahannock."

They ate unhurriedly. The serenity gave Elizabeth a relaxed feeling she had not experienced since leaving Fredericksburg. Ever since their wedding, she felt they had been pressed for time. First, they had to get to Detroit soon enough to claim an established farm; then, buildings had to be readied for cold weather, feed had to be gathered for animals, and now, firewood must be stockpiled for a winter much more severe than in Virginia.

After eating they laid back, closed their eyes, and held each other's hand to enjoy the tranquility surrounding them. A distant woodpecker tapped at a dead tree, and high overhead, through the thinning leaves, they could see parts of a giant wedge of geese. Elizabeth, exhausted by weeks of unaccustomed heavy work, dozed as tension eased from her body. Richard slipped his hand from hers and sat up to maintain a vigil.

Fifteen minutes later, Elizabeth's eyes fluttered open. Richard bent down to kiss her. "You're a sleepyhead," he said, rubbing his nose against hers. "Molly'll think we've left her."

"I know," she replied, looking into his eyes. "It sure felt good." She sat upright. "You know what else would feel good?"

"Not here. Never know who might be watching." He paused and kissed her again. "And I wouldn't want some red buck to see your white bottom."

"Richard!" she said, slapping his arm and grinning with embarrassment.

When they started back, Richard saw an unusually large beech tree a short distance away. He had never seen a tree so large. Fully thirty inches in diameter, it dwarfed all hardwoods in the area. He walked over to inspect it and found a large hole eight feet off the ground in its gnarled trunk. Rapping on it with the butt of his musket, it sounded hollow. He assumed it was a living shell that had suffered from years of internal decay.

"It's mighty big, but there's not much left to it anymore!" he called back to Elizabeth.

"You'd better get away, quick!" she shouted, pointing to the hole above his head. "There's a lot of bees coming out!"

"By God, it's a bee tree!" he yelled.

He grabbed her by the hand, and they ran back to the wagon.

The ride to the house was one of the most pleasant Elizabeth had experienced. She felt safe and secure, and everything was falling into place. She was proud of how well she had adapted to the frontier. As the shadows lengthened and the afternoon sun warmed her back, she wanted to place her head against her husband's shoulder. But showing affection in public was frowned upon, so she sat with half closed eyes, submerged in the wonderful feeling that engulfed her.

When they bounced across the ruts of the river road and entered their driveway, Elizabeth grabbed Richard's wrist. "What is that against our door?" she asked hoarsely.

Squinting to filter the light coming into his eyes, Richard recognized his Indian friend squatting on his haunches. "It's Naseeka," he said, straining to make out the impassive face staring at them. "The Wyandotte I told you about."

Pulling Molly to a halt not far from the door, he jumped down and extended his hand. "Naseeka!" he shouted, a broad grin flashing across his face.

The red man rose slowly to his feet, seized Richard's hand firmly and gave it his characteristic single, vigorous shake. "My brother," he said huskily, his face showing no emotion. "Good to see you."

He was dressed in low-cut moccasins and loose fitting deerskin leggings that were covered by a breechclout. His shiny, black hair, parted in the middle and made into a single braid, hung down his bare back and was crowned with a brightly beaded leather band and two eagle feathers. Several mosquito bites marred the smoothness of his deeply tanned, bronze skin that shone with a dull luster from the residue of perspiration and body oil.

He pulled the thong up from inside Richard's shirt collar and fingered the contents of the pouch at its end. As he looked at the fading picture of its symbolic arrow, he grunted and nodded. "No enemy can hurt you," he said, a slight smile forming on his lips.

"It protects me," Richard assured him, feeling thankful he insisted on wearing it over Elizabeth's objections. He'd removed it in Fredericksburg, but put it on again after the charivari.

Elizabeth had informed him she thought it was just so much meaningless superstition. Besides, it was not very clean. However, after he explained what it meant to the Indian and told her it would harm their friendship if he did not wear it, she acquiesced with the provision he not wear it to bed.

"Your woman?" Naseeka asked bluntly, pointing to Elizabeth as she got down from the wagon.

"My woman, Elizabeth," Richard stated. Turning to her, he said, "This is Naseeka."

She nodded and smiled, but Naseeka merely stared at her.

He was taller and lighter complexioned then the Oneidas she'd seen on the Mohawk Trail, and his facial features were of a finer nature. But still, he had the dark, piercing eyes of a savage. It frightened her.

Remembering what Richard told her about the Indian woman's position in the tribe, she turned away, unhitched Molly, and led the horse to the barn.

When she returned to the house, she found her husband and Naseeka sitting cross-legged on opposite sides of the rug they had slid to the center of the living room area. She could smell the smoky odor similar to that of the Comptoir Grillon. Perhaps, she thought as she busied herself in the kitchen, it was common to the forest people. She hoped she would not acquire it since it was an unpleasant smell to her.

"I expected you sooner," Richard said, indicating he was certain the Wyandottes knew he had arrived.

"Naseeka was away on a hunt with braves," the Indian informed him. "Must smoke much meat for the long winter." He took a leather bag from his side and placed it in the center of the rug. "For you," he said.

Richard unpuckered its top and peered inside. "Pemmican," he smiled.

"A gift from the Wyandottes to our brother. Matoka made it."

"How is your father?" Richard asked, continuing the subject of Naseeka's family

"Nasingah is not good. His spirit will leave the Wyandotte village before the first white blanket covers the ground."

"He is very sick?"

Naseeka nodded. "He sleeps much of the day."

Richard took a pinch of pemmican and motioned for Naseeka to have some.

"That is a gift for the white brother. Naseeka must not eat it."

The discussion dragged on until Richard became uneasy. They talked about British–Indian policy, pack trains through Wyandotte territory, and their mutual friends, Flip and Frenchy. Elizabeth listened as she prepared biscuits and venison for supper but considered most of it to be repeated prattle.

She placed a plate on the rug in front of each man. Naseeka emptied one into another, pushed it into the center of the rug, and handed the emptied plate back to her. For a moment she watched as the Indian, eating with his fingers, motioned for Richard to do likewise.

Shortly after the sun went down, Elizabeth, feeling exasperated with the long discussion but assuming it was necessary when dealing with Indians, lit several candles and sat down at the table to work on a shawl she had been knitting. With a sudden abruptness that startled her, the two men stood and shook hands. The conference was over. Naseeka lifted the latch and strode into the darkness, not bothering to close the door.

"Was he upset?" Elizabeth asked as Richard closed the door.

"No," Richard replied. "Indians are that way. You'll get used to it after a while."

"Maybe," she said, shaking her head. "But it'll take some doing." She picked up the plate and slid the rug back into position. "You sure have some unusual friends," she muttered.

◆

It was early November, and winter was near. A heavy frost came every night giving the dead plant life a tawny color, and the ground froze deeper, frequently taking until noon before the sun could thaw it again. Containers of water became solid, and occasionally Richard and Elizabeth arose to find the area powdered with a light snow. The prevailing wind had shifted from southwest to northwest, and according to Naseeka, the heavy husks on corn and the large quantity of food being stored by squirrels were sure signs of a long, hard winter.

The *Huron* and *Michigan* stopped running for the season, causing an increase in the number of pack trains traveling the river road from Niagara to Detroit.

Then, the pack trains stopped. Detroit would have to sustain itself until spring.

Elizabeth knew of the fine garden Richard's mother had grown, and when she saw what Marie harvested from a small piece of land, she was determined to have one of her own.

Richard decided to plow the little plot before the frozen crust made it too difficult for Molly to pull the plow. Then the winter moisture could combine with the loose soil and compost the heavy crop of weeds. With a loop of thick rope attached to the plow, he drew the tall sweet clover down so it could be turned under by the steel-tipped share.

When he finished, he went into the house. "That'll be the last plowing until spring he said.

Elizabeth poured him a cup of tea, then sat down beside him. "Oh, thank you!" she said, her voice ringing with excitement. "When spring comes, I'll be ready with plenty of seed."

In the morning, a pale, yellow sun ascended slowly from the dark horizon across the Detroit River. Its warmth melted the coating of frost that grew during the night. As Richard walked toward the barn, he sniffed the air, then stopped to look at the steamy vapor rising like thin, white smoke from the roofs of his buildings. The trapping season was only a week or two away. He would have to get some traps and a supply of powder and shot.

At the Comptoir Grillon he saw an old musket hanging on the wall behind the counter. "That for sale?" he asked, thinking of a firearm for Elizabeth when he was on the trap line.

"Oh, yes," Frenchy replied, turning to look at it. "Do you need it?"

"I want it for Elizabeth."

"For the madam?" Frenchy asked soberly.

"For her when I'm away."

Reaching beneath the counter, the Frenchman withdrew a light-weight, short-barreled weapon. "For the madam," he said, a broad smile showing beneath his mustache.

Richard examined it carefully. It was used but had been well kept and coated with oil. "Does it shoot good?" he asked.

"Yes," Frenchy assured him. "Take it and try it."

Richard rammed it with powder and shot. Then he went out the rear gates of the fort and fired at a burl on a hickory tree.

After three rounds, he returned to the Comptoir Grillon. "I like it. How much is it?"

"For you, my friend, five pounds."

"Good!" Richard reached into his pocket. "Where did you get it?"

"Courier de bois."

"He sold it to you?"

"He sell me everything. Go back to Quebec." Frenchy shrugged his shoulders. "He say business bad. Indian no longer like the white man."

Richard examined the dents and scratches in its walnut stock. "Well," he said, "it's a good one."

At that instant the door burst open and Flip stepped inside. Throwing his arms into the air, he shouted, "Hello, you sons-o'-guns!"

He was dressed in new buckskins, was clean shaven, and had his hair cut so it was up off his collar.

Richard, startled momentarily, recovered and replied, "Come on in!" Then, as Flip made his way toward him, asked, "What brings you here?"

"Just comin' in on the back trail ta pick up a few things and thought I saw ya out there firing your musket."

"Yah," Richard explained. "Getting it for Elizabeth."

"Good idea," Flip agreed. He paused, then said, "I told ya one o' these days I'd be droppin' by for a visit."

"Good! Could use your help on a few things."

"Anytime! What did ya have in mind?"

"Got a bee tree to cut down and a pig to butcher."

"That shouldn't be too hard." Then, winking at Richard, he added, "Maybe Frenchy could help us with the pig."

Frenchy, smiling as he watched the verbal exchange from behind the counter, suddenly raised his hands and shook his head. "I am a businessman," he said solemnly. "I eat the animals, but I do not kill them."

Richard walked over and sympathetically placed his hand on the Frenchman's shoulder. "We will take care of it," he said. "And then we'll bring you some."

The smile returned to Frenchy's face. "Thank you," he said meekly.

At the Black Swan, Richard and Flip were told the Hudson's Bay Company would buy all the prime pelts they could get at premium prices. The officials also wanted all the trappers to know they had a large stock of general merchandise to sell or barter.

"Gonna give Frenchy some competition," Flip said. "But he'll survive. There's some people who won't buy from an outside company."

"Do you think Hudson's Bay will have any chickawees for sale?" Richard teased, a sly smile showing on his face.

"Who you been talkin' to?" Flip grinned.

"Oh, just heard they're good at keeping the bed warm."

"Yah, I got one," Flip confessed. "She's an Ottawa. Not as fat as the Chippewa we had. A little neater."

"Well," Richard said, "Naseeka says it's going to be a long, cold winter. So you'll probably need her."

"You seen Naseeka?" Flip asked, pleased to change the subject.

"He's been to our place a couple of times. Says his father is pretty sick."

"I've been meanin' ta go see him, but just never got around to it."

"More than likely it's his wanton sister you want to see," Richard said, smiling as he poked Flip's arm.

"She's all right," Flip replied. "She's a nice girl, and I like her a lot."

On the way to Richard's farm, they stopped at the LaCroix's to borrow a scalding kettle.

"I will butcher one of my pigs in two days," Louis said. "We do them at the same time."

In a boastful moment at the Black Swan, Flip had volunteered to do the stabbing, a technique requiring skill to sever the jugular vein with precision. Although he had helped with butchering, he'd never stabbed a pig. "Can't beat a deal like that," he said energetically, relieved Louis would do it.

◆

With preparations for winter nearly complete, Elizabeth felt relaxed. She stayed inside much of the time making curtains, knitting socks, and finishing work on a heavy shawl. Protected from the wind and sun, her skin again became smooth and soft, and the calluses disappeared from her hands. Her hair, no longer dry and brittle, returned to a rich brown color accented with gentle highlights that enhanced its soft, natural waves. And she had more time to think about family and friends in Fredericksburg.

Although she had written three letters to her parents, she had received but one, a note sent by her mother shortly after they'd left. It had buoyed her spirits, but a loneliness was developing. She missed the social activity of Fredericksburg, so when Richard returned with Flip, she was pleased to have a guest.

Smelling ale on their breath, she poured them a cup of tea and told them to sit at the table. Then she went into the second bedroom to make a place for Flip's bed among the stored things.

Flip sensed what she was doing. "If your doing that fer me, don't bother. I'm going to sleep in the barn."

His remark startled her. "But we have room right here," she countered. "Besides, it'll get cold out there at night."

Flip felt guilty if anyone went out of their way on his behalf. "I'll be perfectly at home there, and besides, there's a lot of hay ta keep me warm."

"But we've got plenty of room right here," Richard insisted.

"No," Flip said emphatically. "You know I'm an outdoorsman, my friend. So I'll just sleep in the barn."

"Whatever you say," Richard conceded.

Elizabeth, humming happily, wanted to impress Flip with her talents as a wife. She prepared a supper of roast rabbit, boiled potatoes, baked beans, and crab apple pie.

After eating, Flip slapped Richard on the back. "That's the kind of wife a man needs," he said. "Know where I can find one like her?"

"No," Richard replied, beaming with pride. "Not too many like her."

Elizabeth was elated by the compliments. She cleared the table, then sat down and listened as the men talked. She was enthralled by the incidents they had experienced together.

But their description of Naseeka, as they'd found him, sickened her. And when Richard told of the drunken Indian urinating on him, she excused herself and left the table to clean the dishes.

Upon learning of Nasingah's weakened condition, Flip's face mirrored concern. "Let's visit the Wyandottes tomorrow," he suggested, fingering the soiled doeskin pouch that hung from his neck.

"Good idea," Richard agreed.

Elizabeth knew she could not accompany them, but hoped that someday Naseeka would invite her to accompany her husband on a visit to his village.

◆

Although their chief was on his deathbed, the mood of the villagers became festive when they learned of the arrival of Naseeka's rescuers. The young warrior's mother, sister, and fiancee were very pleased the two men had come. They were disappointed, however, when informed the visitors planned to return home the same day.

Naseeka raised his arms for silence. "This should be an occasion for celebration," he told them. "But due to respect for Nasingah, the visitors will be accorded a warm, friendly welcome without feasting, singing, or dancing. Our white comrades, brothers of the Wyandotte, will understand."

Those standing before him became humbly subdued.

Naseeka realized that soon, probably before midwinter, he would have to assume the duties of tribal chief and enforce the traditions and customs of his people. He wished to remind them that, at a time when their leader's spirit was preparing to leave on its long journey, tribal decorum must be maintained so the body and soul would be ready when the final moment comes.

Since his father no longer was able to take food and remained in a coma except for brief moments of lucidity, the young warrior knew death was but days, perhaps hours, away. Members of the tribe were not aware of the chief's debilitated condition, for they were not permitted to see their leader in a state of helplessness.

Naseeka stood before the two men, his arms folded beneath a wool cape that hung over his buckskin jacket. "You wish to visit Nasingah, chief of the Wyandottes?" he asked in a strong, inflexible voice.

He sounded harsh and looked severe enough to be less than cordial, but Richard and Flip knew his behavior was designed to impress members of the tribe, not indicate a coolness toward his white brothers. They knew he was a warm person who looked upon them as equals in the Wyandotte village.

"Yes," Flip answered, standing erect and looking directly into his dark eyes. "We wish to pay a visit to our good friend, the mighty Nasingah."

When they approached the chief's tepee, Naseeka waved his hand, and the brave standing at its entrance pulled the flap aside. Flip removed his raccoon hat and Richard his tricorn as they stood in the dimly lighted quarters. A brightly painted medicine man sat cross-legged in front of a small fire burning in a recessed ring at the lodge's center. He was chanting in a low voice and sprinkling bits of feathers and colored nutshells on the flame.

Through the smoky haze they could see the comatose Nasingah lying on an upraised pallet of skins at the rear of the tepee. The chief's neatly braided gray hair rested on top of the woven blankets that covered him. His wrinkled, ashen face appeared calm and serene. The only sign of life was the irregular rise and fall of the blankets from his shallow breathing.

Dropping to their knees, the two men watched the once stalwart leader for a full minute. Between chants of the medicine man, they could perceive a gurgling rattle from his fluid-filled lungs and, mixed with the smoke, smelled the offensive odor of pneumonia. A trace of blood oozed from the deeply creased corners of his mouth.

When they emerged from the tepee, Naseeka looked into the faces of his friends. "He is very sick?" he asked.

"Yes," Richard replied. "Very sick."

"Can the white man's medicine make him well?"

"No," Richard said flatly. "The Great Spirit is calling him."

They walked in silence through the crowd that had gathered, passed the outdoor fire ring where they had cooked fish on a previous visit, and entered the longhouse of Naseeka's mother. Expecting their arrival, she had placed barley, wild rice, and water in a cooking basket, then dropped in two heated stones.

While waiting for the grain to cook, Matoka placed a bowl of pemmican before them. As she dropped to the kneeling position, she looked into Flip's face. Richard saw the sparkle of love in her eyes when Flip smiled at her.

They sat for an hour and nibbled at dried sturgeon and boiled grain while talking with Naseeka. It was longer than intended, but as a courtesy they could not leave sooner. Naseeka told them his people had stored enough food to last through the winter, even if it was longer than usual. When Richard informed him he planned to butcher a pig the next day, the Indian's eyes beamed. "Good!" he said, a burst of enthusiasm showing in his face. "Naseeka will come with you!" It would give him a chance to learn more about the white man's ways. Besides, he could expect to be given some of the animal's organs to take home to his family.

Richard and Flip stood. "Tomorrow," Flip said, grasping Naseeka's hand, "you come to us."

"When the sun comes up," Naseeka replied, the handshake jarring the smoothness of his last two words.

"When the pig is finished, we will get honey from a tree," Richard said as he shook the Indian's hand. "You like honey?"

"Honey? " Naseeka questioned.

"Sugar of the bee," Richard explained, noting the curious look on the faces of the women.

"Yes, sugar of the bee," Naseeka repeated, still looking puzzled.

Before they left, Matoka, with Lahana standing at her side, gave Flip a bracelet made of small clamshell discs strung on a sinew of deer tendon. When they left the village, Richard asked if it had a particular meaning.

"Not sure," Flip replied. "But I think, if I put it on, it means we plan to marry."

———————◆———————

The next morning shortly after sunrise, Richard was walking along the icy, frost encrusted path to the barn. Looking up, he saw Matoka, a shawl of brown wool covering her head and shoulders, slip from the building and walk hurriedly toward the River Rouge bridge.

He pulled the latch string and, stepping inside, was met by Flip who had just descended the hayloft ladder. "Little late getting up today" he said, as he walked over to untie Bessie from the manger.

"Yah," Flip replied slowly. "Slept a little overtime." Then, suspecting Richard knew about Matoka, he continued. "Did you see her?"

"Yes," Richard said, turning to face him.

"I sure like her. Like her a lot." Flip raised the left sleeve of his buckskin blouse to expose the clamshell bracelet on his wrist.

"She's nice," Richard said, showing a smile of satisfaction. "She'll be a good woman for you."

Richard was not sure how Elizabeth would react when she learned Flip was marrying an Indian, even if it was the sister of a

280

prospective chief. Her parents were opposed to mixed marriages, especially between blacks and whites. He had seen Mr. Harrington nod in agreement when his wife concluded such a discussion with, "Even the birds have more sense than that."

But Elizabeth knew life on the frontier was much different than it was in Virginia. And Flip, unlike the farmer or merchant living in a settled area, had spent most of his life among Indians and roughneck trappers.

With these thoughts in mind, Richard decided to break the news at the breakfast table. "Notice the bracelet Flip's wearing," he said, pointing to the exposed wrist.

"Looks nice," Elizabeth said, reaching over to finger the discs.

"Means he's engaged."

"Really? How nice." A smile broke across her face. "Who to?"

"Matoka," Flip said, continuing to eat the pancake on his plate.

"That's Naseeka's sister," Richard explained, noting a surprised look suddenly appear on his wife's face. "She's a nice woman."

"Oh, I'm sure she is," Elizabeth said. Her response was more a matter of courtesy than agreement. Then, turning to Flip, she asked, "When will you be getting married?"

"Don't know. Probably afore spring."

She did not know of Matoka's visit to the barn, but Richard was pleased of her response to the marriage. The next thing, he thought, would be to have a wedding ceremony instead of Flip merely taking the Indian woman to his cabin.

By the time the men had finished breakfast and were crating the pig for the ride to LaCroix farm, Elizabeth had concluded it was probably a good match. After all, she reasoned, it would take an unusual woman to keep house for a man who had lived in the forest for so many years. Now, she was anxious to meet Matoka.

———————◆———————

Louis LaCroix arose early after a fitful night of sleep. Using flint and tinder, he lit a fire beneath the scalding kettle he had filled with water the night before. After milking his cows and feeding the remaining pig and chickens, he returned to add more wood to the fire. A thin layer of ice that had covered the water was gone, and steam was beginning to rise from its surface. Satisfied with its progress, he went inside to eat a breakfast of porridge and fried eggs Marie had waiting for him. Tomorrow they would have pork to go with the eggs. Their children, ten year old Pierre and eight year old Mimi, would like that.

Hearing the clatter of Molly's hoofs on the hard ground and the rattle of springless wheels and axles, Louis stepped outside to greet Richard and Flip. "Water should be about ready," he said, pointing to the steaming kettle.

"By the way, Naseeka said he was coming," Richard informed him.

Louis looked up, somewhat surprised. "He'd better hurry," he said, shrugging his shoulders, "or he'll miss it."

They unloaded Richard's crated pig and led Molly to the other side of the house. "Horses get nervous when they see a butcherin'," Richard explained to Flip as he tied her to a small tree. "Don't like the smell of blood, either."

Louis threw a piece of old canvas over the crated pig to keep it quiet; then they walked over to the kettle. After tossing more wood on the fire, he bent down to see through the steam. The water had just begun a rolling boil. He placed his hands on the table located next to the kettle. "We put him on here," he said, "then slide him in and out of the water so we can scrape the hair off."

As they walked toward the pigsty, Naseeka, followed by three braves, trotted up. Smiling, he shook hands with the white men. His companions stood expressionless in the background, little clouds of steam spurting from their nostrils.

Richard and Flip grabbed the pig Louis selected and wrestled the squealing animal to the ground near the gate of the enclosure. With surprising speed, Louis ran the eight inch blade to its hilt into the animal's throat. After tipping the handle back and forth, he removed it.

The released pig, squealing loudly, jumped to its feet and ran out the gate, a large stream of thick blood issuing from its wound. After a hundred feet, its high pitched squeal turned to a raspy gurgle. Then it collapsed.

Naseeka, with arms folded beneath his cape, stood a short distance away and watched. The other braves trotted after the faltering creature.

Richard saw delight in the Indian's faces as they stood over the pig and watched the final struggles of the dying animal. Turning to Flip, he asked, "Did you see how those three acted?"

"That's the savage in 'em," Flip replied out of the side of his mouth. "That's why you've gotta watch 'em. Can turn on ya in a minute." He emphasized the last sentence by snapping his fingers.

When the cumbersome pig was placed on the table, Richard and Flip grasped a hind leg and slid the animal into the boiling water. After a moment, it was withdrawn, and Louis, using a scraping blade, began removing the hair. Fifteen minutes and four dippings later, the animal was shaved smooth.

Strung up to a clothesline pole by the tendons of its rear legs, the pig was quickly eviscerated.

Used to throwing the whole animal onto a blazing fire, the three braves were amused at the removal of hair, and when the entrails dropped into a waiting pan, they chuckled audibly.

Naseeka studied the procedure carefully, hoping he could learn how meat was made to taste like that he had sampled from the white man's kitchen. Sensing the dissatisfaction of his hosts with the response of the three braves, he glared icily at the warriors. They immediately changed to solemn observers.

Louis handed Richard the stabbing knife. "Now, it's your turn," he said.

When Richard was finished, he felt a twinge of distress at killing an animal he and Elizabeth had raised and nurtured.

Richard and Flip placed the dressed pig on a canvas in the wagon box. Then Louis brought a bottle of blackberry wine from the house. He poured drinks for his white guests and Naseeka. As the men drank and chatted, the three braves kicked and chased an air inflated bladder Louis gave them.

Richard knew the warriors should have no wine, but he wanted to give them something. Dipping into a pan in the wagon, he handed them the sweetbreads. They quickly abandoned the bladder and stood about the steaming kettle, grunting, smiling, and talking in their harsh language as they ate pieces of the organ.

Although Naseeka felt equal to the white man, and incidents with the military commander showed he was held in high esteem, the offering of a glass of wine confirmed his status. He wanted to show his braves he was not only their superior, but stood on the same plane as the white man. Invited to ride on the wagon to Richard's farm, he instructed them to walk behind in a single file as he climbed aboard the seat. They, he knew, would spread the word throughout the Wyandotte village.

The wagon was halted near the cabin door, and Elizabeth, interested in the amount of meat there was, stepped outside onto the stone landing. She was visibly startled at the sight of the braves behind the wagon, but quickly regained her composure. Walking over to the wagon, she peered inside. "Looks good," she said, eying the cleaned animal.

"We're going to cut it up and hang it in the smokehouse," Richard informed her. "Probably could use something to eat after that."

"Would you like some fried liver?" she asked, looking at the pan of organs.

"That'd be good!" Flip said.

The leaf lard and kidneys were stripped from the animal before it was cut into sections. While Flip carried the pieces to the smoke-house, Richard held out the severed head to Naseeka. "For you," he said, watching carefully to gauge the red man's reaction.

The Indian looked at Richard with straight-faced sincerity, then replied, "This is good for Naseeka's family."

Grasping the head by the ears, he wheeled and handed it to the braves. After barking instructions, he watched as they found a pole and slipped it through the open mouth. Two of them shouldered it and the three walked briskly toward the River Rouge bridge.

Having been meticulously taught how to fry fresh pork liver at the age of twelve, Elizabeth was anxious to demonstrate her skill. Humming as she worked, she honed a knife on the hearthstone, then sliced the slippery organ. Thin slices, her mother had taught her, were essential to make it cook firm and absorb the flavor of the seasoning.

After rolling the slices in a mixture of flour and corn meal, she placed them in a hot skillet and topped them with slices of a large onion Marie had given her. Occasionally as she set the table, she looked at the liver, turning some pieces, adding others, and placing those that were done on a warm platter.

Then she made a large bowl of thick, brown gravy from the fat and juices. With the table ready, including a pot of tea next to the platter stacked high with liver, she opened the door and called out, "Time to eat!"

"Let's go!" Richard shouted, motioning to the others as he slammed the door on the smokehouse.

Naseeka, not sure he was included, stayed back, a questioned look covering his face

Richard went to him. He placed a hand on the red man's shoulder. "Naseeka will eat, too," he said.

They sat at the table, Richard and Elizabeth on one side, Flip and Naseeka on the other. All waited for someone to begin.

"Let's not let it get cold!" Richard said, spearing a piece of liver from the platter.

Naseeka, dropped his fur cape to the floor behind him, then hesitated as he watched the others. He wanted desperately to learn the white man's ways. This would be a good opportunity.

He had no trouble getting the liver to his plate and spooning gravy onto a piece of bread, but, as Elizabeth watched obliquely, he was unable to coordinate the knife and fork to cut the meat.

After a few minutes, he looked up into the eyes of the others. They had stopped eating to watch. Frustrated and embarrassed, he dropped the utensils to the table. Picking up food with his fingers, he stuffed the liver and gravy-soaked bread into his mouth. He gulped wolfishly, grunted, and smacked his lips. This was the kind of food he wanted the Wyandotte women to cook. Perhaps Elizabeth could teach Matoka and Lahana.

He cleaned his plate quickly, then lifted the teacup to his mouth. The hot liquid burned his lips and tongue, causing him to jerk his head back and stare at the steaming cup. He quickly put it back on the saucer, then sat erect to watch the others cut up their food and place it, piece by piece, into their mouths.

"Have more, " Richard urged, pointing to the platter.

Naseeka filled his plate again, but hesitated before eating. Holding his fork in his hand, he was trying to decide if he should try the utensils again or use his fingers.

"Flip," Richard said, pointing to Naseeka's plate, "why don't you show him how to use the knife and fork."

"Sure," Flip replied coarsely.

Flip placed the fork in the red man's left hand and the knife in his right, then helped him cut a piece of liver and insert it into his mouth. When, for the second bite, Naseeka did it himself, he looked up at Richard and Elizabeth. His face beamed a broad smile of satisfaction.

As she watched the red man eat, Elizabeth experienced a great sense of reward. This red man was a human being after all, she thought, and when she looked into his eyes, they seemed dark and warm instead of fierce and penetrating. Now, if there was some way to eliminate the smoky odor he emitted.

Except for a second helping taken by Flip and Richard, Naseeka devoured all the remaining liver, bread, and gravy. Occasionally as he ate, he looked at Elizabeth, smacked his lips, smiled, and nodded. He liked the way she prepared food.

"He must have been very hungry," she said to Richard in a low voice.

"Probably hasn't had anything since yesterday," Richard said with a shrug.

Flip looked at Naseeka and patted him on the shoulder. Then turning to Elizabeth, he said, "That's why ya don't find any fat Indians. They're hungry as dogs most of the time. Eat their fill when they find it and then run it all off huntin' for more."

"They probably could make it taste better, too," Elizabeth added, as the three men got to their feet and started for the door.

"Be back in a couple of hours with a batch of honey" Richard told her, laying a hand on her shoulder before stepping outside.

◆

While driving the springless wagon across the rough, frozen field toward the distant, somber woods, Richard looked back at Naseeka. The Indian was sitting among the buckets and kettles, his body quaking from the jarring ride. Reining Molly to a halt, Richard asked if he wanted to sit on the seat. Naseeka refused, indicating the seat was too narrow for three men in heavy clothing. Richard then stepped back and showed the red man how to stand with bent knees to cushion the bumps.

286

When they started again, Naseeka stood as directed. Placing a hand on Richard's shoulder to steady himself, he smiled. He had learned another lesson from his white brothers.

At the bee tree, Flip stood and looked at it. "By God!" he exclaimed. "That's a big damned tree! Biggest hardwood I've ever seen!"

"It's got a lot of bees in it," Richard warned, wiping his nose as he picked up the bow saw.

The leaves had fallen from the deciduous outcropping. Only a scattering of pines and firs broke the dismal gray of naked trunks and bare limbs that reached skyward. The pond at the bottom of the little hill was dark, its smooth, leaf-dotted surface broken occasionally by paths of ripples from wind gusts that dipped down to race across its chilly water. A fringe of ice crystals, growing stronger and extending farther each night, surrounded the lonely muskrat house. It was a lull, an in between time, a quiet period after a busy fall of preparation. Most activity had come to a halt, awaiting a plunge in temperature that would freeze the ground deep enough so the snow would stay and accumulate. Then winter creatures would emerge to romp, to forage, and to play.

"This is just a shell," Richard said, a surprised look on his face as he stopped sawing to tell Flip.

"Hell yes, your blade is covered with honey already," Flip replied, sticking his finger on it to taste the sticky residue.

Flip used an axe to complete the notch that would make the tree fall uphill.

"Not as bad as I thought it would be," Richard said, halting to catch his breath.

Naseeka watched with intense interest, noting a few bees flying dazedly about the large hole in the trunk. The cold had stunned them so they would not attack, but as a precaution, he gathered moss and leaves for smoke.

Richard shouted a warning. Then he stepped back and watched the contorted agony of the massive limbs as they tried to cushion the final descent.

"Just some seepage here," Richard said, looking at the mixture of honey, leaves, and decayed wood that plugged the huge end of the trunk.

"We'll run a couple of slits down its length and lift off a strip," Flip said.

Grabbing the axe, he swung the implement with a precision that surprised Richard and amazed Naseeka. The powerful strokes came down with a resounding ring, each exactly in line with the previous one. He cut through the tree shell in a straight line from one side of the hole to the severed base. As he began the second cut at the opposite side of the hole, Naseeka left for the wagon to fetch the containers for the honey.

"He's a damned nice sort," Flip said, nodding his head in the direction the Indian had taken.

"I like him," Richard said. "I really consider him a brother."

"Well," said Flip, hesitating a moment. "I guess I do, too."

When the strip was pried from the trunk and set aside, they looked down in disbelief. Submersed in honey that had accumulated for decades was the body of a human being.

Richard was the first to speak. "Good God! Some poor bastard got himself trapped in there!"

Naseeka and Flip removed the honeycomb containing the hibernating bees. Then, using their hands as scoops, they exposed the body. It was a young, perfectly preserved Indian brave. He was dressed in moccasins, leggings, and a breechclout, his face and bare chest heavily painted with the stripes and symbols of war. The colors were as bright as if they had been newly applied.

"Never met any of that tribe," Flip said, scratching his head. "That hairdo and paint is completely different."

Naseeka squatted and studied the body carefully for a full minute. Standing, he looked at Richard and said in a loud, firm voice, "Mascouten!"

"Mascouten?" Richard questioned. He had not heard of the tribe.

As they stood over the mummified warrior, Naseeka explained he had never seen one, but when he was a boy, his father had told him the story of the Mascoutens. "They were a small tribe of great warriors," he said. "They lived across the big river where the sun rises. One day the Hurons came, and there was a great battle. The Mascoutens fought well. But after four days when great numbers of Hurons were about to kill them all, they fled to this side of the river. There they again built their village and lived for many years as neighbors of the Wyandottes.

"Where was this village?" Richard asked.

"Where you and Louis have your farms," Naseeka replied tersely. Then he continued, "And again they were besieged by great tribes of Chippewa and Ottawa. They were forced to abandon their village. As they fled they were chased for many days."

"Where are they now?" Flip asked.

"Far away." Naseeka pointed to the west.

"Did the Wyandottes fight the Ottawas and Chippewas then?"

"No!" Naseeka replied sternly. "They see Wyandotte braves across the river, the Rouge River." He swept his outstretched hand before him. "They dare not come."

"You are sure he is Mascouten?" Richard asked.

"Yes," Naseeka nodded. He pointed to the dual mane of short-cropped hair on the shaved head. "My father said no other brave has hair like that." Then he pointed to the war paint on the chin and chest. "Mascouten!" he confirmed.

The body had stripes of red and white to outline raised tattoos on the forehead and about the eyes. Skin from the bridge of the nose to the base of the neck was painted a bright blue, and its black chest was decorated with three red X's that covered other raised tattoos.

Flip bent down for a closer look at the head. "The Mohawk's the only one I ever saw with hair like that. But they had only one strip." He shook his head. "And all that paint," he muttered. "Poor soul! Must have been a rear guard and got caught."

"Cornered, more likely," Richard added.

"What the hell should we do with 'im? Bury 'im?"

Richard thought a moment before replying. "Let's take him to the fort. Maybe Major Rogers would like to see him."

Flip looked at his friend and sighed.

After scooping away most of the honey, Flip looked down at his sticky hands and cuffs. "Isn't this one helluva mess!" he declared. "Maybe we should just leave 'im here and let the bears take care of 'im."

Such a thought was counter to Richard's Christian upbringing and the reverence for human life his mother had taught him, but he realized that, when one has lived a long time among savages who take pride in killing and mutilating others and who must kill forest creatures to survive, the sanctity of life has a tendency to diminish. "No," he said firmly. "We'll see to it he gets a proper burial."

The stiff, slightly shrunken body was lifted from its syrupy tomb and placed on the strip they had cut from the trunk. They washed their hands in the pond, then carried the heavy wooden litter to the wagon.

As they approached the house, Elizabeth, who had been listening for the clatter of the wagon, stepped out onto the landing. When Richard drew Molly to a halt, she called out, "Get much honey?"

"There was lots of it," he answered, shaking his head. "But we can't use it."

"Why not?" she asked, a puzzled look coming over her face as she walked toward the wagon.

"Because of this." Richard pointed to the body.

Much of the honey had flowed from the remains and was slowly running in a small stream off the end of the curved log section. Features of the cadaver were becoming more discernible. Teeth showed clearly through parted lips, and eyelids sagged into sunken sockets.

Elizabeth gasped and paled. "Oh, Lord," she said softly, twisting at her apron. "How horrible."

She looked up at Richard, then walked briskly into the house. Richard jumped from the wagon and followed, leaving Flip and Naseeka to take Molly to the barn. Sitting beside her at the table, he placed an arm around her shoulder to ease the shock she was experiencing.

"How did it happen?" she asked. The color was returning to her face.

"It's a very old body. Been stuck in that tree for years."

She looked at him questioningly. "It doesn't look very old."

"The honey must have preserved it."

After several minutes she felt strong enough to get up and walk about. Thinking it best to keep busy, she wiped the moisture from her eyes, then began to make a pot of tea. Her mother had told her that making a pot of tea was a good thing to do whenever something needed to be done but there didn't seem to be any reason to do it.

"Do you feel all right?" Richard asked, concern still showing on his face.

"I'm all right, now," she assured him. "Just surprised me. Thought I was going to see a lot of honey. Kind of silly, I guess."

◆

In the morning they would take the body to the military headquarters. Meanwhile, they could eat the meal Elizabeth was preparing. And Naseeka would spend the night in the barn with Flip.

That evening Flip built a blazing fire in the fireplace. Then he pulled the rug to one side so he and Naseeka could sit on it with their backs propped against the wall. Richard sat nearby in a chair. They talked about the Mascouten and how he'd met his fate.

"Maybe he got stung ta death," Flip suggested, packing tobacco into a corncob pipe.

"Maybe," Richard said. "But if he did, wouldn't there be some signs, some swelling?" He thought momentarily, then added, "Maybe he was in before the bees took to livin' there."

The discussion went on all evening without changing the topic. They wondered why he, a young brave in good physical condition, could not have outrun his pursuers, be they man or animal. Had he become wedged in such a position he could not crawl out? Or could he possibly have sunk into the honey and drowned? Was his demise quick and merciful, or had he died a long and agonizing death?

"Whatever happened to him," Flip concluded, watching the smoke from his pipe drift slowly toward the fireplace, "his life was cut short."

He handed the pipe to Naseeka. "Naseeka, my friend, what say we go to bed so we can get up early and go to Detroit."

Naseeka, sucking noisily at the pipe, grunted and nodded.

Thankful the morbid conversation had come to an end, Elizabeth handed Flip two blankets. "For Naseeka," she said.

"Thank you," the Indian said haltingly. He bowed his head and smiled.

Flip grabbed his musket from beside the door, then he and Naseeka stepped out into the pale blue moonlight. "Goodnight," he said, drawing the door closed. "See ya in the morning."

He glanced at the glistening frost crystals covering the barn roof, sniffed the smoke from the smokehouse, then looked over at the wagon with its mummified cargo. He pulled his collar up around his neck, shuddered, then strode off toward the barn. Naseeka, carrying the blankets, followed close behind.

He climbed into the loft and, before sitting down to remove his moccasins, showed Naseeka a place several feet away to spread his blankets. In the darkness he could see his exhaled breath in the crisp air as he slid into the snug pouch that served as his bed. It felt warm. Matoka had been there waiting for him. She must have run away when she found Naseeka was with him.

At first he hoped she would come back, but realized she wouldn't. He inhaled a deep breath of the juniper scent that welled up from within the bed and wondered where she had gone. Knowing Indian women, he assumed she was trotting along the trail back to her village. He felt guilty, but didn't know what he could do.

He pulled the blankets up around his neck, but sleep came slowly. Routine noises he readily recognized seemed amplified.

He listened to the shuffling of Molly and Bessie in their stalls, heard field mice, driven inside by the cold, chasing along the rafters, and he tried to decipher the calls of two distant wolf packs. He thought about the events of the day and, finally, about the soft, warm arms of Matoka.

◆

On the way to the fort they stopped in front of Louis' house and called him from the barnyard where he was feeding chickens. When he saw the Mascouten, he shrugged. "A dead savage?" he asked. He had seen many, and this one didn't seem so different.

Then he looked more closely at the coating of honey. Some of it had flowed onto the wagon box floor. "What's this?" he asked, pointing a finger.

"Honey," Richard replied.

"We found him in a bee tree," Flip said.

Naseeka nodded confirmation.

Louis suddenly realized it as an oddity. He called to Marie. When she came, he stopped her short of the wagon and explained what she would see.

Sidling up to the vehicle, she gingerly peered inside. "*Mon dieu!*" she gasped, putting her hands up to shield her eyes. Slowly she withdrew a few steps, a look of shock registering on her face.

"He used to live here," Richard explained, pointing to Louis' house.

"Here?" Louis asked, pointing a finger toward the ground.

"He is Mascouten, and his village once stood here on our farms."

"That is so," Naseeka assured the French couple. "Long time ago. My father told me."

Richard and Flip explained how they found the body and were taking it to Detroit. When they drove away, the LaCroix stood, hand in hand, shaking their heads as they waved goodbye.

At first the major, a lean, wiry young man, clean shaven except for a thick, brown mustache, was not interested enough to step outside for a look. He thought it just another in a series of wild tales he had heard over the years. But then, these men were sober and showed a sincerity others did not possess.

Dressed in a bright, new uniform, he walked out to the wagon. After peering carefully at the body for a full minute, he looked at Richard. "Well preserved, 'e is. Must be old. Never seen any like 'im."

"Naseeka says he's a Mascouten," Richard said.

Major Rogers looked at Naseeka, then back at Richard and nodded. "Heard of Mascoutens around the mission at St. Joseph. Not many supposed ta be left. Friendly lot."

As they walked around the wagon, Richard related what Naseeka told him about the Mascouten tribe.

"Very interesting," Rogers said. Then his piercing blue eyes stared directly into Richard's. "And now, what do ye plan ta do with 'im?"

"I guess we'll bury him." Richard was disappointed at the major's response.

"Seems like a sensible thing ta do," Rogers agreed. He sensed Richard's letdown. " 'Tis an unusual case all right, but I don't know what else we can do."

They took the body to the Church of Ste. Anne. Perhaps they could bury it in the parish cemetery at the rear of the church, but Father Ault informed them the consecrated grounds were reserved for members in good standing.

The Church of England, temporarily housed in a wooden cabin, also refused. "You see," the pastor explained sympathetically, " 'e is a heathen savage, and they 'ave no soul. Only persons with souls can be buried in our cemetery. If 'e would 'ave converted, would 'ave been baptized, 'e would 'ave acquired a soul. Then 'is body could be buried 'ere and 'is soul could enter the kingdom of 'eaven." He paused and looked into the dejected faces of the three men. "I'm afraid you'll 'ave ta take 'im outside the wall to the pauper and 'eathen plot." He pointed to the north gate of the fort.

Richard, his face red with frustration, set his jaw and climbed up to the wagon seat. "Come on," he called to Naseeka and Flip. "We'll take him back home. Back to the home that was once his."

When they stopped at the Black Swan, they sent Naseeka to visit Frenchy at the Comptoir Grillon.

"Mornin' men," Henry said, as they pulled the door of the smoke-filled room closed behind them. "What'll it be?"

"Ale," Flip replied, walking up to the bar.

Henry placed two filled tankards before them. "I 'ear ye found a petrified savage."

"We did," Richard said coolly, sipping at his drink. "And now we're trying to find a place to bury him."

"Where is 'e?"

"Outside, in the wagon."

They picked up their tankards and walked through the door. Four tavern patrons followed.

Several men had gathered around the wagon.

" 'Tis the damnedest thing I ever saw," Henry said, shaking his head. "And ye don't know where ta bury 'im?"

"Neither church'll take him in," Flip said, taking a stick from a crusty, old man who was trying to lift the Mascouten's breechclout.

"Toss the bloody savage into the river," suggested one of the customers, a middle-aged man with a heavy fur coat who wheeled on his heels and went back into the tavern.

"I'm going to bury him proper," Richard said, looking sternly about the crowd. "Come on, Flip, let's go in and drink our ale."

After their second tankard, the two men pushed their way through the crowd that had gathered. Richard ignored questions that were shouted at him. He was disgusted with the unchristian behavior of his fellow man. He flipped the reins to start Molly. Several men walked alongside the wagon, continuing to stare at the Mascouten.

When they picked up Naseeka, they spoke with Frenchy. Again a crowd gathered. And when they drove away, it followed them down the street as far as the Savoyard bridge.

Driving south on the river road, they sat quietly on the overburdened seat for a long time. Then Richard turned to his two companions. "We'll take him to my place and bury him there!"

Using an axe to chop through three inches of frozen crust and a shovel to dig the remaining four feet into the sandy loam, the men, including Louis, dug a grave near the edge of a low bluff at the confluence of the Rouge and Detroit rivers. They lowered the body, resting imposingly on its curved, beechwood bier, to the bottom of the hole. Then they covered it with a thick blanket of pine and spruce boughs.

They were compacting the soil into a mound when Elizabeth and Marie walked up.

With a cold, yellow sun midway down in the blue western sky and a chill wind blowing at their backs, they stood, quietly looking down at the freshly turned earth. Richard broke the silence. "May the gods of this Mascouten brave watch over him and lead him to the land of the Great Spirit."

Then the LaCroix and the Lockes, lowering their heads against the cold wind, started back toward their homes.

Flip tossed the tools into the wagon and climbed onto the seat. He waited for Naseeka, who stood with arms folded and legs apart, looking across the grave to the treelined shore on the eastern side of the Detroit River. After a few minutes the young, Wyandotte brave wheeled about and climbed up beside Flip.

Flip snapped the reins. "Let's go girl. We've done our duty for the day."

Chapter 11

New Year

Flip sat across the breakfast table from Richard and Elizabeth lingering over a second cup of tea as he contemplated the walk back to his cabin. The wind had shifted to the northeast during the night, raising the temperature to just below the freezing level and driving in a heavy layer of billowy, gray clouds. Shortly before daybreak the air became calm, and snow in large damp flakes began to fall, slowly and softly at first, then like a deluge of heavy, white feathers. He hoped it would slacken or, better yet, stop. If it didn't, he'd be soaked to the skin by the time he reached the fort. Perhaps, like a spring shower, it would pass. He finished the tea, then packed his pipe and lit it with a firebrand from the fireplace.

"Where did you get your tobacco?" Elizabeth asked, sniffing the aroma as he sat down again.

"From Frenchy," he replied, holding the pipe away so he could watch the smoke curling up from it. "I think he got it in a shipment from Virginia."

"Smells good," she complimented. Then turning to Richard, she said, "Maybe you should smoke that kind."

Richard looked at her thoughtfully. He wasn't a steady smoker, but occasionally brought out his clay pipe. He liked the relaxed feeling it gave him. His tobacco was of poor quality and dry with age. And it wasn't very aromatic, but certainly didn't smell like the moldy hay she sometimes mentioned. "Might just do that," he said.

By the time the tobacco in Flip's pipe was half consumed, the snow had nearly stopped falling. He looked at the door, then back at Richard. "I'd better get goin'," he said, rising to his feet to look out the window. "Got a long way ta go."

Thinking he saw movement in the distance, he pushed his face close to the window and squinted to filter the white glare. Suddenly his face tensed. "There's somebody comin'!" he said. "Runnin' hard and headin' this way!"

Both men grabbed their muskets and returned to the window. Elizabeth stood back a few steps, sighting between their heads for a glimpse of the stranger.

"Why, that's one of Naseeka's braves," Richard stated, looking at Flip for a reaction.

"Sure is," Flip agreed. "One of them that was with him at the pig butcherin'."

They stepped outside and pulled the door closed.

The young Indian's knees buckled as he halted before them, but he quickly regained his balance. "Nasingah *mort!*" he gasped, vapor spurting from his nose and mouth.

Flip waited for him to take a few more breaths, then asked, "When did your chief die?"

The lightly clad brave stared with a blank expression. He didn't comprehend French. Naseeka must have told him what to say. Switching to the Wyandotte dialect, Flip haltingly asked the red man several questions. As they talked, the brave's heavy breathing subsided.

"Says the chief died during the night," Flip stated, relaying the information to Richard. "His people want their white brothers there for the burial."

He turned back to the brave. "When will Nasingah be placed in the ground?"

Steam rose from the brave's jacket as his dark eyes roved across Flip's face. "He must be placed in the ground before darkness comes," he replied, shuffling his feet, anxious to leave.

Richard motioned for him to come inside and dry his buckskins before the fireplace. The red man shook his head. He turned to Flip. "Naseeka says I come back quick."

He gulped down a cup of tea Elizabeth handed him, then changed the wet grass insulation in his knee-high moccasins for dry hay Richard gave him.

"I guess it's no use asking him to wait and go with us," Richard said, looking at the brave who was beginning to shiver.

The Indian sensed what was being discussed. He looked at Flip. "I run back to the village," he said. "When I run I will get warm and dry." He whirled on his feet and started toward the River Rouge bridge, leaving a trail of pigeon-toed tracks in the moist snow.

◆

The trail beyond the bridge was a white tunnel of heavily burdened, overhanging branches, the smoothness of its clean floor broken only by the straight line of evenly spaced footprints made by Naseeka's messenger. Richard wrapped the reins around a peg in the wagon box giving Molly her head as he quietly pondered the situation. He hoped the burial would not take long, and he didn't want to become involved in a wild celebration for the new chief. He would trust Flip to see to it.

A small cascade of snow fell from an overhead branch and landed on Molly's back, disrupting his train of thought. It quickly melted, and he watched it steam for several minutes as it evaporated. "Damn good horse," he said, breaking the silence.

"Good horseflesh," Flip agreed, puffing lightly on his pipe.

"By the way, what do you know about burying the chief?"

"Not much," Flip replied, smoothing the coat collar about his neck. "Never seen the buryin' of a chief afore. But I think each tribe does it their way." He looked ahead up the trail, then added, "Just have ta play it by ear."

◆

Naseeka emerged from the chief's tepee where several women under direction of the medicine man were sewing Nasingah's corpse into a deerskin shroud. He had to make sure the body was dressed in new, buff-colored buckskins and adorned with a beaded headband containing four white-tipped eagle feathers.

He stared at the heavy layer of snow. Dozens of footprints crisscrossed the area before him and circled the large fire ring. Why did his father have to die in winter? Why couldn't the Great Spirit have waited until spring or summer when it wasn't so miserable to do what had to be done? But it was not to be. Now he was chief of the Wyandottes, a tribe facing growing pressure from the white man and mounting hostility from the Ottawa and Huron. He was grateful, however, for the counsel and guidance of his tribal elders. They would show him the ways of a new chief. It lessened the anxiety surging through him.

Looking toward the snow-clad ridge of sandy soil that ran along the broadening channel of the Detroit River, he concentrated on the young braves digging the twenty foot circular grave. Nearby, older men were stacking the remains of countless dozens who had died since the burial of the last chief. Initially sewn in shrouds of cloth or animal skin and placed on pole-supported platforms in the sacred plot in the forest, they would now join their chief in the ground. Nature and animals had dispersed the remains, but he hoped the old men and boys could find them all so they could be placed around his father to offer protection and show their loyalty.

Suddenly, he felt a damp chill seeping through the soles of his moccasins. He whirled on his toes and walked briskly to the longhouse of his family. Looking inside, he saw a dozen women, including three of the chief's wives, gathered about his mother's fire ring. They were loudly wailing a mournful dirge. That was good. It would bring the rest of the village to the proper funeral mood.

He turned to leave and saw Richard and Flip approaching the big fire ring. Their presence elated him. Although he had to retain a look of sorrow, inside he felt better.

When he declined their outstretched hands, they looked at him questioningly. Gazing into their eyes, he said soberly, "The Wyandotte people are pleased their white brothers are with them at this time of sadness."

He motioned for them to follow him to the guest tepee. When they reached the entrance, he said, "I will come for you when it is time." Then, quickly, he shook their hands.

There were glowing coals in the fire ring but no food or water. Sitting on short logs, the two men spoke in muffled tones, their voices occasionally overwhelmed by the wailing women in the nearby longhouse.

"Sounds awful," Richard said, shaking his head.

"Some's grievin', others is actin'," Flip advised. "I'm sure there's a batch of them who's glad the old man's gone."

Naseeka came. He motioned for them to stand a short distance in front of the chief's tepee.

With a suddenness that startled Richard, the entrance flap opened, and four braves, dressed only in breechclouts and moccasins, emerged carrying a pole pallet bearing the encased body of Nasingah on their shoulders. Richard clenched his fists and shivered as a chill rose along his spine to the nape of his neck. He looked at Flip for direction.

Flip nodded and motioned for him to join the procession that quickly formed for the short walk to the grave.

The wailing, initially done by the small group of women, soon involved everyone in the village except Nasingah's family. The moaning, screaming, and crying that filled the cold air was deafening. Richard felt his pulse pounding in his temples. He wished he hadn't come.

The villagers gathered around the freshly dug hole and looked down on the rotting shrouds of several bodies that had been placed among the large number of skulls and other skeletal bones. The chief's pallet was gently lowered onto a cleared area in the center. As a covering of evergreen boughs was put in place and earth tossed upon it, the wailing reached a crescendo.

The family stood, dry eyed and without signs of emotion, watching from the edge of the hole. When the last basket of soil had been placed on the grave, the wailing stopped abruptly.

The medicine man stepped to the edge of the grave and extended his arms. Speaking slowly and loudly, he said, "Oh mighty leader of the Wyandottes, may your ride on the Giant Bird take you swiftly to the bountiful hunting ground of all great warriors." He lowered his arms, then plucked a small bale of jerked venison from his robe and tossed it onto the soft mound of fresh earth.

Naseeka, standing beside hin, immediately changed his stance. No longer the humble son, he was now a leader with authority. He brought his arms up from his sides, folded them across his chest, and stood with his feet apart. With jaws firmly set and eyes sternly ahead, he stared across the grave at the slowly flowing, gray waters of the river as members of the tribe walked around the grave in twos and threes. Each tossed a token gift onto the foot of the grave before starting back to the village.

Lahana, Matoka, and Naseeka's mother stood at his right side. Two other wives stood on the left. Although they held their eyes open wide, Naseeka's mother and sister could not keep the tears from forming and running down their cheeks.

Like a bad dream, Richard felt he and Flip were caught unaware. If he had known they were obligated to contribute to the growing pile of food, leather bands, nature symbols, and straw dolls, he could easily have brought something from home. He watched Flip search his pockets, then shrug as he gave up his doe-skin tobacco pouch.

The only thing Richard had in his pockets was lead shot. That would be inappropriate for this occasion. He took off the mittens Elizabeth had knitted and tossed them onto the pile.

"We must wait a few minutes for Naseeka," Flip said as they stood in the cold near the big fire ring with Matoka and Lahana. Naseeka had been escorted into the chief's tepee by the medicine man to meet with his council of braves.

In a few minutes Naseeka emerged. He was dressed in fitted buckskins and wore a brightly colored leather headband which held four eagle feathers in an upright position at the rear of his head. Centered on his forehead among the painted decorations of the band was the head of a vicious timber wolf portrayed in glass beads.

A cry of jubilation arose from the hoarse throats of three hundred emotion-charged members of the tribe. "Naseeka, our leader! Naseeka, our leader!" they shouted.

Richard and Flip watched in awe. How quickly they had forgotten Nasingah.

Lahana leaned close to Richard's ear. "I made his headband," she boasted, shouting so he could hear.

"It's nice," he complimented.

"You like it?"

"Yes. It is very pretty."

Naseeka raised his hand for silence. In a clear, authoritative voice, he said, "I am Naseeka, chief of the illustrious Wyandottes!"

The tribe roared approval.

He walked across the packed snow and stood before Richard and Flip. "To you, my brothers, I promise the friendship of the Wyandotte people."

As Naseeka shook his hand, Richard studied his face. The red man's eyes still appeared dark and intense, but somehow they didn't seem so fierce. Richard was cold and anxious to return home, but he was glad he had come.

◆

Elizabeth stepped outside and tossed the dishwater around the corner onto a growing slick of gray ice. She hung the pan on its peg, then dropped into a chair in front of the crackling fire Richard had built before leaving to walk the trap line. It was only midmorning, and already she was tired.

She looked up on the wall at the short-barreled flintlock Richard had bought for her. Winter life on a frontier farm was a combination of adventure and boredom. There were so many things she had to learn to do that women didn't do in Fredericksburg, but she was proud to be able to hit a six-inch bull's-eye at fifty yards with constant regularity. She enjoyed ramming the ball down the polygrooved barrel with a greased patch and shooting it, even if it covered her shoulder with bruises.

She also had assisted Richard in the delivery of Betsy's calf, then learned to milk the cow. When he insisted she couldn't do the milking because she lacked sustained grip-strength, she protested. "But I've got muscles," she remembered saying, holding a clenched fist at arm's length.

"A Baltimore oyster!" he had teased, feeling her biceps before drawing her to him.

"But it's growing," she said meekly, as they hugged.

When he showed her how to wean the frisky little animal by teaching it to drink from a bucket, she insisted on trying it. At first she was hesitant. Perhaps she was pushing things too fast. But she wanted to be a good farm wife, so she shoved two fingers into the creature's eager mouth and forced its head into the bucket. "Eek!" she squeaked. "What a sandy tongue!"

She looked down at the two small wooden tubs near her feet. Tomorrow was wash day again, and Richard would fill them when he got back. Washing clothing in the winter was a harsh task she faced every two weeks. Before the river froze, Richard carried water up whenever it was needed, but now he tried to do it only in the morning or late afternoon when he watered the livestock. That way, he wouldn't have to chop through the ice so often.

The two wooden tubs were filled so she could heat a portion of the water in an iron caldron, changing it throughout the evening. In the morning, she would heat the kettle over the morning fire until it boiled. When she added it to the tubs, they would be ready.

But the worst part was hanging the steaming items over the clothesline in the bitter cold, then collecting them, frozen stiff in the afternoon. The wind chapped her hands. And her fingers, often so numb with cold she felt no pain, were cut by the sharp edges of the frozen garments as she pried them from the line.

Brought inside, the clothing would quickly thaw and rapidly dry, but her hands would be sore for several days. She studied them for several minutes, then slowly rose to her feet. She would bring in more firewood so Richard wouldn't have to do it when he got back.

When Richard returned, he sat down in a chair in front of the fireplace. Elizabeth handed him a cup of tea, then returned to the kitchen area.

He had caught two beavers, three muskrats, and a skunk. Unhappily, the trap line was less productive than anticipated. The area had been over-hunted during the past few years by the white man with his more efficient rifle and steel-jawed trap, and there was the concentration of Indians who moved in to trade and barter at the fort.

He stared at the fire and recalled the winter on the Tittabawassee. Rarely did he find empty traps, but here on the Rouge the animals were less plentiful and more wary. Often the traps went untouched, many with tracks in the snow indicating the animals sensed the danger and left their usual trail to traverse a safer route.

And skinning the animals was different than at the cabin he'd shared with Flip. On the first day, he brought in eight beavers, three muskrats, and a fox. After he stripped them of their pelts on the table, Elizabeth cleaned up the mess. "There must be some other place you can do this," she sighed.

"It's too cold to go it outside," he protested, his hands still covered with a greasy film of caked blood from carrying the carcasses to the riverbank.

"But, Richard," Elizabeth explained, placing her hands on her hips, "I don't want to scrub this floor and table every other day. Besides, it smells awful."

She didn't mention it, but she didn't like to look at the contorted faces of the little animals, some having died in great agony. Her love for Molly, Bessy, and the calf made it painful to see them hurt. She realized that trapping and hunting had to be done, but she preferred to have it remain more distant from her.

His decision to use the smokehouse for skinning and storage pleased her so much that the next day, while he was doing the skinning, she baked a batch of honey and butternut cookies, his favorite.

———————◆———————

Richard flipped the reins so they rippled across Molly's back to begin the ride home. On his face was a smile of satisfaction. He had delivered a bale of pelts to the Hudson's Bay warehouse for a good price. Although the air entering his lungs was crisp and cold, the bright sun felt warm, on his face. He turned to Elizabeth, "Next time we'll sell them to Frenchy."

Elizabeth knew he sometimes sold to Frenchy, although the price was lower. She looked at him, smiled, and nodded. "Yes," she said, removing her hands from beneath the robe that covered her lap. "We must keep him as our friend."

Every two or three weeks, Richard hitched Molly to the wagon and delivered a bale of furs to Detroit. Usually he went alone and sold to Hudson's Bay, but occasionally he took a bale to Frenchy, especially if he wished to buy something from the Comptoir Grillon. The Frenchman understood and appreciated the favor, even though the bales weighed only eighty pounds instead of the standard hundred the hinterland trappers brought in at the end of the season.

Richard enjoyed the frequent trips to Detroit, and it kept the smokehouse from becoming congested with pelts and thawing animals waiting to be skinned. Each bale brought enough money to buy needed supplies, and there was always a some money left over. In a contrived game, when he entered the house he tossed the pouch of coins into Elizabeth's spread apron. As they counted it at the table, he related the events of the trip. Afterwards, he placed it in the secret cache of the hearth.

Sometimes he encountered a party of Wyandotte braves on the road, or in the Comptoir Grillon where they bartered furs for grain, ammunition, and hand tools. They grunted and nodded recognition but wouldn't speak unless he spoke first. Because of his limited knowledge of their language, the conversation was restricted to an inquiry about Naseeka and their terse responses.

Previously, the trading had been done by Naseeka, but since becoming chief, his trips to Detroit were elevated to conferences with the commandant, Major Rogers, or the aide, Captain Campbell.

When they reached the intersection of Rue St. Jacques, Richard reined Molly to a sudden halt. Coming toward them from the narrow side street were three Indians dressed in heavy fur clothing. It looked like Naseeka, flanked by two braves.

When they were near enough to be sure, he handed the reins to Elizabeth and jumped down. "My brother," he said, extending his hand.

The Wyandotte chief grasped the outstretched hand and gave it a snap. As he released it, he looked up at Elizabeth. Elizabeth smiled and nodded.

"What brings you to the fort?" Richard asked, glancing at the two stern-faced braves.

Naseeka's smile vanished from his thin lips, and the muscles of his jaws tensed. "Naseeka cannot get guns and powder from the English!" he snapped.

Richard did not want to let on that he knew British policy and understood the reason for it. "Did Major Rogers tell you why?" he asked innocently.

Naseeka's eyes flashed. "He says the English sells no guns to Indians!"

"Do Wyandottes have many guns?"

"We have some," Naseeka explained, placing a hand on Richard's shoulder. "But each year there are fewer deer. Wyandottes need guns to eat." He hesitated momentarily, then jerked his head. "Naseeka will get guns from the Frenchman!"

Richard knew that, over the years, Frenchy had bartered and sold guns to anyone who had the price. During the French occupation there had been no restrictions, but now it was illegal to sell firearms to the red men. He thought it best to change the conversation. "How is the family of Naseeka?" he inquired.

"All Wyandotte people are well. They have a good chief!" He snapped his head to emphasize the point. "And they are looking forward to my marriage with Lahana."

"When?" Richard asked, smiling and nodding to indicate approval.

"When the white blanket goes away, Naseeka will marry Lahana, Flip will marry Matoka."

Richard swallowed hard. He managed a smile as he shook the red man's hand again. Matoka would make a good wife for Flip, but he wondered if his friend knew of Naseeka's plans.

"You will come," Naseeka stated flatly. Then pointing to Elizabeth, he said, "You bring your woman!"

Richard smiled broadly. "We will wait for your message."

Naseeka grunted and turned to leave.

"You want to ride with us?" Richard asked.

Naseeka turned to face him again. "Naseeka will ride! Braves will walk!"

Richard glanced at the wagon. There was plenty of room for everyone. "All will ride!" he stated firmly with a sweep of his hand.

Naseeka grunted and nodded. He climbed into the back of the wagon and motioned for his companions to join him.

———————◆———————

The heavy snow had halted the weekly convoys to and from Fort Niagara, but Elizabeth continued to write letters to her mother for Richard to deposit at military headquarters. She didn't write as often as before, but when they were delivered she wanted her parents to know she had not stopped thinking of them.

Then, one day Richard came back from the fort with a letter. She was pleasantly surprised. It had been delivered by an army courier who, taking advantage of the frozen lakes and rivers and traveling alone to elude the treacherous Hurons, traversed the more direct route along the northern shore of Lake Erie. Her heart leaped to her throat. She popped it open and quickly scanned it.

Richard waited, watching the expression on her face. His concern was for bad news. Since there was no way to go back in winter, there was little he could do except comfort her. When she looked up, he saw no sadness in her face. "Everything all right?" he asked, still waiting to be sure.

"Yes," she said, smiling.

"I'll put Molly away," he said, starting for the door.

The letter was little different from others she had received from them, but it buoyed her spirits. It ended by stating they hoped she could find a way to return because they missed her very much.

She sat down at the table and read it again, more slowly this time. When she finished she looked blankly out the window. Life had been easy and pleasant in Fredericksburg. Maybe she and Richard should have stayed.

Her thoughts were interrupted by the sound of Richard stamping his feet as he approached the door. She released a big sigh. It would be nice to go back for a visit, but she didn't want to return and let them think she and Richard had failed. Until it could be arranged, she would work hard with her husband to make a success of frontier farming and trapping.

Richard hung his coat and hat on a peg and walked over to the fireplace. "Glad everything's all right at home," he said, warming his hands before the blaze.

"They'd still like us to come back," she said. She paused, then added, "If only for a visit."

He was pleased the letter had lifted his wife's spirits, but Mrs. Harrington always included a suggestion they return. That was impossible. They could not travel in winter and had to work the farm the rest of the year. She could go back in the summer, but he was sure she wouldn't go alone. It would be better to change the subject. "Do we go over to the LaCroix's, or do they come over here Saturday?"

They tried to get together with the French couple on Saturday evenings to play euchre, a game the LaCroix became enthusiastic about when Richard brought out his cards and taught them how to play. The visits alternated between the houses with the LaCroix bringing their children when they came to the Lockes' cabin. Early in the evening the children were put to sleep on the bed, wrapped in blankets brought for the purpose. During the three or four hours of card playing, the host served popcorn, nuts, and cider or wine

When they finished playing, they drank hot tea and ate cookies while energetically discussing how the game might have gone if certain cards had been played differently. Then it was time to light the candle in a tin lantern, bundle up against the crisp night air, and walk home through the powdery snow. The host couple watched through a window to track the light until its final wave indicated the visitors had arrived safely.

◆

A few days before Christmas, Elizabeth spread holly sprigs on the windowsill around a large red candle she had purchased in Detroit. Satisfied it looked all right, she returned to the kitchen to finish the honey and butternut cookies she was making. She missed the bells, the caroling, and the gathering of friends that occurred in Fredericksburg. Here on the farm, the distance from the church and people of the fort made it difficult to generate a holiday spirit.

When Richard returned from the trap line, she watched for his reaction. He stood before the fireplace and looked at the decorated window, but said nothing. She was disappointed. Maybe it was because his father had done little to make holidays a special occasion after the death of his mother. She didn't know. But she would bake a cake and roast the goose Marie gave her anyway.

In addition, she was making a black and white blanket coat for him. Several weeks before, she'd noticed they were the fashion for men in Detroit, so she'd secretly purchased the material. Although she worked on it only when he was away, it would be finished in time to give as a present.

On Christmas eve, a short time before they were to leave for the LaCroix's, Richard went outside. When he returned, he had a pair of brown, high button shoes and a hanging lamp which he had hidden in the barn. He had overheard Elizabeth tell Marie how she would like to have a glass-lined copper lamp suspended by a chain from the ceiling of the living room area. The next time he'd gone to Detroit, he had a metalsmith make one using a design he remembered from his father's shop in England.

"For you, my darling, on this, our first Christmas together," he said, his face beaming with a broad smile. He was sure she hadn't expected anything.

Elizabeth was astonished. Tears appeared in her eyes as she held them up before placing them on the table. She looked at him with a sly grin, then got his coat from the spare bedroom.

"And for you, my wonderful husband."

As he put it on, he saw a smile of satisfaction spread slowly across Elizabeth's face. He gathered her in his arms and said, "The Detroiters wear these." He kissed her warmly. "You make me so proud to be your husband."

Thirty minutes later, they stepped outside for the short walk to the LaCroix cabin. Richard carried the musket and a kettle of hot wassail; Elizabeth had a small rum cake.

A bright moon centered in the cloudless canopy of brilliant stars made a lantern unnecessary. In the calm air, the only sounds came from squeaking snow beneath their feet and the far-off howls of a distant wolf pack. Ahead, they could see dozens of cottontails chasing about, enjoying the safety of the well lighted, snow-covered fields.

"Merry Christmas!" they called out as they stamped their feet in the wedge of light issuing from the open doorway.

"Come in! Come in!" Louis smiled, holding the door open with one hand, greeting them with the other.

Before giving her coat to Marie, Elizabeth took two small packages of cookies from her pocket and gave them to the LaCroix children.

"*Merci! Merci!*" they responded in unison, each bowing slightly as their mother had taught them.

Elizabeth watched as they placed the cookies with other packages in front of a small nativity grouping in one corner of the living area. When the children stepped back, she looked down at the ceramic figures. A candle at each end of the scene made the exquisitely painted statues glow softly in the dim light. It reminded her of the church in Fredericksburg at Christmas. A surge of warmth rippled through her body.

Marie's voice interrupted her thoughts. "Normally, they would open their gifts after the evening mass," she explained. "But here they'll open them in morning."

"A very fine coat," Louis said, as Richard slipped it from his shoulders.

"Elizabeth made it for me for Christmas."

"How nice," Louis said as he and Marie examined its soft texture and fine stitching.

Startled by a sudden knock at the door, Louis grabbed his musket. Richard picked up his weapon and motioned for the women and children to stand back. Cautiously, Louis lifted the latch and peered out. Then he drew the door fully open disclosing a middle-aged man standing with a cast iron kettle in one hand.

"Come in, Hiram," Louis said, motioning the man inside.

Hiram Jackson, the farmer on the other side of the LaCroix, explained that he and his family had just returned from the fort. When he tried to relight the fireplace, he discovered he didn't have his tinderbox and flint. "Musta lost it someplace along the way," he said, shaking his head to indicate disgust with himself. "Hafta borrow some coals."

Hiram was an Englishman who considered the French less than his equal. He worked his farm, occasionally waving or nodding to Louis, but never made an effort to become acquainted. The warm welcome he received surprised him. In a few minutes he had been introduced to the Lockes, given a cup of hot wassail to drink in front of the roaring fireplace, and handed a slab of rum cake to take to his family. He smiled broadly, his red nose and cheeks shining in the light of the fire as he enjoyed the friendly reception.

"Gotta get back ta m'family," he said, handing the empty cup to Marie. "They're a-waitin' fer me ta light the fire."

Louis filled his kettle with glowing coals and covered them with a thin layer of ashes. "That should do it," he told Hiram in broken English.

"Thank ye! Thank ye!" Hiram repeated as he stepped toward the door. "Merry Christmas!"

"Merry Christmas to your family!" Richard and Elizabeth called to him.

"*Joyeux Noel!*" the LaCroix chorused.

For two hours Richard and Elizabeth sat before the fireplace, absorbing the warmth of radiating heat and enjoying friendly conversation with their French neighbors. They nibbled on candy and nuts and sampled a variety of sweets as they sipped spiced wassail and Louis's blackberry wine. "Do you know about the New Year's eve party at the Detroit Council House?" Marie asked.

"Oh sure," Richard replied, holding a cup of wassail on his knee with one hand while eating a piece of cake with the other. "Didn't think we'd go, though. Awfully far, and it'd be so late."

"We go every year," Louis said, his face showing dismay at Richard's negative reply. "Lots of fun."

"Yes," Marie added. "We take the children with us. It's a big celebration."

The thought of a party sparked Elizabeth's interest. She and Richard had been working hard and staying close to home for a long time. She was ready for a big evening of entertainment. Besides, she was anxious to wear the party dress she had brought from Fredericksburg. She turned to Marie. "Will there be music and dancing?"

312

"Oh, yes," Marie answered. "It's a *big* party." She spread her arms to emphasize the size.

Elizabeth turned to Richard. "Sounds like fun. Why don't we go?"

Richard could see the longing in his wife's eyes. He sighed. "It's all right with me," he assented, showing little enthusiasm.

Louis brightened. "I have a sleigh big enough for all of us." He paused, then added ruefully, "But other than my oxen, I have only a very old plow horse to pull it. It will be a slow ride."

Richard's face suddenly showed a degree of eagerness. "We'll use Molly! She'd like that!"

"Then it is settled!" Louis said, holding up his glass of wine. "We'll go together—your horse, my sleigh!"

On the way home, Elizabeth experienced an inner feeling of warmth and contentment. She clutched Richard's arm tightly and looked at the snow-covered fields that were bathed in a pale blue light. "You know," she said, "the LaCroix are like family to us."

Richard also felt a close kinship with the French family. "I think we *can* consider them family. They've been awfully good to us." The snow squeaked a singsong tune beneath their feet as they walked slowly toward their dark cabin. "Besides, we can use all the friends and family we can get out here."

◆

Elizabeth took her satin and velvet dress from its hanger. It had to be aired, and she wanted to pin small packets of lavender sachet to its inner folds. It had been worn twice before, once at her birthday party and again at a piano recital she had given at Widow Wright's school. Holding it against the front of her, she smiled. Its light blue color went well with her complexion.

This was the first party of any magnitude since leaving Virginia, and she wanted to look her best. For the past week she had been giving her skin special care. Each day, she applied chicken fat to her face and hands, and she was training the natural waves of her hair so the curls and ringlets hung loosely about her face and neck.

She slipped the dress on to see if the buttons and seams were in order. It fit just as it had the last time she'd worn it. Humming to herself, she whirled and took a few steps across the floor, gliding gracefully before the fireplace. Stopping to look out the window, she wondered if she should leave it on to get Richard's reaction. No, it would be better to wait until New Year's eve when she could get completely dressed.

Confident, even with her meager wardrobe, she could match the elegance of anyone at the fort, she pressed her party petticoat and the pair of embroidered pantaloons her mother had made for the wedding.

And she would have to get Richard's clothes ready. Selection would not be difficult since the only dressy things he owned were those from the wedding. All others were work clothes. She placed his shirt and tie on the bed beside his suit, then stepped back to look at them. How handsome he'd looked on that special day in Fredericksburg. Suddenly, she was anxious to see him wear it again.

◆

When Richard returned from the trap line, he carried two beavers, a raccoon, and three muskrats. Although it was a sunny day, the freezing temperature kept the heavy covering of snow from melting. It was December 31st, and he had to get ready for the party. Most of the day he had been thinking about it. At first he hadn't been interested in going, but as the time approached and he watched Elizabeth's spirits soar while she made preparations, he could feel an excitement rising within.

At the smokehouse, he hurriedly skinned the beaver and stretched their hides on wooden hoops; then he tacked the raccoon pelt to a board frame. He looked at the muskrats. There was no reason why they couldn't wait until tomorrow, or even the next day. He tossed them into a corner and went out the door. As he walked toward the house, he hummed the refrain of a folk song his mother had sung when she worked in the kitchen at Christmas time.

It was nearly dark when he backed Molly into the thills of Louis's sleigh. She was skittish at first, but he stroked and patted her back until he and Louis could fasten the traces. Then he led her to the door of the LaCroix house.

Louis placed wrapped buckets of heated stones on the floor before the front and rear seats. When he finished, he stepped back, nodded and winked. Now his Virginia friend would know how heat could be retained beneath the lap robes.

The LaCroix boy, Pierre, wearing a heavy black coat and red knitted hat like his father's, sat in front between the two men. For several minutes he watched the flashes of sparks from the steel capped runners as they contacted protruding gravel. Then he slid down in his seat and pulled the coarse wool blanket up beneath his chin.

"How do you like it, Son," Louis asked with a nudge.

The boy was enjoying the warmth from the stones. "*Bon!*" he replied, giving his father an enthusiastic grin.

"Speak English, Son!" Louis demanded.

"Good!" Pierre responded with a noticeable accent.

"That's better!" Louis grinned. Then, turning to Richard, he said, "We will learn to speak English now."

"That's very nice," Richard agreed. "And we will learn to speak French."

After the women and children got off at the door of the well-lighted council house, Richard led Molly to a hitching rail amid several snorting, shuffling animals harnessed to a variety of conveyances. Louis helped him cover her with a blanket, and he placed a pile of hay at her feet. As he patted her on the nose, he wondered if she could stand the cold. Louis had lived in this climate for nearly five years, so he turned to him. "She will be all right?" he asked, hoping his French friend would concur.

Louis sensed his concern. "She'll be fine," he said with an air of authority.

The two men stepped inside and let the warm, smoke-tainted air fill their lungs. Blazing fires were crackling in the two huge fireplaces that flanked the large hall, sending great tongues of flame into their chimneys. The glowing highlights they emitted darted about the walls and ceiling and made the cheeks of those standing nearby gleam in the reflection. Several women, wearing a diversity of dresses and hair styles, were at a long table setting out cider, tea, cookies, and cake. At an adjacent table, a number of men were slicing roasted meats that had been prepared earlier in the day, and across the room, a counter was being readied to serve ale, rum, and brandy.

In the distance, they could see Marie and Elizabeth leading the children to a special area at the rear of the hall.

"Doesn't look like the Trapper's Ball," Richard observed, scanning the room for someone he knew.

"Oh, no," Louis replied as he removed his heavy coat and hung it on a peg. "This is very nice. For the family."

He fingered his red hat to be sure it was square on his head and that the front edge was cutting across the center of his forehead. Noting Richard's questioning look, he pointed to it and said, "The badge of Quebec."

"Ah, yes," Richard smiled. Just then he saw the women and beckoned for them come over.

In thirty minutes, after some hundred people had arrived, Major Rogers, nattily attired in a freshly powdered wig and striking red and white uniform stepped to the center of the floor. With a wave of his silver-sheathed saber, he ordered the music to begin. As the sounds of violins, lute, and harpsichord filled the room, talking paused briefly, then commenced again.

Elizabeth held Richard's arm as they watched the major escort Mrs. Sam Taylor, wife of a general store proprietor who was playing a violin, to an area in front of the musicians and begin to dance.

As a dozen other couples joined in, Elizabeth, her eyes sparkling, looked up into her husband's face. "Oh, let's dance!" she said eagerly.

Richard's face flushed. If only he could dance better. But then, these people weren't all that adept either. "All right," he consented, "Remember, I'm not too good."

"You'll do just fine," Elizabeth assured him. "Besides, this is a good place to learn."

When they began, Richard caught himself watching his feet. But Elizabeth was graceful, and she had the balance and perception to sense his movements and follow them precisely. After a few steps, he gained the confidence to dance by listening to the music.

They glided back and forth before the musicians, being careful to maintain a respectable distance between themselves. As the

LaCroix shuffled mechanically past, Richard nodded and smiled. Out of step with the tempo, he thought, but nice people. He listened dreamily to the music, the chatter of conversation, and the shuffle of dozens of feet on the rough floor. He was enjoying a feeling of inner warmth, a satisfaction with his lot in life. Suddenly, there was a surprised look on Elizabeth's face. Then he felt a tapping on his shoulder.

Turning his head, he looked into the smiling, bewhiskered face of his old friend. "Flip, you old son-of-a-gun!" he shouted. He wheeled about and extended a hand.

"Say," Flip said, a broad smile exposing a span of white teeth, "you two dance real well."

"Didn't know I could until she showed me."

"Mind if I try?" Flip asked, stepping back to look at Elizabeth's dress before scanning his new buckskins.

Richard looked at his wife. When she nodded, he consented.

"Might be a bit awkward," Flip warned. "Haven't had much occasion ta dance."

Richard walked over to the bar for a tankard of ale. He took a sip, then turned to look over the crowd. His eyes suddenly focused on Sarah standing with Agatha a short distance away. They were talking to a soldier. Plying their trade, he assumed. When she saw him looking at her, she nudged Agatha. The two of them smiled, waved, then beckoned him to join them.

Embarrassed, he turned back toward the bar. He'd often wondered how they were faring in this isolated outpost, but if others thought he was acquainted with them, there most certainly would be a wagging of tongues.

A short time later the music stopped, and Elizabeth, Flip, and the LaCroix joined him. "Want a drink?" he asked, holding up his tankard.

As the men stepped forward, Elizabeth shook her head. Feeling out of place at the bar, she turned to Marie. "Let's go over for some tea," she suggested.

Flip explained he came in for the celebration because of loneliness. "Damn awful quiet out there in the woods," he complained. "Sometimes wake up at night and have ta make noise ta be sure I haven't gone deaf." he took a drink, then smiled as he looked at Richard. "Besides, hoped I'd find you here."

"By the way," Richard began, curious about the news he had learned. "Naseeka says you're going to marry Matoka this spring."

Flip stepped back and stared into Richard's face. "Where in hell did he get that idea?" he asked, hoping his friend was joking.

"Naseeka told me a couple weeks ago. Said he was marrying Lahana and you're taking Matoka."

At that moment, Frenchy came up behind and slapped them on the back. Turning to face him, the three of them shook his hand. "Good to see you," Frenchy grinned, picking up a glass of wine. "How you do, Flip? " he asked.

Before Flip could respond, Richard broke in. "Just telling him about marrying Matoka."

"Ah, yes," Frenchy beamed. "Naseeka say so."

Flip appeared stunned. "Damn funny nobody asked me," he stormed. He hesitated as thoughts raced through his mind. "Maybe it's not such a bad idea. She'd make a good woman."

"Very good woman!" Frenchy agreed, lifting his glass.

"A very good woman!" the others chorused, quaffing their drinks.

Elizabeth stood with Marie near one of the fireplaces, watching the people who were standing in small groups talking. They didn't seem so different from those in Fredericksburg, she thought, except perhaps for the diversity of dress. Some were smartly attired, such as Henry of the Black Swan. He was conservatively dressed in a white shirt, brown tie, and tweed cape as he talked with the Hudson's Bay man who wore a silk top hat and had a cane dangling from his wrist. Most wore their Sunday church fashions. A few appeared in soiled work clothes.

When the music resumed, Elizabeth spotted Major Rogers walking toward her. Several times during the intermission, she had seen him looking at her. And now he was going to ask her to dance; she was sure of it. Her heart jumped, and she tried to look away as he approached.

"May I have the pleasure of this dance?" he asked, bowing slightly from the waist.

She scanned the crowd for Richard, but could not see him. How could she refuse with all these people looking on? Besides, he was impeccably dressed and did exhibit good manners. She nodded and smiled.

As they danced, he told her he had asked who she was and knew her husband. "You dance so well," he said. "So you must understand music."

"Yes," she said nervously, concentrating on her dancing. "My mother taught me to play the harpsichord."

He smiled. "Then you will honor us with your talent?" Leading her toward the musicians, he added, "After all, this instrument belongs to Captain Campbell. I'm sure Mrs. Campbell wouldn't mind."

"Not at all," the young Mrs. Campbell agreed, rising from the stool.

Elizabeth felt a nervous perspiration break out on her upper lip and forehead. She wished she hadn't mentioned she could play, but now felt obligated. She sat down on the warm stool, hoping she could remember the popular tune she'd played so often in Fredericksburg.

As a hushed group gathered about her, she calmly told them, "I'd like to play 'Heather on the Highlands.'"

There was a light applause mixed with a few audible sighs.

When she finished, the applause was loud and prolonged.

"Do one more, will ye please?" the major asked.

"One more" she consented, feeling more confident.

She played a lively jig taught to her as a little girl by her mother. It prompted hand clapping and foot stomping by some, dancing by others. When she finished, she stood and bowed. Major Rogers graciously kissed her hand, then handed her to Richard. Looking into the face of her husband, she saw he was beaming with pride.

Shortly before the hour of midnight, the musicians stopped playing, and the crowd formed a large circle. Their attention was directed to Major Rogers at its center. Staring at the opened, gold watch in the palm of one hand, he held his gleaming saber aloft with the other.

With a suddenness that startled some, the weapon was forcefully lowered. "Welcome to the year of our Lord, one thousand seven hundred and sixty-two!" he declared.

The music began with a flourish. Toasts were given and drinks guzzled. The shouting, stamping, and dancing raised such a din that several children sleeping on blankets at the rear of the hall awoke with alarm.

Where Flip and Richard stood, two grizzly trappers wearing soiled sheepskin coats and decrepit coonskin hats began shouting and shoving one another. Instead of trying to stop the attention-seeking combatants, Flip and Richard seized them by their smelly coats and shoved them out the door. "If ya want ta fight, do it outside!" Flip shouted as the disgruntled pair staggered off. "Go to the livery stable and sleep it off!" Then he turned to Richard. "Too much free rum. Damn fools could start a brawl."

A half hour past midnight, the two families decided it was time to leave. After one last dance, Elizabeth helped Marie bundle up Pierre and Mimi and lead the sleepy children to the sleigh. She was delighted with the way the evening had gone. She'd met many townspeople she had heard Richard mention from time to time, and the dancing was wonderful. Too bad they had to leave, but it was a long way home.

Standing with Richard beside the sleigh, she asked, "Flip, where are you staying tonight? After all, it was cold, and his cabin was deep in the forest. "You could stay with us, you know."

"The Black Swan. Got to get back tomorrow." He looked at Richard. "Will drop by for a visit one of these days, though. Probably when the trappin' season is over and I bring in my catch." He smiled. "Maybe I can help with the plantin'."

I'll depend on it," Richard said, boosting Elizabeth into the sleigh. He knew Flip detested farming and would be of little help.

The sky had cleared, bringing out the stars and dropping the temperature several degrees. Two extra guards had been posted at the palisade gate, which had been left partially open to accommodate the late revelers. As Richard guided Molly through the opening, he waved.

"Goodnight, sir,"the guards chorused.

After dropping off the LaCroix, Elizabeth climbed into the front seat. She pulled the carriage blanket up and snuggled against her husband. She was still basking in the pleasant feeling of having had an enjoyable time at the party and was especially pleased at the way they were received by the local people.

"Cold?" Richard asked, turning Molly into the driveway.

"No," she replied, squeezing his arm. "I've got something inside to keep me warm."

"Oh?" Richard responded, looking down into her face pressed against his shoulder.

"Tell you about it when we get inside," she teased, trying to arouse his curiosity.

He led her inside, brushed aside the ashes covering the banked fire, then laid on several pieces of dried wood. As the flame rose, he ignited a wooden taper and lit the candles. Looking at Elizabeth, who was standing with her back to the fireplace, he said, "Gonna take care of Molly. Be back in a few minutes."

As the warmth of the flame seeped through the heavy coat she still wore, she wondered what his reaction would be when he learned the news. Perhaps she should have waited until being more sure, but this was a joyful night and she had to tell him. A momentary tremor, starting in the calves of her legs, rippled upward through her body as the excitement rose within.

Richard stamped his feet at the threshold and hung his coat and hat on a peg. Then, rubbing his cold hands as he walked toward her, asked, "Tell me about this warmer you have."

"Well," she said, pursing her lips, "we're going to have a baby."

A startled look came over his face as he held her at arm's length. "Are you sure?" he asked, not quite believing what he heard.

"As sure as a woman can be," she replied matter-of-factly.

"Wonderful!" he said, hugging her. Then the tone of his voice changed. "Maybe we shouldn't have danced tonight."

"Nonsense," she said. Smiling, she added, "So maybe we'll have a boy to help you in the fields."

"Or a girl as pretty as her mother."

◆

In the early morning hours of a day in mid-March, Elizabeth was suddenly awakened by a series of pulsating abdominal cramps.

Reluctant to disturb her husband, she tried to lie still and remain quiet. Richard sensed her discomfort, but she told him she would be all right in a short time.

Richard got out of bed, dressed, and lit the fire. As he watched the flames build, his fear grew. He didn't want to lose her. He loved her so much. Maybe if he went to Detroit, he could find a doctor that would come out, but he wasn't sure there was a doctor in Detroit.

By the time the sun broke over the horizon, the pains had become much more severe, and Elizabeth noticed a spotting of blood. "Oh, Richard," she sobbed, "I wish mother was here to tell me what to do."

Richard ran to the LaCroix's and told Marie what was happening. She abandoned the breakfast she was preparing and rushed to the side of her good friend.

In spite of her best efforts of prayers, compresses, and sips of warm wine, the French woman could not stem the course of nature. Life on the frontier was destined to take its physical and psychological toll. "It's God's will," Marie assured the softly weeping Elizabeth. "It happened to me four times."

Richard heard them talking and went to the foot of the bed. "Will she be all right?" he asked, concern showing on his face. He knew the baby was gone, but he had also heard of women bleeding to death.

"She will be fine," Marie assured him. "Now you can start over again."

◆

Two weeks of mild, south wind melted the snow and sucked the frost from the ground letting puddles of accumulated snow water percolate into the soil. It aroused the earthworms, and they rose to the surface in great numbers. Ice on the rivers broke into pieces, and the swollen, swirling currents pushed it out into lake Erie where it became porous and disintegrated. Pussy willows, awakened by a flow of fresh sap, burst forth with plump, furry catkins. At the same time, yellow outcroppings of crocus forced their way through layers of rotted leaves and webs of dead grass, and birds, dressed in bright colors, returned and hopped among the budding trees, happily singing their loud, melodious mating songs while eagerly anticipating the fulfillment of spring and abundance of summer.

In a stump-studded field across the road, Richard struggled to hold the plow as it turned the neglected, weed-infested sod. Stopping to wipe his brow and give Molly a rest, he looked toward the house. Elizabeth was energetically preparing the garden plot he had plowed for her last fall. He knew she was trying to shed the melancholy over losing the baby. He had told her it was not her fault, that many women have the same problem during the early months. He knew she wanted to give him a son and Elizabeth thought she had failed him. She had been carrying his seed within her body and lost it, had expelled it.

Leaving Molly standing in the furrow, he walked over to her. "Let me help," he said, taking the shovel to spade in a top dressing of manure.

When he had finished, he looked at her. Her face was still tired and drawn, but she smiled warmly. She was feeling better. Looking across the road, he saw Molly was still standing quietly. He would stay a while longer.

As they prepared spaced beds for the pumpkin and squash seeds Naseeka had given her, he knelt and grasped a fistful of the sandy loam. He squeezed it, rubbed it between his palms, and let it sift through his fingers. It held an abundance of rich humus and clay, and was mixed with just enough sand for good drainage and ease of root growth. "This is mighty fine soil," he said, looking up at her. "Should raise good crops."

"Won't have to buy so much," she replied, a sparkle seemed to appear in her eyes.

During the winter he had received a hundred and fifty pounds for his furs, but most of it had been spent on food and clothing for themselves and feed for the livestock. By fall he expected to be self sufficient except for a few staples. The surplus wheat, corn, and millet would be more than enough to offset that. "Won't have to buy much of anything after harvest time," he said, feeling a sense of satisfaction.

———————◆———————

It was late in the afternoon when Elizabeth answered a knock at the door. It was Flip who had come for his promised visit. She hardly recognized him. Wearing new clothing, he was clean shaven and had hair that was neatly trimmed.

Without waiting for Richard to greet him, he stepped inside and unrolled a prime wolf pelt. As he held it up for her to see, he said, "For your bedroom, ma'am."

"Oh, how lovely," Elizabeth said, stroking its long, gray hair.

He handed it to Richard, then pulled a leather pouch from his shoulder bag and set it heavily on the table. The sound was that of many coins. "My winter take," he said, placing his hands on his hips. He looked first at Elizabeth, then at Richard. "Minus, of course, a bit I spent. Nigh on two hundred pounds. Want ta leave it with you folks for safekeepin'."

"Be glad to," Richard said, understandingly. "We'll hide it in the fireplace with ours."

"Not as much as it should be," Flip said, shaking his head as he sat down at the table with Richard. "Too many Indians around this year."

"Same here," Richard agreed. "You'll probably have to go farther north again for good trapping."

"Guess so," Flip agreed, sipping at the steaming tea Elizabeth had poured for him. "Didn't know there was so many damn Ottawas in the world." He put the cup down. "Anyway, I'm glad you'll keep my money. They've probably already looted my cabin."

A few days later, a Wyandotte brave arrived with the message that Naseeka's wedding would take place in four days. Flip listened intently as the Indian explained it was the time of the full moon, the one that signaled the optimum period for planting, seeding, and germinating. It would smile down with favor upon the chief and his bride.

Flip nodded that he understood.

"And your woman, Matoka, will be waiting for you," the messenger told the young trapper. "She will make you a good wife! She will make you a good baby!"

Flip's face reddened. He grinned as he looked at Richard.

Chapter 12

Feast of Friendship

Elizabeth was absorbed in thought as she finished washing the last dish. She was concerned about what to wear to the wedding. Her party dress wouldn't be appropriate, and she didn't like the idea of wearing buckskin. She dropped the dishcloth into the basin and turned to the two men at the table. "Flip," she began, "what do white women wear at Indian weddings?"

Flip stared at her with a puzzled look. "Don't rightly know. Never saw a white woman at an Indian weddin'." He reflected momentarily. "Indians don't dress up much. Oh, the bride and groom might don new buckskins. But mostly they go in fer feastin' and hollerin'." He stroked his clean shaven chin. "Besides, every tribe does it different."

"It's not like the Harvest Ball at Fredericksburg," Richard said, shaking his head. "They're forest people. Do things real simple like."

There was a knock at the door. It was Louis. Richard invited him in, then asked, "Louis, what do white women wear at Indian weddings?"

Louis looked at Elizabeth, then at the two men. He didn't know much about women's apparel and cared less about Indian weddings. "They don't have a real wedding," he said, gesturing with his palms up. "They're heathens! Not joined by God! We've never gone to one." He paused for a moment. "Never been asked to go to one."

After the men went outside, Elizabeth looked over her meager wardrobe. Since there were very few occasions to dress up, nearly everything she had was for working around the farm. There was, however, one dress she thought would be right for the occasion. It was a plain, ankle length design she had made last fall from a medium gray, nubby-weave linen. With it, she would wear her waist-length jacket of wine velvet.

------------◆------------

The Rouge River was running high, carrying a heavy burden of red clay silt from its upper tributaries. As Molly pulled the wagon across its noisy plank bridge, Elizabeth experienced a feeling of apprehension. Although she had occasionally studied the thickly forested area from her yard, she had never thought of entering it. To her, it seemed so dark and foreboding, the domain of the red man, a place to avoid. People at the fort had told her all Indians were savages, that they were devious and could not be trusted. She knew it was Wyandotte territory and they were friendly, especially toward Richard and Flip, but still she felt uneasy. She sat up straight, took a deep breath, and tried to put the thought out of her mind.

"Army's gonna have to fix that bridge someday," Richard observed when the clatter ceased. Looking ahead, he could see that some of the deep ruts left by convoy wagons were filled with water and mud. He wondered if they would have trouble getting through.

A short distance from the Wyandotte village, they came to the ford on the Ecorse River. Molly halted. She was afraid to step off into the fast moving current.

Richard stood, wondering how to get across. Heavy upstream rains had combined with the late spring runoff to make the water run swift and deep. The only sign of the stepping stones were irregularities in the otherwise smooth surface of the rapidly flowing, muddy water.

When he flipped the reins to urge Molly on, he could see the muscles in her strong legs tighten as she braced against any forward movement. Stepping down from the wagon, he patted her on the nose as he assessed the situation.

"Bout two feet deep, I'd surmise," Flip said, tossing a pebble into the water at midstream.

"At least," Richard concurred. "But we'll make it." He stroked Molly's neck. "You get in the wagon to hold it down. I'll ride the horse."

"Sure ya don't want me to lead her?" Flip asked, wondering if Molly would shy in the rushing water and upset the wagon.

"No," Richard replied calmly. He knew his horse. "She'll be all right." He mounted the animal, all the while speaking softly and patting her. He looked back at Elizabeth. Nothing must happen to her. "Just stay on the seat and hold on," he cautioned.

Taking hold of the reins, he said in a low voice, "All right girl, let's go."

He could sense the confidence Molly felt in him as she stepped into the water and gingerly picked her way across the stony bottom. Carefully monitoring depth, he watched the water gradually rise until it touched her belly. When it began to recede, he gave a sigh of relief and hoped they would not be surprised by an underwater hole. Looking up, he saw a group of Wyandotte children approaching on the far side.

When he halted Molly and climbed back into the wagon, he could see that Elizabeth was intrigued by the children. She had never seen a group of them before. Some wore a motley assortment of clothing, many were naked. They stood back and stared soberly at her. She smiled, then much to his dismay, invited them to climb in for a ride to the village.

"Might be a mistake, ma'am," Flip cautioned as they clambered aboard. "They's filthy, and could give us a good pesterin' besides."

They squatted quietly in the rear of the wagon and looked soulfully at him. He, seated on the floor with his back against the seat, stared sternly back at them.

While Richard tied Molly to a budding wild cherry tree, the wagon was surrounded by several dozen curious villagers. Suddenly the medicine man appeared and ordered them away. His costume and painted body frightened Elizabeth. Richard saw her uneasiness and quickly took her hand and helped her down from the seat.

The chattering crowd made it difficult for the medicine man to usher them to the guest tepee. Although Richard knew the Indians were merely enthralled at the sight of a white woman in their village, Elizabeth was terrified when some of the women, no longer able to contain themselves, reached over to touch her velvet jacket. She bit her lip to keep from crying out.

"Well, what do you think of it?" Richard asked as they sat, waiting to be called for the ceremony.

"Wasn't too sure of things when they all swarmed about us," she replied. Then, wrinkling her nose, added, "When they kept touching me, I didn't know what to expect."

Richard knew she was still frightened. "Just remember, we are considered members of the tribe—brothers of Naseeka. They are curious about us, but will do us no harm."

"That's right," Flip assured her. "Nothin ta fear here. Just have ta learn their ways so they don't scare ya."

The medicine man opened the flap of the tepee and beckoned them to follow.

When they stood, Richard looked out at the crowd shuffling past. He had not seen such a number in the village before. It concerned him. "What about our muskets?" he asked.

"Leave 'em here. They'll be all right," Flip answered confidently.

Richard took Elizabeth's hand and followed the medicine man through the throng. The Indians seemed happier than he had seen them before. They didn't smile, but the expressions on their faces were less tense, their jaws less tight.

At a straw mat a short distance from the entrance of the chief's tepee, the medicine man motioned for them to sit. They lowered themselves in a cross-legged position, Elizabeth flanked by the two men. The crowd surged in close behind.

Smoke from the pile of cooking animal carcasses in the big fire ring drifted over them. Elizabeth held her breath and hoped it would go away, but it didn't. The first shallow breaths she took nearly gagged her, but gradually she managed to be able to stand it.

She looked up just as Naseeka emerged from the tepee. He was dressed in buff buckskins and wore the leather headband with its beaded timber wolf emblem. His chest was covered by a triangular reed and quill breastplate that reached the midpoint of his torso. He looked over the crowd waiting in the tree-filtered sunlight, then walked to within a few feet of her.

In a matter of seconds, Lahana appeared from a nearby bark hut and was escorted to his side by two elderly squaws. She was dressed in an off-white buckskin dress and wore knee length, ornately beaded moccasins. Her neatly braided hair, adorned with red ribbons, hung down the front of each shoulder. She, too, wore a leather headband bearing the timber wolf emblem.

"She's a beautiful girl," Elizabeth whispered, nudging Richard. She remembered he had told her about the blond men who had wintered among the Wyandottes generations ago. She could see the skin was lighter and features finer than those of Indians near Fredericksburg or along the Mohawk Trail.

Flip leaned over and whispered in her ear, "Yeah, but she'll be fat and dumpy in a couple years."

As the medicine man stepped before the couple, now standing side by side, a hush fell over the crowd. The only sounds came from the crackling fire in the fire ring and the whimpering of a small child. He placed a deerskin cape over the shoulders of Naseeka and Lahana, then looked skyward. "The union of this woman with the brave Wyandotte chief will increase the wisdom of the tribe, strengthen its leadership, and promote its courage and strength." He paused, then announced loud enough so all could hear, "The great Naseeka and his woman are now one!"

Members of the crowd remained in place, but shouted a roar of jubilation.

He then directed the chief and his bride to step back and sit on a mat that had been placed on the ground for them.

Another couple, wanting to get married with the chief, was brought forward and positioned before the medicine man. Since only the chief could wed fully clothed, they were naked to the waist.

Elizabeth's face reddened as she tried to hide her embarrassment.

"How's that for a beauty?" Flip teased as he gazed at the robust woman.

"She's nice, too," Elizabeth answered. She wished Flip would not make light of the situation or, better yet, say nothing.

After the medicine man again performed his ritual, the couple were ordered to sit next to Richard. He then motioned Flip to stand where the grooms had stood.

Flip slowly rose to his feet. There was a reluctance in his movements. "Wish ta hell you hadn't talked me into this," he said over his shoulder.

"It's a good move," Richard replied. He wasn't sure his friend heard him.

When ordered to remove his jacket, the paleness of his white skin, adorned only by the soiled doeskin good-luck pouch hanging from his neck, created a wave of twittering and giggling in the crowd. Before he had time to react, Matoka, wearing a blue cloth skirt and ankle-high moccasins, suddenly appeared at his side.

Elizabeth stared in disbelief. The young bride was pregnant, probably six months along. Her breasts, shiny and plump with protruding nipples, pushed out from her chest.

Flip looked into Matoka's eyes and smiled adoringly, but when he looked down at her bulging abdomen, his expression changed and he swallowed and reddened. He wished Richard and Elizabeth were not here, especially Elizabeth.

Elizabeth leaned toward Richard and asked, "His?" She had recovered from her initial shock of seeing the pregnant bride, but couldn't comprehend their friend being intimate with an Indian, a savage.

Richard looked up at the smiling face of Matoka who was scanning the consenting faces of her people. How could he explain such a delicate matter to his wife? He would wait until he got home. "Must be," he said, trying to ease past the matter.

The crowd was strangely silent when Flip returned to the mat with his bride and, when he attempted to put on his jacket, was instructed not to. Oh Lord, he thought, not that damned fertility rite.

Matoka had told him of the ritual to insure propagation of the tribe. A male dog, selected for his stamina and virility, had not been fed for two days, then gorged an hour before the wedding with partially cooked wild rice reserved from the fall harvest. Now, they would have to eat the rice.

Two ornately dressed matriarchs stepped forward, killed the animal with a blow to its head, then emptied the partially digested contents of its stomach into small, wooden bowls. The medicine man handed a bowl to each bride and groom.

The odor made Flip's stomach churn. He looked up and saw Lahana and Naseeka eating the rice with their fingers. He turned to Matoka. She gestured for him to eat. He gingerly sampled a few grains of the sour tasting substance, then looked up. Naseeka was watching. He pushed the rest into his mouth and forced a smile.

The chief placed his empty bowl on the mat and rose to his feet. It was a signal to start the celebration. There began a tumultuous commotion of shouting and dancing to the rhythm of beating sticks and thundering drums.

Elizabeth, afraid to move, looked around wondering if she would be trampled. She was waiting for Flip and Matoka to stand, but they remained seated. If they were not concerned, maybe everything was all right. She turned to Richard, a questioning look on her face.

"Let's stand," Richard said, offering her a helping hand. "They're stirring up too much dust."

Richard walked up to Naseeka and placed a leather thong about his neck from which hung a shiny copper disk engraved with the good-luck arrow pointing skyward. Then Elizabeth gave Lahana a small silver sewing box containing needles, thread, and buttons.

As the newlyweds showed each other their gifts and spoke in their native tongue, Elizabeth noted several women look longingly at Lahana's sewing kit. She wished she had something practical to give them.

She turned to Flip and Matoka. They had replaced their jackets and were now standing. "We have something for you when we get back to the house," she told them.

"Come on," Flip invited, pointing to the fire ring where the Indians were pulling pieces from the charred animal carcasses. "Let's get some meat!"

Elizabeth looked at him soberly. Strangely, she had no fear of the frenzied crowd. Perhaps it was because of the nauseous feeling growing in her stomach from the foul odor of the undressed carcasses cooking in the fire ring. Or maybe it was the repulsive memory of the dog butchering. She turned to Richard. "Go ahead, if you want to. I'll just wait here."

Richard knew she didn't want to go near the fire ring. She probably would like to leave. But as a matter of courtesy, he had to eat something. "I'll be right back," he told her.

With folded arms, she stood and watched the celebrating Wyandottes jabber and prance about while stuffing their mouths with food. Occasionally, they dropped a few scraps on the ground for the dogs or handed some to the small children having difficulty approaching the hot fire.

Three young women, reeking from the offensive smoke, walked over to her. She took shallow breaths and stood perfectly still, ready to run to Richard if they threatened her. After looking her over carefully, one of them reached out and gingerly touched her hair. When she did not flinch, the other two stroked her jacket with their grubby hands.

Just curious, she thought. She looked down into their dark eyes and smiled. They grinned bashfully. Just then Naseeka and Lahana walked up, and they shied away.

"You must eat!" Naseeka half ordered in a voice that seemed more suggestive than authoritarian.

Elizabeth chewed her lower lip. She wouldn't think of eating any of the food she had seen. "I do not feel well," she complained, pressing her hand against her stomach.

There was a rapid exchange of words between Naseeka and his bride. Lahana dashed off. "Lahana will bring you good medicine," he said.

Elizabeth didn't want to eat or drink anything. As she pondered the situation, she absentmindedly stared at the copper talisman Richard had given him.

Noting this, Naseeka fingered the disk. "This is very good medicine for Wyandotte chief. Richard is a true brother."

Lahana returned with a steaming cup of liquid in a dented, badly tarnished copper container. "You drink!" Naseeka ordered, thrusting it into Elizabeth's hands.

Sniffing it, Elizabeth was sure it was an herbal tea with a pleasant odor. Still, she didn't want to drink it. She scanned the crowd for Richard, but could not see him. Fingering the container hesitantly, she looked at Naseeka, then again at the crowd. If only Richard or Flip would show.

Noting her reluctance, Naseeka, using a softer tone, again urged her to try the liquid. "You drink. It will make you well." He nodded and smiled.

At that moment, Richard and Flip returned. "What's that?" Richard inquired, pointing to the cup.

"Something for my stomach," Elizabeth answered, holding it up for his inspection.

"Good medicine!" Naseeka stated emphatically.

Flip sniffed it. "Sassafras root tea. Good for the stomach. Go ahead, drink it."

Elizabeth looked at Richard. If only she could leave, just escape these terrible odors and go home. When Richard nodded, she shook her head, then put the cup to her lips.

Flip watched her drink, then turned to Richard. "Should settle her stomach, but ya might have ta let her go behind a bush on the way home."

Disappointed they would not stay for the nightlong celebration, Naseeka and Lahana, standing before the chief's tepee, shook hands with the Lockes. A brave was ordered to bring Richard's musket.

They walked to their wagon, unnoticed by the dancing tribal members who seemed hypnotized by the pounding drums. When they climbed into the seat, Flip, standing beside Matoka, called out, "See ya in a few days!"

Richard nodded and waved. Elizabeth forced a smile.

Two days after the wedding, Richard was carefully cultivating the young plants in his bean field. The sun was hot and the air humid. At the end of a row, he stopped in the shade to let Molly catch her wind. He was pleased with the way the crop was growing. His father would be proud of him. Looking toward the River Rouge, he saw Flip trudging across the bridge. Matoka was close behind. Richard waved, then walked toward the house to meet them.

"What are you doing here so soon?" Richard asked as they shook hands at the driveway. "Thought for sure you'd still be celebrating."

"Celebration's over," Flip replied flatly. "Some braves come in with a jug o' rum, got drunk, then started shootin' guns into the air." He reached back and got Matoka by the hand to draw her up beside him. "Naseeka got some braves ta take the guns from 'em. Then they tossed the drunks into the river. Held 'em under fer a long time, too. Thought fer sure they'd drown."

"That ended it?"

"Yessiree! Naseeka declared the whole thing over. Sent everybody back to their huts."

"And where are you headed now?" Richard looked obliquely at the heavily burdened Matoka.

"Goin' ta my cabin. Gonna fix it up ta live decent like." Matoka watched her husband's face as he talked.

Hearing voices, Elizabeth stepped outside, then hurried over to greet them. As she shook Matoka's hand, she noted the puffiness of the Indian woman's face. They had walked a long way, she thought, and Matoka needed a rest. Probably could use something to eat. "Come on in for a cup of tea." She motioned for them to follow.

In addition to the tea, she served each of them a bowl of stew. Noting the uneasiness of Matoka, she poured herself a cup of tea and sat down with them. "Go ahead," she urged Flip. "Richard will be here as soon as he puts Molly away."

Matoka watched Flip for a moment, then grasped the spoon and began eating.

They stayed with the Lockes three days before leaving for Detroit to get supplies on the way to their cabin. The Indian woman, eager to learn the ways of the white woman, worked closely with Elizabeth who was happy to teach her. The two women became well acquainted, and Matoka, who's command of English was meager, impressed her husband by greatly expanding her vocabulary. As presents, Elizabeth gave her a small leather sewing kit, some blue cotton cloth, and, since she admired it so, the wine-colored velvet jacket.

To express her gratitude, Matoka took Elizabeth's hand into hers and looked directly into the white woman's eyes. "Thank you, my sister," she said in halting English, tears welling up in her dark eyes.

Although they insisted on sleeping in the barn during their stay, Flip and Matoka consented to accept a wagon ride to Detroit. As a departing gift, the Lockes gave them a red woolen blanket.

"Hope they make it," Elizabeth said as Richard turned the wagon around after letting them off.

"They will," Richard replied confidently. "Flip can handle things." He held the remainder of his response until Molly expelled several noisy blasts of gas. "Besides, he's got enough money with him to buy anything."

◆

The summer of 1762 was exceptionally good for farming. The warm, half-hour thunder showers came every seven to ten days to furnish the carefully tended crops with a continuous feeding of abundant nourishment from the rich soil. But weeds, numerous from seeds of previous uncultivated summers, kept the Lockes working long hours during the extended days. When evening came, going to bed was a welcome respite where they were quickly lulled to sleep by a chorus of chirping crickets.

Elizabeth wore a bonnet and long sleeves, but the sun still tanned her face, and the handles of implements made calluses grow thick and hard on her hands. Regardless of the hard work, however, she enjoyed watching the planted seeds sprout and grow into mature plants, and she was enthralled by a brood of chicks hatched by a setting hen from a dozen eggs Marie had given her. But on the morning that she awoke to find one of the babies had died during the night, she sobbed uncontrollably.

"They're just animals," Richard explained, taking the chick from her cupped hands. "Here, I'll take it over and throw it into the river."

"No," Elizabeth declared emphatically, the tears still running down her cheeks. "Let's bury it on the other side of the garden." It had been her charge, and she would be responsible for its disposition.

As the summer wore on, Richard observed more Indians, primarily Wyandotte, walking the road, and when he was in the fields, he could see them, singly and in small bands, making their way through the adjoining forest. Were they just traveling to the fort and hunting in the woods? Or was there something unusual about their activity?

When he asked Louis about it, Louis shrugged and threw up his hands. "These red men know us as a friend. They will not harm us."

But Richard remained troubled. He noted that, when new families emigrated to the area, they settled north of the fort. His farm was still the southern limit of white settlement.

Early one afternoon after he had finished his lunch, he stepped outside and was confronted by three Wyandotte braves. One had a string of fish, another a basket of blueberries, and the third a freshly caught rabbit. When they held their items up to him, he asked what they wanted. By studying their response, he determined they wished to barter for tobacco, powder, or a knife.

He looked at them sternly. "I only have enough for myself," he told them. "Go to the Frenchman at the trading post."

They stared at him coldly, then turned and walked away, talking among themselves. He wondered if they would be back.

Elizabeth had watched and listened from just inside the door. Although she tried to keep it hidden, she harbored an inner feeling of uneasiness when the savages were near. She felt no fear of Naseeka and his family, but there was a fierceness she saw deep in the eyes of other red men that triggered a sense of cautious alarm. She would continue to practice with her rifle to maintain her skill with the weapon.

◆

In late July the laborious effort against the weeds and quack grass had nearly ended. The planted crops had reached that state of maturity where their roots could not be disturbed by hoeing and cultivating. It gave Elizabeth a respite from the fields until the harvest. She now had time to work about the house and tend her garden.

And she looked forward to the leisurely visit with Marie each Wednesday. They drank tea, talked, shucked peas, or baked bread in Elizabeth's outdoor oven. Sometimes, they donned their bonnets and picked blackberries and huckleberries. Her French friend always knew where the sweetest and plumpest ones grew in the filtered sunlight at the edge of the woods.

336

Most of all, however, she liked the days she could spend with Richard. She filled a jug with a drink made with apple vinegar, honey, and water and took it to the field where he was pulling weeds. There she could sit with him beneath a tree, lolling in the pleasantness that surrounded them.

Sometimes they strolled up and down the rows of corn or traversed the hayfield. Once, they entered the forest and climbed the hill where they'd found the bee tree containing the Mascouten brave. As they sat looking down on the quiet pond below, Elizabeth sniffed the pine scented air and speculated, "Wouldn't it be nice to build a house here?"

"Have to clear these trees away so you could see," Richard replied, showing little enthusiasm as he placed his hands behind his head and laid back. "Probably wouldn't be too good, though, being so far out of the way."

"You mean because of Indians?" she questioned, remembering the friendly innocence she had seen among those at the wedding but also recalling the advice she had repeatedly heard.

"Yah. Their friendly all right, but you never know for sure." He sat up again. "Best we stick by the river."

And there were other times, when Richard was away at the fort or chopping firewood in the forest, that Elizabeth experienced a feeling of loneliness and depression. It was then that she reflected on life in Fredericksburg. She thought of her family and friends and wondered what they were doing. Although letters were exchanged every four to six weeks, she found with the passage of time that recollections faded and aspects of events became distorted. She was remembering things as she wished them to be.

It was then that she found herself walking to the bank of the Detroit River. Sitting beneath a large oak tree, she watched the river traffic and looked for activities of the natives on the far shore. Sometimes she saw the *Huron* or *Michigan* sail past and speculated about the cargo being carried or the destination of the passengers.

When she saw a ship sailing south on its return to Fort Niagara, a strong yearning developed to be aboard, taking the first leg of the long journey back to Fredericksburg. She would remain for several minutes, dreaming of such a trip, then jump up and walk briskly back to the house. As she walked, she mentally chastised herself for thinking such thoughts while Richard was working hard to make a permanent and successful life here.

And when Richard mentioned Flip and Matoka and wondered how they were getting along, it pained her by magnifying the disappointment of not conceiving again.

◆

By mid-August the harvest had begun. She was glad. She could return to the fields and be close to her husband, and she could keep her mind on things that made her feel better.

Using a scythe, Richard cut the hay for a second time. Then, attaching a cradle to the blade, cut the wheat and oats while Elizabeth tied the bundles. In three weeks, everything but the corn, which remained in shocks, had been harvested and hauled to the vicinity of the house and barn.

Of the nine young chickens remaining from the original brood Elizabeth had raised, one suffered from an accident of nature. It grew no feathers except a light fringe about the neck and a few pinfeathers on its wings and tail. After one of the many times of applying grease to the peck marks made by other chickens on its sunburned body, Elizabeth looked up to see Marie watching her. She held the unconcerned pullet up to the French woman. "What's going to happen when it gets cold?"

Richard, standing nearby, chuckled and said, "Well, it'll probably lose its sunburn."

"Men!" Elizabeth snapped, giving Richard a look of disgust as she lowered the unfortunate fowl to the ground.

Two days later Marie returned with a small, knitted sweater. Louis had come along to witness this *act of foolishness*, as he put it.

Elizabeth caught the tame but frightened bird and slipped the sweater on it. When released, the chicken stood for a moment and stretched its neck. Then it trotted off to join the rest of the flock.

Louis shook his head. "First thing you know, we'll have to dress all the animals."

"That calls for a drink," Richard declared as he beckoned toward the house.

"I don't care," Elizabeth told Marie as they walked. "That poor thing needs something like that."

Marie nodded agreement.

It was early in the evening, after milking Bessie and tending the other animals, that Richard took Elizabeth by the hand and strolled over to the Detroit River. He wanted to rake the soil and clear the weeds from the grave of the Mascouten, as he and his father had done so many times for his mother and sister.

When finished, they stood for several minutes gazing at the blue-green water as it flowed past. On the distant east shore, thin columns of smoke rose lazily from Huron campfires. And a half mile upstream, two canoes were crossing the broad expanse. Indians or French traders, Richard mused.

Elizabeth was especially fond of this spot. From here she could wave at the *Huron* and the *Michigan* as they sailed past, and she liked to watch the full moon rise, big and yellow from the dark, tree-lined skyline, to cast its bright reflection on the flowing water. "Let's sit down for a while," she said, dropping to the ground and pulling Richard with her.

Behind them, having been awakened by a whippoorwill, crickets and tree frogs were beginning their nightlong opera.

"Sure," he agreed, a relaxed feeling of contentment rising within.

He suddenly had a feeling someone was approaching. Slowly turning his head, he thought he heard voices. "Come," he whispered, pulling Elizabeth to her feet.

As they approached the house, he could see two forms walking in the driveway.

"No light. Wonder if they're here," a voice said.

It was Flip. He would recognize that voice anywhere. "Hello, you trapper!" he called out.

"Hello, yourself!" Flip replied, dashing up to meet his friend.

Elizabeth, smiling nervously as the tension left her body, shook hands with Matoka. "So nice to see you again."

"We're on our way ta visit her family," Flip explained. "Thought we'd drop by."

Inside, Elizabeth lit several candles, then turned to Matoka. The barefooted Indian woman was wearing the wine velvet jacket and a long skirt of the material she had given her. Noting her slimness, Elizabeth peered around her head into her backpack. "What do we have here?" she asked with a smile.

"Papoose!" Matoka declared enthusiastically. "Boy baby!" She turned so Elizabeth could see the infant. A broad smile stretched across her face.

"Look at this, Richard," Elizabeth said as she gazed into the large, dark eyes that dominated the full, round face.

"Let's get the rascal out here so you can see im," Flip said, stepping over to lift the baby from the carrier.

"What's his name?" Elizabeth asked, taking the child to cradle it in her arms.

"Matt," Matoka replied.

"Yah, Matthew," Flip interjected. "Wanted ta name 'im Gordon, but she couldn't pronounce it," he said, tossing his head in the direction of Matoka.

The baby, dressed in a lightweight shawl and smelling as Elizabeth remembered babies do, appeared healthy and alert as it scanned her facial expressions. His complexion was lighter than the reddish-bronze of other Indian youngsters, leading her to assume Flip was the father as Richard had told her. "Matt, you're one fine boy," she said. She turned back to Matoka. The Indian woman had a heavy coating of dust on her feet and the edge of her skirt. She reeked with a musky odor of perspiration. "Have you had supper?"

"Oh, yes," Flip replied. "Ate with Frenchy a couple of hours ago."

"I'll make some tea, anyway."

"That would taste good," Flip said with a smile.

Matoka nodded as she took the baby from Elizabeth.

While they sat at the table, Flip explained he and Matoka had to do considerable work on the cabin. "Damn Ottawas! Thought I was just another one-season, British trapper. Tore up the building and carried off most of my utensils and equipment." He paused to sip at the tea, spilling some down his front. "And ta top it off, she decides ta have Matt right in the middle of it all!" He chuckled and shook his head.

Matoka looked down at the child cradled in her arms. She nodded and smiled.

"But it's in pretty good shape now," Flip added with a satisfied grin.

They spent the night in the barn and were awakened in the morning when Richard tended the animals. At the house, Elizabeth had a breakfast of fried eggs and biscuits waiting. To her surprise, both Flip and Matoka had bathed and were neatly groomed. And Matoka, wanting to impress Elizabeth with how well she cared for the gifts from her white sister, had also washed her clothing in the river the night before.

That evening the LaCroix came over. When a discussion arose about the future of the Detroit settlement, Louis wrinkled his brow. "Many more Indians here than there was." His face took on a look of concern, and he shook his head. "Some of them are not happy. There are many signs of discontent."

"That may be so," Richard said. "But the Wyandottes are good. They are friendly neighbors."

"I hope so," Louis replied. "But I hear the Huron and Chippewa are getting restless."

"And the Ottawa have been a bit nasty this summer," Flip added.

Elizabeth sat quietly holding Matt, stroking his cheeks and rubbing his chin, feeling a special kinship toward him. She was surprised at the conversation, not certain what to make of it. Matoka, it seemed, was such a nice person. She was making outstanding progress with the English language. Even this morning, she had noticed the Indian woman watching intently as she worked about the house. Matoka really wanted to learn the ways of the white woman.

She studied Matoka's face for a moment. Then she asked, "What do you think, Matoka? "

Matoka looked at her and shrugged. "Matoka does not know."

Louis looked at her questioningly. Perhaps she didn't know anything about the situation. Or maybe, he thought, she didn't want to offer an opinion.

Elizabeth listened to the conversation a few more minutes. She felt the Wyandottes were trustworthy people. Perhaps it would be wise to have them as special friends. "Why don't we invite some of Matoka's family to have dinner with us?" she said.

Conversation ceased abruptly. Slowly, she searched the faces staring at her.

After several seconds of silence, Marie responded with a smile. "That would be nice. A big feast for them."

Louis thought for a moment. "Why not?" he said with a nod, turning to Richard and Flip.

"I think it would be a good thing to do," Elizabeth stated, enthusiasm showing in her face.

Marie nodded agreement.

Flip turned to Matoka, who had sat expressionless during the discussion. "Would your family come?"

"I think so," she replied with sober look. "Naseeka would want that."

◆

The women placed a large venison roast into the outdoor oven. It would be early afternoon before it was done. Elizabeth turned to Marie. "Just wished we knew when they'll come."

"They'll be here when they get here," Marie said, wishing her friend would stop fretting. "You worry too much."

But Elizabeth was still concerned. She knew Indians didn't worry about time. After Flip and Matoka had left with the message, it was a week before a runner arrived to inform her that Naseeka and other Wyandottes would "honor the invitation to eat at the wigwam of his white brother." At first she thought the long delay meant Naseeka would ignore it, but Richard knew better and told her so. He had a deeper feeling for the chief and his family and knew an invitation would be ignored or refused only to administer an insult. Naseeka would not do that to him. He also knew the Wyandotte chief would determine the date. It would demonstrate his authority.

"If they come too early, what will we do with them?" Elizabeth fretted. "If they don't come until late afternoon or evening, things will be overcooked or cold. And the bread will be dry and hard."

Richard gave an audible sigh. His wife was too meticulous about details. "They'll eat anything. Won't matter if its hot, cold, raw, or burned."

"But I'd like to show them how to do it right."

"It won't make any difference to them." He shook his head to show his exasperation. "We're as ready as can be. You and Marie have been cookin' and bakin' for three days. And we've got three tables up there under the big oak." He paused, then continued, "Well, if you're that worried, we'll go up there and eat ourselves. Don't have any tables in our houses anymore, anyway."

Marie had placed her hands on her hips to listen. When he finished, she nodded agreement, then headed for the kitchen.

It was mid-morning when Flip and Matoka trudged up the driveway. "Thought we'd come early ta help out," Flip said as he approached Louis and Richard. "Besides, Matoka wanted to learn more about cookin' from Elizabeth and Marie."

"When are the others coming?" Elizabeth asked anxiously.

"Gonna leave at noon. Be here two hours after that."

"Like I said," Richard told Elizabeth, "everything would be all right." He turned to Flip. "She was worried about when they'd be coming."

"I told 'em when ta come," Flip explained. "Figured ya wouldn't be ready 'til afternoon sometime." He paused, then added, "If I hadn't, they mighta come yesterday. Sometimes they come a day early ta get in the mood."

When he saw his wife watching Elizabeth mixing dough in a wooden bowl, Flip grinned and pointed to her. "She just pours a cup of water into the flour sack and rolls up whatever sticks together."

When Elizabeth heard him, she showed the Indian woman how to add lard, salt, and honey to the mixture.

Marie watched disdainfully for several minutes, then shrugged and walked off. To her, trying to teach a savage civilized ways was a waste of time.

It was early afternoon when Richard sighted the Wyandottes crossing the River Rouge bridge. "Here they come!" he called to Elizabeth.

Elizabeth was in the house, chatting with the other two women. "They're here," she said, rising to her feet.

Since her table was beneath the oak, she had placed the dishes of prepared food on the floor. Matoka shouldered the carrier holding Matt, then the three of them grabbed a pan or dish and started for the bluff overlooking the Detroit River. A few minutes later, Richard, Flip, and Louis, carrying the remainder of the food, escorted Naseeka, Lahana, Naseeka's mother, and three stone-faced braves to the tables.

The chief, his wife, and the mother were dressed the same as they had been at the wedding, but the three braves, one badly pock-marked, wore a garish mixture of soiled leather, cloth, and fur. Two of them carried rusted muskets and, at the direction of Naseeka, presented Richard with two fox squirrels they had killed on the way.

When Elizabeth looked up from the table she was setting and saw the three motley braves, she grimaced. They looked like the unfeeling type that made her nervous. Sidling up to Richard, she whispered, "Who are they?"

Richard replied in a low voice. "Flip says they're Naseeka's half brothers. On his war council."

As Richard spoke, the LaCroix children, fascinated by the Wyandottes, asked their father if they could sit at the table with the braves. "Yes," Louis replied, patting them on the back.

"Let's sit down and give thanks," Elizabeth suggested, anxious to serve the Indians.

Assuming the white man's God was being summoned, the Indians sat sober-faced and watched. As they waited, the eyes of the three braves darted about, suspiciously watching the curious acts.

Elizabeth rose to her feet. She wasn't about to let the Indians serve themselves. "Come on, Marie. Let's feed them."

The Indians watched intently as she went to the LaCroix children first, asking what they wanted from the serving dishes. When she approached Naseeka and Lahana, she felt they were trying to imitate the white man by requesting but a few of the courses, aware they could get more later. The three braves, however, grunted and nodded to each item brought before them, resulting in plates heaped with venison, smoked ham, chicken, fish, wild turkey, and corn bread.

Elizabeth noticed that Matoka spoke continuously to her mother and Lahana. She could tell by Matoka's hand movements that she was describing how the food was prepared.

As they ate, Lahana and Matoka proudly showed Naseeka's mother how to use a knife and fork. Reluctantly, the older woman tried, but soon gave up and returned to using her fingers.

The three braves, to the amusement of the children, used their soiled hands to stuff their mouths, then bolted their food. And Matt, hanging in his carrier from the nub of a dead limb on the oak, was given a strip of ham skin to suck. Relishing its flavor, he smacked his lips and drooled.

When the three braves had emptied their plates, they took more food from the serving dishes, stuffing it directly into their mouths. Noting this, Matoka stood, admonished them, then filled their plates for them. After consuming a third helping, they grunted and nodded to one another, then walked off to lie down in the grass a short distance away. As they walked, they patted their distended stomachs and farted and belched several times. Elizabeth looked in their direction disdainfully, but others ignored them.

Richard, sitting across from Naseeka, saw that the copper talisman he had given the chief at the wedding was discolored. He pointed to it. "Do you want it made new again?" he asked.

"Naseeka says yes," the red man replied, removing it from his neck.

Motioning for the chief to join him, he rose from the table and led the way down to the river's edge. After rubbing the disk briskly with a handful of gray silt, he rinsed it in the water. Then he held it up. The sunlight flashed from its gleaming surface.

Naseeka smiled with elation and grasped Richard's hand. Again, he had learned from the white man. "Thank you, my brother," he said. "Now I will keep it looking like the fire of the sun."

The women cleared the tables, then brought out several loaves of nut bread and a kettle of tea. Elizabeth was certain the braves were in such a state of discomfort they would not want more to eat. However, they returned to the table and consumed several large pieces of the nut bread.

Flip was amused. "Means it tasted good and the hosts are good friends," he told Richard. "Like animals with an uncertain supply, they eat too much when there's a lot of it."

Elizabeth thought it disgusting. "Did you ever hear of the sin of gluttony?" she asked Marie as they carried a basket of dishes to the river for rinsing.

"I saw it for the first time," the French woman replied from the side of her mouth.

◆

Richard, Flip, and Naseeka sat in the lengthening shadows of the oak and smoked their pipes, Flip giving a spare he carried to Naseeka who didn't have one. Noting the smoke rising from the village on the far side of the river, Richard was interested in knowing what the Wyandotte chief knew about it. He pointed and said, "Big Indian camp."

Naseeka took two quick puffs from his pipe, then withdrew it from his mouth. "Huron," he replied hoarsely.

"Many braves?"

"Many braves." Naseeka paused. "Huron not a good fellow."

"They are bad?" Richard asked, looking the chief in the eye.

"Sometimes bad. Sometimes good."

Flip, who had been listening to the exchange, said, "What I guess he means is, they're all right but you gotta watch 'em. At least any I've dealt with seem kinda sly."

When the Wyandottes departed, Naseeka expressed his appreciation to the Lockes and LaCroix, calling them true friends. The braves wanted to stay overnight in the barn with Flip and Matoka, but he ordered them back to the village. Then he looked into the eyes of Richard. "Someday soon, my brother, we will eat and smoke together again."

Richard, with Elizabeth at his side, replied, "Someday soon."

Chapter 13

Great Council of Warriors

Naseeka sat on his raised pallet in the chief's tepee, patiently listening to the monotone of utterances of the fur-draped medicine man. Suddenly, the medicine man became quiet. His eyes followed the little curls of smoke upward from the small blaze in front of him, then focused directly on Naseeka. "There will be a long, hard winter," he said with a raspy voice. "Cornhusks are very thick, fox squirrels are storing large amounts of acorns and hickory nuts, and the green bark of poplars has a telltale cast. In the flames there is an angry white wolf spirit."

He paused for a response from his chief, but Naseeka looked over his head at the faces of the old men behind him. Then one of the elders spoke. "Seven years ago there were the same signs. Nasingah ignored them. A terrible misery followed."

The other old men puffed their pipes, grunted, and nodded agreement.

He went on. "A deep snow and bitter wind descended on our village in early fall. It did not leave until it was time for summer."

Again the others nodded and grunted.

"The deer starved because they could not move to find food. They froze stiff in a standing position. Then the fluffy snow covered them. Our hunters could not find them. Other animals could not find them." He paused. "We used up our wood supply, and the long-house fires went out. Our people ate the village dogs. They scraped what they could find from hides and boiled cornhusks from their beds. Even our sacred burial grounds were ravaged by an emaciated pack of wolves."

There was silence in the tepee as all eyes turned to Naseeka.

He was younger then, but he could remember the gloomy cloud of desperation that had covered the village. He rose slowly to his feet. "We don't want to be like the Chippewas or the Potawatomis who are lazy and always run out of food before the white blanket goes. The signs have been placed before our eyes by the Great Spirit. We have read them, and now you must exhort the people of our village to prepare themselves."

When the elders transmitted the predictions to the people and told them what they must do, the young chief was surprised how well they obeyed the order. Women dried and smoked meat brought in by hunting parties, children gathered nuts and berries, and others harvested armloads of ferns to increase padding in family sleeping pallets. Lahana, who was carrying his child and not expected to work beyond his tepee, led a group of young wives to the secret mineral springs three miles west of the village. There they filled baskets with dirt-encrusted chunks of scarce salt.

After two weeks, the Wyandotte chief thought efforts were lagging. The villagers must do better. He summoned them to a meeting around the large fire ring. In the light of a blaze that warded off the brisk chill of a fall evening, the elders repeated long, embellished tales from tribal lore that told of other severe winters.

When the last elder had finished, Naseeka rose to his feet. "You have done well, my people." His voice was calm, barely audible above the crackling fire. He was very proud of how well they followed his leadership. Then his eyes flashed, and his jaws tensed. His voice became loud and stern. "But you must do more! Search again for corn, squash, or nuts that were overlooked. Gather up every kernel of grain." He paused and looked into their faces. "Bring in every pitch-soaked knot from the fallen, rotted trees! And make clothes that will keep the cold wind from your skin!"

As he spoke, his mother sat on a log at the back of the crowd and listened politely. She had already done her part and refused to be ruffled by her son's dire predictions. She had accumulated nearly a cup of earache medicine by repeatedly filling a doe bladder with little yellow mullein blossoms and letting the sun rays distill it. She was ready, ready to care for the afflicted who would come to her as they had for many years to receive a warmed drop of the amber, herbal oil in a troubled organ. She also had a supply of the plant's woolly leaves to be moistened and applied to their boils and carbuncles. Others could scurry about and make preparations. She would linger about the village, inhale the wonderful aromas of fall, and enjoy the relaxed feeling the season always gave her.

———————◆———————

Early one morning during the waning days of October, Naseeka waited at the water's edge as six braves of his war council prepared the canoes. He wished he didn't have to go, but when summoned, he knew he must comply.

He had been invited to attend a council of local chiefs to discuss problems caused by intrusions of the white man. It was called by a chief of the Ottawas known throughout the territory as the one who had organized and led resistance groups against the English from Fort Pitt to Sault Ste. Marie. Naseeka had met him before and knew he could hold an audience in rapt attention for two hours or more. He was also capable of leading their minds through a sequence of plausible chains of thought to arrive at conclusions he desired. His name was Pontiac, Lord of the Country, head of all Ottawas.

Naseeka shivered slightly as he removed the deerskin cape from his shoulders and stepped into the first of two canoes. He wanted to get past the Locke farm without being detected. It would be better that way. The fiery tongue of Pontiac was not good medicine for the Wyandotte, and he knew the white man was even less trusting of the wily Ottawa.

They paddled northward for several minutes, then entered the fog shrouded mouth of the River Rouge. Naseeka pulled his cape over his head and slouched low in the lead canoe as the sleek craft sliced through the smooth surface of the slow-running current and glided silently beneath the wooden bridge. In a few minutes he was beyond the settled domain of the white man. Now he would have to watch for more cunning enemies.

The next morning, Naseeka rubbed his eyes and peered out from beneath his overturned canoe. Although deep in Potawatomi territory, he had slept well. His trusted braves had maintained a vigil during the night.

He crawled out and rose to his feet. Tossing the deerskin cape over his shoulders, he turned to look at the bright fireball rising above the eastern horizon. The warm rays felt good on his face. They would soon take the chill from the air.

As he waited, the braves threw off brush that camouflaged the canoes and quickly slipped the vessels into the water. They must travel swiftly to reach the rendezvous by nightfall. Besides, in enemy territory it was better to keep moving. They could eat pemmican as they traveled.

Several miles upstream, a fallen tree blocked their passage. Naseeka walked along the river for several hundred feet, pondering the situation. The river had narrowed to a dozen feet, and rocks broke the surface of its shallow water. He looked at the sun, now halfway down in the western sky. There was only a short distance to go, he was sure, and he wanted to get there before nightfall.

Turning to his braves, he said, "We will travel on foot from here."

Quickly and quietly they slung pouches of pemmican and jerked venison across their shoulders, then divided the powder and shot they would carry. When they started to walk, a young Ottawa brave, armed only with a bow and quiver of arrows, appeared suddenly from behind a clump of witch hazel.

Naseeka had seen other red men at a distance as they made their way up the river, but this one was close, guarding their path. The Wyandotte chief froze in his tracks and stared at the Ottawa as his braves moved in with their muskets ready. He did not fear the Ottawas, but knew the Potawatomis, his longtime enemy, would be attending the meeting. He would take no chances of being ambushed.

Seeing the Ottawa was scarcely more than a lad, and noting the fear beginning to show in his eyes, Naseeka called his braves back. He raised his open hand in the sign of peace, then beckoned the young man forward. "Why are you here?" he asked, looking sternly into the brave's eyes.

"I am to show you the way to the Ottawa village."

Naseeka could see the tension drain from the young warrior's face. "Good! We will follow you!"

The Ottawa smiled, then wheeled and started off along a lightly used trail beside the river.

Where the stream became a trickle, oozing from a marshy spring on a hillside, he led them to an area of rolling hills covered with a profusion of oaks and maples in their final stages of shedding leaves. A few squirrels, busy storing food, chattered briefly at them, and from a distance, a small group of deer cautiously watched their progress.

Naseeka liked the openness. It would be difficult for an enemy to set upon them, but he knew his braves would remain alert for telltale signs. He sniffed the air. "The white blanket will come soon," he said. His voice rang with authority, but the preoccupied braves didn't hear him.

In less than an hour, they arrived at the shore of a large lake surrounded by a dense growth of pine and spruce. An elderly Ottawa led them to a bark covered lodge, one of several spaced along the south shoreline. At a distance, across the water, they could see the activity of a large Ottawa village.

———————◆———————

A soft drizzle was falling as Naseeka, accompanied by two braves of his war council, made their way along the lakeshore to a cluster of Ottawa tepees and round huts where the longhouse was located. Stepping inside the smoke-filled building, he halted and let his eyes carefully scan the circle of men. They were sitting around a fire on reed mats placed to avoid dripping water from the leaking roof. Sitting in the background was Nagammee, chief of the host village, quietly signaling orders for the positioning of mats and serving food.

Naseeka knew Nagammee. He had met him three years before when the Ottawa chief visited his father in their village. Naseeka nodded to him, and Nagammee pointed to the mat where he and his braves were to sit.

The Wyandotte chief was the youngest in the circle. He knew that his status would be less because of it, but he would not be bullied or humbled.

As each chief was introduced by a brave beside him, Naseeka watched the reaction of others. He knew all the chiefs, but they knew him only as the son of Nasingah. Now, he was a chief. How would they consider him?

First there was Teata, chief of the Huron village across the Detroit River. A slender, middle-aged man, he had met with Pontiac many times. As his aide identified him, he barely looked up from his eating.

Next sat Sacco, chief of a Chippewa village, a friend of Naseeka who had permitted Richard and Flip to trap on his land two winters ago. He was introduced by his fierce-eyed war chief, Naghee, a man whose harsh facial features gave the appearance of one ready to do battle with little provocation. Naseeka gave Sacco a pleasant look. He liked the Chippewa chief, but thought Naghee could not be trusted.

Sacco rose to his feet. Pointing to a frail, elderly man sitting beside him, he said, "This is Minavavana, the great chief of all Chippewas!"

All in the circle looked at Minavavana and nodded. He was chief of the vast Chippewa nation to the north, a man who commanded great respect because of the many villages he ruled.

Sitting next to Naseeka was the gray-haired, pockmarked Seetonka, chief of the Potawatomis. When introduced, he nodded to each chief in the circle, then glared at the young Wyandotte. Old Nasingah was dead, but he remembered Naseeka as the leader of the fierce battle that drove his people from its village on the banks of the River Rouge, forcing them to relocate two days walk to the west. For all these years, he had harbored the thought of revenge. Now, he sat beside his enemy, forced to treat him with respect.

When Naseeka was introduced by one of his braves, Pontiac looked up and nodded. The Wyandotte chief was pleased the great Pontiac chief recognized him, but he knew the Ottawa expected something in return.

For a fleeting moment, Seetonka glanced at him, looking coldly into his face. Naseeka stared back. He knew that, when the Potawatomi war council thought the Wyandottes could be overwhelmed, they would attack. He was determined the time would never come.

For nearly an hour they sat, eating strips of meat and roasted nuts, smacking their lips, nodding, and grunting. As Naseeka looked around, he saw that little was being said except within tribal groups. Pontiac sat with his hands folded between his crossed legs, his dark, deep-seated eyes scanning his guests. Twice, Naseeka saw the Ottawa chief studying him. He was sure it meant something special.

Nagammee stepped forward and handed Pontiac a lighted pipe. Pontiac held it about his head, and the circle became quiet. "I pass to you the calumet of peace!" The sound of his voice commanded immediate attention. He took two puffs, then handed it back to Nagammee.

During the several minutes it took to reach Naseeka, the Wyandotte noticed that its harsh smoke caused an occasional cough or snort. That would not happen to him; he would see to it. As he took it from Seetonka, he could see the eyes of others watching. He drew on it carefully, held the smoke in his mouth, then exhaled it. There was no effect. Not even his eyes watered.

Pontiac rose slowly to his feet. A man of medium stature, the muscles of his hard-set, square jaws rippled as he looked at the assembly before him. His bronze skin, smoothly stretched over high cheekbones, belied the forty harsh years he had lived, and his black hair, neatly plaited in braids that hung halfway down his broad chest, shone dully in the smoke-filled shelter. As he started to speak, a gray blanket dropped from his shoulders, exposing brown buckskins and a sleek otterskin vest.

"My fellow leaders," he began, arms folded across his chest, "we meet today to consider the problem that bothers us all, a problem that grows worse with each passing day, a problem that multiplies with each new moon. I speak of the English leader at Detroit."

The sound of his voice was of such quality it commanded rapt attention from those sitting before him. It had a texture of tone that was forceful yet mellow, totally different from the deep, raspy, guttural sounds that issued from the throats of many red men.

"Every summer he brings more of his white friends to take our land. They hunt and trap the forest game that used to be so plentiful and now are so scarce and frightened that we can no longer walk among them. He takes much more than he needs. And he bribes the weaker among us to work for him for little or nothing. He poisons their minds with firewater. When we ask for fire sticks and powder to hunt the frightened deer so we can eat, he will sell us none."

He paused for the nods and grunts of agreement, then continued, his voice producing a new and stirring tonal quality. "The French who lived among us for many years were our brothers. They ate with us. They slept with us. And they took our women as their wives. When they traded with us, they gave us good merchandise at fair prices. They, too, have come under the yoke of the English."

Raising his voice in a passionate plea, he spread his arms. "Today, I call for us to unite. Each alone, we cannot drive the English commander and his soldiers from our land. I speak with a voice of experience. I have fought beside the Iroquois. They discovered too late that the English leader tells lies and does not keep his promises."

He looked directly at Naseeka. "I invite you, Naseeka of the Wyandottes, and Teata of the Hurons, to join with us. We, the Ottawas, the Chippewas, and the Potawatomis, the Three Fires, need your help so we can rid our land of the white tyrants, the English!"

As Naseeka and his braves searched the faces of the others, he noted repeated grunts and nods.

Naghee, attempting to upstage the others, leaped to his feet with his musket in his hand. Thrusting the weapon above his head, he shouted, "We go now and gather our braves! In five days, we can storm the fort!"

354

Sacco, surprised by the outburst of his war chief, motioned for him to sit down.

Pontiac nodded. He was pleased with the show of enthusiasm. "Our victory must be quick!" he said. Then, he became somber. "If it is not, a long battle will follow. We will need more food and more weapons." He shifted his stance and looked around the circle. "We must make careful plans! We must be successful!"

The rain stopped, permitting them to go outside. Several red men stood in a cluster and spoke quietly. Naseeka did not join them. He walked to the edge of the lake to ponder the proposed alliance. He thought of the brave warriors of his small village and of the hate-filled Seetonka and his Potawatomis. And there was Richard and Flip.

The sun, breaking through the clouds, formed a bright rainbow that spanned the lake and reflected from its glass-like surface. A fish leaped from the water to catch a low flying insect, generating a series of ripples in concentric circles that rapidly made their way toward the shore. Naseeka was impressed with the beauty of the scene. How wonderful it was to have a village here.

When they returned to the longhouse, Pontiac told them there would be another meeting after the coming white blanket had gone. He would send runners to inform them. In the meantime, they should gather extra food and weapons.

Again they ate, and again the calumet was passed. Naseeka took a gentle draw from the plume-decorated stem and felt the harsh smoke gnaw at his throat. When he handed it to Seetonka, as much as he tried to stifle it, a muffled cough burst from his lips.

With a sneer, the Potawatomi seized the pipe and drew on it twice, the second with such force it made a strong gurgling sound.

Naseeka knew a mouthful of the potent liquid had been ingested by the scurrilous chief. He watched as Seetonka, with eyes watering but determined to act unconcerned, returned the pipe to Pontiac. In seconds, the Potawatomi chief convulsed and gagged, forcefully splattering the ground before him with tobacco juice and vomit.

Pontiac glanced at him, then calmly looked over the heads of others as he put the calumet to his lips for the last puff before handing it to his aide. He rose slowly to his feet, stretched to his full height, and waited for the others to stand with him. "This meeting is over," he said matter-of-factly. "Go to your people. Prepare them. Wait for my call."

As he watched representatives of each tribe trudge off in separate directions, he was satisfied he had acquired allies for his campaign. When spring came, he would launch his final, maximum effort to dislodge the white man from his forested domain.

◆

Naseeka stood quietly at the edge of the mound where a few moons before he had placed the body of his father. So many things had happened since, and now he needed to call upon Nasingah's wisdom. He would communicate with his father's spirit, and it would seek advise from the chiefs who had gone before. First, he would think about the things that would please them.

He recalled the winter that had passed. Although bitterly cold at times, it was not as severe as the medicine man had predicted. Hunting and trapping had been good, and by trading pelts with Richard and Louis, the Wyandottes had accumulated a reserve of wheat and corn. Then, there was the Frenchman at the fort. A true friend, he sold them powder and shot when others would not.

Naseeka looked up at the sun, a blazing ball midway up in the eastern sky. It was a bright and sacred fire. His mind became troubled. Again, he stared at the mound.

With the spring thaw had come a new commandant to the fort, a tall, sandy-haired major, a strange and distant man. Naseeka was not satisfied with the contemptible treatment his people received at the hands of the English, but hoped he could develop an accommodation with the new commandant like that he'd had with the French. He thought of how well their cultures blended. Perhaps it was because they had been in the red man's world longer and their dark features more closely matched those of the Indian than did the light complexion of the English. Some of their trappers had lived with the forest people and, although it had never happened to a Wyandotte maiden, occasionally married one.

When the English came, they promised many gifts and a life of peace and harmony. However, the gifts of blankets, beads, cloth, and utensils were given in much smaller quantities than he was told, and peace and harmony existed only as long as the red man obeyed English orders, orders for the benefit of the white man.

He closed his eyes and again looked toward the sky. A pleasant feeling flowed across his body. The spirit of his father was calling for him to think of more good things.

His mind searched his concerns. Yes, there were more. He was grateful that, when additional white men came, they settled north and west of the fort. No one claimed land below the River Rouge. And he was proud of the rapport he had established with Major Rogers who invited him to discuss the red man's concerns.

And, of course, there were his two white brothers, Englishmen who demonstrated they could be loyal and trusted friends.

For them, he was deeply concerned. If Pontiac proceeded with his plan to attack the white settlement, they would be in great jeopardy. He, then, would be caught in the agonizing position of either obeying the code of the red man or alerting them and violating his sacred Indian oath. He hoped Pontiac would not initiate his plan of war.

Although his scouts had told him they had seen Ottawas around the fort, they were only trading or begging. There was no sign of trouble. Pontiac had spent the winter on a little, tree-covered island to the north where the big water funneled down to the Detroit River. Maybe he had changed and wanted to live in peace with the white man.

His thoughts were interrupted by running footsteps behind him. It had to be a matter of extreme importance. His people would not disturb him when he was at the burial mound communicating with his father's spirit.

He turned around and saw a runner, sweating profusely and breathing heavily, slow to a halt a short distance from him. With a wave of his hand, he motioned for the young man to approach.

"Ottawa chief and braves come this way!" the runner gasped.

Thoughts raced through Naseeka's mind. They certainly would not attack without the other tribes. But then, these were not ordinary times. Not wanting to alarm his village, he walked up close to the runner. "Where are they?"

"They cross the River Rouge."

Naseeka quickly gathered two dozen braves and ran north on the river road. Before leaving, he gave orders for others to prepare for battle.

When they reached the Ecorse River, he saw the Ottawas approaching on the far side. It was Nagammee, chief of the large village where they had met last fall. He was accompanied by eight braves.

Nagammee raised his hand in the sign of peace.

Naseeka was relieved. It was a friendly meeting. He returned the sign. Then, determined to keep the Ottawas on the other side of the river, he ordered his braves to follow him across the ford.

Nagammee instructed his braves to spread two blankets on the ground. Then, with a polite nod, he invited Naseeka to sit.

Naseeka eyed him carefully. His actions seemed genuine enough, but why would a chief of the proud Ottawas treat a Wyandotte with courtesy? Naseeka would have to find out.

As the two groups of braves stood back and eyed each other, Naseeka and Nagammee sat on the blankets. The Ottawa chief explained that his village, with a larger than normal population, was running low on food. He wished to get some from the Wyandottes.

"But why do you come here?" Naseeka asked, voicing suspicion. He wondered if there was another group of Ottawas approaching his village from another direction. But there couldn't be; his scouts would have informed him. All the same, he was glad he had alerted the braves of his village.

Nagammee let his cape, a dangling patchwork of pelts, slip from his shoulders. "The great Pontiac, he says the Wyandottes always have food. They prepare well for winter."

"Why do you have more people?"

"Pontiac, he brings arrowsmiths from distant villages. They bring their wives and children. They work very hard."

This information alarmed Naseeka, but he did not show it. Pontiac must be forging ahead with his plan by building a supply of weapons. In the past, when the Ottawa ran low on food, they sought help from the Hurons or Chippewas. "He has not asked for help from the Wyandotte before," he responded coolly.

"Pontiac, he says the Wyandottes are now brothers of the Three Fires. They will help."

Naseeka asked Nagammee if he would wait while he went back to his village and talked with his people. Nagammee nodded and waved him off. Then Naseeka waded back across the Ecorse where he ordered half of his braves to remain and watch the Ottawas.

For three hours, Naseeka sat in conference with his war council and the village elders. They did not like the haughty Ottawas and, most of all, did not want to be involved in Pontiac's designs for personal power. The arrogant Ottawa chief looked upon them as inferiors, and he was sure to turn on them when they no longer served his purpose.

But this was not the time to refuse such a powerful tribe. With reluctance, they agreed to give Nagammee two sacks of corn, two sacks of wheat, and one sack of chestnuts.

When presented with the sacks, Nagammee ordered his braves to run their fingers through them. Satisfied with the inspection, he walked up to Naseeka. He took a six-inch square of birch bark from a pouch and held it out. "From the great Ottawa chief, Pontiac!" he declared with a snap of his head.

Naseeka examined the carefully painted figure of an otter that decorated its back surface. He had seen one before in the hands of a Chippewa. It was the red totem of Pontiac. The debt would be repaid someday in furs, food, or wampum. Such was the law of the red man.

He also knew that Pontiac would consider him an ally. As such, he, too, would have to activate his arrowsmiths.

◆

In the early dawn of Monday, April 25, 1763, Seema and a friend, Chowchow, slipped a canoe silently into the water and paddled south toward the nearby Isle aux Cochons. He would steal a fat goose from the fenced barnyard of James Fisher, one of the English farmers who lived there. Then he could treat his mother to an exquisite meal of delicate taste.

The teenage brave, whose father had fallen through the ice and drowned several years before, lived with his mother in Pontiac's village on the Isle aux Peche. Since the father's death, the doting woman spent much of her time gathering and cooking food and sewing for her son. He had always lived a life of plenty. Even when food was scarce, he remembered how he ate well because she sacrificed from her plate. Now that he realized what she had done for him, he would regale her with a meal like that enjoyed by the white man.

He and Chowchow had paddled past the island on numerous occasions, always seeing the geese strutting about. It would be easy to take one. Besides, he reasoned, the Fishers had other animals and should not miss one goose.

Working his paddle noiselessly in cadence with his friend squatted in the prow, he thought of the many things they had done together. He had known Chowchow all his life. They were like brothers, neither having a father. Chowchow had been orphaned as an infant and reared by an aunt. He remembered the long days of many summers when they had played together. He was glad Chowchow was with him.

The warm sun was thrusting its yellow ball above the horizon as they guided their canoe close to the eastern shore of the river, keeping in the long shadows. Suddenly, Seema whispered, "Now!"

Turning abruptly to the west, they began the final approach to the island. Ahead in the haze, Seema could see the fenced compound that held the animals. By the time the canoe nudged against the shore, his heart was thundering within his breast.

They pulled the craft into the shrubs at the water's edge, then crept along in a low crouch to the picket fence. Heavy dew soaked their moccasins and chilled their feet, but it also muffled the sounds of their travel.

They stopped and carefully looked about. The farmhouse was quiet. The Fishers were still asleep. Inside the compound, cows lay on the ground, contentedly chewing their cuds and exhaling white vapor from their nostrils. Two geese, standing a few feet away, stretched their necks to watch the intruders.

Chowchow leaped the fence and seized a goose about the neck. There was an intense flurry of beating wings and a chorus of hissing and honking. The startled cows rose clumsily to their feet and trotted away.

Seema reached over the fence to take the struggling goose from Chowchow when he saw Mr. Fisher, still dressed in his nightgown, pull open the rear door of his house. Raising a musket to his shoulder, he took quick aim and fired. Seema heard the ball hit its mark with a sickening thud.

He fled to the canoe, paddled around the corner, and hid in some reeds. If only he could have pulled Chowchow back over the fence and brought him along. But the Englishman would have shot him, too. He would wait. Maybe Chowchow would appear, and he could rescue him.

He watched the activity and listened to the shouting for a long time. Finally, peering through the shrubs, he saw Chowchow's body being tossed into the river. His first impulse was to paddle after it, but he knew he would be killed. Tears filled his eyes as he watched the current carry it away.

At the village, the frightened young brave told only his closest friends what had happened, but before the sun had reached its zenith, he was standing rigidly before Pontiac.

"I have been told your friend has been killed by the English," the chief said, looking directly into Seema's face.

"Yes," Seema replied humbly.

Seema's affirmative reply sparked an intense fury within the chief. With set jaw and fiery eyes, he walked over to the distraught lad and placed a hand on his shoulder. "The white man will pay for this!" he vowed. "Soon you will return to the Isle aux Cochons to seek your revenge!"

The day following the death of Chowchow, Pontiac, riding amid a flotilla of canoes carrying many members of his village, including his three wives and their children, glided quietly through the thick fog that shrouded the east shore of the Detroit River. It was essential that he get past the fort without arousing the suspicion of the rampart lookouts.

Three weeks before, he had sent his fleet-footed runners carrying small belts of red and black war wampum to all the tribes he thought he could rally. They contacted the angry southern ones and those in dark, dank pine forests of the north, telling them he was assembling the Council of Warriors as he had promised. They would meet on the fifteenth day of the Green Moon on the northern banks of the Ecorse River, a short distance upstream from where it emptied into the Detroit River.

When he arrived to establish his camp, Pontiac found several hundred fellow red men already there, and band after band were continuing to drift in. They came on foot and by canoe, in large parties and small groups, and selected sites on the perimeter of the clearing for their shelters.

Late in the afternoon, the Ottawa chief stepped from his hide-covered wigwam and surveyed the scene that stretched before him. He was pleased. The large bowl-shaped glen was dotted with makeshift huts, tepees, and wigwams, the temporary shelters of people from many nations. And they were in a festive mood. It would be easy for him to kindle their passions.

Among the motley conglomeration were the elders who sat about in tribal clusters, thoughtfully smoking their pipes as they talked. Lounging about, groups of veteran warriors gestured with their hands as they ate and told exaggerated tales of daring feats. And there were scatterings of gaudily dressed young fops who had little status, since their bravery had not been tested in battle. Bedecked with beads, bells, and feathers, they were noisily prancing about in a vain attempt for attention. Nearby, maidens, their faces coated with bear grease and vermilion and their bodies smelling of juniper, displayed their lures of enticement. Waddling among them with bent bodies and scrawny, bowed legs were several wrinkled, toothless hags who shrieked with jealous disdain at the young ladies' behavior.

For several minutes Pontiac watched dozens of naked children, their black, mischievous eyes and grubby little hands searching for excitement, teasing one another and pestering the adults. Then he inhaled a deep breath and smiled. Soon, he thought, they would be part of the great confederation he would create.

As Naseeka approached the river, he could hear the clamoring assembly on the other side. Although he could return to his tepee at night, he would camp with the others. That way, he reasoned, there would be no excuse for outsiders, especially the Potawatomis, to approach his village.

Followed by a war council dressed in long buckskin blouses and carrying stone-tipped lances, he halted at the edge of the meadow to get his bearings. The sight he saw through the blue-white haze of smoke was awesome. He had never seen so many people. The air vibrated with the sounds of rattle beads, hollow gourds, ankle bells, and thong-tied thigh drums. Above the pervasive babble of countless conversations, he could hear the prattling voices of mothers and the squeals of their children.

Early the next morning, shortly after the dew had lifted, elderly camp supervisors walked among the lodges and called in loud voices for the warriors to assemble. As the summons sounded, braves emerged from their shelters. There were the tall, naked Chippewas, four thousand in number, half of those present, with loaded quivers on their backs and slender war-clubs cradled in their arms. The stocky Ottawas had wrapped themselves in gaudy blankets, and the Potawatomis wore brightly painted shirts, feathers in their hair, and bells attached to their leggings. And there were representatives from two dozen other tribes, some having traveled great distances to heed the call.

When the Ottawa chief appeared, they seated themselves upon the grass in sweeping arcs, one within another, creating a silent and solemn assembly. Occupying a slight knoll, Pontiac sat erect and watched for several minutes as decorated pipes, with plumes and ornaments attached to their stems, passed from hand to hand.

Naseeka scanned the gathering. Eight Frenchmen, the only white men he could see, were seated a short distance behind the great Ottawa chief. He recognized three of them as longtime courier de bois, hangers-on and troublesome malcontents, who frequently harangues the Indians to overthrow the English so the French could return to power. They would be working with Pontiac to arouse the forest people.

But the presence of the others bothered him. They were prominent persons who lived in and near the fort. How did they know of the meeting? Could they be trusted? Maybe Pontiac had French spies on the inside to help.

After a time, Pontiac stood. Plumed and painted in the full costume of war, he appeared darker than Naseeka had remembered.

Slowly, with a bold and stern expression, he scrutinized the vast crowd before him. He inhaled deeply, taking an instant to savor the odors of smoke, food, and bodies. Now they could see he was a man of substance, a leader of power and character. He turned admiringly from left to right, causing the porcelain beads and wrought silver ornaments he wore to flash in the sun, now halfway up in the morning sky. Then, slowly and deliberately, he raised his arms, a signal he was going to speak.

"Several moons ago I spoke with the great Abnaki prophet," he began. "He told me many things. He told me the Great Spirit would give direction to a chosen one. I, Chief Pontiac, have received the sign. Friends and brothers, the Great Spirit has destined us to meet here today for our common good." He spoke in a low voice, causing those at the perimeter to strain to hear. It would give him total and complete attention.

He paused to allow interpreters to murmur translations to their fellow Shawnee, Delaware, Sioux, and Osage. Then, raising his voice so it was clearly audible to all, he launched into his delivery in earnest. His words were clear and precise. "The sun shines bright so we can see clearly, the wind is quiet so we can hear unmistakably, our minds are quick so we can reason without confusion."

When the interpreters had finished, he heard loud grunts of agreement. Enthusiasm was building in the faces of those who now waited eagerly for his next words.

He attacked the arrogance and injustice of the English and contrasted them with the French who had been driven from the land. Complaining that the English commandant had treated him with contempt and his people with neglect, he charged that the soldiers were specially trained to abuse the red man. With a loud, impassioned voice and fierce gestures, he related the death of Seema's friend, Chowchow. The cause of the shooting was not mentioned.

He lowered his voice and continued. "The French have always been our brothers. And now their Great White Father from across the sea has heard our voices and understands our troubles. One day soon, his great war canoes will return and attack the English criminals to drive them from our land. We must fight beside our French brothers so they can complete the task quickly and punish the oppressors severely."

Halting momentarily, he hoisted a huge red wampum belt emblazoned with shiny, black symbols above his head. Holding it in his outstretched hands, he turned slowly so all could get a measure of its magnitude, could see that it nearly reached the ground. A ripple of grunts and sighs fluttered across the gathering.

"This," he shouted, "has been sent by the Great French Father. He promises more. He also promises to oust those vile English who tell us we have simple minds, who have taken our source of food, who have robbed us of our furs, who have denied us good weapons, and who have destroyed our pride and self respect! He sends word that, when we raise our tomahawks to the English, his great war canoes will appear in our waters to assure our victory!"

Now that he had aroused their anger and stirred their thirst for revenge, he appealed to their superstitions and religious beliefs. Using all the cunning of his vivid imagination and fiery, dramatic oratory, he told them he had taken an arduous journey through the forests and mountains to meet the Great Spirit. "He seated me before him, and ordered me to bring his message to you!"

The audience was spellbound with eager anticipation.

He waited for a series of low-level vocal undulations to subside, then continued with a deeper tone to his voice.

" 'I am the Maker of heaven and earth, the trees, lakes, rivers, and all things else. I am the Maker of mankind, and because I love you, you must do my will. The land on which you live I have made for you and not for others. Why do you suffer the white man to dwell among you? My children, you have forgotten the customs and traditions of your forefathers. Why do you not clothe yourselves in skins, as they did? And use the bows and arrows and stone-tipped lances which they used? You have bought guns, knives, kettles, and blankets from the white man until you can no longer do without them.' "

Pontiac raised his voice to its maximum volume and flung his arms skyward.

" 'And what is worse, you have drunk the poison firewater which turns you into fools!' "

Breathing heavily, he paused and looked at them, his dark eyes flashing. There was not a sound. Then, with a lowered voice, he continued.

" 'Fling these things away. Live as your wise forefathers lived before you. And as for these English, these dogs dressed in red who have come to rob you of your hunting grounds and drive away the game, you must lift your tomahawk against them! Wipe them from the face of the earth, and then you will win my favor back again! And again you will be happy and prosperous! The children of our father, the king of France, are not like the English. Never forget they are your brothers. They are dear to me, for they love the red man and understand the true meaning of worshiping me.' "

His body glistening with perspiration, Pontiac again raised his hands. "Such is the word of the Great Spirit."

He paused to catch his breath, then proceeded more solemnly. "He ordered me to gather the great warriors of all tribes and direct them to rise as one against the red-jacketed devils and strike them down. We must be cunning, deceive them, and give them no warning so we can easily destroy them. When they are gone, driven from our beautiful, bountiful land, we will discard his weapons, his clothes, his vices. Once again, we will return to our proper way of life."

Again his voice changed to a high-pitched shout. "My brothers, we must vow never to fight each other again! We are one people! We are one family! My mother was Chippewa, my father Ottawa! The same blood runs in all our bodies! United, we will tear the hearts from our common enemy! Go home now and prepare yourselves to eliminate the English from your lands! When you are told that I, the great Chief Pontiac, have struck the fort at Detroit, take to the warpath and destroy those English dogs! Eliminate every one you find!"

Pontiac whirled on his heels and strode rapidly to his wigwam. Suddenly it was quiet. The warriors turned to look at one another, then rose to their feet.

Mesmerized by hearing directly from one who had spoken with the Great Spirit, and buoyed by the thought of retaking their hunting

366

grounds, they talked in small clusters while the women spent the afternoon and evening loading the canoes.

When the sun rose the next morning, the savage swarm had melted away. The lush grass of the great meadow had been trampled flat and littered with frail shelter frames, bits of cloth, scraps of leather, and broken utensils. But silence and solitude had returned, and nature would heal the scars.

Chapter 14

Fury Unleashed

When Naseeka, leading the contingent of his war council, neared his village, he could hear the sound of dozens of excited voices filtering through the trees. He knew it was his people, but thought it strange they were so aroused. Approaching the fire ring, the group was beset by a large number of villagers asking questions. He stood back and listened for several minutes. What he heard did not please him.

Although forbidden to attend the Council of Warriors, many of his braves had stood guard and watched from the thick growth along the south bank of the Ecorse. They heard Pontiac's loud, dramatic call for an all-out, united attack on the fort. Rushing back to the village, they spread the word of an impending assault. Now, they stood in the crowd and boasted how the attack would let them display their courage and prove their prowess.

Dismayed at their blind hunger for war, Naseeka raised his hand for silence. "Do not be so anxious for the taste of blood," he warned.

The braves looked at him questioningly. Why was their chief speaking words of caution? He was a proven warrior. Certainly he was not afraid of danger.

Naseeka continued. "The English have many muskets. Much of the blood spilled will be that of the red man. Their swivel guns can tear apart the bodies of many braves with a single shot."

He scanned the sobered faces surrounding him. At their age, he, too, did not comprehend the dangers of battle. They with the questioning eyes would be among the first to fall.

"We must also think of our tribe. The Ottawas, the Hurons, and the Chippewas have many, many braves. They can lose a large number and still remain strong. We are a small tribe and cannot waste our braves." He paused, then continued. "And remember, my courageous warriors, our mortal enemy, the Potawatomi, will be lurking nearby."

One of the anxious young men straightened to his full height and asked in a tone that seemed to question his chief's spirit, "That means we will not fight?"

Naseeka glared at him. It was a reminder that he, Naseeka, was chief. Being both brave and wise, *he* would make tribal decisions. "The war council will consider the matter very carefully. When a determination has been reached, Naseeka will inform you."

The braves grunted and nodded acceptance.

"Go now," he told them. "Repair our palisade and make weapons for yourselves. Should the time come, we must be ready!"

Although heavily burdened by the momentous problems confronting him, he knew he must maintain a firm stance in the eyes of his people. He turned and strode briskly to his tepee.

For the next two days the young chief sat cross-legged before a small fire ring. As he sat, he stared at little tongues of blue flame rising from ash-covered brands fueled at a low level by Lahana. She knew the fire was not needed for warmth, but when her man was troubled it cleared his thought processes and gave inspiration.

As evening approached, she placed a blanket over his shoulders. He gave her a nod, a show of appreciation for her comfort and concern. Attempting to raise his spirits, she handed him their four month old son. Although Naseeka ate little of the food she brought, he smiled as he held the boy and shared a bite with the cooing, drooling infant.

Naseeka was proud of his child. In a very painful delivery, it had been born strong and healthy, like the medicine man had requested

370

in a dozen special rituals. Confident the Great Spirit wanted to insure the future of the tribe, Naseeka selected the boy's name and ordered a breechclout and bow and arrows for his puberty rites two months before he was born. He would be called Chawkimree, Preserver of the Tribe.

He held the boy up and looked at the infant's dark eyes and fat cheeks. He would like to show Chawkimree to Richard and Elizabeth. They knew of him only from what he had told them when he stopped for a visit on the way to the fort. But the Council of Warriors had changed things. He handed Chawkimree back to Lahana.

His deliberations pursued thoughts ranging much farther than Pontiac's goal of chasing the English from the territory. He had been astounded by the large gathering the Ottawa chief assembled, a greater number of red men than he knew existed. It would be folly to oppose the rising tide of resentment he had witnessed. Perhaps Pontiac was right. Maybe it would be better to rid the land of the English and return to the old ways.

But then he thought of the comforts they brought—the woolen clothing that was soft and warm in winter, the musket that reached out to kill the deer, and copper pots for heating water and cooking food. If the Wyandottes adopted the English way of constructing buildings, raising animals, and preserving food, they could live with greater ease and more security than they had ever known.

And there was Richard and Flip. He knew the Wyandottes would not harm them, but once Pontiac had raised the war axe, roving bands of renegades intent on wanton bloodletting would scout the area in search of anyone who did not have dark hair and eyes.

As he lowered his head, a large gas pocket burst forth from wood in the fire ring. The hissing noise startled him, and the sudden flash of light reflecting from the copper disk hanging from his neck smarted his eyes. When he looked up, he saw the momentary rays focused on the skin of a timber wolf hanging near the door.

This was the sign, the omen for which he had been waiting. The Great Spirit had reminded him of the friendly Norsemen with their white wolf's head and shiny breastplate.

On the morning of the third day, after consulting with his war council, he stepped from his tepee into the warm, filtered rays of a rising sun. The brightness made him squint, but he was satisfied the Great Spirit had given him solutions to the difficult problems facing his people. He was tired, his body drained of its vigor, but he could feel it being revitalized by the resolutions he had concluded, answers that would be accepted by his people and serve their best interests.

He sat on the seat before his tepee as the war council assembled the tribe before him. When he stood, a somber hush came over them. He knew they would follow any decision he had reached. But he also knew they realized, from what they had learned of Pontiac's passion-kindling speech, that the life they had come to know would forever be changed.

"My brothers, my sisters, my tribesmen," he began soberly, "the Wyandottes have always been a proud people blessed with wisdom, strength, and courage. We now face a moment of great decision, a next step fraught with serious and far-reaching consequences. Pontiac, the great Ottawa chief, will soon attack Detroit, and he has asked for our help."

He waited for a wave of murmuring to stop. "He wishes to rid the land of the English, a noble task for the red man. But we, being a small tribe, must also remain strong to protect our people and our land." He paused, then continued in a louder voice. "There are red men who wish to reduce us to nothing and take our territory. They want to turn us into slaves. We must not be misled! We must protect ourselves! We will help Pontiac, but we must do what is best for us!"

He waited for it to become quiet again. "We will let the Ottawa, the Chippewa, and the Potawatomi, the Three Fires, attack the fort. We will help by foraging for food and giving them supplies. Our warriors will watch the river so the English war canoes from across the Big Sea Water cannot come to the Englishmen's rescue." He lowered his voice. "And we will protect our two white brothers, Englishmen who are true friends of the Wyandottes." He surveyed their somber faces. "Naseeka, your chief, has spoken!"

He entered his tepee, then summoned his most fleet-footed and trustworthy runner. "Go to the wigwam of my sister, Matoka," he ordered. "Tell her she must return to our village at once. She must bring all her family. Tell her there is great danger coming."

———————◆———————

When the new commandant, Major Henry Gladwin, took over the fort, it was immediately apparent to Richard that he was an excellent military officer. He put his troops through practice exercises to keep them in top fighting form, laid in a large supply of food and ammunition, replaced weak timbers in the palisade, and remodeled the water gate so it was safe and practical for river traffic, especially the schooners, *Michigan* and *Huron*.

At the Comptoir Grillon, Richard mentioned how highly he regarded the major.

Frenchy nodded. "Oh, yes," he replied. Then he smiled knowingly. "But, my friend, he has a keen eye for beautiful women."

Richard raised his eyebrows.

"When he dances, he whispers little endearments into the ladies' ears, hoping for encouragement. They are courteous, of course, but they know they must be careful not to start a scandal. The married women stay close to their husbands, and the single ones are always chaperoned." Then the Frenchman smiled. "Now, Sarah and Agatha, they are interested in such a liaison, especially with the commandant, but they are beneath his status."

———————◆———————

Early in the spring, Major Gladwin was walking past the Comptoir Grillon when an Indian maiden of rare beauty caught his eye. She was selling exquisitely crafted elkskin moccasins that had been chewed to an unusual softness. When his eyes met hers, a magnetic attraction occurred. He wanted to make her acquaintance. Unable to communicate his wishes, he asked Frenchy to act as interpreter.

He purchased a pair of moccasins for six shillings. As he did, he scrutinized her carefully.

Dressed in an ornately beaded buckskin dress, she was tall, slender, and long-waisted. A generous head of neatly braided black hair was decorated with bits of red satin ribbon. Although she stared at the ground, he saw her eyes were brown, a soft, sensitive, dark brown. And to accent her straight, narrow nose, she had highlighted her prominent cheekbones with a touch of vermilion.

Gladwin's pulse was rising. "Find out where she lives," he ordered.

Frenchy asked several questions, then turned to the major. "She say she was born a Chippewa. Her name is Makki. Now she lives with an Ottawa family in Pontiac's village."

A few minutes later she followed Gladwin to his quarters, assured that others were interested in moccasins.

Summoned by their commandant, Captain Campbell and Lieutenant MacDougal reluctantly bought moccasins. When they left, Makki looked into Major Gladwin's eyes. She wanted to return again, and knew she must.

When Makki visited the commandant's quarters two or three times a week, she carried a pair of moccasins as a symbol of her mission. Frenchy was sure she was indulging in torrid sessions of passionate release, but only smiled when someone mentioned it. When the wives, however, noted that she carried the moccasins in both directions, her activity became a matter of intense interest and common gossip.

"How brazen!" protested Mrs. Sam Taylor, wife of the general store proprietor.

But her friends in the church choir questioned the sincerity of her outrage. She seemed to derive too much joy from talking about it.

And when they asked Mary Stanton if she knew, the stocky little wife of the blacksmith indignantly replied, "Disgraceful! Simply disgraceful!" Bound by a tight corset, she paused to catch her breath, then added, "Imagine! Our commandant taking up with such a person!"

"A trollop!" a member of the choir echoed.

Cupping her hand beside her mouth to project a loud whisper, Mary said, "She's just an Ojibwa whore sent by the devil to corrupt our men!" A ring of jealousy sounded in her voice.

At the Comptoir Grillon, the affair was a topic of jokes. When Richard asked about the authenticity of the rumors, Frenchy shrugged with his palms up. "The major, he calls her Catharine, not Makki. He say she is like a beautiful woman he knew in England."

A sly grin drifted across his face. "The major is a brave soldier. He has strong English sap. I think, maybe, she have little papoose in her belly soon."

———————◆———————

Richard drew on the reins. "Whoa, girl," he called. Molly snorted her pleasure at being able to rest in the shade of the big oak.

He removed his hat, wiped his forehead on his sleeve, then looked back at the long furrow. The field, now half plowed, would produce an abundant crop of corn. He was proud of what he had accomplished.

He was raising sufficient grain to feed his animals with enough left over to sell and barter. Four cows, including Bessy, grew fat on lush grass and produced enough milk to fatten several hogs when it was mixed with grain and garbage, and now there was clover and timothy to feed another horse through the winter.

Louis, working in the field across the road, waved.

Richard held up his hat. The LaCroix were good friends, and he was grateful for all their help. And ever since Elizabeth had invited the Jacksons to dinner, the three families had become quite close. It pleased him to see the children teaching one another their native languages as they played together.

He thought of Marie and Elizabeth and the amount of time they shared together, especially during the busy summer months. When he recalled how they prevailed in getting him and Louis to drive them to church on Sunday, he smiled. It eased their conscience about showing respect for God, a deep-rooted duty ingrained since childhood, and gave them an opportunity to wear their best clothing. The trip, however, was made but once a month and only during good weather.

Looking at the distant woods, he wished there was a way to let Elizabeth visit her parents. Although her yearning had abated, he knew she still wanted to go. During the winter, when he could get someone to tend the animals so he could go, too, the trip was too arduous and risky. Perhaps by using their savings they could go during the summer, letting Louis work what he wanted of the farm.

He sighed and was about to slip the reins from the plow handle when he looked up and saw Louis approaching. "Hello, Louis," he greeted. "Nice day."

"Oh, yes," Louis replied, putting a stem of grass in his mouth. "It will be a good season for farming."

"Farming's getting better, but the trapping's getting worse." He paused, then added, "And from the looks of things, it's not going to get any better." For the last two seasons the trapping had become progressively less productive. During the past winter, he had barely cleared one hundred pounds. "Not enough seed animals left. Too many Indians moving in around the fort. Stripping the place clean to sell to Hudson's Bay." He drew a deep breath and threw up his arms. "Something had better be done soon! The damn fools are gonna wipe out their food supply."

Louis nodded. "But they don't know any better."

"And Hudson's Bay don't care!" Richard declared. He looked at the position of the sun. There was still time for two or three more rounds, but he didn't feel like it now. "Think I'll call it a day," he said, walking over to unhitch Molly.

Louis accompanied him to the road, then departed for his house.

As Richard was about to turn into his driveway, he looked up and saw Naseeka, accompanied by two braves, coming across the Rouge bridge. He pulled on the reins to wait for the Wyandotte chief.

"Hello, my good friend Naseeka," he greeted, extending his hand.

Naseeka shook his hand and nodded. "My white brother," he said. His mood was somber, his face expressionless.

Richard was surprised. Something had to be wrong. Then he recalled their last meeting at Detroit when Naseeka had appeared to have a gloomy attitude. At the time, he'd thought the chief was not feeling well. He placed a hand on the Indian's shoulder. "Naseeka, my friend, you seem uneasy. The great Wyandotte leader seems troubled. Is there something wrong with your family?"

Naseeka knew his deep loyalty and affection for Richard made it impossible to disguise his feelings. Richard knew him well enough to recognize his personal turmoil. "Family is good. But my white brother can see through Naseeka's eyes." He hesitated, looking at the distant river as he searched for a reply. He wished he could warn Richard of Pontiac's plan, but he could not betray the obligation to his fellow red men.

He turned and looked directly into Richard's face as he had in the past. "Naseeka can speak no more," he said flatly. "You, my brother, will soon know more." He shook Richard's hand firmly, then strode off to join the braves.

Puzzled by the evasive answer, Richard watched as they walked away. It gave him a feeling of uneasiness.

✦

"Want to ride to the fort with me?" Richard asked Elizabeth. He had broken two teeth on a harrow when it snagged on a stump while preparing a field for wheat. David Stanton would have to forge new ones for him.

She had planned to work in the garden plot he had plowed for her. "Not this time," she told him. "I'm going to plant some peas and turnips." Besides, she wasn't feeling well, a slight upset. Maybe she was pregnant, but she didn't want to tell him until she was sure. "You could sell some eggs and bread for me, though," she said as he walked off toward the barn to harness Molly.

"All right," he called back, halting momentarily to speak. "I got an extra bag of seed corn and some beans I can let go, too."

He brought the wagon to the door and loaded her straw-filled basket of eggs and a canvas bag of bread. Then, going inside, he emptied the powder and shot from her musket. "Want ta make sure it won't misfire," he explained as he reloaded it.

After he set it back in the corner, he told her, "Keep powder and shot handy. Been seein' more Indians than usual wandering about this spring."

"They haven't bothered any, have they?" she asked calmly.

"That's true. Maybe more of 'em movin' in to hang around the fort during the summer." He paused, then added, "Have to be especially careful of the drunk ones."

She walked with him to the wagon and watched as he placed his musket on the floor beside the seat. Noticing a wrinkle in the tan sweater she had knitted for him, she straightened it. Then she grasped the lapels of his corduroy jacket and looked up into the smooth, cleanly shaven face she loved to caress. Pulling him down to her, she kissed him warmly. "Take good care of yourself. Hurry back."

"I will," he said convincingly as he wrapped his arms about her shoulders. "Should get back by late afternoon."

He stopped to chat briefly with Louis and waved to Hiram as Molly energetically pulled the wagon up the rutted river road. Spring was a favorite season for Richard, a time for renewal, a time when the juices flowed freely in plants and animals. He liked fall, too, when abundant harvests rewarded him for the summer's labor, but it was also a reminder that the harsh, restrictive times of winter lay just ahead.

Smiling, he sniffed the air. It smelled fresh and clean. The trees, covered with new, tender leaves, were alive with wrens boldly singing at the top of their tiny lungs. Fragrant, carefully pruned orchards were buzzing with thousands of bees combing the fully blown blossoms for nectar, and there were robins, with mates already chosen, making numerous trips to and from the hayfields carrying dried grass for nests they were building.

Looping the reins loosely around the armrest to give Molly her head, he inhaled deeply. He thought of the handblown vase, a surprise present he was going to buy for Elizabeth. She could use it for the roses growing from rootstock Marie had given her. He had taken an extra silver crown from the fireplace cache to pay for it. How wonderful it was, he mused, just to be alive and enjoy the wondrous world about him on this Monday, the ninth of May.

Near the fort, he encountered an unusually large number of Indians wandering idly about. When they looked up at him, some smiled, others scowled. Molly hastened her pace as she threaded her way through them.

A few hundred yards from the palisade, he entered the downwind drift from the encampment. The intense odor of smoke, bodies, and waste matter told him their number was large, and he thought he saw other families moving in.

Beside the Savoyard River bridge, a middle-aged woman using a twig broom was trying to keep the wandering braves from trampling her recently planted garden. He wanted to stop and help, but thought he should get the wagon inside the fort first. But he found the gates of the fort heavily guarded and closed so they had to be opened to admit him. A wave of apprehension swept over his body.

Going directly to the Comptoir Grillon, he rushed through the door and called out to Frenchy, "What's all the Indians doing out there?"

Frenchy stepped from behind the counter, extended his hand, then calmly replied, "My friend, the pot, she boils."

"But the Indians out there!"

"The work of Pontiac, the Ottawa chief."

Richard looked at him questioningly. "There's Hurons and Chippewas out there, too!"

Frenchy shrugged. "Pontiac, he brings them all."

Pontiac sensed a high state of excitement as he led his contingent of sixty Ottawa chiefs and warriors toward the west gate, but he dared not show it. This was supposed to be a serious meeting with Major Gladwin and all his officers, to smoke the pipe of peace and speak of friendship and mutual trust. This time, however, things would be different. When he gave the signal, he and his chiefs would slay the officers. At the same time, they would alert the three hundred braves who had been assigned to casually infiltrate the fort and surprise the rest of the garrison. After all, he had laid careful plans to be certain it would succeed.

A week before, he had brought forty warriors to perform the annual calumet dance for another summer of harmonious coexistence between Indian and white man. It was the first in his planned progression of events to allay any fears of the residents and lull them into a complacent state of trust. He, himself, had boldly driven the stake into the middle of Rue St. Louis near Gladwin's quarters. Then, as the major and his officers smoked the peace pipe, several of his braves had danced around the stake to draw a crowd. In the background, his war chief had slipped away to find the location of swivel guns and cannon, of storehouses and arsenal, and of the thatched roofs that burn easily. The two houses of worship were also pinpointed. They were the white man's connection with the Great Spirit. When the battle came, they would be spared. He wanted no arousal of spirits to cast an evil spell upon the attackers.

After his war chief had returned to the crowd, Pontiac brought the dance to a close, and he spoke of friendship and good will as he gave Major Gladwin and Captain Campbell the peace pipes with soapstone bowls. He remembered how proud he'd felt when he led his warriors in a single file out the west gate after completing the first step of his plan. Captain Campbell trusted him, and now he had acquired the confidence of Major Gladwin.

◆

As Major Gladwin walked back to his office from the calumet dance, he was puzzled. In spite of Captain Campbell's assurances that meetings with the Ottawa chief were routine and Pontiac was trustworthy, he felt uneasy every time they met. Although he saw no outward signs when sitting across the circle from the red man, he perceived a sense of deceit in the Indian's dark eyes. He hoped Campbell was right, but defense preparations would continue.

He removed his hat and was about to sit at his desk when he heard the familiar voice of Sam Taylor speaking to the orderly in the outer room. "Must see the major right away." The words carried a sense of urgency.

Gladwin opened the door. "Ah, Mr. Taylor. What brings you here?"

Taylor walked quickly over to him. "Some disquieting news, I believe." He paused as Gladwin looked at him soberly. "Mrs. Beaudreau was in today."

"She's the Frenchman's wife. Downriver, I believe."

Taylor nodded. "Said she crossed the river yesterday to sell eggs and buy meat from the Hurons. The Hurons was using files to cut a foot off the ends o' their muskets."

"Believe 'er?" Gladwin queried.

"Oh, yes sir! She wouldn't lie." Taylor took in a deep breath. "And David Stanton says he's sold a number of files to the Ottawas and Chippewas, as well."

Gladwin looked into Taylor's anxious face. "Thank you, Mr. Taylor. I'll look into it."

Two days later, Catharine came to his quarters. He took her by the hand and looked into her face. She appeared troubled. A few minutes of passionate release would undoubtedly cure that. It always had in the past.

But it didn't. Usually she smiled and caressed him as she cuddled against his side, but this time she had remained still and stared at the ceiling. "What's the matter?" he asked, rising to his elbows to look into her eyes.

She shook her head.

"But you must tell me," he said, kissing her. He wasn't sure she understood the words, but certainly she sensed his concern.

"Catharine love you," she muttered, tears flowing down her cheeks. "Catharine talk, they kill her."

"Who? You can tell me."

Assured he would not betray her, she looked into his eyes. "Pontiac meet with many chiefs. Soon he take fort," she said, her sobs becoming audible. "He kill all Englishmen."

After they had dressed, he hugged her warmly and let her out the door.

The next day he summoned Captain Campbell to his office and told him what he had learned. "What do you think?" he asked.

" 'Tis evil sounding," Campbell replied, stroking the hair back from his graying temples. "We must remember, the savages don't think like civilized humans. Besides, that bloomin' Pontiac is known as a troublemaker."

Gladwin sat quietly for several minutes pondering the situation as Campbell packed and lit his pipe. He thought about his location, the great distance from help, and the length of his vulnerable supply lines. He knew he had some excellent soldiers in his command, but only a hundred and twenty against hundreds, perhaps thousands, of Indians. The thought of such numbers made him shudder.

Properly organized, he reasoned, the fort could repel any assault Pontiac might mount. Indians don't like to stand and fight. They must win quickly or lose interest. The only thing to do was to get ready.

"As I see it," Campbell said, thoughtfully puffing his clay pipe, "we 'ave no choice. If they attack, we either fight or surrender." He shifted in his chair. "I don't fancy surrenderin' ta no savages. Seen too much o' what they do."

Their thoughts were interrupted by a knock. "Man ta see Captain Campbell," the orderly reported, sticking his head inside the partially opened door.

Gladwin nodded. "Send 'im in."

"Been told ta report ta Captain Campbell," the man said, removing his brown fur hat.

"I'm Campbell," the captain said, rising to his feet. The odor and soiled buckskins told him the man was a trapper.

"Name's Harper," the man said, stroking his heavy beard. "Was bringin' me load o' furs downriver. 'Bout two mile ta the north, came through a whole fleet o' canoes, dozens of 'em crossin' from the east. Only two braves kneelin' in each one. And they was painted!" He winked and nodded. "But they can't fool me! They's loaded 'cause they's settin' low in the water! They's other braves under the blankets in the middle, if ya ask me!"

Campbell turned to Gladwin.

Gladwin nodded, then turned to Harper. Extending his hand, he said, "Thank ye, Mr. Harper. We appreciate that kind of information. We'll look into it."

After Harper had gone, he turned to Campbell. "That bloody red bastard. He wants ta take our scalps!"

When Major Gladwin was informed Pontiac was approaching the gate, he and Campbell, in full dress uniform and armed with saber and pistol, casually emerged from his headquarters. At Rue Ste. Anne, he halted. "Get the French trader and meet the Ottawa at the gate," he said solemnly. "I want to be at the council house when he gets there."

Campbell shook his hand and left.

Gladwin watched for a moment. Then, in a slow, deliberate manner, he walked toward the council house. Although he appeared outwardly calm, his mouth was dry, and he could feel a tightness in his stomach.

◆

Pontiac, his head held proudly high, led the single file of Ottawas to the open gate where Campbell and Frenchy, squinting in the bright sunshine, waited to welcome them. The faces of his chiefs were heavily painted with soot, vermilion, and white clay. Beads, bells, and bones, hanging from their wrists, ankles, and ears, made an undulating, discordant din. Their hair was closely cropped, many with skulls shaved except for a few tufts decorated with hawk, crow, and eagle feathers.

The haughty chief ignored the extended hands of his greeters. He no longer had to be nice to them. When he gave the death cry, the Frenchman would be spared, but Campbell would not see another sunrise; he would see to it. The captain's scalp would hang from his belt. Too bad, because Campbell treated him with respect, even learned to speak the Ottawa language, but he wore the hated red jacket of the English.

The stern-faced chief continued his march as Campbell and Frenchy fell in on either side of him.

With his first step inside the fort, a distant drumbeat, from deep inside that matched his stride, began. When he looked to the left and right, he saw a dozen soldiers in dress uniform standing at attention with fixed bayonets. His eyes widened, and he inhaled deeply. Had he been betrayed? Did the English know?

No matter. This was not the time to appear weak and lose face among his tribesmen. He would continue on and prove to all that he was Lord of the Forest, Chief of Chiefs, a leader who had the courage and ability to sack the fort and expel the English.

He casually glanced up. A soldier was patrolling the perimeter catwalk. Allowing his eyes to follow the plank platform, he saw that the swivel gun at the corner watchtower was manned.

At Rue Ste. Anne, he looked to the left. It should be bustling with Saturday afternoon shoppers, but it was deserted except for small groups of armed merchants. The shops were locked and barred. Behind him, the loud jangle of the brave's disdainfully proud march had softened. He knew they were uneasy.

In an open field beside the council house, a platoon of redcoats, bayonets bristling on the ends of their muskets, were practicing close order drill under direction of two officers armed with pistols and sabers. Behind them, Pontiac spotted the rotund drummer who was beating a heavy cadence timed to his pace. He swallowed hard. The hot stomach acid was burning in his throat.

He led his band of blanket-shrouded followers into the large hall where Major Gladwin, sitting in a chair, awaited him. A quick glance around the room showed a dozen soldiers standing against the side walls. After ordering his group to sit on the floor, he bowed to the major and seated himself. With lips noticeably tight, he waited for a word of greeting.

"I welcome you in peace," Gladwin said soberly. Then he ordered the distribution of quarter loaves of bread and slices from tobacco twists.

When the Indians seated themselves on the floor, Gladwin detected a number of muffled thumping sounds. The information he'd received about the shortened muskets must be correct. And there were the shaved heads and short-cropped hair. He had heard that Pontiac commanded his Ottawa chiefs to groom themselves accordingly when preparing for attack so their scalps would never hang from an enemy belt. The group seated before him was prepared for war, not peace.

While his chiefs chewed on the bread and mumbled among themselves, Pontiac looked about sourly. As he pondered his predicament, he placed his bread on the floor, then withdrew a stained clay pipe from beneath his blanket and lit it.

Although the Ottawa leader was careful in his movements to keep himself covered, Gladwin thought he spotted, for a brief instant, the shiny muzzle of a rusty musket beneath a fold in his blanket. Looking up, the major noted that the guard at the door, a sharpshooter assigned to kill Pontiac at the first sign of trouble, had moved a few steps to the side so the commandant was not in the line of fire.

"What's the situation outside?" he asked, leaning toward Captain Campbell sitting beside him.

"The gates is closed," Campbell replied, shifting uneasily in his chair. "But there must a couple hundred Ottawas roamin' the streets."

The major looked over the head of Pontiac. "Trouble?" he asked out of the side of his mouth.

"Aye. We're outnumbered but can 'andle 'em, sir. This bloomin' bastard seated before ye, though, is up ta somethin'."

Gladwin sat back and waited for Pontiac to begin the dialogue. He was confident the chief, after seeing the fort's preparations, would not risk the lives of his tribal leaders. The expressions on Pontiac's face told him the red man was trying to find a way to get out of the plight he had led his chiefs into. Hopefully, it would not be something foolish just to save face.

For nearly an hour, the Ottawas sat, some conversing in low voices, others looking about aimlessly, waiting for a signal from their leader. Gladwin and Campbell tried to appear relaxed, patiently smoking their pipes and listening to the beat of the big drum outside and the intermittent clinking of beads and shells the Indians wore. Vigilantly, they kept Pontiac under close observation, since he was in absolute control of the group.

Suddenly, the silence was broken. The Ottawa chief, sitting erect and speaking in a loud voice so all could hear, said, "The many chiefs of the the Ottawa tribes come in peace." He tried to make a sweeping gesture with his hand while keeping his blanket tightly pulled about him. "They are true friends of the English." He paused to look around the room before continuing. "But they are surprised to find the streets empty of people and filled with armed soldiers and trappers."

Gladwin stood and raised his hand. "It is only a military exercise that should not concern the great peace-loving leader, Pontiac."

After fifteen minutes of verbal maneuvering, Pontiac reached inside his blanket and withdrew a short, wide belt of wampum.

A hush descended over the gathering. The rhythmic beating of the drum sounded more ominous as all eyes focused on the Ottawa leader. Soldiers along the walls, who had been resting their muskets on the floor, lifted the weapons and held them with both hands. The sharpshooter at the door leveled his so it was aimed directly at the head of Pontiac, and as Gladwin and Campbell stared intently into the chief's dark eyes, they allowed their right hands to drop slowly to their thighs near the grips of their sidearms.

The chiefs sitting behind Pontiac, their breathing nearly halted, watched their leader carefully to see how he held the belt. Would it be with the peaceful white side up, or turned over to reveal a deep green color, the signal to spring to their feet and give the eerie, blood-curdling death cry?

Pontiac rose nimbly to his feet, holding the belt over his outstretched hand.

Before Gladwin rose to receive it, he whispered to Campbell, "Cover me."

"For you, my friend," Pontiac said as he transferred the belt, white side up, to the hands of the English commander.

Gladwin, knowing Indians found it difficult to lie when looking into their eyes, searched the Ottawa chief's face for a telltale sign of deviousness. He could find none. "I will keep it always to remind me of your friendship."

By withdrawing, Pontiac knew he had lost stature in the eyes of his subordinates, but he would regain it when he returned in a day or two. He looked soberly into Gladwin's eyes. "And Pontiac will bring some of his people to visit you soon," he promised.

He wheeled around and led his sullen-faced, mumbling contingent from the room.

Gladwin and Campbell, walking a short distance behind, watched as the gate was opened to allow the chiefs, and those who had been loitering in the streets waiting for the death cry, to leave.

Gladwin signaled for the drum to be silenced. "That plan worked out," he said with a nervous smile.

Campbell nodded. "But I think we 'ave a blighter on our 'ands, sir." He took his pipe from his coat pocket. "A bloomin' rotter with an evil streak in 'is 'eart."

The next morning Pontiac, accompanied by three of his chiefs, came to the gate. Captain Campbell ordered they be admitted, then escorted them to Gladwin's office. After seating them in chairs across from the commandant's desk, Campbell stepped back into a corner to watch.

Pontiac removed a carved stone calumet from his jacket and held it at arm's length. "The sacred symbol of the Ottawa. The lips that smoke it speak only the truth."

He lit it, puffed on it briefly, then handed it to Gladwin. Gladwin took three light puffs and handed it back.

Holding the pipe in his two hands, the Ottawa chief rose to his feet. "You must ignore the lies that evil birds sing in your ears. Pontiac and his chiefs visit in the name of peace. The Ottawa love the English as brothers. The Great Spirit wants us to share the same sky, the same land, and live in harmony."

Gladwin stood. Looking into Pontiac's eyes, he replied, "The English want to live on this land in harmony with the Ottawas and their great chief, Pontiac."

Pontiac nodded, handed the pipe to Campbell, then led his chiefs out the door.

◆

With a sense of urgency, Richard flipped the reins and drove to the military headquarters.

Captain Campbell, seated in a corner chair talking with the desk orderly, rose to his feet as Richard entered. "Mr. Locke," he said, extending his hand.

"Captain Campbell," Richard replied. "Came to see what the commotion's about."

"Oh, that," the captain said with an air of reserve. "Seems Pontiac's been actin' up lately." He put his hands behind his back. "Matter o' fact, 'e was in 'ere the last two days. Brought a bunch with 'im. Kinda thought 'e was gonna start something. But 'e didn't, though. Saw we're ready for 'im."

"Do you think he'll try again?"

"Maybe. A 'ard one ta figure, 'e is. We've recommended any Englishman livin' outside the fort might be safer comin' inside until 'e settles down again."

"Anybody come in?" Richard asked, thinking about Elizabeth.

"Very few," Campbell replied with a shrug. "Just don't feel the need. Course, you, bein' so far from the Ottawas, might be all right." He paused and looked away. "But ye might wanta consider it. At least get ready"

The sun felt warm on Richard's back as he descended the wooden steps to the street. He didn't think Elizabeth was in any danger at the moment, but he would get back to her as soon as possible. As he climbed into the wagon, he heard a distant clamor at the gate. His concern began to mount. By the time he reined up at Taylor's General Store, he sensed a genuine fear for her safety.

Instead of lingering at each establishment to talk with the proprietors and customers as he usually did, or taking time to savor a tankard of ale at the Black Swan, he hurriedly completed his errands. After carefully tucking the blue, handblown vase under the seat, he drove directly to the gate.

The gate was closed and barred. Major Gladwin, with several troopers at his side, was standing on the rampart talking with Pontiac.

The Ottawa chief had approached the gate and requested that he and four hundred of his followers be admitted. "These Ottawa tribesmen wish to have a peaceful meeting with our English friends," he said, looking up at the redcoated major.

"Pontiac can enter, but the others cannot," Gladwin told him matter-of-factly.

Pontiac stared with a straight-faced expression. "But they want to enjoy the fragrance of the friendly peace pipe we smoke."

"The great Ottawa chief is welcome," Gladwin repeated. "But those with him cannot enter the fort today."

Pontiac's dark eyes widened and flashed as he looked into the set-jaw face of the English commander. With a grin of hate and rage, he wheeled about and strode back toward his followers who lay in wait just beyond range of the sentinels' muskets. Although he could not get them inside the fort, it was time to begin the orgy of bloodletting he had promised. Raising his tomahawk above his head, he inhaled a deep breath, then screamed out the eerie scalp cry of the savage.

Gladwin watched in awed silence as the frightening multitude, painted in bright colors and carrying a variety of arms, rose to their feet. In groups large and small, they waved their weapons above their heads and charged off in many directions, yelling, whooping, and prancing as they ran.

One group of eight went straight to the cabin of the widow who had chased them from her garden. They beat down the door, dragged her outside, and thrust two flint-tipped lances into her chest. After scalping her, they tossed her limp body into the Detroit River.

Richard, hearing the war cry for the first time, raced up the stairs to the catwalk, taking three steps with each stride. As he watched the brutal death of the widow and saw smoke rise from her cabin, he shook his head and muttered, "My God!"

The braves swarmed from the surrounding forest by hundreds, some whooping and dancing in circles, others running off as if directed on a mission. All kept out of musket range of the fort.

Richard, his face ashen with shocked disbelief, turned to Major Gladwin who had walked to his side. "They've gone crazy!" he said. "Completely crazy!"

"That's the savage in 'em," Gladwin explained calmly, trying to conceal the concern he felt.

"But my wife is home on the farm!" Richard cried out.

"Perhaps they won't go that far," Gladwin replied. He was certain the uprising would encompass the entire area, but couldn't bring himself to tell the young farmer.

"Can we take some soldiers and see?"

"There is no way until the situation stabilizes," Gladwin replied. "We need all the help here we can muster." He thought for a moment, then added, "Besides, no Englishman, soldiers or not, can stay alive out there at this moment."

Richard's heart sank. He had to save his wife. Or die trying.

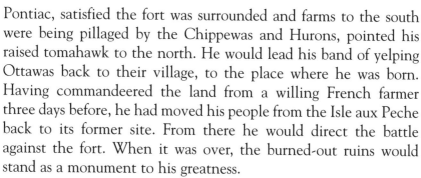

Pontiac, satisfied the fort was surrounded and farms to the south were being pillaged by the Chippewas and Hurons, pointed his raised tomahawk to the north. He would lead his band of yelping Ottawas back to their village, to the place where he was born. Having commandeered the land from a willing French farmer three days before, he had moved his people from the Isle aux Peche back to its former site. From there he would direct the battle against the fort. When it was over, the burned-out ruins would stand as a monument to his greatness.

As the howling mob proceeded along the road, he stopped to watch as they pillaged the land and slew the English, and it gave him special pleasure to see their swift canoes dart out to seize the river travelers. The French, however, would be spared. They were friends of the red man.

When he arrived at his wigwam, he summoned his runners. "Go," he ordered them. "Travel to all the villages you can reach in one day. Tell them to come to the fort. Tell them now is the time to rise up and cut the evil head from the English snake that lies coiled across our land. Pontiac will show them how."

Then, gathering ten of his most able warriors around him, he sent for Seema. When the lad arrived, he placed a hand on the young man's shoulder. "You," he said, looking into the eyes of the group facing him, "will go with our young brave to the Isle aux Cochons. There, he can avenge the death of his friend, Chowchow. If he bloodies his tomahawk well, he will join your ranks as a seasoned veteran."

With a series of enthusiastic whoops, the grotesquely painted contingent, armed with primitive weapons and dressed only in breechclouts, boarded canoes and paddled toward the forested northern tip of the island. Pontiac watched for several minutes, then returned to his lodge, a wry smile stretching across his face.

Using the cunning of a fox, four lean, wiry braves, with faces hideously painted, crept up to the barn and seized James Fisher. The terrified man opened his mouth to call a warning to his wife and daughter, but no sound would come. The strong fingers of a harsh hand pressed against his throat, stopping all but the slightest breathing. They spread his arms apart and bound him to the barnyard gate.

Making certain he could see what was happening, they watched his horror-filled face as others pulled the women from the house and hauled them out of sight. Then they stepped back so Seema could exact the revenge for which he had been rehearsing the past three weeks.

The young brave, standing directly in front of Fisher with a well-honed hunting knife in one hand, scornfully eyed the frightened man from head toe. Brusquely, he cut and tore the clothing from the pale body. To impress his fellow warriors, he yanked his tomahawk from his belt, raised it above his head, then paused to watch the Englishman's eyes open wide as the fear-filled victim waited for the blow to come.

Swinging with a strong, sweeping motion, he buried the sharpened weapon to its handle at the base of his captive's neck, severing the carotid artery. Then, with one of his savage tutors at his side, he released his grip on the handle of the imbedded weapon and carefully watched Fisher's ashen face as blood gushed from the man's open mouth and flared nostrils. Drowning in his own blood, Fisher's head dropped upon his chest, the thick fluid forming large, red bubbles as he exhaled for the last time.

Taking his knife from his belt, the young brave quickly shucked Fisher's testicles from the scrotum. He looked at his admiring colleagues, then shoved the bloody organs into his mouth. Already he felt more powerful. He had added the strength of the Englishman to his.

The heart, the center of a man's courage, was supposed to be next, but Fisher's courage had not been tested since he was taken by surprise without the opportunity to do battle. Still, any white man who chose to live on the frontier possessed much courage. If only he had fought to defend his land or, better yet, if he had killed one or two of the raiding party. Seema stood before his unconscious victim, now hanging limply from the gate, not certain how to proceed.

An older warrior standing beside him, noting the confusion showing in the young brave's face, quickly shoved him aside. With a razor-sharp knife he slit Fisher's abdomen from navel to sternum. He reached into the bloody cavity and drew forth the man's heart. After severing the arteries restraining it, he thrust the slippery organ into Seema's hands.

Surprised how quickly and easily it was done, the young brave looked at the others, smiled, then took a bite from the warm, dripping flesh. It smelled dully sweet and tasted slightly salty, but it gave him a feeling of great exhilaration. Now he was a seasoned warrior, one who had acquired the added measures of strength and courage from his enemy. He took another bite and handed it back to to the older warrior so it could be passed around.

At that moment, those who had taken the women joined them. On his blood-smeared biceps, one wore an armband covered with golden, down-like hair that had been excised from the virgin pubes of Fisher's daughter. With faces and torsos already splattered with blood, they, too, took bites from the heart.

Before departing the island, each warrior adorned his belt with a tuft of hair hanging from a one-inch circle of scalp that had been cut and yanked from an English head. Seema knew Pontiac would be pleased.

Chapter 15

Death of a Chippewa

When informed of Naseeka's order to return to the Wyandotte village, Flip became indignant. "Hell," he sputtered, looking at the sweating runner standing before him and Matoka. "Nothin' ta be afraid of out here."

"I go!" Matoka replied abruptly. Then she turned to gather up some cooking pots and a blanket. "Naseeka hears and sees many things."

He was further incensed when the runner insisted they use a back trail to keep out of sight. They would not go past the Locke farm. "If something's wrong, we should warn them!" he protested.

"Warn them later, after we speak with Naseeka," Matoka said, hurrying to keep pace with the runner.

Reluctantly, Flip agreed to stay at the village to show he cared about the safety of his family. "But, we'll move back to the cabin in a few days," he sternly informed the Wyandotte chief. "Pontiac just makes big talk."

"Pontiac makes big talk in front of *all* the red men," Naseeka told him with a sweeping wave of his hand. "Now, Pontiac makes war or he dies!"

Flip did not believe Pontiac would start an uprising. Otherwise, he would have gone directly to Richard and told him, Indian code of secrecy be damned! The safety and well being of Richard and Elizabeth superseded his loyalty and obligation to the red man's custom even though he was an intimate member of the tribe.

◆

An hour after Pontiac sounded the war whoop, two runners arrived at Naseeka's tepee. They told him the Ottawa chief had surrounded the fort and Richard was among those trapped inside.

Certain the rampage would spread south, he summoned twenty-five of his most stalwart braves. "Go to the bridge," he ordered. "You will let no one see you. But if the Ottawa or the Potawatomi come to the Locke farm, you will stop them!" He set his jaw. "No red man will harm our white brother and his woman!"

After they left, he sat quietly for several minutes. He wished he could have warned Richard and Elizabeth. Now, he would try to protect them.

He walked over to the wigwam Matoka and Flip occupied. When he informed them of Pontiac's action, Flip jumped up. "My God!" Flip shouted. "We must help them! They are brother and sister of the Wyandottes!"

"Richard is at the fort. Elizabeth at the farm," Naseeka said calmly.

Flip's face paled, then reddened. "Oh Lord!" he moaned. "She's alone!"

"No harm will come to her," Naseeka said assuringly. "Naseeka has sent warriors to protect her." He forced a smile, then continued. "We go now to our brother's house."

When they reached the River Rouge bridge, Naseeka's war chief told him a runner had been sent forward. "When he comes back, we will know where the Ottawa marauders are."

Naseeka nodded. "No Ottawa must cross the river!" he ordered.

"No Ottawa will cross the river!" The war chief's jaws were set and his voice firm.

With Naseeka at his side, Flip knocked on the door of the Locke house. As he waited nervously for it to open, he hoped he would find Elizabeth home.

The latch moved and the door opened, just a crack, then fully. "Flip!" Elizabeth said with a smile, wiping her hands on her apron. She glanced at Naseeka and nodded.

"Hello, Elizabeth," Flip said hastily, trying to smile. "Richard around?" He knew he wasn't, but thought he should ask anyway.

"No. He went to Detroit this morning." Then, looking at the stern-faced Naseeka and back again at Flip, she sensed trouble. "Is there anything the matter?"

Flip quickly briefed her on what he knew. "Maybe you should get ready to leave," he said, trying to be as gentle as possible with the suggestion. "Nothin' lost if everything's all right." He looked at Naseeka, then back at Elizabeth. "And, if there is trouble, you'll be ready ta leave."

Elizabeth stared at him in disbelief, yet felt he would not have come without concern. A greater fear rising inside, however, was for Richard. If Flip's information was correct, he had been caught in the vortex of the uprising, but she was thankful he was inside the fort and hoped he would not endanger his life trying to get back to her. She tried to appear calm, but could not disguise her apprehension.

At that moment, the runner came to Naseeka. He excitedly reported that a raiding party of seventy-five Ottawas, with a few Chippewas and Potawatomis, were five farms away, three miles up the road. They were burning the buildings, driving off the animals, and killing the inhabitants. Those who tried to flee up the river in canoes or boats were caught and murdered.

As Naseeka relayed the information to him, Flip noted Elizabeth's face whiten with fear. After assisting her to a seat at the table, he took a glass of water from a wooden bucket near the door and placed it before her. "Stay put, he ordered. "We're goin' ta tell Louis. Be right back!" He paused at the door. "We'll take you outta here. Think about what you want to take along."

When Flip and Naseeka spoke to Louis, the Frenchman became very excited. He called his family together to explain the situation. He had heard rumors that Pontiac was thinking of such an adventure, but never gave them credence. Since he was French and had bartered with the Ottawas, he felt his farm would be spared. He looked at Flip and his eyes turned sad. "Bring the Locke's animals to me," he said. "I will keep them safe until Pontiac's rage has passed."

Elizabeth hugged Bessy. The cow was like a member of the family, and she hated to let go. Then Louis tugged at the rope and led the animal away.

"I will take good care of your animals," Louis assured the sobbing woman.

Elizabeth, unable to speak, patted Louis' hand to indicate she appreciated what he was doing.

When all the animals had been moved, except Elizabeth's flock of chickens running loose, the men took Richard's canoe from the barn and placed it in the river at the water's edge. They loaded it with the gun, bedding, clothing, and other items she had selected. Then Flip waved to her. "Time ta go!" he called.

Reluctant to leave, she stood for a moment and looked out over the tidy farm she and Richard had worked so hard to transform from a group of neglected fields. She shook her head, then turned to hug Marie and the children. They kissed her on both cheeks.

"We will keep everything for you until you return," Louis told her as he shook her hand. His eyes glistened with tears.

Then they heard the distant report of gunfire to the north. It was followed by an eruption of wild shouting and yelping. As they strained to listen, Naseeka spoke in a low voice. "The Ottawa. They come."

Before leaving his house to gather the Locke livestock, Louis had slipped a red knitted hat into his pocket. He knew the Indians recognized it as the badge of a French-Canadian. Maybe Flip could use it. Then, uncertain how his English friend would accept the gesture, he had second thoughts.

But when he heard the terrifying sounds coming from the Jackson farm, he thrust it into Flip's hand. "Take this, my friend," he said anxiously. "Perhaps it will be of use to you sometime."

"Thank you," Flip replied, as Elizabeth looked on. "Maybe I *can* use it."

While the LaCroix scurried back to their house and Flip and Elizabeth headed for the canoe, Naseeka assembled his warriors on the river road. "Do not let the Ottawa raiders cross the river!" he ordered. His eyes flashed as he spoke.

When he saw two columns of smoke billowing above the distant trees that hid the buildings of the Hiram Jackson farm, he dispatched a runner to his village for reinforcements. He hoped they would not be needed, but he must be prepared. He was determined no Ottawa would enter Wyandotte territory.

He walked to the LaCroix driveway to await the arrival of the Ottawas. He could inform them that the LaCroix were French and should be left alone. If their wanton carnage had run its course in this direction, he would try to dissuade the raiders from burning the Locke's buildings and get them to return to Detroit. It would also avoid encroachment on Wyandotte territory.

Richard watched the violent rampage from the southwest corner blockhouse and could hardly believe his eyes. Many times he had heard stories of Indian savagery but thought they, like so many other accounts, were overly dramatized by the teller. It was difficult to comprehend that such plain forest people could suddenly be transformed into ferocious, brutal butchers by a few yelps from their leaders.

He could see the warriors, mostly Ottawa and Chippewa, working their way down the river road, attacking the English farms but sparing those of the French. Everywhere, people were being cruelly clubbed, speared, and shot, their hacked bodies dismembered and scattered about or tossed into the river. Domestic animals were killed or driven off and buildings looted and burned, the contents littered across the countryside. After the warriors had committed their bloody deeds, hundreds came from the forest to gather whatever struck their fancy, sometimes using the plunder to dress in a gaudy, frightening manner.

The fort, a quiet, solemn island surrounded by a sea of violent, noisy agitation, had prepared as best it could for an assault Major Gladwin was certain would come. From all sides the sounds of many drums, some distant, some near, combined with the excited yelling and singing to reverberate back and forth across the river. Richard, aghast at what he was witnessing, turned to the sentry beside him and said in a voice loud enough to be heard, "The damn fools have gone crazy!"

With a thick brogue, the sentry replied, "Aye. But ye notice they keep their distance lest they get a lead ball in their bloomin' asses!"

"I've got to get to my wife," Richard explained. "She's on the farm down the road a piece!" He tried to remain as calm as possible, but inside, his fear for Elizabeth caused his stomach to knot and his thundering heart to race the blood through his veins.

The sentry turned to him. " 'Tis a bad time fer an Englishman ta be out o' the fort," he said seriously. "And where might she be?"

"On our farm by the River Rouge."

"Oh, that's a bit o' distance. She's probably all right." He thought for a moment, fingering the barrel of his musket. "But ye should think about gettin' 'er 'ere as soon as ye can."

"That's why I want to get to her," Richard said, feeling some relief from the sentry's reply.

"Maybe a break'll come a bit later when the savages get tired from their jumpin' and yellin'. Then ye can slip out."

Richard moved along the plankway, now being manned by a growing number of soldiers. Periodically, he looked over the pointed logs for some place in the fields or woods free enough of Indians to allow him to get through. Everyplace he looked, however, including the river, was teeming with the aroused natives. When he explained his plight to Captain Campbell, he was told nothing could be done at the moment since certain death awaited anyone who left the fort. "Indians don't like long fights," the captain explained. "Maybe they'll go 'ome in a day or two."

"But, I can't wait a day or two!" Richard exclaimed, fear reflecting in his eyes. "That might be too late!"

Calmed by Major Gladwin, the young Virginian realized he had no other choice. He would have to wait for a more opportune time. If he was to try to make it past the Indians and be killed, he would be of no value to his wife or anyone else. He drove Molly to the Hudson's Bay warehouse, parked the wagon under a shed roof, and turned her loose in the enclosure with several other horses.

By joining those filling water barrels and sprinkling thatched roofs, he attempted to keep busy. His mind, however, could not rid itself of concern for Elizabeth. Several times, he mounted the ramparts to peer out over the surrounding area, hopeful the activity was subsiding. But it was spreading, and the noise made by the Indians was increasing.

Bodies, some terribly mutilated, were floating down the river. One, that of a graying, bearded man, became wedged between the riverbank and the hull of the *Michigan* tied up at the northeast blockhouse. It was retrieved by four soldiers, under protective fire-power from the blockhouse sentries and swivel guns of the *Michigan*.

"A lucky one," said one of the sentries who came down from the blockhouse to see it. "Just 'ad 'is 'ead bashed in and tossed in the river."

"Why, that's John Earns," said one of the residents who had come to look. "Owns a farm upriver a couple mile. Lived alone, 'e did."

"Lucky?" retorted another. "Dead 'e is! *Not* lucky, if ye ask me!"

"Killed quick," the sentry explained. "Sometimes they turn 'em over to the squaws. Strip the skin from 'em whilst they's still alive, they do. And sometimes they burn 'em with glowing sticks."

As the afternoon wore on, Richard's concern grew. He helped those strengthening barricades at the gates and saw that Molly and other animals had ample hay and water. Frequently, he climbed up to watch the siege.

The Indians kept a safe distance from the fort, content to keep it surrounded while bands of warriors roved the area and raided the farms. Occasionally, a young buck, overwhelmed by firewater or the sound of drums, dashed forward a few paces to hurl a lance or shoot an arrow, then race back out of range of the sentries. Most of the time the missiles fell short of their intended target. Although the sentries had their muskets properly aimed, they rarely returned the fire.

Late in the afternoon Richard walked to the Comptoir Grillon. Frenchy handed him a bowl of bean soup and a piece of dark bread. "Eat, my friend; it is good for you," Frenchy said, trying to console him.

As they talked, Frenchy tried to think of a way to help. "The Indians, sometimes maybe at night, they do not watch the river. Maybe you get in a canoe and go to your farm."

"You think so?" Richard's face brightened.

"Frenchy go with you!"

They consulted Captain Campbell and Major Gladwin. "Very dangerous," Gladwin warned. "The savages are in a high state o' agitation. Why not wait a day or two? They should calm a bit by then."

Richard listened patiently, but explained to the officers he wished to try anyway.

"Pick your time, and we'll keep watch," Campbell replied with a sigh.

When the sun went down, dew appeared on the grass, and smoke from a hundred campfires rose above the forest and blanketed the area with a blue haze. The dense pall limited visibility and irritated the eyes and throats of those inside the fort. When Richard looked out over the countryside from the plank walkway, he could see but fifty yards. Even so, activity around the ring of glowing campfires confirmed the besieged bastion was tightly surrounded. The only possible way to escape the encirclement was to make his way to the middle of the river and hope he could glide through without detection.

Looking up, he saw the stars becoming brighter with only a scattering of clouds to hide them. He cursed to himself and wished it was overcast to dull the reflection of the water.

"Maybe the smoke, she hide the river later," Frenchy said, placing a hand on Richard's shoulder.

"I hope so," Richard replied with a sigh. "Right now they would certainly see us. Besides, I think I saw some of them still crossing the river."

"Maybe we try empty canoe first," Frenchy suggested with a shrug. "Frenchy have two."

Frenchy was not concerned for his safety. He was French, and many Ottawa and Chippewa had come to know him over the years. If they caught him with a fleeing Englishman, however, he was not sure of their reaction. His English friend would have to use extreme caution. If detected, he knew Richard would be pursued relentlessly until caught. There would be no way to get back to the fort and no place to hide.

Frenchy wanted to launch the canoe from the boat dock at the water gate between the tied up *Michigan* and *Huron*, but Captain

Campbell felt the empty vessel would not have the necessary distance to drift far enough out from shore before passing the ring of Indians a hundred yards downstream.

"Gotta get upstream as far as possible," Campbell explained. "Launch it above the big schooner."

Richard and Frenchy carried the two canoes to the north gate and set them down. Sam Taylor looked them over in the light of his lantern. They were not in good condition. The seams needed repitching to make them watertight. "Might be all right empty," he said. "But wouldn't go far with you in it." He looked at Richard. "I got a real good one in the back of my store. Kinda small, but it's in good shape. Sure welcome to it, if ye wish."

In a few minutes Sam, with Henry of the Black Swan, placed it beside the other two.

By nine o'clock the glow of the Indian circle had subsided. The fires were no longer being fueled by large quantities of wood. Although drums continued to beat in several locations and war songs could be heard on all sides, it was apparent to Richard the Indians were relaxing their vigil. Turning to Frenchy, he said, "Let's try the empty one."

The north gate was unbarricaded and opened enough to let the two of them get out with one of Frenchy's canoes. As a precaution, torches and lanterns had been removed so they would not show through the open gate or silhouette the men as they left. Keeping close to the wall, they reached the riverbank, then moved upstream a few feet across the grass-covered mud until they cleared the prow of the twin-masted *Michigan*. Sentries, standing silently in the blockhouse and lying on the schooner's deck, watched.

Silently, they squatted and looked across the shining ripples moving slowly past them. For several minutes they watched and listened for telltale signs of the red man. Richard quivered as he felt an impulse to get into the canoe, lie down, and let nature provide the means for his return to Elizabeth, but when he thought of the possible consequences, he realized he must not take the chance.

Satisfied they were undetected, they slid the canoe into the water and gave it a shove to clear the schooner. When certain it was under way, they crept back to the gate.

Racing to the southeast blockhouse, they watched the dark, elongated form glide past scarcely a hundred feet from shore. When it reached a point where it was barely discernible in the darkness, Richard's hopes grew to near elation. If it could pass the ring of Indians undetected, he and Frenchy would get into Sam Taylor's canoe and be on their way.

Suddenly there was a sequence of whoops and cries, culminating in loud yelling of a general disorder. Drums in the sector fell silent as sounds of the commotion moved toward the riverbank.

"The bastards!" Richard exclaimed under his breath. "They've spotted it!"

"I think so," Frenchy agreed with a sigh.

Squinting to sharpen their vision, they could make our the dark outlines of several canoes darting about, searching the area.

"Well," said the young blockhouse sentry, "it seems ta 'ave stirred 'em up a bit."

The Indian campfires again glowed brightly against the darkened forest. The entire sector had been fully aroused and alerted.

The two men tried again at midnight, but the second canoe could not escape detection. Not sure whether the Indians suspected their encirclement was being tested or whether they thought the canoes were loose strays, the two men decided to get get some rest. In the morning, they would plan their next move.

Frenchy invited Richard to join him at the Comptoir Grillon, but the young Virginian declined, deciding instead to put some hay in his wagon and sleep there. Try as he would, however, sleep would not come as events of the day raced through his mind.

The first gray of dawn found him stretched out in the wagon bed looking up at the dark plank roof through the half-open lids of his burning eyes. He was pondering a way to get through the confining ring of savages. Molly, faithful to her master, stood statue-still beside the wagon, her nose hanging over the box a few inches above his head. "We've got to find a way, old girl. Got to find a way," he told her softly as she moved her head in recognition of his attention.

Straining to hear what he thought were sounds of distant voices, he lay perfectly still to listen. Then, certain they were words being spoken, he sat upright and turned his head to sense their direction and detect any sign of urgency. Suddenly, he leaped from the wagon and ran toward the water gate, his sore feet and aching body causing him to wince.

The sentry on the rear deck of the *Huron* had quietly alerted others that a canoe with two persons aboard was approaching from the south. Racing to the southeast blockhouse, Richard squinted to see through the layer of mist floating above the surface of the river. Just then the graceful little vessel, paddles dipping rapidly and quietly front and rear, made a turn from midstream and headed for the boat dock at the prow of the schooner.

He could see a Frenchman, wearing a tasseled, red knit hat and gaudy sash, sitting in the rear, and a squaw kneeling in front.

When he arrived at the dock, those in the canoe were being assisted ashore by several men speaking excitedly in jubilant terms. Recognizing the voice of Flip, he pushed forward and shouted, "Flip! You old son-of-a-gun!"

Then he saw Elizabeth smoothing her buckskin dress after stepping from the canoe. Leaping forward, nearly pushing one bystander into the water, he gathered her into his arms and swept her off her feet.

Momentarily startled before recognizing him, she pushed back to look, then wrapped her arms about his shoulders and buried her face in the hollow of his neck. Suffering from the terrible strain and lack of sleep, she released the pent-up stress by sobbing convulsively for several minutes.

Weak from paddling and drained by emotion, she had to be supported by Richard as they walked up the ramp and into the fort. Steam rose from her hair and clothing that had become damp during the long night in the fog, and her body trembled periodically from the morning chill.

Richard lifted her hands and examined the large blisters she had acquired. Then he hugged her. "Oh, Lord," he said, "I'm so grateful you're all right. I tried to get back to you."

She looked up at him, her soot-darkened face streaked by rivulets of tears already shed. Her lips and chin quivered. "I was afraid something had happened to you," she told him, her voice breaking as tears welled up again in her reddened eyes.

While Flip left to report to Major Gladwin, Richard and Elizabeth were escorted to the council house to stay with six other families who had fled nearby farms. As they walked, she tried to explain how Naseeka and Flip had rescued her a few minutes before the Ottawas arrived.

"Tell me about it later," Richard insisted. "You've got to get some rest first."

At that moment, a young man ran up with a blanket, and Richard draped it over her shoulders.

In the council house, Elizabeth stood before a rekindled, blazing fire to absorb the radiating heat. A bevy of women, some still in their night robes, awakened by the commotion and touched by news of her ordeal, scurried about getting a change of clothing and a basin of warm water.

When she emerged from a blanket-shielded corner of the room, soot-free and wearing an oversize blue linen dress and heavy wool socks, Richard again wrapped his arms about her. He was so happy to have her safely at his side again. "They've fixed a bed over there for you," he told her, pointing to the wall. "You get some sleep while I go out and see how things are."

She nodded wearily as he kissed her hand.

"Think I'll get our wagon fixed up again like it was when we came," he said. "Then we can sleep there."

She nodded again, then walked toward the pallet of blankets.

◆

Frenchy was awakened by a loud pounding. Cautiously, he peered through a crack in the trading post door, then flung it open. "Flip, I am so happy you are safe!" he declared, motioning the two men inside.

Richard explained what had happened. "To celebrate, we've decided to make a big breakfast—eggs, biscuits, side pork, and porridge. We'll buy everything from you."

"Frenchy eat, too. You buy nothing!"

As Frenchy brought the ingredients, Richard and Flip cleared the small stove of its accumulation of pots and dishes, some partially filled with caked food.

Although Flip moved about with considerable vigor, Richard noted how tired and drained he appeared. After igniting the kindling he had placed in the stove, Richard turned to his friend. "Why don't you slow down," he suggested. "You didn't get much sleep last night."

"I know you didn't, either," Flip replied with a shrug. "Besides, I haven't had a chance to cook like this in quite a while."

"You used to do pretty well on the trail," Richard reminded him.

Flip snapped a spoonful of lard into the skillet. "This, my friend, is gourmet cooking compared to that."

Frenchy laughed at the bantering exchange and waved his hand up and down at Flip's clothing. With strong facial expressions and a thick accent, he said, "He makes very good Frenchman!"

Nearly an hour later, having eaten their fill, they sat back and lit their pipes with firebrands from the little stove.

Richard was so pleased Elizabeth was safe, he gave little thought to the problems they still faced. One step at a time, he reminded himself, feeling certain everything would be all right. "Tell me, Flip," he said, taking a long draw on his pipe, "how did you get Elizabeth here? Musta taken some doing."

"Wasn't that bad," Flip replied. "Went to the farm, me and Naseeka. Put her in your canoe and took her ta his tepee." He thought for a moment, then continued. "Decided ta make a run fer it after dark. She'd be an Indian, me a Frenchman."

He related how Lahana and Matoka dressed her in a buckskin dress, braided her hair, then darkened her complexion with soot. He darkened his face, put on Louis knitted hat, then found a piece of bright red and blue cloth to wrap around his waist. Under cover of darkness they paddled north, keeping in midstream to avoid detection.

"But wouldn't ya know it," Flip said, slapping the table, "just about the time we could see the fort, the Indians found an empty canoe floating downstream."

"Good God!" Richard said, looking at Frenchy. "Musta been the second one we sent." He shook his head and sighed. "If we'd only known."

Flip related how they quickly darted for cover in one of the numerous fingers of fog that settled over the mouths of streams emptying into the river. At the first light of dawn, after waiting the chilly night with the canoe wedged against a clump of young reeds, they made a quiet, but quick, dash for the fort. Two young braves sleeping on the riverbank rose to their elbows for a look as they passed, but dropped down again and pulled their blankets up about their necks.

"Just a damned good thing we know that Wyandotte," Flip said, snapping his head to emphasize it.

They sat for several minutes, watching the smoke rise from their pipes and exit a small window that had been propped open.

"And I told ya," Flip said, "Louis has yer animals." His eyelids blinked more slowly.

"That's good!" Richard said with a smile.

As Flip's eyes gradually closed, Richard sat back and enjoyed the pleasantness that came from knowing his wife was now safely with him. And he was grateful his animals had been taken in by the LaCroix. As for the land, it would always be there. He just hoped the buildings would still be intact when he returned. It shouldn't be long, he mused. Just a few days, possibly a week at the most.

He looked up at the dusty beams overhead. The thunder of drums made him think about the rampaging Indians, and he wondered about the condition of his house. Suddenly, his face assumed a grave look of concern. Leaning forward toward Flip, he asked abruptly, "Did you get our money from the fireplace?"

Flip's eyes slowly opened. "Don't know," he answered wearily. His facial expression became serious as he tried to recall Elizabeth's movements when they left the farm. "Don't think so, though."

"Oh, my God!" Richard exclaimed, his arms falling to the sides of the chair. "That was all we had!"

Flip looked at him for a moment, then calmly said, "Hell, it'll still be there when ya get back. Those red bastards will never find it." He grinned, then added, "Maybe ya ought ta be like me. Still luggin' most o' mine around wonderin' what I'm gonna do with it."

The grating sound of the safety bar being removed from the west gate caught their attention. They stepped out into the street to investigate. Although the rhythmic beat of a distant drum could be heard, the immediate area seemed strangely quiet. There was no longer the sound of musket fire from the enemy guns that had begun when Pontiac stomped off in his livid rage, and the yelping and singing of the aroused savages had ceased.

Two Frenchmen, farmers living north of the fort, were being admitted. They carried a message of apology from the Ottawa chief and requested a meeting between himself and Major Gladwin to discuss problems that exist between the white man and the Indians.

Since the meeting was to be held in a farmhouse a mile north of the fort, Gladwin declined, suspecting a ruse to take him captive.

The Frenchmen went back to report to Pontiac, then returned to assure Gladwin that Pontiac was sincere. The Frenchmen would guarantee the major's safety. Once again, Gladwin refused to go, suspicious of the wily chief.

"Major," Captain Campbell began as they sat in Gladwin's office, "let me see what this is all about. I've been a friend o' Pontiac for a long time."

Gladwin shook his head. He knew Campbell spoke the language fluently and was a trusted friend of the Ottawas. But Pontiac had changed. He remembered looking into the chief's eyes when he had charged out of the council house. The savage in him had returned. He turned to Campbell. "I can't afford to lose you," he said.

"Won't 'urt ta try," Campbell insisted, leaning forward in his chair. "I know the French farmers. They said there'd be no 'arm. They promised it." He paused, then went on, "Besides, what they do ta me wouldn't 'elp 'em get the fort."

"All right," Major Gladwin replied. "But remember, we can't 'elp if ye find yourself in trouble."

"There'll be no trouble, major," Campbell said, smiling as he rose to his feet.

───────────────◆───────────────

When Captain Campbell and Lieutenant George MacDougal entered the farmhouse, they found themselves seated cross-legged on the floor among a circle of ruling red men. Pontiac sat alone with his back against a wall.

"Good day, my friends," Campbell said, nodding to the chiefs.

The Chippewa sitting across the circle glared at him. "The English must leave this land," he said bluntly. "When they came, they promised many things. But they give nothing." He waited for the nods and grunts of the others.

The tirade continued for twenty minutes, telling Campbell and MacDougal the English were white devils who could not be trusted. "You lie, you steal, and you abuse the red man!" the Chippewa shouted.

Campbell could feel the perspiration breaking out on his forehead. He looked at Pontiac, but the Ottawa stared at him impassively. "The English wish to treat the red man fairly," he said. Again, he looked at Pontiac. "The great Chief Pontiac knows Captain Campbell is an honest man."

The Chippewa chief scoffed. "Pontiac's Ottawas are not strong enough to defeat the white man," he said, waving his hand.

Campbell realized Pontiac was not in charge of the conference. He turned to MacDougal. "This is serious," he told the profusely sweating lieutenant.

"We will keep you here until the English leave," a Huron chief said. "Then we give you to them!"

Pontiac objected, but the other chiefs nodded and grunted approval.

"But we were told no harm would come to us," Campbell protested, looking toward Pontiac.

"No harm will come to you," Pontiac said.

Captain Campbell and Lieutenant MacDougal knew they had made a terrible mistake.

When word spread that two English leaders had been taken prisoner, the area again reverberated with sounds of pounding drums and the wild whoops and yells of savages working themselves into a frenzy.

◆

To the north, in the southernmost pocket of Saginaw Bay, was a village Naseeka called the Black Chippewas. They possessed an innate, feisty temperament different from other Indians in the area. Although they enjoyed brawling among themselves, they derived their greatest pleasure attacking and torturing others with little or no provocation. Under leadership of Bokaar, they had developed their fighting skills as a form of recreation. To obtain captives for their sadistic pleasures, they raided other villages, sometimes great distances away.

Bokaar had become chief two years before when he killed a large, pain-crazed black bear that had invaded his village. As a member of the warrior group, when confronted by the rampaging animal outside his wigwam, he had attacked and stabbed it repeatedly with his knife, managing to inflict mortal wounds in the throat and chest of the large beast.

The bear, however, suffering pain from a broken tooth, had succeeded in slashing deeply into Bokaar's legs and torso with its sharp claws. As soon as he recovered, his comrades, wanting a dynamic leader, had installed him as their village chief. They buried his elderly predecessor, Lactoma, to his neck outside the village and poured honey over his head to attract insects and animals.

The light-colored welts and scars that now laced the dark skin of Bokaar's body provided a grotesque badge of courage, and his pock-marked face and large, curved nose emphasized a pair of deep-set, black eyes which glared with a resolute fierceness. These qualities served to intimidate those who faced him, giving him a power he enjoyed using.

Learning of Pontiac's plan to attack Detroit, he had set out to join the fray. The sun was just settling below the treetops when he arrived at the Ottawa village. He halted momentarily, took a deep breath, then strutted to the front of Pontiac's lodge.

"Bokaar's braves have come to fight the English!" he declared, certain of a warm welcome.

The Ottawa chief gazed at him with a cold stare, then shifted his eyes to the motley line of warriors that trailed behind. As he pondered the situation, his eyes again focused on Bokaar. So this was the crazy chief the Wyandotte called the Black Chippewa and the feisty braves who torture their neighbors. How, he thought, could such undisciplined ruffians win a battle? Perhaps they fight only women and old men.

Bokaar could see he had not impressed Pontiac. Refusing to shrink back even from someone as powerful as the Ottawa chief, he boldly announced, "Bokaar's warriors will spend the night in the Ottawa village. It will let them rest for tomorrow's battle."

Pontiac continued to stare at him.

Seeing the Ottawa chief still unmoved, Bokaar looked at the large yellow ring rising in the sky across the river. To the white man it was Wednesday, May 11, but to Bokaar it was the time of the dark of the moon, the time when victory was certain. He turned again to Pontiac. "Tomorrow, Bokaar's warriors will capture the fort. Then Bokaar will give it as a present to the great chief, Pontiac!"

Pontiac did not believe in the stocky, dark-skinned chief's invincibility, but was aware of his nasty deviousness. He looked at the two hundred young bucks prancing about behind him, then ordered the Chippewa chief to make his camp in a meadow a half mile to the west.

Giving Pontiac a sour stare, Bokaar whirled and led his horde away.

The astute Ottawa chief entered his wigwam and sat down. He was the experienced fighter of the white man and was not about to have some young upstart overshadow him, but he would permit the wild-eyed Chippewa to exhaust himself hammering at the fort. If the attack was succeeding, he would send his legions in to lay claim to the seizure. If it failed, he would boast to his recalcitrant tribal leaders that his plan to obtain surrender by convincing the English commander he was hopelessly surrounded would be the best strategy. Regardless of the outcome, he would gain from Bokaar's actions.

◆

The next morning, after spending the night glutting themselves on food obtained by raiding the farm and terrorizing the family of a French friend of Pontiac, Bokaar's unkempt contingent set out noisily for the fort.

As he hurried along the smoke covered trail, the blood rushed through Bokaar's veins. He thought of the impending battle, his first against an organized group of white men. Swaggering pompously at the head of his column of rowdies, he sensed the adulation he would receive when he handed Pontiac the captured fort.

410

At the edge of the clearing, he halted to survey the scene. The size of the fort astounded him. It was the largest structure he had ever seen. He had been to the missionary village of St. Joseph, but its palisade had poles as big around as a man's leg and only slightly taller than he was. Here, he felt overwhelmed.

But this was not the place to show weakness. Turning to face his braves, he raised his musket over his head. "Prepare for battle!" he yelled, his voice barely audible above the clamor.

Following the example of their chief, the warriors stripped naked and coated their bodies with a black, shiny mixture of bear grease and soot. While adorning each other with grotesque stripes of white clay, they began a slow, rhythmic war chant that continued until the body painting was finished and they had rearmed themselves.

Bokaar raised his hand, a signal to wait silently until he appraised the situation. His darkened skull, shaved clean except for a shaggy mane of black hair along its center, glistened in the morning sun as he scanned the fort for weak points. The sounds of Ottawa and Chippewa drums thundered in his ears as he searched the thick walls, the heavy gates, and the threatening blockhouses. He could see no easy place to mount his attack.

Slowly, he advanced his warriors to within a hundred yards of the structure. Then he halted them again. The massive, complex edifice was very intimidating, but his pride would not let him back away. Tasting the bitter acid rising from his knotted stomach, he swallowed hard, thrust his musket upward, and gave a terrifying war cry that bounded from the fort and echoed through the surrounding trees.

His ferocious warriors, whooping and yelping, charged the north wall. Spreading out as they ran, some halted long enough to fire their muskets at exposed heads of soldiers manning the ramparts and blockhouses. While they reloaded, others flung spears, tipped with stone, steel, and fire-hardened points, that cleared the wall and landed inside.

A few of the red men, in a wild frenzy, attacked the upright logs with dull hatchets and tomahawks, screaming loudly with each chip they managed to dislodge.

Bokaar stood in the middle of the charging warriors and flailed his arms wildly as he screamed encouragement. An older brave, wanting to demonstrate loyalty to his chief, stood beside Bokaar and fired a brass-barreled blunderbuss he carried. An excessive charge of powder in the corroded weapon knocked the old warrior flat on his back. Frightened and embarrassed, he looked through the thick blue smoke at his surprised leader, then ran into the forest, abandoning the ruptured weapon. The onlooking Ottawas chuckled and sneered as he fled through their line of encirclement.

After losing a dozen men, Bokaar ordered his fighters to attack the west wall while he probed for a crack, an opening, or even a knothole. Again, they were driven back into the forest by gunfire from an increasing number of sentries.

While his sweating braves rested, Bokaar paced back and forth at the edge of the clearing, his dark eyes glaring at the monstrous structure that defied him. How could anything made of poles stop his braves? He wondered if Pontiac was watching. Certainly the Ottawa chief knew of his difficulty.

He gave a loud shriek and waved his braves to the south wall. This time they would concentrate on the heavy gates. He searched for notches or protrusions that could afford hand or toe holds, but none could be found. After trying a human pyramid, with devastating casualties, he had them build a fire of dry brush against the massive doors.

But again, several sentries, dodging bullets, spears, and arrows, drove them off and doused the fire with buckets of water poured from the top of the wall.

Leaving more than a dozen of his fallen warriors on the gravel roadway and in the trampled grass, the frustrated Bokaar took refuge in an abandoned cabin just across the Savoyard River. From there, he ordered his braves to loop barrages of fire-arrows tipped with burning tow into the center of the Detroit complex. Perhaps the white man would surrender if his village was burned. The massive flights of arrows would make it difficult for the fires to be put out.

---◆---

With the onset of the commotion brought on by Bokaar's first charge, Richard, who was in Sam Taylor's store, grabbed the musket he had left leaning against the door frame and headed for the Comptoir

Grillon where Flip was staying with Frenchy. Approaching the trading post, he saw the two men standing in the street trying to sense the direction of the yelling and shooting.

"Attack on the north wall!" a sentry standing on the plank walkway shouted down to them.

While Richard waited, Flip ran inside, grabbed his musket and tossed on an ammunition bag. Then he returned to the street. "Let's go!" he said, looking at Richard.

"Moment!" Frenchy yelled, running after Flip.

Frenchy did not want to fight the Indians, but to demonstrate his loyalty and support for the English, he handed Flip and Richard extra bags of shot and powder.

The two men climbed the stairs, two at a time, and mounted the walkway. They were met by a sergeant near the southwest blockhouse. "You men stay 'ere in case they 'it us from the south!" he shouted. "We got the north wall pretty much under control!" He dashed off along the west walkway.

As soon as Flip saw the charging red men, he began firing at Bokaar's braves. Having fought the Mohawks and Hurons, he calmly aimed and fired at targets he was sure he could hit. In his mind, he was able to get along with most people, Indian or white, but figured anyone coming at him was a threat to his life. He would take no chances.

Richard had never shot at another human being. During the past few days, however, he had witnessed the savage fury of the Indian. He stood back and watched Flip fire three times, but was still reluctant to pull the trigger even once. Then, a few feet to his right he saw a soldier hit in the throat with an arrow, its blood-smeared flint tip protruding from the back of the man's neck.

The soldier turned toward him, his bulging, terror-filled eyes pleading for help. As the trooper's legs buckled, the blood began to spurt from his gaping mouth and flared nostrils.

Richard rushed over and knelt at his side, but the wounded man was exhaling his last, gurgling breath.

Richard remained for several seconds, watching the blood run across a plank and drip through a crack. Then he rose slowly to his feet and looked between the pointed tips of the logs. Squinting, he saw a grease-blackened brave about to fling a spear. He took careful aim and fired. The Indian slumped to the ground, dropping the spear at his side. Richard immediately reloaded his weapon. He did not wish to watch the brave die.

As the attack progressed, Major Gladwin came by. He was walking the ramparts to direct the fire and supervise the evacuation of the wounded. "Wait until they're close enough. Don't waste ammunition," he repeated as he strode past each sentry.

He was confident the fort could defend itself until he could get word to Fort Niagara and relief arrived, but in all his Indian battles, he had never encountered such a reckless, fanatical assault as he was now facing.

Each flight of fire-arrows brought on another ringing of alarm bells and triangles, and again young men climbed the roofs to quench the fires that were started. Bucket brigades, primarily women and children, brought water within their reach, and sentries on ramparts pointed to the imbedded arrows still flaming that could not be seen by those on the ground.

Although the system of firefighting satisfied the major, it involved much shouting and confusion. Added to the beating drums and Indian yelps, it created a din he was certain could be heard a great distance up and down the river.

With Captain Campbell absent, Gladwin decided to confer with Sergeant Fitch. "What do ye make of it, sergeant?" he asked.

Fitch was a career soldier who understood Indian tactics. " 'Tis me guess, sir," he began, standing rigidly at attention, "that 'e's used most of 'is ammunition. Must be a renegade. 'Tis plain the others aren't 'elpin' 'im."

They dodged another barrage of fire-arrows. "And 'is fire-arrows must be about gone, too," Fitch said, looking to see how many fires had been started.

An hour later, with fire-arrows continuing to fly in great numbers, Gladwin studied with his spyglass the cabin Bokaar was using. "My word!" he exclaimed, turning to Fitch. "The Ottawas are resupplyin' 'im!"

"Good God!" Fitch replied, waiting to use the spyglass. "Let's 'ope it's not powder and shot, too."

"And let's 'ope the rest o' them don't join in on the fight," Gladwin added, squinting into the bright sun as he peered between the pointed tips of two logs.

Gladwin ordered a small cannon mounted on the firing platform of the southwest blockhouse. He had it loaded with red hot spikes that had been heated in David Stanton's forge. When he gave the order, it was fired directly at the cabin, starting fires in several places.

Bokaar screamed in a fit of rage. He climbed upon the cabin roof and shrieked his defiance at Gladwin. Just then the cannoneer lowered his torch to the touchhole of the weapon, sending a second volley of hot spikes at the building. One of the missiles hit Bokaar in the head, penetrating his skull. First a puff of vapor, then a spurt of blood, issued from his head as he toppled to the ground.

A great cheer arose from the parched throats of those manning the ramparts of the fort. Flip stood calmly and watched, but Richard, shaken by the experience, leaned against the blockhouse wall.

Bokaar's warriors were frightened and bewildered by the loud, fire-spitting weapon the English were using. They knew they had fought bravely, having lost half of their number, and still believed their chief to be invincible, but when they discovered the twisted body on the ground beside the cabin was lifeless, most became terrified and fled into the woods in frantic disarray.

A few, stunned and enraged, gently hoisted the glistening, black body of their chief to their shoulders. In a show of fearless indifference, they slowly retraced the route by which they had come.

As they made their way around the southwest blockhouse and along the west wall on their way to the river road, the drums fell silent, and the English, out of respect for the reckless but brave chief, allowed them to pass unmolested.

When Major Gladwin assessed his casualties from the fierce, three-hour battle, he found three dead and twelve wounded. But it had broken the fighting spirit of the Black Chippewas. He knew they would never again enter Ottawa territory.

Chapter 16

Treasure Recovered

Pontiac, deep in thought, sat cross-legged on a bearskin in his lodge. As he pondered the outcome of the battle, he studied the thin strands of smoke rising from dying embers in the fire ring. He had stood at a discreet distance to watch the futile charge of the Black Chippewa against the north wall. They had shown unusual courage, he had to admit, but now that their chief was dead and they had returned to their village, he knew he had to organize a new plan of action if he was to remain chief of chiefs. This had been but the first skirmish.

There were already over a thousand warriors ringing the fort who had heeded his call; many, supported by their families, camped in the adjacent woods. Each day, scores more arrived. Although they were mostly Ottawas and Chippewas, he was pleased to see several dozen Hurons from across the river, and there were some Potawatomis whose camp was assembling in the forest a day's journey up the Rouge River.

He wished the English would realize the hopelessness of their position and surrender, but they didn't appear ready to accept his terms. Perhaps another assault like that of Bokaar would make them consider it. If only his allies were more reliable, more united and loyal to his leadership. He had already sensed resentment from some chiefs.

He rose to his feet and walked to the edge of the river. The cadence of distant drums echoed in his ears as he watched several children playing with frogs in the mud. He assessed the promised support he had received at the Great Council of Warriors.

He concluded that Teata, who was never enthusiastic about having his Huron braves fight the English, would continue to pay lip service to the cause each time the tribes met. The Hurons had a long history of fighting the English, but they were devious rascals. Teata liked his good trading relationship with Detroit, enjoyed the rum, blankets, and axes it brought to his village. He would probably help in a superficial way, taking what spoils he could easily obtain, but leave the primary assault to the Ottawas and Chippewas.

Seetonka had another goal in mind. He was obsessed with reestablishing his Potawatomi village at the mouth of the River Rouge and considered the elimination of the white man as the necessary first step. Perhaps Seetonka would direct an assault on the fort, but would he then expect the Ottawas to later assist him in his feud with the Wyandottes as payment for his pivotal role? This option, Pontiac reflected, would be bold but risky.

And there was that light-skinned Wyandotte, Naseeka. Pontiac felt Naseeka's mind had been poisoned by the tongue of the French conjurer, Father Pothier, who had told the Wyandottes not to fight the English because the white man would eventually win. Then the Potawatomis would be driven away, and the Wyandotte village would be safe. Although few in number, the Wyandottes were fierce warriors. Too bad they would not fight at the fort. But Naseeka had promised to blockade the river so Gladwin could not get supplies. Pontiac knew that, although not enthusiastic, Naseeka could be counted on to uphold his stated obligations.

He clenched his fists. For now he would let things as they were because he desperately needed help from the Wyandottes. But if they didn't do more, he would destroy their village after he drove the English away. Then, the Potawatomi could have the land.

As he returned to his lodge, he thought of the Chippewas. They were arriving in great numbers and could be his greatest resource, but because he failed to get his warriors inside the fort, their chiefs were becoming less patient and more arrogant. He decided it would be wise to call a meeting and get them to intensify their attacks. Then the English, out of fear, would surely agree to surrender.

◆

Gladwin stood on the firing platform of the west wall and peered cautiously over the logs. With his spyglass, he could see intense activity among the painted savages at the edge of the woods. At the first dim redness that tinged the eastern sky, a furious war whoop sounded, bringing with it an increase in the strength and tempo of the incessant drumbeat.

The major was thankful he had detected Pontiac's ruse in time to foil the chief's attempt to infiltrate the fort. After Bokaar's defeat, it should have been evident to the savages they couldn't capture it. Besides, he thought, Indians were not noted for long sieges. By now they should have released Campbell and MacDougal and started returning to their villages. Suddenly, his reverie was disrupted as guns blazed and bullets rapped hard and fast against the fort walls.

The savages concealed themselves behind bushes and fences or lay flat in depressions in the ground. Each of those with a firearm had his mouth filled with shot for loading and firing. Occasionally, a brightly painted dandy would jump up and race about, whoop and fire his weapon or throw his lance as he went within range of the fort. Several sentries manning the walls waited for such targets. Half the time their volley of fire killed or wounded the young warriors.

In the afternoon, Gladwin posted a special guard at the southeast tower to watch for the cargo canoe flotilla that was due any day on its routine supply mission.

◆

Major Gladwin sat in his office fingering the soapstone pipe Pontiac had given him. Day after day had brought little change within the fort. Outside, the Indians were growing steadily in numbers, and the din and clamor of their assault continued with varying intensity throughout the day. A week had passed, and the cargo canoes had not arrived. They must have been captured. He concluded he would have to notify Fort Niagara of his plight and request assistance.

He rose to his feet. "Orderly," he called, "send for Sergeant Fitch."

"Yessir!" the orderly replied from the other room.

When Fitch arrived, Gladwin motioned for him to sit down. "Sergeant, we can hold out for a month. By that time the savages will have tired of fighting."

"I 'ope so, sir."

"You don't sound convinced," Gladwin said, waiting for the sergeant to voice an opinion.

Fitch shook his head. "They should 'ave gone away by now. But 'tis different than I've seen afore."

Gladwin took in a deep breath. "Well, I've decided to send one o' the schooners to Fort Niagara for 'elp."

Fitch nodded. " 'Tis a smart move. And which one will it be, sir?"

"The *Huron*. And load enough ammunition to blast 'ell out o 'em on the way downriver!" He paused. "And, sergeant, spread the word that any resident who wants to leave should get ready.

"Yes, major," the sergeant replied. "But I don't think many will."

———————◆———————

A small crowd stood at the gangplank and watched the handful of passengers board. When Sarah and Agatha, dressed in brightly colored dresses and carrying parasols, reached the ship's deck, they turned to wave at the gathering.

"We'll miss you, ladies!" Flip shouted, nudging Richard with his elbow.

"We'll miss you, too!" Sarah replied. Then she turned to Agatha. "But I'm glad we're goin'. Business wasn't all that good here, anyway!"

Although she had lowered her voice, several of the women standing at the foot of the gangplank overheard and responded with a sneer.

Agatha raised her head and brushed back her hair. In a voice loud enough for the women to hear, she said, "Some o' those tight-ass wives are simply gonna 'ave ta loosen up a bit now that we're leavin'!"

When the *Huron's* crew lifted her gangplank and hoisted her sails, Richard and Flip climbed to southeast blockhouse to watch. In less than a minute, her heavy guns were blazing away at the shoreline, raising havoc with the Indians unfortunate enough to be in its line of fire. The two men could hear yelping and shouting as the shot sliced a swath through the brush and trees. When it tore through the Indians' makeshift shelters, frightened warriors fled in wild disarray, and screaming squaws grabbed up their children and scurried inland.

Richard turned to Flip. "I just hope they don't shoot up the Wyandottes."

Richard placed his outfitted wagon in a small space between a young pine and Ste. Anne's Church. It would be in the shade and have some protection from the arrows and spears that occasionally cleared the walls of the fort.

He expected the uprising to be over in a few days. Then he could return to the farm in time to plant the crops if seed was available. Flip had told him the buildings were still intact, at least they hadn't been set afire, and since his livestock was safe with Louis, he figured he could get under way with little difficulty. The furnishings would be gone or broken, of course, but they could be replaced in due time. A matter of serious concern, however, was the money, some three hundred and fifty guineas, by Elizabeth's count, that had been left in the hearthstone cache. He would go after it at the first opportunity.

While he waited, in addition to serving his turn each day as a sentry on the ramparts, he would work with David Stanton casting lead shot and making and repairing hand knives most people wanted to carry as personal weapons.

He was pleased Elizabeth had recuperated from her ordeal. And now she was working on the food distribution program Major Gladwin had set up in the Hudson's Bay warehouse. Soldiers had gone to every house and collected supplies of food, tallow, and grease so they could be doled out as needed. She had to monitor the requests and approve the disbursement which was then carried out by other women volunteers. It gave her the satisfaction of helping during the crisis.

Two young Chippewa women, wives of white men who worked the charcoal kiln and had fled to the protection of the fort, also worked in the warehouse. Initially looked upon by others with distrust, they had redeemed themselves by daring work on the bucket brigade during fire-arrow attacks. Normally silent in the presence of others, they became communicative with Elizabeth when they discovered her relationship with Flip, Matoka, and the Wyandotte tribe. "If the fort is captured," they explained, "we die a long death. Much torture."

Elizabeth nodded that she understood.

As the days passed, Elizabeth thought more and more about returning to Fredericksburg. At first she feared they would be overrun and killed, but after Bokaar's fierce attack had been repulsed, she felt confident the fort could be defended until the *Huron* returned. At one point, feeling the warmth of a child growing within, something she still had not reported to Richard, she planned to suggest they go with the ship, but she knew he would not consent to do so as long as he thought there was a chance of recovering his land in time to plant a crop.

◆

By the time the second week had passed, Pontiac realized the fervor of his attacks were lessening. He urged the other chiefs to maintain a constant, unrelenting barrage of bullets, spears, and arrows from dawn to dark, to recoil only long enough to prepare for the next onslaught. Instead, he watched as the warriors took long periods to rest, smoke, or wander about.

Another problem was the growing shortage of food. As the multitude of tribes drifted in, many bringing their families, the numbers quickly grew to more than four thousand. They initially lived off livestock taken from English farmers, but instead of conserving their booty, most was wasted on their wanton rampage, making flies and maggots the primary beneficiaries. And now the deer and rabbits were gone, and fish were becoming scarce.

He managed to get some corn and jerked venison from the Wyandottes and Hurons, which he paid for with his birch bark promissory notes, but he knew they gave it reluctantly. They had never been strong allies of the Ottawa and Chippewa, and he knew they gave only to avoid his wrath.

And there was the matter of small bands of Chippewas going to friendly French farmers, threatening violence if they did not get the provisions they demanded. The angry farmers came to him and remanded the raiders cease their foraging.

Efforts were then directed across the river where a number of enterprising Hurons, as well as some Frenchmen, bartered food for beads, furs, trinkets, and amulets. At night, river traffic became heavy as sleek canoes, each making several trips, traversed the gently flowing water.

◆

South of the fort, just beyond the Savoyard bridge, were two rush-filled ditches, a short length of wooden fence, and the burned remains of the cabin Bokaar had used for his attacks. They provided cover for the assaults of Pontiac's warriors. Major Gladwin, wanting to eliminate such hiding places so he would have a clear field of fire as far as possible from the fort, decided to ask for volunteers to fill the ditches and remove the remains of the cabin and fence. "I'll send twenty-five of me men along to protect ye, and we'll assemble plenty o' firepower up on the wall," he told a group one evening at the Black Swan Tavern. "Spread the word," he urged. "See who'll 'elp us."

When Flip heard of the request, he went to the Locke's wagon and informed Richard. "Wanna go?" he asked, enthusiasm showing in his face.

"Maybe," Richard replied, looking first at Elizabeth, who appeared surprised at his response, then back at his buckskin-clad friend.

"Richard!" Elizabeth scolded. "That's dangerous!" Then turning to Flip, she asked, "Aren't you afraid to go out there in the daylight?"

"Not really," Flip said, looking her square in the eye. "Not afraid of man or beast. Besides, this won't amount to anything 'cause there's gonna be a lot of guns behind us." He picked up a handful of dried pine needles and let them sift through his fingers. "And when they clear that stuff out, it'll keep those redskins farther back."

While the two men continued to talk at the plank table Richard had made, Elizabeth steeped some tea.

Confinement within the fort made Richard anxious for some form of activity. He did not want to be left out, especially if Flip was going. There would be some danger, of course, and he realized he had an obligation to Elizabeth but, after listening to Flip, decided the risk was small.

Elizabeth was reluctant to let her husband take chances that could cost him his life, especially since she was with child and so far from Fredericksburg, but after listening to the conversation for several minutes and noting the eagerness building in the two men, she reached over and grabbed Richard's hand. "Go ahead," she said, forcing a smile. "It shouldn't be bad with all that protection. Besides, it will make it safer here."

Richard knew she wasn't as comfortable about the situation as she pretended, but he was pleased to have her consent. He squeezed her hand, then turned to Flip. "Let me know when they plan to go."

The following day the sun rose bright and clear, sending vivid rays to search the heavens and warm the earth. In less than two hours it dried the grass and swallowed the delicate film of fog that had crept into creek beds and hollows during the night.

Sergeant Fitch, standing beside Major Gladwin at the southeast blockhouse, peered over the pointed log ends as his eyes scoured the area for Indian activity. "Seems ta be nuthin' 'appening this side o' their line, sir," he said, still searching the terrain.

"Are we ready, then?" Gladwin asked.

"We are, sir. I've got twenty-five grenadiers waitin' at the gate, and twenty volunteer workers should be there with 'em by now. And as ye can see, this south wall is manned by every musket and swivel gun we can spare."

"That's good, sergeant," Gladwin complimented with a snap of his head. "And remember, no shots to be fired unless absolutely necessary! We want the least expenditure of ammunition and minimum risk to the men." He paused. "But should the savages be riled and attack, we'll send 'em a curtain o' fire, and you get the boys back quickly! Understood?"

"Aye, sir!" Fitch replied, anxious to get under way.

Gladwin nodded, then turned and waved his hand to signal the captain of the *Michigan*. The schooner would anchor fifty yards downriver so its heavy guns could be used if necessary.

The sergeant checked the buttons on the front of his coat, then descended the stairs to meet the detail nervously waiting on Rue Ste. Anne near the south gate.

By the time Richard was ready to leave the wagon, Elizabeth was having second thoughts about him going. She had never been enthusiastic about the operation, but after discussing it with Flip the previous day, she had felt there was little danger involved.

During the night, however, she had been awakened by a field mouse cavorting on the wagon canvas. She was suddenly frightened when she remembered Richard was soon to go with the volunteers. She looked at his sleeping form lying beside her and noted the outline of the thin blanket that covered them rise and fall with his breathing. Many thoughts chased about her mind as she mentally made her way through the sequence of events he might face, occasionally picturing some terrible, unsuspected danger that could present itself. Finally, after finding herself silently weeping, she set her jaw and decided to put it out of her mind. Turning on her side, she placed an arm over his chest and snuggled against him, determined to think positively until he returned from the operation.

In the morning, they walked together as far as the Black Swan where Henry and David Stanton were standing. Forcing a smile, she kissed her husband on the cheek, then watched the three men, muskets in hand, walk down Rue Ste. Anne.

Turning slowly, she walked back to the wagon. She would clean the breakfast dishes before going to the warehouse to wait with the other wives for the volunteers to return.

◆

One of the massive doors of the south gate was unbarred and opened enough for two men at a time to pass through. The troopers, led by Sergeant Fitch, took up positions on each bank of the sluggish Savoyard, concentrating on the portion between the gate and the Detroit River.

Once the soldiers were in position, Fitch, resplendent in his brightly colored uniform, strutted with military precision to the midpoint of the bridge. There he halted, looked left and right into the eyes of his men scattered along the river to show he held no fear, then did an about face. Then, looking up, he gave a snappy salute to Major Gladwin standing on the rampart above the gate.

With the protective screen of soldiers in place, Sergeant Manners led the volunteers from the fort. Each man was armed with a musket or pistol and carried a shovel, sickle, axe, or saw. As they crossed the bridge and fanned out, Manners assigned each a task to complete. Richard and Flip were ordered to turn left and fill in a depression a dozen yards from the Detroit River.

Walking rapidly, the two men kept a wary eye for Indians on the smoke-laden tree line a hundred yards to their right. When they reached the depression, they found its lush reeds and grass trampled into a protective nest capable of shielding two warriors and hiding them from view of sentries manning the ramparts and blockhouses.

As he tossed the first spadeful of dirt into the depression, Richard thought he noticed movement near the Detroit River bank. Remembering the lesson he learned from Flip on their trip from Fort Pitt, he pretended not to have seen it. "Something in the tall grass to the right," he said quietly as he dug the second spadeful.

"I see it," replied Flip, tossing a shovelful of dirt.

Stooping for their muskets lying on the ground, both men looked obliquely in the direction of the movement. There, fleeing the reeds and grass, scurried two brightly painted braves.

"Potawatomis," Flip whispered. "Let 'em go."

The red men ran toward the riverbank for protection, but when they saw the *Michigan* drifting slowly downriver, they veered sharply to their right and, in a low crouch, raced through a thicket and across an orchard toward the tree line. Although in full view of the work party and the ramparts, no shots were fired.

"Let's get this damn job done!" Richard said, grabbing his spade.

A few minutes later his nose perceived the approach of a trapper. He looked up to see a huge, barrel of a man with long, matted hair and a heavy black beard.

"Gonna cut all these weeds and grass down to a nubbin so those red-assed bastards can't hide in it," the man said, swinging a scythe in a wide arc with ease.

Richard waited for him to blow his nose and wipe his hand on buckskins that were already saturated with grease and blood. "Flushed two out of here."

"Saw 'em," the man replied, sweat seeping from beneath his badger-fur cap as another wide swath of grass and reeds toppled behind his vigorous swing.

Richard continued to shovel, mindful of the man's strong, gamy odor. "I'm Richard Locke, and this is Flip Wade," he volunteered.

The trapper looked at them and nodded but did not reply. With the handle of the scythe held in a vise-like grip by fingers that looked like sausages, he continued to cut, gradually working away from the two men.

Soon the Savoyard was discharging fence posts, tree limbs, cut reeds and burned logs into the more rapidly flowing Detroit. While most of the debris drifted toward midstream, an occasional piece lodged against the *Michigan*. As some crew members pried it loose, others continued to man the battery of loaded guns.

When the task was completed, Sergeant Fitch, standing on the Savoyard bridge, ordered the men to return to the fort. As they walked, Richard, taking long strides beside the trapper but mindful to stay upwind, asked, "What's your name?"

"Simon," came the terse reply, the trapper looking straight ahead.

"That your first or last name?" queried Flip.

"Me only name," the man replied, his fleshy cheeks jiggling as he plodded toward the gate. "Just plain Simon!"

"Hadn't seen you before," Flip said, looking up at the man's ruddy cheeks.

"Just come two day ago," Simon replied, turning to look at Flip. "Come down the river with a load of furs."

"Thought the river was too dangerous. Didn't the Indians try ta stop you?"

Simon's eyes narrowed. "Not them red bastards! They know Simon never forgets. Know as soon as I dropped off me furs, I'd come after 'em!"

"Where are you staying?" Richard asked as they passed through the partially opened gate.

"Made me a bed in the hay at the livery. Best sleepin' around," Simon replied, veering around the waiting crowd.

When the gates were closed, the volunteers were slapped on the back and hugged, and there was much talking and laughing as the pent-up nervous tension subsided. Frenchy, who had furnished many of the shovels and axes, elbowed his way to Flip and Richard as they talked with Elizabeth. "The Indians," he said, a smile on his face and a sparkle in his eye, "they get tired. Soon they go home. We then can go outside the fort."

Flip looked down into his face. "They may be gettin' tired," he said, digging for the pipe in his breast pocket, "but they's not ready ta leave yet. The Potawatomis we saw carried too much paint ta be thinkin' o' givin' up."

Most of the crowd who walked down Rue Ste. Anne stopped at the Black Swan to drink from Henry's dwindling supply of ale and rum. Elizabeth, Richard, and Flip, however, continued on to the wagon.

Elizabeth served the men tea and biscuits she warmed on the hot ashes in the fire ring. She was grateful they had returned unharmed. Now that the dangerous mission was over, she would tell Richard about the baby as soon as Flip left.

When they finished eating, she picked up the dishes and placed them in a pan of water on a bench beside the wagon. Then she sat down and waited for Flip to leave.

Instead of leaving, he lit his pipe and leaned back to enjoy the moment of tranquility. Exhaling audibly so it could be heard above the monotonous beat of drums, he scrutinized his battered pipe. He watched the smoke curl lazily upward from its scarred bowl, then looked overhead at a robin feeding her young in the branch above. Richard, sitting across the table, was drawing an imaginary design on its top with a twig that had fallen a moment before.

Elizabeth noticed a distant look suddenly appear in Flip's eyes as he watched the robin. Then, he broke the silence. "Ya know," he began, "startin' ta miss that boy o' mine." Computing the days, he stared at Richard before continuing. "Been a week or two since I saw the little fellow. Yessir, little Matt! Bet he's growed six inches since then." He smiled and looked at Elizabeth.

"Still kind of dangerous to make the run back," Richard reminded him.

"Well, maybe," Flip replied. Richard could see the desire to return growing in him. "But I bet a lot o' them Indians aren't so anxious ta fight anymore." He took a couple of slow drags on his pipe. "I think we could even go down and get your money."

Elizabeth's heart skipped a beat. She had hoped Richard would not get involved in any other dangerous adventures. "The money can wait until this thing's over," she protested, twisting the hem of her apron with tense fingers.

"Practically all over now," Flip replied. "Those red devils aren't so alive now as they used ta be." He looked over at Richard, knowing his friend knew better. "Just get in a canoe at midnight and slip down the river. Doubt they'd even bother ta take after ya now, even if they saw ya."

Again Elizabeth objected, stating she didn't want to take a chance of losing her husband—didn't want him to go anywhere without her.

Flip reached over and took her hand. "It'll be all right," he assured her. "Have 'im back hardly afore ya know he's gone."

Feeling a tight knot of anxiety building within as she looked back and forth at the two men, Elizabeth gave a deep sigh of resignation. She knew Richard was extremely concerned about their money, and she felt guilty for having overlooked it when she fled. "All right," she said soberly, nodding her head.

Her consent pleased Richard. Now, he was anxious to go. He was sure he and Flip could accomplish the task with minimum risk.

◆

Shortly before dawn the two men, wearing red knit hats and blue wool jackets, pulled their canoe from the water at the landing of Louis LaCroix. They had to find out if Indians were on Richard's farm. After hiding the craft beneath some shrubs, they took up their muskets and cautiously climbed the bank. Moving in a low crouch as noiselessly as possible in their moccasined feet, they strained to recognize the outlines of buildings, trees, and fences in the dim, gray light.

Richard's heart was beating furiously in his chest. He could feel every irregularity in the soil through his thin soles, and he worried about the effect of dampness on the powder in his musket. He inhaled a deep breath of the moist air. It was heavy with the smell from the barnyard. He was in his element. Suddenly, he wanted to return to his farm and get on with his life. Right now, however, they had to be careful. What if Louis thought they were intruders and fired on them?

As they neared the house, the LaCroix dog, aroused from a mat beside the door, barked once before recognizing them. The lone bark, however, triggered a flurry of squawking and hissing from three geese standing stiffly a few yards away. With a suddenness that surprised Richard, Louis, clad in suspendered trousers and underwear, his musket at the ready, peered from the partially opened door.

"Louis!" Richard called out in a loud whisper. "It's me, Richard!"

Louis kicked the door open farther, then stood motionless, his sleep-filled eyes straining to identify the two shadowy forms standing a few feet before him.

"*Mon dieu!*" he uttered, lowering the musket. "Come in!"

Louis lit a crackling fire in the fireplace so Marie could make biscuits and eggs for breakfast. As he watched the flames build, he told the two men how happy he was to see them. "We have not left the farm since Pontiac's attack," he explained. "The Potawatomis, they would loot it."

As he talked, Pierre and Mimi, still in nightclothes, appeared in the doorway of their bedroom and looked shyly at Richard and Flip. Richard waved and smiled. The children grinned, then scurried back into the bedroom.

"Yes," Louis said, seating himself across the table from his visitors, "that Seetonka, he wants to take my farm. But Pontiac says he must leave me alone. He dreams of building the Potawatomi village here again. With you gone and Jackson gone, I am here in the middle. He needs my farm." He shook his head. "He tells his people he will take it someday."

"Do they come here much?" Richard asked, biting into a hot biscuit.

"Some. For now, Seetonka has his village at the back of your farm, by the woods. But many of his braves are at Detroit." He paused long enough to tell his wife to refill the teacups. "Sometimes the old men of the village get drunk when the braves bring wine and brandy from other Frenchmen. When that happens, the women chase them from the wigwam. They spend the night in your barn or house."

"Have you seen Naseeka?" Flip asked.

"No," Louis replied. "But his braves are always on the other side of the river." He pointed toward the south.

"Ya see," Flip said, looking at Richard. "No Potawatomi will ever cross the Rouge as long as there's a Wyandotte tribe left." Then, turning to Louis, he continued. "If we'd have run into any trouble, we'd have made a beeline ta get south o' the Rouge. Knew we'd get help there!"

"Pontiac's been getting meat and corn from the Wyandottes," Louis said, hinting Naseeka was lending support to the Ottawa war effort. He tossed two squares of birch bark onto the table. They were decorated with Pontiac's red otter totem. "Got these when a party of painted Ottawas made me give them a bag of barley and a goat."

"How are my animals?" Richard asked, feeling an urge to visit them.

Louis smiled. "They are good. All here except your chickens. They roost in your barn yet." He shook his head. "They come here every day, and I feed them. But they go back every night."

"It's a wonder a skunk or weasel don't yet them."

"They roost high in the barn. They spend the day over here because the Potawatomis tried to catch them. They know they are safe here."

Then Richard told him he had come for his money.

Louis watched him intently as he spoke, then shrugged and shook his head. "I do not think they find it," he said. "When they find something like that, they yell and throw it around. I see them throw only your furniture." He hesitated, then added, "I see them take some clothes. They wear them like crazy people."

"Did they burn anything?" Flip asked.

"They burn nothing." He shook his head in a negative manner. "They do not come often."

Louis rose from the table and got his white cotton shirt from the bedroom. As he buttoned it, he told the two men, "You stay here. I go over to your farm to see if Indians are there." He put on his jacket and slipped out the door.

The two men watched as he walked rapidly across the pasture field that lay between the two groups of buildings. "I sure hope it's there," Richard said anxiously as he looked at his house.

"It's there," Flip said convincingly, trying to ease the tension he felt building.

Ten minutes later, Richard spotted Louis coming back across the pole fence that separated their farms. He squinted to see through the haze that the sun, which had just broken over the horizon, was lifting. He hoped to see a smile instead of a frown on Louis' face.

When Louis reached the barnyard, he could see the two men's faces in the window. He signaled for them to come out.

"We can go!" Richard called out, bolting for the door.

Bessy, through a mysterious sense, recognized her master as soon as he came out the door. She rushed to the fence to meet him. While Louis explained he had searched the buildings and found no one, Richard reached over the top rail and rubbed her forehead. She nuzzled his hand, sniffed deeply to confirm her recognition, then shook her head with excitement. With his other hand, he scratched beneath her chin. She stretched her neck to accommodate him.

432

"You must go quick!" Louis warned in a low voice.

"Yah, let's go," Flip echoed impatiently frowning at Richard's attention to Bessy.

"Let me milk her when I come back," Richard suggested as Bessy licked his palm.

"Yes, of course," Louis replied, his face and voice expressing an understanding for the bond he knew existed between Richard and his animals. "Go now, and I'll wait here for you."

They walked in a low crouch through the damp overgrowth of grass and weeds that surrounded the buildings, hoping the Potawatomis, who had to face the morning sun from their village, could not detect their presence through the haze. Approaching the house, Richard saw the first signs of reckless destruction. His heart sank. The window glass he had collected and installed was broken and missing, and the curtains Elizabeth had worked so hard to make were hanging out, dirty and torn.

Rounding the corner, he found the door half open. With the barrel of his musket, he pushed it open and stepped inside. Flip halted outside and scanned the surrounding area for any movement, any sign of life.

The interior was a shambles. Torn cloth, dented pans, and cornhusks ripped from mattresses littered the floor. Chairs had been smashed, the table overturned, and cushions Elizabeth made lay partially burned in the fireplace.

As he walked, several field mice scurried to hide. He saw two places where the debris was splattered with vomit that had dried and stained the floor. The hearthstones, however, appeared intact and undisturbed.

He leaned his musket against the wall, knelt down and carefully examined the moveable stone that concealed the cache. It appeared secure. He pressed against its corner, and the face moved forward so he could grasp it. He could feel his pulse throbbing in his throat as he reached into the hole and fingered the two coin-filled leather pouches.

"They're here!" he said excitedly, turning to face Flip who was standing just inside the door.

"Good!" Flip said with a grin. "Now, let's get movin'."

Before leaving, Richard picked up the front of a broken dresser drawer and examined it. He dropped it gently to the floor, shook his head and sighed. "It's a shame," he said disgustedly. "A damn shame!"

He thought he saw something shiny just barely visible in a pile of cornhusks. Bending down, he uncovered one of the ornate brass sconces Elizabeth had purchased on her first trip to Detroit. He looked it over carefully, found it undamaged, then quickly glanced around the rest of the room. "Where's the other one?" he asked.

"Don't know, but let's go," Flip urged.

Richard kicked the debris about on the floor but could not find it. "They must have run off with it," he said, his voice showing disappointment. "Elizabeth sure liked those."

"We must go," Flip exhorted, peering out the doorway. "You'll be back soon and can straighten everything up. Buy a new one if ya need it."

"I hope so."

When Richard showed Louis the two pouches, the Frenchman beamed. "What I tell you," he said. "Me, Louis, take good care of your place!" He paused, then added, "And your Naseeka, he help, too!"

Richard had just finished milking Bessy when Louis ran over to him "The Potawatomis, they come!" he said, alarm showing in his face. "You must hide!"

Richard and Flip peered around the corner of the barn, searching the fields across the river road in the direction Louis had pointed. In the distance they saw five painted braves casually walking in their direction.

"Don't look like they seen us," Flip observed. "Else they'd be actin' different." He studied them a moment longer. "But we'd better be goin', anyway."

"You can stay," Louis protested, his expression pleading for a longer visit. "I hide you."

Richard placed his hands on the Frenchman's shoulders and looked him in the eye. "Louis, you are my good friend," he said soberly. "But if they find us here, you will be in big trouble." Louis looked at the ground as Richard continued. "We will go now. Then, we can come again."

Louis looked up. His eyes were glistening as he nodded agreement.

Once in the canoe, the two men paddled furiously to get beyond the Rouge River into Wyandotte territory.

◆

Naseeka, having been alerted by scouts that the two men were at the LaCroix farm, brought many of his people to the secluded Wyandotte canoe landing to greet them when notified of their approach. Although delighted to see them, because of the unique role his tribe was forced to play in the uprising, he felt he should temper any overt display of enthusiasm. Although a few stood back and silently watched the men disembark, most of the villagers were nodding, smiling, and chattering, eager to get closer to the visitors. A group of children surged forward to touch them and nearly toppled Matoka as she waited with Matt in her arms.

Flip kissed his wife on her forehead, then grabbed his son and held the little, dark-haired boy aloft. "How's this for a strong, young trapper?" he beamed, turning the child so its dark eyes focused on Richard.

"Just like his old man," Richard said with a wry smile. "Will probably be a killer with the girls, too."

As they walked into the village, Richard did not think it reflected the war the Indians were waging against the English.

The activity appeared routine, the same as when he was here before. The women worked, the children played, and the elderly observed, advised, and did light, menial tasks about the encampment. Although Naseeka wore his headband and shiny talisman, he was dressed in plain buckskins and wore no paint. The only painted Wyandottes he could recall seeing were two scouts he had spotted near the River Rouge bridge.

Flip and Matoka went directly to the wigwam he had constructed for his family from poles, skins, and bark. After they had gone, Naseeka beckoned Richard to come with him to his tepee.

Lahana, who had been waiting for them, welcomed her guest with a nod and smile, then motioned for him to sit on the skin-covered floor. Richard knew protocol required Naseeka to speak the first words, so he waited as the Wyandotte chief slowly packed and lit the clay pipe he had acquired from the Comptoir Grillon. Then the red man nibbled at the food Lahana placed before them.

Richard did not like the long palavers Indians seemed to enjoy. To him, they were a waste of time. As he waited for Naseeka to go through the preliminaries, he tried to sit still but fidgeted with his fingers and hands.

"My brother," Naseeka began, "the Wyandottes are pleased you have honored them with your visit."

He paused to let Richard respond.

"The Wyandotte people, my true brothers and sisters, are my friends," Richard replied, trying to ease the stiffness of the meeting. "I am always honored to walk among them."

"Good!" Naseeka said, his sober face breaking into a smile. He took two puffs from his pipe, then placed it on the mat between them.

Richard, who sensed his Indian friend was having difficulty with his next statement, decided to speak again. "Naseeka, you are my true friend, my true brother. I know you face grave problems with the Potawatomi, the Huron, and the Chippewa." Naseeka looked at him and nodded agreement. "And the big chief, Pontiac, hovers above like a black cloud."

"And now I do not know how much storm the black cloud will bring," Naseeka said solemnly.

"Justice will prevail," Richard answered philosophically. "The Wyandottes are honorable people."

"The Wyandottes fear no one," Naseeka boasted.

Richard waited for him to pick up his pipe and relight it.

"But the Wyandottes must be careful," Naseeka continued, his eyes narrowing to emphasize the tightrope of deceit he was walking. "The Potawatomi and Huron are mere children. But Pontiac and Sacco have more warriors than there are stars in the sky."

Richard nodded that he understood.

When Richard rose to leave, he extended his hand. Naseeka seized it firmly, looked him squarely in the eye and said, "My friend. My blood brother. You and your family will always be welcome to walk among the Wyandottes. You may live among us, if you wish."

This is a savage of different dimension than most, Richard thought. Knowing him is to realize that he is warm, caring, and a true friend. "Thank you," he replied. "I will always remember."

"And," Naseeka added before releasing his hand, "should Pontiac get to your door and raise the tomahawk over your head, Naseeka will be there to see that it does not fall. You are a Wyandotte!"

Outside, in view of his people, the chief changed his posture to that of a sober-faced leader. He asked two elderly men, who were waiting for him at the fire ring, if the the women had completed their task. When informed they had, he turned to Richard. "You are dressed like a Frenchman. But that does not mean you will not be harmed. Naseeka will send his braves to protect you."

A group of women, supervised by the old men, had painted symbols along the prows of two canoes, including the one Richard and Flip had brought from the fort. Using reed brushes to apply paint to the dull white bark, they had drawn a dark gray wolf's head. It was followed by a green pine tree, a wavy blue line, and a bright, red sun.

Naseeka pointed to the canoes. "The symbols represent a fearless people who live among pine trees at the waters edge. They will continue to do so as long as the sun rises to light the heavens and warm the earth." Then he pointed to four nearly naked braves decorated with bright war paint. "These warriors will take you back to the fort. You will be safe!"

Lahana walked up and placed a shell bracelet in Richard's hand. She spoke not a word.

"For your woman," Naseeka stated with a smile.

Matoka, with Flip at her side, handed Richard a pouch of pemmican. "For your journey," she said, looking at him admiringly.

"I will eat it," he promised.

"You'll find some clothes in your canoe," Flip informed him. "Some Elizabeth saved from your house."

Richard looked at him questioningly.

"When the Ottawas came, we loaded the canoe with as much as we could. She took a few things with her when she went up the river. Afraid to take too much, though."

Richard recalled Elizabeth saying she left some things with the Wyandottes. He recognized his jacket spread over a small pile of clothing in the bottom of the canoe.

"This is all of it," Flip continued, "except for some bedding we still have. Get that to ya someday, too."

"Thanks," Richard replied, bending down to get into the light craft. "Hope it won't be too long."

He shook hands with those present, including some chattering boys, then knelt down in his canoe with the two braves who were to man the paddles.

"You'll get no blisters this time!" Flip shouted as the sleek vessels got under way.

When Richard looked back to wave for the last time, a sudden feeling of apprehension swept over him. He sensed it would be a long time before he spoke to any of them again, but he must not let it bother him now. He pulled the red knit hat down against his ears, wrapped his arms about his knees, and tried to relax. The only sounds he could hear came from the smooth, rhythmic dipping of paddles and the intermittent staccato of a woodpecker searching for its midday meal.

◆

Late in the afternoon at a point midway between Pontiac's encircling warriors and the fort, the two Wyandottes in Richard's canoe handed him the paddles and transferred to the other vessel. Quickly swinging around, they headed downstream at a rapid pace, behaving as they had during the entire trip—they uttered not a sound and showed not the slightest sign of emotion. They had, however, answered the question Richard had asked himself several times as to what they would do upon reaching the heavily armed fort.

Sentinels at the fort who had been watching the wet paddles flashing in the sunlight were elated when they saw the Wyandottes abandon Richard to his own canoe. At first they thought he was being held captive, but when Sergeant Fitch identified the braves as Wyandottes, a tribe yet to appear on the battle line, their fears were lessened. Some among them, however, including a few who understood Richard's relationship with Naseeka, remained skeptical until he was on his own. They contended that savages, like wild dogs, were simply unpredictable.

Chapter 17

Leave of Absence

Pontiac paced slowly around the cold fire ring in his wigwam, then halted at the open flap of the doorway. For several minutes he gazed across the smoothly flowing Detroit River, then stepped outside into the warm morning sunshine. Tired from the lack of sleep, the light hurt his eyes, and he could taste the bitter gall rising from his troubled stomach. The wily chief was agonizing over a waning enthusiasm among the tribal leaders his fiery oratory had whipped into a bloodthirsty fervor.

He had been so sure he had gained the confidence of Detroit's inhabitants when he'd started. It should have been easy to infiltrate the isolated bastion with a few select warriors, then subdue it in a short time when his horde of followers stormed through the gates held open by the infiltrators. But it didn't work. And when he tried to lure Gladwin into being taken hostage, he was foiled again. Then, there was the succession of furious assaults that were repulsed with heavy losses.

Returning to his wigwam, he sat down and wondered what he should do now. He had even sent an emissary, a French farmer, to the commandant with an offer of safe passage if he would load everyone onto the big ship and leave. What was the reply to this sensible offer? Gladwin said he was going to stay and would defeat Pontiac and his Ottawas if they did not release the two English officers and have the red men return to their villages where conditions were much better for them.

He shook his head as he recalled his disappointment when the two officers had come instead of Gladwin. He wished he could release them, not because of Gladwin's response, but because they were serving no useful purpose. He had wanted to send them back after a brief conference, but the other chiefs, especially those of the northern Chippewa, thought they should be held for ransom. To avoid a confrontation with his overly zealous allies, he had to permit their detention. He wished he hadn't allowed it, because Captain Campbell was a brave soldier and a good friend of the red man.

Again, he thought of the worsening food shortage. The English farms had been stripped of livestock, grain, and produce, and wild animals had been so decimated that his hunting parties had to travel great distances to find more. He resolved to prod, threaten if necessary, Seetonka, Naseeka, and Teata. They must give more help.

He went to the door and, with a wave of his hand, summoned two ever-present warriors standing a short distance away who served as bodyguards and aides. "Get Pontiac three swift runners and twelve birch bark totems," he told them. "In two days we have a council of tribal leaders. This time, it will not be held in an Ottawa camp. We will gather where the two rivers meet, on the farm of that Englishman called Locke."

◆

When Louis LaCroix saw fifty painted Indians assembled on the bluff near the grave of the Mascouten, he became alarmed and barricaded his door. As he watched nervously from a window, he saw Pontiac, followed by a small entourage, climb the bluff and join them. With a feeling of relief, he watched from his partially opened door as the red men bickered about the seating arrangement before squatting down to sit cross-legged in a large ovate ring.

The Indians sat for some time smoking and eating before Pontiac, seated between Sacco and Naghee of the Chippewas, stood. For a full minute his dark, penetrating eyes looked into the faces seated about him.

Folding his painted arms across a quill breastplate, he told them victory would already be his if he had not been betrayed by a woman whose heart and mind was bewitched by the English commander. "When the Great Spirit told Pontiac who she was," he beat his breast forcefully with his fist, "she was killed, cooked, and fed to the dogs." He paused, observing the rapt attention he was receiving. "And the dogs were killed and burned. Their ashes were thrown into the great river so the bad spirits would depart from all our territory."

Grunts and nods of approval were given by most of those present. Naseeka, mindful of the special stare he had received when Pontiac stood and suspicious of the Ottawa chief's ambitions, sat impassively observing the reactions of those around him. He was concerned about any move by Seetonka to gain favor with the powerful Ottawas since the Potawatomi chief often stated he planned to reestablish his village on this very spot.

Pontiac described the actions of the Ottawa and Chippewa braves surrounding the fort at great length, calling them daring, valiant, and courageous. "The English have suffered many casualties; their food and ammunition are running low, and their spirit is broken. They will surrender soon," he promised. He thought of the brusque refusal by Gladwin to his offer to allow the inhabitants to sail away. His jaw tightened. "But they must remain isolated!" he shouted. He paused while a murmur of comments arose from the circle.

Naseeka fingered the shiny copper disk hanging from his neck as he awaited Pontiac's next declaration. He knew it would express dissatisfaction with the assistance the Wyandottes had given.

"Some of our friends have not supplied warriors to do battle at the fort," Pontiac continued, making a sweeping motion with his hand. "That is acceptable because the Ottawas and the Chippewas have many, many braves who are not like old women afraid to do battle! They are true warriors! They fight! And they die if they must!" He lowered his voice. "But some of you," again he waved a hand, "have given little to the cause. Now, you are being asked to give more."

He walked to the center of the circle and turned to face Naseeka. "From the Wyandottes, we must have more food!" He paused again to allow another murmur to subside. Pointing to Naseeka, he shouted, "And you will stop the supply canoes that will soon come from across the big water!"

Without waiting for a reaction, he wheeled and quickly aimed his finger at Teata. "And the Hurons will help the Wyandottes!"

While another murmur rose and subsided, Naseeka looked sternly into the eyes of Pontiac, then Teata. He did not like the manner in which he was being ordered to do things, and he detested the idea of working with the Hurons.

The Ottawa chief took a few steps and stood, looking down at Seetonka. "The Potawatomi will be responsible for the great ship that moves with the wind. It, too, will come from the across the big water. It must not reach the fort! It must be destroyed!"

Seetonka jumped to his feet and looked into Pontiac's face. He beat his glistening, painted breast vigorously with both fists. "I, Seetonka, and the brave Potawatomi warriors will seize the great ship and present it to Chief Pontiac as a gift!"

Pontiac smiled and nodded grateful approval. He knew Seetonka did not understand the awesome firepower of the great ships. "We are all red men," he said, his voice soft, his face solemn, "who fight a common enemy, the English. We agreed on the banks of the River Ecorse to unite in this task. The time has now come for the Huron, the Potawatomi, and the Wyandotte to stop any help the white devil-friends of the English send them from across the big water. Our red brothers must know this now." He paused to look at Naseeka, Seetonka, and Teata. "If these supplies get through to the fort, the great Ottawa and Chippewa tribes will bring their full wrath down upon you."

Sacco and Naghee rose and stood beside him as he waited for a response.

Seetonka got up quickly and walked over to face him. "The Potawatomi tribe will serve you well," he said enthusiastically, extending a hand for a quick shake to seal the promise.

As Pontiac accepted Seetonka's handshake, he carefully observed the movements of Naseeka and Teata. Relieved to see the two of them rise slowly to their feet, he redirected his attention back to Seetonka so he could finish with the Potawatomi chief and allow the other two to approach him.

Naseeka was willing to send additional food to the braves surrounding the fort to satisfy the agreement he had made, but was reluctant to intercept the canoe flotilla for fear of engaging in a shooting battle with the English. But he knew, if he didn't halt the canoes, Pontiac would attack his village and overwhelm it, and he was sure the Potawatomis would then sack it. He reluctantly informed the Ottawa chief with the customary single shake of hands that he would have his braves halt the canoes.

As he turned to walk away with the two braves who paddled his canoe, Teata told him, "My Huron warriors will be waiting in readiness for the long canoes to arrive!"

Naseeka glared at him momentarily, then strode off down the path to the landing. The Hurons, he thought, were a treacherous, deceptive lot. The memory of being strung up and left to die by them still haunted him. He would avoid them if possible.

◆

Gladwin climbed to the firing platform and looked back over the village he vowed to defend. As the days passed, the weary inhabitants had settled into a monotonous routine of crowded living in a confined area while waiting for help to arrive from Fort Niagara, and his sentries were manning the guard stations around the clock, frequently calling the rest of the garrison to fight off assaults that occurred almost daily with varying degrees of intensity. He recalled how soiled and threadbare their uniforms were the last time he inspected them. The clear sparkle had left their eyes, and lines were developing in their gaunt faces. They were aging much beyond their young years.

Although the food supply was low, he was grateful to a sympathetic French farmer across the river. Each night under cover of darkness, the farmer quietly ferried beef, pork, and grain to the water gate dock. But Sergeant Fitch would have to keep a close eye on the inventory of powder and shot. He slapped his thigh and set his jaw. If only the supply flotilla would come.

Then, he wondered if complacency had developed over the weeks. Perhaps the village had lost its spirit, its vitality. As he looked, the streets appeared narrow, abandoned, and silent. People were keeping to themselves. They no longer rushed out to take their defensive stations when an attack was signaled, but waited to be summoned if their muskets were needed on the firing platform or a flaming arrow landed on a rooftop.

When he visited the Hudson's Bay warehouse, Elizabeth learned of his concern. She remembered how lively people were when she'd played Mrs. Campbell's harpsichord at the New Year's party. "If you will bring the instrument to the council house, I'll conduct a recital," she told him.

But to her disappointment, her spirited recital and songfest generated little enthusiasm. Many people attended, but few bothered to dress in anything except their everyday street clothes. And when she played, most sat glumly watching instead of singing and dancing as they had in the past.

An event that attracted a large number of people was the daily prayer service. Elizabeth attended those held beneath an oak tree by a self-appointed Congregational minister. She was often accompanied by Richard, but he was more inspired by the Latin prayers and chants he heard from the daily mass in Ste. Anne's Church next to their wagon. "Let's attend a mass," he suggested.

"We shouldn't," she said, shaking her head solemnly. "We're not Catholic, and everyone knows it." But she was pleased he was expressing a reverence to God—glad he wasn't like those men without religious convictions who sat around in small clusters talking, whittling, and honing their knives while drinking what little brandy and rum still remained.

◆

On the bright, sunny morning of May 30th, loud shouts from a sentry in the southeast blockhouse alerted the garrison that the long-expected flotilla of cargo canoes had come into view. It was making its way up the far side of the river.

"But why the far side?" Sergeant Fitch asked, as he and Major Gladwin put on their coats.

Gladwin shook his head, but said nothing.

In a few minutes everyone within the confines of the fort knew of their approach. Amid shouts of jubilation, the water gate was opened, and a contingent of stately soldiers, crowded together, assembled on the small dock to greet the relief contingent.

The soldiers gave three hearty cheers, and the *Michigan* fired its cannons as a welcoming salute. The salvo landed in the Indian positions below the fort.

In response, naked, painted braves rose to their feet in each of the eighteen canoes and wildly shouted defiant war whoops.

Those occupying the dock, along with a large number standing on the ramparts, watched in frozen horror as the vessels, flying the flag of England, continued on. They were being paddled by dejected, captive Englishmen who had been subjected to brutal beatings.

As the third canoe in the convoy pulled even with the fort, the four Englishmen in it began a struggle with their three Indian guards. One Indian was tossed overboard but managed to grasp an Englishman's clothes and take him along. In a wild struggle of choking and stabbing, both disappeared beneath the surface.

When the two remaining Indians leaped into the water, the Englishmen began paddling feverishly toward the *Michigan*. Other canoes in the convoy took up the chase, the Indians aboard them yelping, whooping, and firing their muskets wildly at the haggard, fleeing white men.

Richard, watching from the walkway next to the southeast blockhouse, raised his musket and yelled, "My God! Let's help them!"

"What tribe are they?" a man standing beside him asked.

"They're Hurons!" the blockhouse sentry replied as he leveled his musket.

Richard aimed and fired, but the distance was too great.

"Gotta wait 'til they's closer," the sentry advised.

"We have to do something before that!" Richard yelled.

"The Ottawas is comin' after 'em, too!" the sentry shouted, pointing to a canoe pushing off from the riverbank below the fort.

"Oh, Lord!" Richard moaned, squinting to see through the reflective glare of the water.

At that moment there was a loud report of a rifle-like weapon, followed by a deep, resonating *whomp*, the two sounds blending and reverberating back and forth across the river. Gunners on the rear deck of the *Michigan* had fired a swivel gun at the Ottawas, tearing a large hole in their canoe and forcing them to retreat in terror back to the shore. At almost the same instant, other gunners had fired a below-deck cannon at the pursuing cargo canoes.

Richard watched in amazement as the iron ball made a hissing streak of spray and foam, skimming through the water among the vessels in the convoy. Although it did not hit anything, the frightened Hurons fell silent and directed the canoes to return to the far side of the river. Men on the dock immediately paddled out to rescue the three grateful captives.

◆

When Naseeka had received word from a runner that a flotilla of twenty long-bodied cargo canoes had entered the lower river, he dispatched the trusted head of his war council, Rosatt, with twenty-five braves. They were to intercept the convoy off the southern tip of a long, narrow, overgrown island close to the far shore opposite his village. The braves were purposely not decorated with war paint so Rosatt could peacefully approach the English and tell them they could proceed no farther and must return to Fort Niagara.

As the two clusters of canoes, separated by fifty feet of water, held steady, Rosatt had explained to the English that the relief flotilla would not be allowed to reach the fort. Suddenly, there was a loud commotion, directing everyone's attention to the northeast. A short distance away, from around the tip of Little Turkey Island, there appeared an aggregation of swift war canoes. In them were two hundred brightly painted, heavily armed Hurons.

Rosatt knew there was little his band of lightly armed braves could do against such a force. He yelled to the English, "Go back! Go fast!"

After watching the English exchange shots with the charging Hurons, he ordered his braves to retreat so he could report to Naseeka.

The Huron horde, whooping and yelping, quickly overwhelmed the English convoy. Their leader ordered a warrior into each cargo canoe, then directed the captives to paddle upstream.

At the Huron village, the forty Englishmen were securely tied to trees and logs so they could watch the drunken orgy of their captors. The frenzied women and whooping braves were soon in the mood to torture and kill them, but Teata had other plans. He rose to his feet and lifted his hand. When they became silent, he said, "Do not harm them. Tomorrow we give them and their cargo canoes to the Ottawas. The grateful Chief Pontiac will look upon the Huron with great favor!"

The stunned villagers looked at him questioningly.

Again he spoke. "Then, Chief Pontiac will know the Hurons are not little boys and old women!"

The Englishmen were relieved by Teata's statement. They would live a little longer. It would give the British army more time to rescue them.

But as the night wore on, they could see the orders were not strictly enforced. Squaws squabbled with one another over blankets they found in the cargo. Old men rolled kegs of gunpowder into their wigwams, and a large group of jubilant braves emptied several casks of rum and brandy into one of the canoes and swilled it like hogs at a trough. In their state of maudlin drunkenness, they fought among themselves, kicked and beat their captives, and hacked holes in two of the canoes. At times, some of the more crazed braves ignored Teata's orders altogether and spirited off one or two of the captives.

◆

For two days Major Gladwin and Sergeant Fitch paced the ramparts and watched a procession of badly mangled sections of bodies from men, women, and children, buoyed by small stick rafts, drift past the fort from the north. The terrible torture endured by the captives was evident by punctures, gashes, and burns appearing on the floating parts and on the many slightly submerged, cleanly scalped heads from which the eyes had been gouged out and tongues removed. One eviscerated torso, its hands, feet, and head crudely hacked off, had been partially skinned and cooked. Gluttonous birds rode the human flotsam, ravenously pecking at the flesh, gorging themselves until flying was difficult. Fish darted about, nibbling at the dangling skin and clotted blood which clung to the lacerated undersides.

Of the half dozen women who ventured to look, two became ill. Mrs. Taylor, embarrassed because she vomited in public, secluded herself in her home and vowed to remain there until the crisis was settled.

A group of men who saw the grizzly sight became more angry than frightened. They assembled at the Black Swan to form a plan of action. After a brief discussion, the burly trapper, Simon, stood. "By God, let's take a bunch of volunteers and attack Pontiac's war camp head on! We'll grab the sonofabitch, skin 'im, and hang is hide on the south wall ta dry!"

Gladwin, who learned of the meeting, had just stepped inside the door. "That," he warned, "would be playing right into 'is 'and."

"You could send the *Michigan* upstream ta back us up with artillery fire," said David Stanton, looking about to gauge his support by the number of nodding heads around him. "We'd rescue Captain Campbell and Lieutenant MacDougal ta boot!"

"I'm afraid we're no match for that number of vicious savages," Gladwin replied. "If 'e did you in, and I'm sure 'e would, we'd surely fall." He paused to look into their faces. "We'll wait for reinforcements. Then we'll give it to 'im. Just can't stand ta think o' what 'e'd do to our families if 'e ever got in 'ere."

The men held a brief discussion, then concluded they should follow the major's advice.

◆

As the days dragged on, Richard became restless. The best time for planting crops had past. He doubted there was enough time left to get a decent harvest. "Summer's too short here," he told Henry at the Black Swan. "Back in Virginia we'd have the time."

"I think most o' the people are gonna 'ave to rely on the sup-plies that can be brought in this summer," Henry replied, halting his sweeping to reflect on the situation. "And from the looks o' it, they're gonna 'ave a time doin' it."

Elizabeth understood her husband's concern, but was pleased he could spend a lot of time with her. She still worked at the warehouse when he took his turn on the firing platform, but morning sickness made her curtail her activities. To avoid another miscarriage, she sat around the wagon enjoying a closeness with her husband they hadn't known since being married. Unable to merely sit, however, she vol-unteered to mend clothing for the soldiers.

To be certain Elizabeth did not overexert herself, Richard carried the water, made the bed, and helped with cooking and dishwashing. And he constructed a pole canopy over the table to protect her from stray arrows when she sat outside.

Late in the afternoon, using a sickle, he gathered an armful of grass and clover that grew profusely at the base of the palisade. "Come on," he said, grabbing Elizabeth by the hand. "Let's visit Molly."

When Molly saw them approach the Hudson's Bay corral, she neighed and trotted to the gate. Richard brought her outside and dropped the green feed at her feet. While she ate, he brushed the loose hair and dirt from her body, and Elizabeth spoke softly as she petted the horse's head.

When he finished brushing her, Richard reached into his pocket and took out a handful of wheat. "Try this, old girl," he said.

"Richard!" Elizabeth scolded. "That's against the rules laid down by Major Gladwin."

"I know," Richard replied with a smile as Molly chewed the grain. "But this little bit won't matter."

A moment later, Simon came by. He looked down at the green feed, then at the brush in Richard's hand. "My God!" he thun-dered. "You'd think it was human! Such coddlin'."

"She is pretty special," Elizabeth replied indignantly.

———————◆———————

Gladwin sat in his office, pondering his situation. He wondered what he could do to bolster the spirits of the inhabitants. He looked at his date book. It was Thursday, the last day of June, the end of a month that had seen a pall of gloom grow steadily worse. He reviewed the events of those thirty days that had made a grim situation become even more ominous.

The month had started with Father Jonois, dressed in his brown capote, arriving from the north to tell them of the demise of Fort Michilimackinac and the savage massacre committed by the Chippewas. Then, a French trapper had informed them that Fort St. Joseph had been overrun by a Potawatomi war party which had sacked and burned the missionary outpost. They had killed everyone except four men, including an Ensign Schlosser, whom they intended to exchange for two Potawatomi captives Gladwin held in the brig.

But the most disheartening display had occurred yesterday afternoon. He shook his head as he thought about it. The sentry at the southwest blockhouse, hearing a dismal death chant, had called for help. When he and Sergeant Fitch arrived, there was a line of painted Huron and Chippewa warriors emerging from the forest to do a snake dance. A scalp fluttered from the tip of a pole each carried. The leader, a war chief, had his pole adorned with the battered, rotting head of a blond Englishman.

Thirty minutes later under a flag of truce, a French interpreter approached the fort. "Fort Sandusky has fallen," he shouted. Then he scurried back to the Indians.

There was a light knock on the door. "Some men to see you, sir," the orderly reported.

"Give me a minute, then show them in," Gladwin said, rising to put on his coat. His movements were slow and deliberate. Light rations and little sleep had robbed him of much of his vigor.

"Mr. Stanton, Mr. Taylor," he said, stepping around the desk to greet the two men. "What brings you 'ere?"

David Stanton looked at Sam Taylor. "You tell 'im, Sam," he said.

"Well, it's like this," Sam began. "Some of the people are gettin' nervous." Embarrassed, he paused, not sure he should continue. He

452

took in a deep breath. "They's thinkin' maybe we should take up Pontiac's offer. His offer for safe passage if we all go."

"Very many?" Gladwin asked.

"Quite a few. Especially after seein' that awful thing yesterday."

Gladwin looked at them soberly. He was sure they meant well, but to him, retreat was a military disgrace. Being a proper English officer, he had complete confidence in the army and was sure help was on the way. He knew the *Huron* could make it back, fighting if it had to, and there was the possibility a column of foot soldiers had been dispatched from Fort Niagara. But his primary reason for concern was that he had no faith in the word of the crafty Ottawa chief. "First of all," he said firmly, "Pontiac's word is no good. A bloody lyin' bastard, 'e is." He forced a smile. "Tell your friends we're strong enough to 'old out for a while. Tell them help will arrive soon."

He stopped speaking just as the sound of three distant rumbles echoed through the compound. He listened for an instant, then his face brightened. "Must be the *Huron* announcing 'er approach!" he said, heading for the door. "We've got to answer!"

When the sentry at the southwest blockhouse saw him approaching, the young soldier shouted, "Cannon fire from downriver, major!"

"Good! Fire one round into the Indian positions," Gladwin said, pointing to the small cannon beside the soldier "That'll let 'em know the fort is still in English hands."

In less than three minutes, there was another distant cannon report. "That's them!"

A cry of elation went up around the ramparts, and the streets began filling with jubilant people.

Smiling, he turned to Sergeant Fitch, now standing beside him. "Get ready to receive 'em, sergeant!"

The crew of the *Michigan* pulled the vessel forward with its capstan to clear the water gate, and all able-bodied men were alerted to stand by to counter any Indian attack.

◆

When Captain Loring headed his ship into the mouth of the river, he had hoped he could reach Detroit by nightfall. He carried sixty troopers and a heavy cargo of supplies he knew were desperately needed by Major Gladwin, but as the sun touched the western horizon, the wind that filled the *Huron's* sails had stopped. He would have to drop anchor and spend the night in mid-river by the LaCroix farm.

When Seetonka saw the *Huron* halt a hundred and fifty yards downstream, he was disappointed. He had been lying in wait with two hundred of his Potawatomi braves for nearly a week watching for it to come past. For several days he had forced the indolent warriors to construct a dirt-filled breastwork of poles at the landing of Jackson's burned out farm. He was certain it would afford protection from the *Huron's* heavy guns when he made his attack.

But maybe it was better this way. Under cover of darkness, he could send three dozen lightly armed men to board and capture the ship. Then, it would be intact when he presented it to Pontiac.

It was shortly after midnight when one of the guards that ringed the deck quietly gave the alarm that canoes filled with Indians were approaching. The alerted soldiers waited until the red men were near enough so they could not miss their targets, then fired a thunderous volley.

Captain Loring stood at the rail and watched the yelping braves scramble to get away. When the dark outline of the last of six bodies floated slowly out of sight, he turned to the soldier standing beside him. "Tell the men they've done a fine job." He started for his cabin, then stopped. "And tell 'em to keep their eyes open for any that might try swimmin' out."

The next morning when, under clear skies, a gentle southwest breeze refilled her sails, the anchors were hoisted, and the *Huron* began the slow passage upstream. Moments after she began to make headway, she came under heavy attack from muskets, fire-arrows, and flint-tipped lances at the hands of two hundred Potawatomi assailants.

Captain Loring spotted Seetonka, plumed and painted, pacing back and forth, giving commands and shouting encouragement to his warriors. Turning to an ensign standing on the deck beside him, he ordered three rounds of grapeshot fired at the breastwork.

The sudden broadside rocked the *Huron* and made it shudder. On shore, there was an immense eruption of poles, sand, and bodies. The awestruck Seetonka stood and watched as his braves, terrorized by the heavy smoke and loud noise, panicked. When he regained his composure, he flailed his arms and shouted for them to stay and fight, but they ignored him and fled inland.

As the ship's crew laughed at Seetonka's predicament, the muffled, reverberating sound of the fort's response reached their ears. They gave an enthusiastic cheer.

Captain Loring, standing on the poop deck in a resplendent blue uniform, called out. "Good news, m' lads! But keep a sharp eye! Those treacherous savages could trouble us yet!"

———————◆———————

After firing a harassing round of grapeshot into the ring of Indians it had recently pierced, the *Huron* tied up near the water gate. The fort's joyous inhabitants descended from the ramparts and ran to the dock to greet the newly arrived soldiers and sailors. Richard, mindful of Elizabeth's condition, ran back to escort her to the scene. He wanted her to enjoy the momentous occasion with him.

Major Gladwin boarded the *Huron* as soon as the gangplank was lowered. He conferred briefly with Captain Loring, then turned to the elated crowd. "There's another fleet of cargo canoes on their way!" he called out. "They're heavily armed and will arrive here in two weeks!"

The people raised their hands and sounded a loud cheer. Elizabeth looked at her husband. "Oh, Richard!" she declared. Touched by the wonderful feeling that others were aware of their plight and making an all-out effort to come to their rescue, she buried her face in his shoulder and sobbed.

It took two days to unload the *Huron*. After seeing the supplies it brought, the villagers assumed a jovial mood. Included in the cargo were one hundred and sixty-five barrels of pork, seventy-five barrels of flour, and a large supply of ammunition, rum, and brandy.

The garrison soldiers donned the fresh, bright uniforms it delivered. Once again, to Sergeant Fitch's critical eye, they appeared neat, clean, and well regimented. The streets and shops came alive as freshly groomed civilians bought, sold, and chatted in carnival spirit. The Black Swan filled with revelers who joked, laughed, and played cards and dominoes as they drank from the new supply of spirits. For those of a more serious mind, Father Pothier said mass at Ste. Anne's garbed in a new chasuble made with silk and silver thread. The contingent on duty, however, did not relax its guard.

Later in the day, when the Indians launched another assault, Richard did not go to the firing platform as he usually did. Instead, he looked at Elizabeth, smiled and waited. Like other residents, he was confident the army, its strength boosted by new reinforcements, could manage.

When Major Gladwin's orderly had sorted the messages, dispatches, and reports the *Huron* brought, there were two dozen letters for the residents. One was delivered to Elizabeth.

Sitting down at the table, she nervously opened it. She scanned it quickly, then read aloud to Richard. A cheery letter which had been written in March, it described the budding of the trees and the greening of the grass. It also told of several new buildings under construction. "You just couldn't believe the changes that have taken place. Probably won't recognize the town when you come back." Elizabeth paused to wipe a tear from her eye.

It detailed the wedding of one of her friends, then closed with a sober notation. "Tell Richard his father is ailing." She slowed and read cautiously. "He still gets around, but his movements are much slower and more laboured."

She handed it to Richard and looked longingly into the distance as he read it.

"That is pretty country," he said, handing it back to her.

She placed it in her pocket and got up to make some tea. Richard noted the redness of her eyes.

———————◆———————

In the early morning hours of July 2nd, Richard was aroused by a commotion. He slipped into his clothes and ran to investigate. Lieutenant MacDougal had escaped from the Frenchman's house where he was being held captive and was at the north gate. After the sentry let the officer inside, Richard assisted the bedraggled man to military headquarters.

When the villagers learned of MacDougal's return, they were elated. Father Pothier led them in a prayer of thanks, then said the rosary for the release of Captain Campbell. Afterwards, he walked among them, expressing confidence the captain would come back unharmed.

But the hope and joy was short-lived. On the afternoon of July 4th, the horribly mutilated body of Captain Campbell drifted along the riverbank and wedged against the *Michigan*. It was quickly recovered by the sentries, wrapped in a blanket, and gently interred in front of military headquarters. His grave would serve as a reminder to all who passed of the wicked savagery that confronted them.

◆

Major Gladwin, sickened by the vicious brutality Pontiac had inflicted on the men of the canoe flotilla, then stunned and shocked by the atrocious savagery of the Chippewas against Captain Campbell, went to his office and closed the door. As he sat, his mind searched for ways to punish the Indians and boost the morale of his troops. With the reinforcements and supplies delivered by the *Huron*, he should be able to stage a raid on Pontiac's village, and Captain Loring assured him more was on its way. If he could get the *Michigan* to sail north and shell the Ottawas with its six-pounders, it might make Pontiac relent on his siege. He breathed a heavy sigh, then walked over and opened the door. "Orderly!" he called out in a voice ringing with eagerness. "Get Sergeant Fitch."

The next morning, walking stiffly erect in a new uniform, he went to the water gate dock where the sergeant was waiting with two dozen grenadiers. He smiled. "New uniforms," he said. "Just like the king's guards."

"Yessir!" the sergeant beamed. Then he whispered, "Gotta teach 'em pride and discipline. Show 'em they're in an army that can hand it out as well as take it."

After the troopers had been stationed around the deck rail, Gladwin strode to the prow to watch the ship leave the dock.

As it tacked from shore to shore, he looked at the cleared decks and stout masts of the tight vessel and studied the busy crew who manned her. A shiver of exhilaration swept through his body as he thought of its superior power and the punishment it was capable of delivering.

Braves manning the containment line came to the river's edge to see the large vessel with big cloth sails. Awestruck, they turned to each other and mumbled questions and comments. They knew it took big magic to propel the ship upstream against the wind.

Making one final tack, the *Michigan* headed straight for the Ottawa village where Pontiac was watching from the open doorway of his wigwam. A large number of braves, including some who had trotted along the shoreline following the ship's northward progress, were gathered at the riverbank. Certain it would run ashore, they were ready to board and seize it.

With a sudden shout of command and flapping of sails, the *Michigan* turned parallel to the river's edge. The black muzzles of her guns belched smoke and fire, and loud reports of cannonading echoed back and forth across the river. Iron balls hissed over and through the crowd, tore gaping holes in their shelters, and smashed through the trees beyond.

Startled and terrified, the red men bounded off in all directions, yelping and screaming as they fled.

Pontiac looked impassively at the pandemonium about him. Then, he turned and calmly walked back into his wigwam.

He had barely sat down on his deerskin rug when the final shot tore through the corner of his lodge, covering him with a shower of bark and twigs. He rose to his feet, and the muscles of his face tightened. Setting his jaw, he vowed he would retaliate with the weapon he had been considering for some time, fire. And he would order a fresh supply of deer liver placed in the rattlesnake pit for more arrow poison.

———————◆———————

The next day Gladwin received word from an army scout that three Indians had been killed and a dozen wounded in the raid. Not many for all the effort he had put forth, he thought, but it did serve notice to Pontiac that his village, too, could be brought under attack.

The following day, the same scout reported the furious Ottawa chief was frantically building a huge fire-raft by binding together four of the captured supply canoes. The major promptly ordered the *Michigan* anchored seventy-five yards out into the river. "At least, they won't get both ships," he told Captain Loring.

◆

Three days later, the night was hot and humid. Gladwin had gone to bed early but, after tossing and turning on his cot for some time, decided to get dressed and go up on the firing platform.

The moon had already settled below the horizon, making the river look like a streak of black glass, darker than the trees that lined its banks. It was quiet, except for the ever-present sound of distant drums. He looked down at the sleeping village, then turned to study the Indian campfires beyond the Savoyard. Suddenly, the air was rent by the shouts of sentries passing the awaited alarm, "Burning vessel approaching from the north!"

In minutes, the village was alive with activity. Sleeping troopers were aroused and ordered to battle stations on the ramparts. Sailors aboard the ships were placed on standby alert to protect their vessels.

Nudged into the current by a dozen warrior-filled canoes, the huge pile of dried pine, birch bark, fagots, and tar was burning furiously. As it approached the fort, its flames built to a height of thirty feet, brightly illuminating the area on both sides of the river. The palisade, the trees, even people in the streets, glowed with a lustrous golden color.

As Gladwin watched the towering inferno glide past between the fort and the *Michigan*, he and others with him crouched low to protect their faces from the searing radiation. Roaring like a thousand wounded lions, the flaming pyre drifted near the schooner, forcing the crew to cut one of its anchor cables so it could swing farther away. The tremendous updraft shot a huge tower of burning embers hundreds of feet into the air where they hovered momentarily before plummeting into the river. There they sizzled and steamed until the water extinguished them.

Gladwin watched it for several minutes as it floated slowly downstream, gently turning as it went. He could see clusters of savages standing along both sides of the river, their bodies glistening in the bright light. Satisfied the immediate danger was over, he decided to walk around the ramparts and congratulate the soldiers on their behavior and alertness.

At his quarters, he took off his coat and laid on his bed. He was tired, very tired, but when he closed his eyes, sleep would not come.

◆

Although her morning sickness was subsiding, Elizabeth continued to mope about the wagon. It was depressing to compare the hardships she and Richard were enduring with the beauty and serenity her mother described in the letter from Fredericksburg. She carried the letter in her apron pocket, frequently taking it out to reread it. Each time she did, her eyes filled with tears. Occasionally, one rolled down her cheek to land on the worn piece of paper and make the ink run.

She knew Richard was getting restless, confined for so long in the fort, and she had heard him wonder aloud about the chances of not being able to get back to the farm in the near future. Others had told him it would be a very long time before an Englishman could farm in peace anywhere west of Fort Niagara. Then there was the terrible proof of the savages' deep hatred for white settlers. Maybe if she talked to him, he would consider returning to Virginia, at least until the baby was born.

While they were eating lunch, she tried several times to talk to him about leaving, but each time, her courage failed. Finally, when she rose to remove the dishes, she said, "Richard, let's go down and watch them load the *Huron*."

"All right," he said, cheerfully.

When they reached the dock, there was very little activity. "Are you loaded?" Richard asked a sailor standing on deck.

"Not much ta load," the sailor replied. "Just some furs and a few other things."

"When are you sailing?"

"Probably in a day or two," the sailor replied.

Suddenly the sky darkened, and the wind started to blow. Richard and Elizabeth reached their wagon just as the rain began to fall.

As they lay listening to the large drops of water that had filtered through the pine tree rattle against the canvas, Richard turned toward her. Carefully placing an arm across her chest, he looked into her face and quietly asked, "How would you like to go back to Fredericksburg?"

Surprised, she turned to face him and, with a startled look on her face, questioned, "Do you really mean that?"

She knew it was getting too late to plant crops, but she thought he still wanted to remain, hopeful of returning soon enough to get the buildings ready for winter. Since she wouldn't be able to help much, it would be a tremendous undertaking. Still, he was a hard, determined worker.

"Yes," he replied. "At least, for the time being. We could come back again in a year or so when Pontiac gets taken care of."

A wave of excitement swept over Elizabeth. As soon as the shower passed, she, with assistance from Richard, stepped down from the wagon. The sun had just come out from behind a dark cloud. Looking at the glistening world about her, she inhaled deeply to savor the freshness of the newly washed foliage. With a sudden abruptness, her expression became serious. "What about Molly?" she asked. "I don't want to leave her here."

"I thought about that," Richard replied calmly. He placed a hand behind her neck. "Thought I'd leave a message with Frenchy to give to Louis first chance he gets. I think he'd be willing to hold the livestock until we get back."

"Can he handle all of them?" She was thinking of the limited barn space LaCroix had.

"I'm sure he can manage," Richard replied, reluctantly believing some could be kept outside near the barn. He thought for a moment, then said, "I'll tell him, if he must get rid of any, to save Bessy for us."

"I don't want to leave Molly here," Elizabeth insisted. "Besides, we could use her on the way back."

"Thought I'd ask Major Gladwin if we could take both Molly and the wagon. The ship is half empty."

Richard went directly to Gladwin and told him of his plans. The major appeared disappointed and didn't want them to take the horse and wagon. When Richard explained that Elizabeth was expecting and he'd be hard-pressed to outfit his farm in time for winter, Gladwin suggested they could be accommodated within the fort.

"I like open spaces," Richard countered. "Been on a farm all my life. Besides, we intend to come back in the spring." He paused, then added, "And at one time you said if anybody wanted to leave, they could."

Gladwin told his orderly to dispatch a message to Captain Loring.

When Richard told Frenchy of his plans, the proprietor of the Comptoir Grillon stared at him. "But, you are my true friends," he moaned, tears flowing down his cheeks. "I trust you completely."

"I know, Frenchy," Richard replied, placing his hands on the Frenchman's shoulders. "You are my true friend, too, and always will be." He pushed on Frenchy's shoulders to get him to look up instead of at the floor. "Besides, we plan to come back next year."

The two of them walked back to the wagon. As they drank tea, Elizabeth wrote a letter to Louis and Marie. She wasn't sure they could read English, so she read it to Frenchy. Then she said, "If there is a problem, have them speak with Flip."

She wrote another letter to Flip and the Wyandottes expressing gratitude for their friendship and favors.

After she and Richard signed the letters, Richard handed them to Frenchy. "I know it might be some time before you can deliver these, but get them there when you can—when it's safe for you."

Frenchy looked at him and winked. "It won't be long."

◆

Four other families, two with children, were also leaving. Their departure was not unexpected, however, since they'd lived north of the fort and their buildings had been burned to the ground. But when word spread that the Lockes were going, disappointed friends came by to see them or stopped to talk with them on the street. It gave Richard and Elizabeth a chance to explain their decision.

"Now you stay below deck going downriver," advised Mary Stanton, her blue bonnet tied neatly beneath her double chin. "Don't want anything to happen on the way, now that you're carryin' your offspring."

Elizabeth blushed. "I'll be careful."

In a four-way discussion at his store, Sam Taylor remarked to Richard, "Hell, if we had any sense, we'd probably *all* pack up and go. At least, until they skinned that red-assed bastard, Pontiac, and tacked his hide to the wall."

"'Tis a good idea," David Stanton chimed in. "Let's skin 'im and dry is 'ide!"

"Be damned if I'm gonna leave!" Henry snorted. "But if the bloody blighter ever fights 'is way to m' tavern, I 'ope I can convince 'im ta 'ave a drink on me afore 'e scalps me."

The group guffawed. Then they shook hands, and the three left.

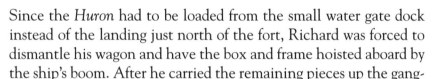

Since the *Huron* had to be loaded from the small water gate dock instead of the landing just north of the fort, Richard was forced to dismantle his wagon and have the box and frame hoisted aboard by the ship's boom. After he carried the remaining pieces up the gangplank, the two sailors operating the boom helped him put it back together, load it, and securely fasten it to the deck.

"I want to thank you, men," he told them when the task was finished. "Guess now I'll have to find a place to sleep tonight."

"See no reason why ye can't sleep right in it 'ere," replied the sailor standing nearest to him.

"Would it be all right?"

"Been done afore," the sailor assured him.

"Good! I'll get the horse on board, then go after my wife."

In spite of Richard's coaxing, Molly refused to walk up the steep, narrow gangplank.

After watching for several minutes, the two sailors came down carrying sticks. "You get ahead 'o the beast," they told Richard. "We'll beat on 'er backside."

Richard shook his head and waved them off. Gently stroking her nose, he fed her a handful of oats he took from a nearby barrel. After speaking to her quietly for several minutes, he draped his coat over her head. When he tugged on her reins, she followed him trustingly up the cleated plankway. The sailors shook their heads and smiled.

Captain Loring, having eaten breakfast, stepped from his cabin and looked up at the bright sunny sky. It was seven o'clock, and already the dew was evaporating and wind rising on this Monday, July 18, 1763. It would be a good day to set sail. He would send out a call for the passengers to board.

He had been prepared to depart the day before, but conditions were not right so he decided to wait. He needed as much speed as possible to go down the river. There had been a heavy, humid, easterly wind, and he wanted to wait for it to switch around to the northwest. Then, the skies would clear, and the wind would blow stronger.

He stood on the forward deck and watched the waving, hand-shaking, and well wishing of the passengers as they bade farewell to those determined to stay. At ten o'clock he told Elizabeth, her eyes reddened and tear-filled, to go below with the other women and children. Then he had the first mate order the crew to set the sails and hoist the anchor.

With a brisk, ten-knot wind propelling her, he steered the *Huron* directly to the middle of the river where the current was most rapid. By the time it reached the line of Indian encirclement, its prow was slicing smartly through the clear, blue water. His confidence building, Loring ordered a harassing round fired from one of its six-pounders.

As the iron ball tore through the trees and shrubs that sheltered the Indians, Richard heard screams coming from the women and children. He ran below to investigate. The cannon blast and sudden lurch of the ship had frightened them. "It's all right," he told them, holding his hands up. "Just one of our guns practicing." He put his arm around Elizabeth. "And there might be more before we clear the river."

When he returned upstairs, he squatted on his haunches with his back against the wheel of his wagon. As he looked at the deck planking, still wet from soaking the rig's canvas top before they sailed, he heard the hushed voices of the sailors. They were of the opinion that, once out of sight of the fort, the ship could cruise along quietly, undetected by downriver Indians.

Richard knew every red man in the area was aware of their sailing. Many would be watching from secluded hiding places along the shoreline. The hair rose on the back of his neck at the thought of it, making a chill race down his spine. He got to his feet and scanned the dense, green foliage they were passing.

He stood at the rail and watched the Jackson farm slip by as the *Huron* approached the rust-colored discharge from the River Rouge. The building foundations, mere heaps of grayish-brown ashes, stood out like little islands in the green fields now fallow and overgrown with grass and weeds. The large maple that had shaded the house wore only half a cover of green leaves. The remaining half, its barren black limbs angling upward as if pleading for help, gave mute evidence to all who passed of the intense heat it had withstood.

When he saw the LaCroix buildings, he watched intently, hoping he could see Louis or Marie. Although everything seemed intact, no one was in sight. There was a cow he thought was Bessy among some animals in the small pasture, but he couldn't be sure.

Thinking Elizabeth would like to see their own farm, he dashed below and brought her up to stand with him at the rail.

"Can't do that," a sailor at a nearby station warned. "Women and children should stay below."

"It's our farm," Richard said, pointing to the buildings coming into view. "It'll be all right."

The sailor shrugged and continued to watch the shoreline.

Elizabeth looked forlornly at the buildings the two of them had worked so hard to put in good order on land they'd toiled to make productive. There, on the little bluff where her husband and Flip had buried the Mascouten, stood the oak that had furnished shade for their festive gatherings and, down below, the canoe landing from which she had fled when the Ottawas came.

For her it was an emotional moment. She felt a kinship to the land, the neighbors, even the animals, but when she recalled the savagery of Pontiac's warriors, then thought of returning to Fredericksburg, a wave of excitement surged through her body, tempering any thought of staying. Tears filled her eyes as she thought of the people remaining and the animals she and Richard had nurtured and tended, only to be left behind.

With her hands on the wooden rail, she squinted to look where Richard was pointing. Suddenly, she saw an Indian who had just stepped to the edge of the bluff beside the big oak.

"That's Seetonka!" Richard gasped, his voice conveying disbelief.

The Potawatomi chief, naked except for a doeskin breechclout, had his chest and face grotesquely painted red, white, and black. His disheveled hair, along with the bands of feathers and shells around his ankles and wrists, fluttered in the breeze as he waved his arms and jumped about, wildly shouting vile epithets.

"How awful," Elizabeth muttered, grimacing to express her disdain.

Fearing an attack, Richard escorted her back to the lower deck. When he returned to the rail, he saw the poop deck swivel gun being aimed. As he watched, there was a loud crack that split the quiet air, and a narrow tongue of flame and smoke spouted from the weapon's muzzle.

Seetonka was standing alone on the embankment, his legs staunchly apart and his arms upraised. In his left hand he held a tomahawk, in his right, a rusty musket. The seven-ounce ball hit him squarely in the center of the chest. It knocked him over backward, and he hit the ground violently. The released musket and tomahawk hung motionless in the air for a brief instant before dropping to the earth.

While a quick cheer from the gun crew faded, the captain's voice could be heard. "Good aimin' m' lads!" Then, he warned, "Now's the time ta keep alert!"

Richard felt a twinge in the pit of his stomach. He didn't like Seetonka or the Potawatomis and was certain it was best to be rid of the beastly chief, but he wasn't prepared for such a sudden and gruesome sight. He was glad Elizabeth hadn't seen it.

With the *Huron* past the River Rouge, Richard felt the perilous part of their journey was past. He got Elizabeth to come back and stand at the rail with him.

" 'Tis a dangerous thing ta 'ave 'er 'ere," a sailor warned.

"It's all right now," Richard replied. "This is Wyandotte territory. Their chief, Naseeka, is friendly to the English."

The sailor shook his head and turned to a fellow sailor. "Taken leave o' 'is senses, 'e 'as," he scoffed, loud enough for Richard to hear.

"Just another bloody red bastard!" a gunner echoed. "They'll be no peace 'til every one o' them's been drawn and quartered!"

"Watch yer foul tongues!" Captain Loring cautioned.

The gunner, chagrined, lowered his eyes. "Yes sir," he mumbled.

Naseeka and his villagers had gathered on the sandy mound in front of their village to watch the *Huron* sail past. Informed by runners that Richard and Elizabeth were aboard, he was puzzled and disappointed. Why were his good friends leaving? They would be key elements in reestablishing the good will he and his Wyandottes enjoyed with the English before Pontiac's attack. Did they plan to return? He fingered the shiny copper talisman that hung from his neck. Deep inside he was sure their presence, or lack of it, would be a decisive factor in the fate of his tribe.

Although the ship was far enough from shore to make identification difficult, Richard readily recognized Naseeka standing at the forefront of the gathering. Dressed in buff buckskins, the chief stood with arms folded across his chest, staring at the *Huron*. Beside him was Flip.

"He's grown a beard!" Richard declared, squinting to more clearly focus his eyes on his friend.

He could see Matoka and Lahana standing nearby. As he pointed them out to Elizabeth, he heard the clicking sound of metal against metal. At that instant, a bright flash of reflected sunlight from Naseeka's talisman caught his eye. A wave of sickening horror shot through his mind. The swivel gun was being readied.

Bounding up the stairs to the poop deck, he seized the muzzle of the weapon and held it down so it pointed toward the water.

"Captain! Captain Loring!" he yelled, trying to get the attention of the ship's master who was standing forward on the main deck.

The captain looked up to see the gunners struggling with the young Virginian.

"What's this?" the captain asked, his eyes flashing.

"Don't fire at those Indians!" Richard shouted. "They are friends of the English!"

"And of what tribe might they be?" the captain asked, walking toward them.

The two members of the gun crew released Richard. Then the three of them stood, looking down at the captain.

"Wyandottes," Richard replied. "Their chief is Naseeka."

Captain Loring smiled. He knew of the Wyandottes, but did not know which village was theirs. "Hold yer fire!" he ordered, loud enough so those manning other guns could hear. "Do not fire at Indians off the starboard side!"

Richard, still breathing heavily, returned to Elizabeth and placed his arm around her waist. The two of them waved at the gathering on the distant shore. To their surprise, Naseeka waved back.

Turning to the gunners, Richard said, "That is my friend, Naseeka, chief of the Wyandottes." His eyes were glistening with tears.

The gunners gave a wry smile and nodded.